# THE ALCHEMIST
# OF
# ALEPPO

A NOVEL

ALSO BY MARIE K. SAVAGE

*The Trouble with Roommates*

*The Oracles of Delphi*

*&*

THE SEEDS TRILOGY

*The Sowing*
(K. Makansi co-author)

*The Reaping*
(K. Makansi co-author)

*The Harvest*
(K. Makansi co-author)

# THE ALCHEMIST OF ALEPPO

A NOVEL

## MARIE K. SAVAGE

Layla Dog Press | Tucson, Arizona

Layla Dog Press
Tucson, AZ 85719



For information, contact:
Layla Dog Press
*an imprint of Blank Slate Communications*
www.kristinamakansi.com

Manufactured in the United States of America
Cover design by Kristina Blank Makansi
Cover images: Shutterstock
Set in Adobe Caslon Pro, Cormorant, and Copperplate

Library of Congress Control Number: 2025900004
Print ISBN: 9780998425993
Ebook ISBN: 9798991272209

*for all those who have loved and lost
and long to love again*

*Time is ephemeral. Only love is everlasting.*
—The Alchemist of Aleppo

*We were young, you were dying, and I was desperate.*
*So, I rearranged the world.*
—Michael Samaan


∞


*My sun sets to rise again.*
— Robert Browning

*Life can only be understood backwards;*
*but it must be lived forwards.*
—Soren Kierkegaard

# ONE

Michael Samaan's phone buzzed and skittered on his desk, jolting him from his research. He tapped the screen and groaned.

*Hellooooo. Hope you're not too far down your rabbit hole to remember Lunch with Leila.*

Damn. He checked the time. Yeah, late again. And he'd hear about it from his obscenely cheery and perpetually punctual little sister who plagued and entertained him in equal measure.

He marked his page and closed the book, *Chemical Analysis of Ancient Glass*, one of a dozen similar titles spread out on his battered dining room table. He stood and flexed his shoulders, aching from too much time hunched over his laptop or bent over a book. Sal looked up expectantly, momentarily distracted from pulling the stuffing from a plush reindeer's nose. Michael bent to scratch the dog behind the ears. "Sorry, buddy. You stay here and guard the place."

Undaunted, the dog clamped the reindeer in his jaws and his short legs churned a path toward the front door, tail wagging as Michael grabbed his wallet, keys, and jacket. "Stay. Be a good boy," he said with a pointed finger, and then was out the door and headed for the Underground.

Michael had no idea where his sister got her preternaturally positive personality. She was disgustingly upbeat while his own thoughts too often spiraled into dark, desolate chambers, rivaling the most gruesome images from Bosch, van Eyck, or Fra Giovanni. Studying art history as an undergrad, he'd become obsessed with paintings of hell from the Renaissance masters, recognizing a darkness in himself that resonated with the landscapes of torture and torment celebrated artists depicted with brushes and paints. Of course, he'd tried to mask his moods with dark humor and glib witticisms, but somewhere along the way his little sister had learned to read him like a book. She could tell when Michael needed a life buoy to keep him afloat and had decided she would be that buoy. They'd never talked about it, but he'd come to rely on her—and their lunches— and was thankful she thought he was worth the effort.

He emerged back up into the sunlight and wound his way toward Mt. Olympus restaurant, their regular meeting place on a busy street teeming with tourists, and London cabs, and double-decker busses and people hurrying to and fro speaking in every possible accent and dozens of foreign languages. Having grown up in a small town, he now felt like he needed the energy of London injected straight into his veins, to crowd out the darkness that all too often stalked him like a pickpocket, ready to grab at him at a moment's notice.

As usual, Leila was already there, sipping a glass of water chock full of lemon wedges and perusing the menu. "Want the kebab again?" She asked without looking up. "I already ordered the mezza platter."

He pulled the menu down to see her face. "And hello to you too, sis."

She flashed him a bright smile. "Punctual as always."

"I'm barely ten minutes late."

"Mum says hi, by the way. Says it's been weeks since you went to see her."

"Oh, please. Sal and I were there last Sunday."

"She's lonely. Next month's their anniversary and it's been five years. We should take her out to dinner."

Five years. Christ, it seemed like five decades since the accident. On every anniversary, their dad had relished telling the story of the day he'd first laid eyes on the green-eyed, dark-haired Welsh beauty sipping tea and drawing intently in a well-worn sketchbook while sitting alone at a coffee shop near campus. A newly arrived doctoral student from Syria bearing an outrageously thick crown of wavy black hair, a nearly unintelligible accent, and a pocket protector, he'd been mesmerized by the young woman. As he'd stared at her over the rim of his coffee cup, he told his friend, *I'm going to marry that one.* When she'd looked up and smiled, he'd stood and wound his way through the tables toward her as if she were his true north. They'd married six months later and had been inseparable for twenty-nine years. Until the accident when he'd been killed in a hit and run on the M23. They'd borrowed Michael's vintage convertible for an anniversary weekend in Brighton and hadn't even gotten past Gatwick when the car was rammed from behind, pushing it off the road where it flipped and came to rest on the driver's side. Most likely a drunk driver, but they'd never know for sure because the driver responsible fled the scene and was never found. CCTV caught it all, but the driver was wearing a hat and glasses, and the car's plates turned out to be stolen.

The accident had knocked Michael completely off-kilter. It had been his first year at City University London teaching a full class load, and he'd had to handle the sale of his father's company to the board of directors, arrange and manage his mother's care while she recuperated from her injuries, and support Leila in her first year at Cambridge, all while slogging through his own personal darkness.

He'd never said a word to anyone. Never revealed the full extent of the desolation—and the nagging feeling that he was to blame for the accident—he so often inhabited. It was his cross to bear, he told himself. Punishment for sins he didn't understand but felt bone-deep he'd committed. Punishment meted out to his father instead of to him, which only added to the weight on his shoulders. He deserved the darkness that ebbed and flowed in his blood. And recently it had returned in spades, calling out to him. Beckoning as if the answers he sought to questions he'd never known to ask were waiting for him. If only he'd let go.

"You pick the place," he said. "I'll pick up the tab. And bring that fiancé of yours too. Isn't he due back this week?"

The server set the mezza platter in the middle of the table. Leila ordered with brusque authority and gave the server a devastating smile. The man walked away with a slightly stunned shake of the head. They were regulars. He should be used to Leila by now.

Michael rolled his eyes. With a diamond stud in her nose, dangling earrings that drew attention to her elegant neck, green eyes set against a flourish of pitch-black lashes, and long, pink-streaked black hair swept up in a tangled nest on the crown of her head, Leila Samaan had the kind of presence that always made heads turn. And she knew it.

"Today, in fact," she said. "I'm heading out to Heathrow after lunch and"—her face took on a dreamy glow—"well, I anticipate an extremely satisfying evening ahead."

Michael groaned. "Must you?"

"Actually, I must." She sighed dreamily. "It's what a fiancé is for, after all. Speaking of, when are you going to get one of your own?" Michael shut his eyes against the inevitable onslaught. "You know I worry about you," Leila went on. "When was the last time you went on a date? Or even, you know...*had sex?*"

He rubbed his temples as if in pain. "Christ, Leila, I'm not talking to you about my sex life."

"That's only because you don't have one." She waved a piece of pita bread at him. "I don't like the idea of you being lonely."

"I know," he relented on a sigh. "I'm fine. Really."

"No. You're not. Let's be blunt. Many of my friends think you're magazine-cover material and would give a limb to shag you. Yet every time George and I try to set you up, you take on some new project and go dark like a Medieval cave hermit. Like with this book. I know you've found your footing and that this project is special, but still, you need to get out. And by out, I don't mean hanging around the V&A for hours on end. What is it with you and that museum, anyway?"

"Um, let's see, it's got one of the most extensive ancient glass collections in the UK, and I'm writing a book on Syrian glassmaking?"

"Please. You've been hanging out there since you were practically in short pants."

"I never wore short pants."

"Maybe you should. Show a little leg, brother. Have some fun. What do you do at the V&A all day anyway? I mean, it's a cool place, but for god's sake, you're thirty-two! Don't you have better things to do with your free time?"

"The collection is…wait. Why do I need to explain to you why an art historian would like to hang out in a museum?" The truth was he didn't understand his obsession with the V&A himself. Well, he wasn't obsessed with the museum, but rather with a single glass goblet that had called out to him from the very first moment he'd seen it. Over the years, he'd spent hundreds of hours just staring at it. Feeling it resonate in his soul like a struck gong. Everyone at the museum knew him, and most likely thought him a bit daft. He thought so too. In fact, he was headed over there after lunch. That's why he'd picked the Mt. Olympus restaurant for their monthly lunches. It was only a couple of Underground stops from home and a nice walk to the V&A. Easy access to his obsession.

She gave him her notorious side eye. "You don't fool me. And you don't fool Mum. She's been busy, by the way. Reading runes. Throwing stones. Tarot. She says something is coming to disrupt your life. A big change. Romance, intrigue, the whole bit. She's quite beside herself with anticipation."

"I hope you and George give her grandchildren soon so she can leave off obsessing about my love life."

"Or lack thereof."

"Whatever."

Leila stuffed an olive in her mouth. "She says your aura was pulsating with energy last time she saw you. According to her, it means you're on the edge of a life-changing event."

"My life-changing event might well be matricide."

"Shall I alert Scotland Yard?"

"Or maybe sororicide." He drained half his glass of water.

"You adore me too much to harm a hair on my head, big brother."

Michael turned in search of the server. "Where's our food?"

"Don't change the subject. You need a date for next Friday."

He raised an eyebrow. "What for?"

She reached out and slapped his arm. "What for? For my thesis show, that's what."

"You're having a show?"

"Wanker."

"I'm sorry. Of course, I know it's your big night."

"And it's the twentieth anniversary of my program so the department's going all out. She speared a cucumber and considered it. "It'll be quite the sophisticated affair."

"I'll bring Mum as my date."

Leila shook her head. "Can't. Mum's bringing her book club."

"No worries." He shrugged. "Just for you, I'll arrange to meet a gorgeous woman and fall deeply in love between now and next Friday." He pulled out his phone and pretended to enter reminders on his calendar. "Let's see. It's still early, so

I can get started today. First on the agenda, meet beautiful woman. Tomorrow: Fall in love. Next: Bring home said beautiful woman and have mad sex. Get engaged. And next Friday? Take her to sister's show." He looked up. "Satisfied?"

"Brilliant. Can't wait to meet her."

# TWO

Kat Musgrave's eyes flew open as she jerked awake, heart pounding as she scanned the room for some clue as to where she was. She pushed her hair back, wiped the back of her hand over her mouth, and swung her legs down to sit up, gradually coming back to herself. She looked around the room, squinting into the brilliant late afternoon Arizona sun slanting in through the blinds. Work. She was at work, in her office. Safe. She drew in a long, cleansing breath and let it out slowly.

How long had she been asleep? The article she'd been reading had slipped to the floor and her little decorative sofa pillow now sported dark wet blotches. Lovely. It had been one of her desolation dreams, complete with tears and, apparently, a bucket of drool. She glared at the wet splotch on the pillow like someone else was responsible, then tossed it toward her backpack. She'd have to take it home and throw it in the laundry.

She jumped when the phone vibrated on the table next to the tiny couch wedged into the corner behind her office door. Whoever was calling could wait. It was probably some telemarketer or politician asking for money anyway. Or her mom. And she could wait too.

She stood, rubbed her eyes, and massaged the back of her neck hard as if she could rub the dream away. Pulling a handful of tissues from the box on the side table, she blew her nose, tossed the tissues in the trash, and headed down the hall to the bathroom. Along the way, she passed a conference room where several grad students were huddled around the table, heads together. Beyond the glass windows of the conference room, the Santa Catalina Mountains rose from the desert plain like jagged stalagmites poking holes in the crystalline blue sky. Now bathed in the sun and shadows of early evening, Kat smiled and thought of the Tucson mantra she'd heard all her life: *When the mountains turn pink, it's time to drink.*

After using the facilities, she washed her hands and grabbed a couple of paper towels to scrub her face. When was the last time she'd slept through the night? When she was twelve? Thirteen? Puberty. That's when the dreams started. That's when everything went sideways. When her body and her brain got together and decided to take her on an adventure she didn't understand and couldn't control. God, she was tired. Twenty-nine and she felt as ancient as Methuselah.

Her mom kept telling her she needed a vacation, and she was probably right. Craig and Isabella had asked her to go to San Diego where a partner in Isabella's law firm had a place on the beach they could use. But a vacation with those two wasn't the answer—especially since they'd been trying to fix her up since she and Daniel had split. Her brother wasn't so bad, but Isabella was determined that Kat find her *special someone*, just as she'd found Craig. *Take up running again*, Isabella had pleaded, *or do yoga, tai chi, or anything to increase energy levels* so she wouldn't look so put upon whenever Isabella mentioned fixing her up with yet another one of their friends. Eight years and four kids later, Craig and Isabella were obnoxiously happy. Frankly, it made Kat a little nauseous.

At her desk, she checked her messages. One telemarketer. A confirmation from a friend about drinks and dinner. Half a dozen texts from her mom; Beatrix Musgrave was nothing if not persistent. A few work calls. Nothing urgent.

She pulled out a drawer, popped a couple of Tylenol for her headache, and washed it down with the tepid remains of a flat Diet Coke. The desolation dreams always made her head pound. In college, she'd lived on pain relievers and pizza, and her freshman year roommate had moved out after three weeks, tired of listening to Kat cry and talk in her sleep. She'd lived alone ever since, self-medicating with pot brownies and banana bread, gummies, yoga, and intensive workouts. It rarely worked. When she and Daniel had tried to spend nights together, he'd taken to wearing earplugs. "Go see a goddamn psychic, a palm reader, a fucking astrologer, I don't care," he'd yelled one night when he'd found her wandering around her house speaking some language he couldn't understand.

Another text from her mom popped up. *Come out to the ranch for the weekend. Craig and Isabella are taking the kids down to Nogales for a family wedding. We can ride in the morning and lounge by the pool in the afternoon.*

Kat smiled. She loved her mom, but she couldn't risk an overnight. Bea was relentless and seemed to be always watching and waiting for Kat to fall apart again. Kat was afraid her mother would wear her down and she'd end up spilling the beans about the dreams, how they were getting…*more*…more intense, more real, more *present* in her waking life. Then her mom would get all worried and start obsessing again about the state of Kat's mental health, reviewing everything over and over again to see if she could have done something differently to help her daughter.

She'd inevitably start at the beginning, like how she'd always wondered about Kat's strange silvery birthmark, a ragged line just below her breastbone, like an old scar that never healed. Or she'd go over all those weird things Kat had said when she was really little, like the time her father had first set her up in the saddle to walk her around the paddock. She'd been about two and a half at the time, all baby fat, brown curls, and curious eyes, and she'd looked down at him and said, *I always hated riding sidesaddle.* Or when her parents had taken her and Craig to Dairy Queen after one of his Little League games and she'd told the teenager behind the counter that these parents were nicer than the ones who'd sold her to the mean man with the nasty teeth. Those out-of-the-blue statements had eventually faded with age, but her father had recorded each odd quip in a journal that he'd shared with her psychologist when the dreams began to overwhelm her just as she was going through puberty.

*Sounds nice, but can't,* she texted back. *Got plans with a friend.*

*A friend or a *friend*?* came the immediate reply. Kat could picture her mother's eyes widening in that *hope-springs-eternal* look she got whenever Kat mentioned any semblance of a social engagement that Bea could conjure into a love life.

Unlike Isabella, neither Craig nor her mother had been enamored with Daniel. *A little too full of himself for my taste*, her brother, a jeans-and-cowboy-boots kind of guy, had told her. *What grown man wears baby blue pants with pink embroidered whales on them, for god's sake*, her mother had asked after she'd first introduced them. Honestly, Kate was surprised the relationship had lasted as long as it had. He'd been charming and handsome and rich and her friends thought she'd hit the jackpot. But it had always felt forced. Maybe dating Daniel in the first place was a testament to her loneliness. God, that was depressing.

*Colleague*, Kat texted. *Sorry to disappoint.*

She scrolled through her email and opened the one that had been sitting in her inbox since last week, an invitation to participate on a panel on epigenetics and trauma at the International Genomics Association conference in London. She'd turned down the offer last month because she'd been up against a grant deadline—that was the story she gave them—but apparently someone had canceled, and they were reaching out again. She chewed on her lip until it started to hurt. London. Could she do it?

She'd flown through Heathrow several times but had never gone into the city. Before he died, her dad had been into genealogy and had dragged her mom to the UK half a dozen times to visit cemeteries and explore old villages his ancestors had inhabited hundreds of years earlier. They always asked her to tag along, but she'd been too busy. College. Grad school. Finding a job. She always found an excuse to say no. Next time, she'd assure them. Even as her parents went on and on about this museum or that exhibit, her skin turned icy and the hairs on the back of her neck stood on end. As if in warning. As if she'd step off the plane and plunge into a rabbit hole from which she'd never escape.

Once she'd heard herself tell her dad, "I can't risk it. Not yet." He'd looked at her as if she'd grown a second head. She'd had no idea where the words had come from. But she *felt* them as if they were true. It was truly weird. Paris hadn't freaked her out. Berlin had been fun. Athens and Barcelona and been amazing. But London? Maybe there really were werewolves there.

She drummed her fingers on the desk. Maybe the invitation was simple serendipity, but something about London finally seemed right. The cancellation and the open space on the panel felt *fortuitous*. Anticipation fluttered up her spine. Taking a deep breath, she typed out a quick response before she talked herself out of it.

> Thank you for the invitation! My schedule has changed, and I'm delighted to accept. I'll make my travel arrangements as soon as I hear back regarding stipend, conference hotel availability, etc. I'm honored to be included on the panel and look forward to participating.
>
> -
>
> Katherine S. Musgrave, PhD
> Associate Research Professor
> James R. W. Bryant Genomics Institute
> University of Arizona

She opened a new tab and pulled up the Wikipedia entry for London, scrolling down the page, clicking on the photos. What had she been so afraid of? It looked like a perfectly normal place. Lots of cool history. Amazing museums. Beautiful city parks. Big Ben and the Tower. She could combine work with sightseeing. Exactly the kind of vacation she loved.

She knew she had a good thing going at the Institute, but maybe it was time for a change. Maybe this conference would be a good place to network, see if there were any other opportunities out there waiting for her.

After her father died, she'd wanted to stay close to home for her mom, but that was six years ago. Now, besides still managing the ranch, Bea was a whirling dervish of activity, on a dozen volunteer committees at church and in the community. What did Kat have besides a cantankerous cat, long days in a lab, and an occasional drink with an equally overworked colleague? Daniel had moved on, her friends were busy with kids and commitments of their own, she could only read so much escapist fiction and watch so much TV. It was her turn for a little adventure now.

She clicked over to her desktop and pulled up her CV. She had to admit, it looked pretty good, especially since she'd included the latest paper accepted for publication. She hit print, tucked a few copies into a folder, and stuck it in her backpack.

The tactile memory of this afternoon's dream still made her skin tingle and the hairs on the back of her neck stand at attention. She tried to shake off the memory of the utter desolation. It always seemed so real. She didn't want to think about the shadowed man who seemed to have taken up residence in her subconscious. Or the scent of roses and jasmine. The pain, sadness, and overwhelming loss. And always the glass vessel, cool to the touch with its gold rim and traceries of green, blue and red and the feeling that it was an extension of herself. Or she was an extension of it, as if she were a phantom limb, a missing piece of something larger.

Something deep within her resonated at the idea of finally making a trip to London. Something portentous and grand. Sweeping. Something…well, she didn't have words for the thing that thrummed at her center, that echoed ever more insistently.

Better to concentrate on one of her desire dreams, rather than the ones that felt like the world had ended. They were much more fun. Maybe she'd finally meet someone like the stranger beckoning to her from the edges of her consciousness. They'd gallop across the countryside on dapple-grey steeds and fall deeply in love. Seemed unlikely in central London, but a girl could dream. Well, Kat couldn't stop dreaming. No matter what she did, her dreams always found her.

# THREE

Sergei Badawi sat in the back of his chauffeured car reading the latest LEH report from Kinkaid, his security chief. *Calm down*, he told himself when he realized his hands were shaking. The report said a new research fellow from the Corning Museum of Glass—a woman—had arrived just days earlier and had already expressed an interest in the Luck of Edenhall. Of course, he knew every expert in the field was charmed by the piece's history, but still, showing an interest in it after just arriving at the Victoria & Albert Museum might mean something more. Something important. Maybe this time around would be different. Recently, Sergei had sensed a shift in the air, as if a sort of energy field around him was gathering force. He didn't know what it meant. He only knew that he couldn't recall ever feeling anything like it before.

"I need everything on the Corning researcher." He glanced over at Andrew Carson, his personal assistant and the only man in the world who knew why Badawi was so interested in the old glass goblet known as the Luck of Edenhall. "I want her academic background, family history, personal details, and a copy of her fellowship proposal. Everything."

Carson nodded, typing a text to Kinkaid.

"Today was Michael's monthly lunch with his sister?"

"Yes, sir."

"Find out if he went to the V&A after and, if so, how long he stayed." Badawi checked his watch. "And if he's still there."

Carson nodded and started another text as Badawi leaned forward. "What's traffic like? How long would it take us to get over there?"

After a moment, Dryden, another member of his security detail, turned toward him from his place in the passenger seat. "No more than thirty minutes if traffic holds."

"He's still there," Carson said, looking up from his phone.

"No telling if we'll get there before he leaves," Badawi said, "but let's head over anyway."

The chauffeur nodded and reprogrammed the nav system to monitor traffic along the new route.

Over the past six months, Badawi's team had noted an uptick in the number of visits and length of time Michael Samaan spent at the V&A. And through Badawi's connections, he'd discovered that Samaan was taking a sabbatical to work on a new book about the history of Syrian glassmaking. That alone set off alarm bells. *He feels it too.*

Sergei Badawi had been shadowing Michael Samaan since the boy—now over thirty—had been in sixth form, watching and waiting for him to realize what he was, *who* he was.

And who Sergei was to him.

He watched as Michael had excelled in school and at university even as he ran himself ragged—rowing and running and playing football and rugby—and doing anything else he could to exorcise the demons and the darkness. The alcohol, the psychedelics, the women. Badawi knew from experience that none of it worked. Michael eventually figured it out too, but Sergei had hated standing by just watching him go through the hard lessons.

Now, Michael was anesthetizing himself through his work, and this latest development, the sabbatical and the book, had Sergei losing sleep. This time around was the first they'd both been in London the same time as the Luck, and the first time he felt there was a chance to finally find what he'd been looking for all these years. Or to finish it once and for all. Although there was only one way to accomplish that, and that required Michael Samaan remembering everything.

Thirty-five minutes later, they pulled up to the curb in front of the V&A and Dryden jumped out of the passenger seat to open Badawi's door for him. It was fifteen minutes until the museum closed. Carson scooted through and climbed out of the back seat to stand beside his boss. "Our man says he's heading up from the gallery now. We should see him exit in…" Badawi was already moving.

He strode toward the steps looking every bit the sophisticated global financier whose money had opened doors and whose pockets had funded galleries, foundations, and research in the arts for over two decades. He made a show of looking preoccupied and in a hurry when he felt Michael Samaan's presence. He looked up.

"Dr. Samaan! What a pleasure to run into you like this."

Michael stopped, familiar eyes dark and haunted. A sharp pang of sympathy shot through Sergei, and he resisted the urge to rub a hand over his heart. He had that same look whenever he caught a glimpse of himself in the mirror, whenever he let his guard down.

"Mr. Badawi. Good to see you." He glanced over his shoulder toward the museum door. "The place closes soon."

"I'm here to have a brief word with the director," Sergei lied. He waved a hand toward his car sitting at the curb. "Won't even be here long enough to park the car."

Michael glanced at Andrew Carson. "I guess billionaires don't need to abide by the same parking rules as the rest of us plebs."

"I'd be glad to give you a ride if you've no other pressing plans," Badawi said with an easy smile. "I heard through a friend that you're taking a sabbatical to write a book. About glassmaking, I presume. I'd love to hear more about it."

"A friend." Michael raised an eyebrow. "You mean another  university donor keeping track of how his money is being spent."

Badawi laughed. "Well, that's another way of putting it."

Michael looked toward the black car with the dark windows, probably bullet proof, and the Badawi muscle standing on the curb, no doubt waiting to open the door as if billionaires don't have working extremities and can't operate door handles.

Michael had never known what to make of Badawi. The man was well known as a generous benefactor and patron of the arts, but his interest in Middle Eastern glassmaking, in particular, had always made Michael uneasy. Yes, Badawi's father had been Lebanese, but that didn't explain all of it. Why had a global financier taken such a personal interest in the career of a young art historian obsessed with glassmaking, turning up at lectures and events that he couldn't even get his mother to attend.

He had to acknowledge that the man was charming and handsome in a world-weary way, but he often seemed… off. One moment hyper focused on what Michael was doing or saying and the next off in some distant place. It was disturbing. Largely because Michael felt the same way much of the time and he recognized the look in the man's eyes, the sense that his attention was both in the moment and in some faraway place. Preoccupied, he'd called it when friends and family teased him about it. A dreamer, they called him. Tormented was more like it.

"I don't want to make you go out of your way."

"It's no problem."

"I'm afraid I'll have to take you up on your generosity another time," Michael said, making a show of looking at his watch. "I'm meeting a friend for dinner. Close enough to walk, in fact. And I better get to it."

Badawi looked away for a moment, then nodded. "Of course. Next time our paths meet."

"Next time."

Badawi and Carson watched as Michael hurried down the steps, nodded at Dryden, and headed past the car and down the street at a rapid clip.

"Shall we make a show of it?" Carson asked, cocking his head toward the museum entrance.

Badawi let out a long sigh. "No need now," he said, turning and heading back to the car. "Make sure he's followed. I suspect the friend he's meeting for dinner is his damned dog."

# FOUR

Kat closed the journal she'd tried to read and raised her seat back and tray table to prepare for landing. Uneasy about sleeping around strangers—or friends and family, for that matter—she shot a quick glance at the man in the seat next to hers. Had she drooled? Snored? Talked in her sleep? Daniel told her that because of her restlessness he'd never slept through the night the whole time they'd been dating. Almost a full year of blissful—ha!—togetherness before it all went kaput.

*What an idiot,* she thought as she leaned her head against the window and watched rivulets of rain race across the pane, leaving silvery trails in their wake. Their relationship had been over way before they'd declared it official. Stasis. Convenience. Fear of being alone. Fear of starting all over with someone else. It was easier to stay than to end it, and less scary than being lonely. And the sex had been fine. Not earth shattering, but maybe earth-shattering sex only happened in romance novels. Daniel hadn't cheated until the very end, but when Kat found out, she realized she didn't care. They'd had a surreal chat about honesty, and he'd gathered his things and left, apparently never looking back.

But Kat looked back. What had he ever seen in her in the first place? And what had she seen in him? Why had it taken an affair to break them up? What had happened to the girl who dreamed of castles, of duels and danger and galloping across the moors—God, she wasn't even sure what a moor was. Yes, she'd been reserved since the dreams started getting really...*real*. Buttoned up, her brother said. Who wouldn't be buttoned up when they had a whole other existence going on in their head? But maybe her reserve hadn't ever been about her dreams setting her apart. Maybe it had just been plain old fear. Of everything. Of being seen. Of risking her heart. She'd never been in a serious relationship—except for Daniel and he didn't really count—and she wondered if the reason was that her heart already felt like it had been broken a thousand times. Why would she want to go through it again?

She reached for her bottle of water and took a long swig. Once again, she gave thanks to the extra points she'd earned on her credit card over the years so she could upgrade to business class without spending a fortune. She couldn't stand feeling penned in and surrounded by strangers. It wasn't claustrophobia, but rather the fear of making a fool of herself. Fear again. This was sounding like a theme. Fear of being alone. Fear of standing out. Fear of exposure. Fear of heartbreak and loss. Fear of sleeping with her mouth hanging open and drooling all over herself. That was a big one.

The man next to her stirred, pulled his noise-canceling headphones down around his neck, and leaned forward to peer out the window. Kat leaned back so he could have a better view of the foggy, rain-spattered landscape. After a few moments of small talk just after takeoff and a snack, he'd clapped his earphones on and closed his eyes, barely moving as they crossed the Atlantic—except for the occasional drumming of his fingers on the armrest.

"Bollocks," he said. "Got to say after a month in L.A., I don't relish returning to London weather."

His accent made her smile. "You from London?"

"Thereabouts. What about you?"

"Headed to a conference."

He glanced at the journal on her lap. "Epigenetics. You're a researcher?"

"Yes. University of Arizona."

"Fascinating. I was just listening to a lecture on Kafka."

"Kafka?" Seemed like a non-sequitur. What did Kafka have to do with epigenetics?

"Yeah," he said as he pulled off his earphones and tucked them into a beat-up backpack. "The meaning of *Metamorphosis*. Transformation. Sudden or gradual. Seen or unseen. Desired or reviled. How you carry the past and the future within you and how it affects everyone and everything around you."

"Wow." She didn't know what to say to all that.

"I mean, isn't that what genetics is all about? Discovering how we're made. How we evolve and change over time? How we understand or manipulate it all? React to it. Live with it. What it means for survival? Of the individual and the species?"

Kat's eyebrows went up. "Yes, but I've never thought about it in terms of Kafka." She pressed her hand against the seat in front of her as the plane bounced on the rain-slicked runway. Engines whined in reverse thrust and her ears popped. As the plane slowed and began to taxi toward the gate, she cast a sideways glance at him. With tousled, dirty blond hair, a chiseled jawline, a diamond stud in his ear, and with his shirtsleeves rolled up and shirt collar open revealing a tendril of ink climbing up his neck, Kat decided he was a very attractive man. "Do you mind if I ask who gave the lecture you were listening to?"

"I did."

"You did?" She couldn't hide the surprise in her voice.

"What?" His voice took on an offended tone which was belied by his bright smile. "Don't I look professorial?"

She stopped herself from rolling her eyes.

"Last time I checked," he went on, "professors came in all shapes and sizes."

"Of course, they do," she said and bent down to gather up her things. When she was done, she turned to him. "I really am interested in the lecture. It's a fascinating take on the subject."

"Seems like there's a lot going on in your field. I'm particularly fascinated by CRISPR and its ethical implications." He leaned over and pulled a card from a pocket in his backpack and held it out to her. "I'd be happy to share my notes or continue the conversation while you're in London."

"That's either very kind or very forward." She looked down at it the card. George Hempstead, III, Faculty of English, Clare College Cambridge. Her eyebrows shot up.

A self-satisfied smirk played on his lips. He hoisted his backpack and stood. "Seriously, I am interested in the science of inheritance and your take on my lecture could offer new insights. If you get tired of geneticists and want to chat about the metamorphosis of the species—either in genetics or in literature—give me a ring. I'll be in London for a few days, and I don't bite. And I've a firecracker of a fiancée who'd most likely tag along and talk your ear off about the implications of art on human development, and vice versa, so rest assured I'm not going to try to get in your knickers. It's just a friendly offer. One academic to another."

Her cheeks flushed. "I'll keep that in mind."

"The more important point is that if you get in a pinch and need a friend, I can be quite resourceful."

"Do I look like a damsel in distress?

"Not at all." He gave her an appraising look. "But I can be a pretty good knight in shining armor."

"Oh, for goodness' sake—"

He adjusted his backpack, leaned toward her, and whispered, "From what you mumble in your sleep, you might need one someday."

# FIVE

"*Khalas!*" Elias Samaan slapped his hands together and scowled at his older brother, tired of having the same, repetitive argument. "You know we must look West, to the Venetian traders and beyond to expand our business. Our glasswork is the best, but we need to sell to buyers who do not look at us and see *kafir*, and there aren't enough new churches or synagogues to fill. This is why I must go to Rome, Madrid, Paris, maybe London, even."

"London?" Boutros's eyes went wide. "Are you mad? The whole of Europe is a backwater beset by war and you want to go all the way to London? They don't even bathe there." He pursed his lips in the characteristic Samaan frown they'd both inherited from their father and his father before them. "Besides, expanding our reach is just an excuse. You simply want to stretch your wings, like Grandfather did."

"Come, are you not curious about what lays beyond the Orontes? Beyond the cedars of Lebanon. Beyond the sea. Are you so bereft of a sense of adventure?" Elias often listened to the stories his friends told—soldiers or merchants, they traveled far and wide and experienced things he would never experience if he stayed in one place. He thought of his friend Sergius, a soldier whom he'd not seen in too long, and wondered where he was.

"I want to make beautiful glass," Boutros said. "I want you to do your job and sell it. And I want to bed my wife, and not necessarily in that order."

"I should hope not." Elias laughed as he looked over the various samples arranged on a table at the front of the Samaan Glassworks shop.

"Speaking of wives," Boutros went on, "you should stay home and marry."

"Since when do you sing the same song as our mother?"

"What about Miriam?"

Elias's scowl told Boutros what he thought of Miriam. "She is a child."

"She's of marriageable age and looks at you the way a little lost lamb looks at her shepherd, though God himself knows not why."

"Lost lamb or not, I am no shepherd, and I will not take her to wife."

"How about—"

Elias held up a staying hand. "Do not start extolling the virtues of all the maidens you know. I am not ready to marry and sire a new generation of Samaans. You're the eldest so that is your job. I'm going to travel, sell our wares where I can, and take my pleasures where I may." He picked up a small lamp and held it up to the light slanting in through a window. "Exquisite. I will never understand how you have the patience for such delicate work."

"You are too like Grandfather."

"A wise man, our grandfather," Elias said with a laugh.

"Wise? As a youth, he was as reckless and intemperate as you."

"An urge to see the world does not equate to recklessness or intemperance, brother. Perhaps Grandfather's wisdom comes from his experience as a man who refused to settle down until—how does he put it?— he'd bedded a beauty in Samarkand, set eyes on the Great Wall of China, and spread his seed from here to Lanzhou. I fear that if the old man were not ailing so, he would saddle up and go with me."

"He fears his wife too much. Grandmother would cast an evil spell on him if he set out on another adventure."

Elias suppressed a shudder. "She is a fearsome thing."

Boutros held a tall glass vessel up to the light. "You know who made this one?"

"No, but Grandfather insists I take it even though it does not carry the Samaan mark." The previous day, when Grandfather had first shown him the piece, Elias had stumbled back as the vision of hands working at the mouth of a furnace, a woman wrapped in a shroud, darkness and more darkness and pain enveloped him. The air became thick. In his hands, the glass quickly warmed and seemed to breathe, pulsing against his skin as if something living within wanted out. He'd quickly set it on the table and wiped his hands on his clothing all the while his grandfather watched with narrowed eyes. Then the old man turned on his heel and disappeared through the doorway without another word.

Boutros held it out to Elias who gave his head a little shake, refusing to take the piece in hand again. Boutros set it back on the table and turned to his brother. "Micah Samaan, the Alchemist of Aleppo."

"Truly?" Elias's eyebrows shot up.

"The one and only."

Without thinking, Elias reached out to run a finger around the lip of the glass. When a bolt of energy shot through him, he jerked his hand back and pressed it against his chest as if it had been licked by fire. "I didn't know we had any of his work left in our storerooms." He tried to keep his voice even. "The piece must go back to, what, 1350 or so? If the stories are true."

Boutros leaned back against the table and watched Elias.

"The Alchemist," Elias went on, trying to marshal his disordered thoughts. "Why would Grandfather risk me taking it on a journey? Wouldn't we want to keep it safe as a tribute to a great artisan?"

"Grandmother insists and Grandfather obeys."

"Poor man. He really is afraid of her."

"We're all afraid of her," Boutros said with a laugh. "After all, the woman claims to be a magus of great power."

"She certainly wields power over this family."

"And you know she claims to communicate with the Alchemist."

Elias winced. The conversation was making his skin prickly and hot.

"She says more than one Samaan has gone mad trying to find his treasure." Boutros picked up the vessel's carrying case and rubbed his thumb over the beautifully tooled leather. "She says this was crafted generations ago by a woman who came all the way from Paris to buy the vessel. The woman knew the piece so well that this—made before she ever arrived in our shop—fit the piece like a tailored glove. The woman claimed it was hers by right, but the Samaan in charge at the time refused to sell. He told the woman that it was not yet time, whatever that meant."

"It meant he missed out on a sale," Elias smirked.

Boutros shrugged. "The woman apparently made such a scene that some of the neighboring merchants came to watch the show. She talked of everlasting love and the transmigration of souls and lost chances and waiting, waiting, waiting. Eventually she settled herself, handed over the case, walked out of the shop, and threw herself into the river. She was found the next day."

"Drowned." The word came out as a whisper. Sweat beaded on Elias's brow, but he did not wipe it away.

Boutros nodded. "Grandmother says the fates were not aligned then."

"Ah, the fates." Elias turned away, his voice dry as the desert wind. "This story grows more tragic by the moment."

"Grandmother says the vessel Micah Samaan made has been waiting all these years."

"God's bones," Elias scoffed. "Waiting for what?"

"You."

Elias's eyes went wide and his skin went cold. "She said that? Truly? Am I finally the Samaan destined to find the Alchemist's elusive treasure?"

"She says it is your destiny."

Elias threw his head back and barked out a laugh. "And why does she not tell me this herself?"

Boutros shot him a harsh look. "And when is she supposed to tell you anything? You avoid her as if her madness is a contagion."

Elias rubbed a hand over his face. He did avoid his grandmother and had done so since he was a boy. The woman scared him. For years, her sightless eyes had tracked his movements throughout the house. He felt her piercing gaze on him even when they were not in the same room. "Her mind is addled from the opium," he said finally.

"Maybe," Boutros admitted.

"Don't tell me you put stock in her superstitions. The more you pay heed to the ravings of old women, the more I fear for your future."

"My future," Boutros snorted. "You're the one about to embark on a voyage across the world and you're the one—"

"Do not worry about me, *akhi*." Elias interrupted before Boutros went any further.

But Boutros had watched Elias struggle against a darkness he could not understand. As the elder brother, he had sought to comfort him, but had always been turned away with a laugh and a jest.

"I have seen it in you, brother," Boutros said. "I have watched you wage war with yourself, watched as you use your vices to soothe the restlessness in your soul. Watched as you searched for…something. Maybe this journey is the answer. Maybe Grandmother is right."

Elias forced a smile. "Here's a prediction for you. When I return, you will be fat and surrounded by babies."

Boutros blew out a breath and placed his hands on his most beloved brother's shoulders. There were places locked away in Elias's heart that no one had ever touched, but their Grandmother understood things—*saw* things—that too often came to pass. Boutros could not ignore what the old woman said, no matter how unbelievable they sounded.

Just that morning she had drawn Boutros aside to warn him that although Elias must make this journey, his return was not guaranteed. The idea of it cleaved Boutros's heart, but he could not show it, could not allow Elias to see the fear and sadness in his eyes.

"Babies take nine months to make," he said finally.

"Maybe you will have twins."

"How long?"

Elias did not answer. He crossed his arms across his chest and leaned back against the table. "I have a mind to visit Roland's home, which he says is as fair a place as any he has seen in his travels. A mighty sea surrounding an island filled with the bluest lakes, the greenest hills, the deepest forests, and cathedrals that reach to the sky."

"Roland Howard talks too much."

"Maybe, but he will be a good traveling companion. He has a gift for languages as well as the sword. He has a fine musket and knows how to use it, and he has a talent for finding just the right place for food and lodgings and," he offered his brother a sly smile, "fine company."

"So, you are to take your destiny in hand and travel to lands I will never see." Boutros fought to keep the emotion at bay. "I will miss you, you know."

Elias swallowed hard. "We have other brothers and sisters for you to worry over."

"They aren't nearly as entertaining as my favorite, troublemaking brother. You've said goodbye to everyone else?"

"Mother and our sisters wept as if I were being sealed into the crypt. Our brothers begged to go along, and Grandfather turned away with tears in his eyes."

"And Grandmother? Did you go to her finally?"

"Grandfather said—"

"Did you go to her?"

Elias stared at his feet and shook his head. "But Grandfather told me that she bade me safe travels and said…"

"Said what?" Boutros waited as Elias bit back some emotion.

"She said it is time."

Boutros studied Elias for a moment then pulled him into his arms for a hard embrace. He would count the days until his brother—his best friend—returned. And would pray that the restlessness of Elias's soul would be eased by whatever he might find on his travels. "I do not know what awaits you, but please, promise that you will return to us."

When Elias stepped back, both brothers' eyes glistened. Boutros waved Elias away and turned back to the assorted glassware on the table. "All will be packed and ready for you at dawn tomorrow. I'll see to it."

Elias nodded and headed to the door to take his leave. It did not escape either man's notice that Elias had promised nothing.

# SIX

The young woman reined in her mount at the crest of the ridge and looked out at the hills and woods unfolding below her.

"Emmaline!" She turned as a man called out from behind her. "You'll have been missed by now. Lady Musgrave will be asking for you, and it is past time for me to escort you home."

"One moment more, Giles," she called back. Her stepmother could wait. The woman had been trying Emmaline's patience more than usual lately—and Emmaline was certain, if asked, Lady Musgrave would say the same of her. It was no secret the woman wanted her married and out from under her roof and was busy trying to sell her to the highest bidder. Every interaction left a bitter taste in her mouth, and Emmaline took every opportunity to annoy her. Daily. "The view is so lovely this time of day." She turned again toward the woods and the road snaking out from beneath its shaded bowers. "Where are you, Roland?" she murmured. "Please come help me decide what to do."

It had been almost two years since she'd last seen Cousin Roland. Well, as her stepmother's nephew, he was not really a cousin. Still, Roland had spent much of his youth at Hartley Castle with Emmaline and her older brothers—half-brothers, as Lady Musgrave was always keen to point out—and Emmaline had always adored him. Now, as he was returning from a trip abroad, she hoped he would help save her from a destiny worse than death: marriage.

She shaded her eyes and scanned the distance. It could be weeks before he arrived, but still her heart leapt as she saw movement along the road. She let out a sigh. It was only a hawk taking flight.

"Emmaline!"

"Coming!" She turned her mount back toward the not-so-patiently-waiting Giles. Poor man. She knew she was a trial and that he only put up with her because he had to. Because he didn't want to spoil his relationship with Mary, one of the laundrymaids who also served as a sort of lady's maid to Emmaline. She was also Emmaline's only true friend.

"Roland will know what I should do," she told her mare as they picked their way down the hillside. Emmaline had attempted to speak with her father before he'd left for London last week, but Sir Philip had more important matters on his mind and had swept her concerns away before thundering off to serve his king.

"Do not worry so," Mary told her just last night. "As much as your father admires Sir Neville, he'll not force you into marrying such a man. Surely, he cannot expect you to…" Mary shuddered and made a face, unable to complete the thought. She had an understanding with Giles and knew exactly what went on between a man and a woman.

"It's not just Sir Neville, Mary," Emmaline said. "Lady Musgrave has recently been singing the praises of Will Beachem. If she can't get Sir Neville to take me off her hands, she'll be happy to sell me to Beacham."

"But he's a brute!" Mary had exclaimed.

The problem, as Emmaline saw it, was that Mary, as a servant, had choices and knew exactly what her place was. Mary and Giles—a veritable magician with horses and therefore invaluable to the estate—were saving their wages to set up a household and have a family of their own in his rooms above the stables. Emmaline, however, as the bastard daughter of a baronet was neither fish nor fowl, servant nor served. Her father had ensured she was educated and charming, could speak Scots, French, and a smattering of Latin, paint, sew, sing and play the harp, and ride like the very devil himself. She'd grown up with six brothers who sometimes adored her and sometimes forgot she existed, treated as family when close acquaintances visited but shunted off to her rooms when more important personages arrived. She was part of a family whose pedigree went back to the days of the Conqueror and yet no one, save her father, knew who her mother was. Emmaline was certain the not knowing drove her stepmother mad and was why she was treated one day as the daughter of a titled lady and the next as the offspring of a tavern whore. Either way, her father wasn't telling.

Lady Musgrave, her father's wife and mother to her brothers, spent her days planning brilliant and profitable matches for her sons and dreaming of the day she could remove Emmaline from Hartley Castle, preferably by foisting her on a man who had lost his first wife to a wasting disease, his second to childbirth, and several of his teeth and most of his hair to the vagaries of age and who lived too far away for frequent visits. Emmaline shuddered. There was still time for Sir Neville to fall off his horse or get run through by brigands, and even though she knew it was a grave sin, she prayed nightly for such an outcome. Emmaline was not opposed to marriage and was certainly eager to be out from under Lady Musgrave's influence, but the thought of wedding someone likely afflicted by gout and windy bowels made her bile rise. The man had more hair sprouting out his nose and ears than on his head, for goodness' sake.

But at least he was kind, unlike the handsome but arrogant Will Beacham. And Sir Neville was a Royalist with a fine estate which would accord her all the protections due the wife of a wealthy man. Will Beacham, in contrast, was the grandson of a notorious border reiver known for his cruelty and had grown into a man with a violent temper who had whipped more than one servant nearly to death. If she married Beacham…no. She could not marry him. He had greedy eyes and roving hands. She shivered. The way he looked at her, as if she were laid out naked on a banquet table just for his feasting, made her stomach roil. She'd rather be a governess. Or join a convent. And she wasn't even Catholic.

Inspiration struck as she rode alongside Giles on the way back home. As soon as Roland arrived, she would convince him to take her along on his next trip. She could ride as well as any man and wield a short blade if necessary. Plus, she'd learned enough of cooking from time spent in the kitchen and would find it an adventure sleeping at a roadside inn. *Imagine*, she thought. *Sleeping under the stars!* Adventure, not marriage, was what she needed.

As a third son, Roland would never inherit a title or lands of his own and so he'd set out to make his own way in the world. Why couldn't she? Nearly thirty and not yet married, Roland came and went as he pleased and was even now returning from his second—*second!*—trip to the Holy Land. She was not yet three and twenty but Lady Musgrave was impatient to have her wedded and bedded and burdened with a brood of children as soon as possible. But why should she be forced to marry when a man like Roland could do as he pleased? The unfairness of it all made her want to spit. And that attitude, she knew, was one more reason her stepmother was anxious to be rid of her.

# SEVEN

Kat tilted her head back to take in the dazzling blown glass chandelier, obviously a Chihuly, hanging in the central rotunda of the Victoria & Albert Museum. Glass had long fascinated her and, according to the website, the V&A boasted one of the most comprehensive collections in the world, covering 3500 years of history. That was why she was here.

She was a Junior Girl Scout when she'd discovered that glass is basically melted sand and that she could take a glassblowing workshop and get a badge to boot. Turns out, she was an unmitigated disaster. Still, she'd persevered until she managed to produce a lopsided little candy bowl for her parents' anniversary that could barely hold a handful of M&Ms. Unfortunately, it was shortly after that when she'd experienced her first desolation dream during which she'd first seen in her mind's eye and held in her dreaming hands the glowing glass vessel with the gold rim that had haunted her ever since.

A group of young schoolgirls swarmed past her as she checked the museum map on her phone. The place was overwhelming, and she allowed herself to drift along in the wake of the chattering students. Moments later, she was in an airy sculpture gallery, smiling at the giggles and stares some of the naked statues elicited.

That morning, she'd been the youngest and only female on her panel and, as usual, she'd failed at managing her imposter syndrome, her fear of being laughed at, talked over, or not taken as seriously as the older, more experienced male researchers. Thankfully, everyone had been welcoming. She'd even received an invitation to visit the lab of a Cambridge geneticist she'd long admired.

The comfort level with her peers didn't translate into the courage to broach her interest in connecting epigenetic inheritance to memory formation, the reptilian brain, and déjà vu. Or to talk about her theories linking epigenetics with deep memories inherited from long-dead ancestors. She'd probably never be friendly enough with anyone to talk about that. She knew that by even entertaining such ideas she was flirting with the far *far* edge of reason and science, but that was what made it so fun, wasn't it? That was where the pioneers and innovative thinkers lived, right? At least that's how she rationalized it. She reveled in asking w*hat if* and using flights of fancy—or in her case, dreams—to imagine and make deep connections between consciousness, neuroscience, and genetics. It's why she'd gone into research in the first place. If only she could figure out how to turn her avocational interest into a solid, fundable proposal.

The sounds of children laughing drew her attention back to the exhibit hall. She wandered away from the group of uniformed students and stepped outside to take in the courtyard where visitors lounged at tables and children played on the grass and at the edge of the reflecting pool. *This might be my new favorite museum*, she thought. She considered getting a cup of tea from the café while enjoying the spring sunshine, but the glass collection was tugging at her. Time to get started on the exhibits.

She headed back to the information desk in the rotunda. One of her favorite things to do in a museum was to ask employees and docents what their favorite pieces were. A bright-eyed young woman with ebony skin, a shaved head, and earrings that looked like they belonged in the collection greeted her—Dayo, her name tag announced—and was more than happy to share her favorites. At the top of the list was a piece known as the Luck of Edenhall.

"In fact," Dayo explained, "The Luck has a charming history as the talisman of a great English estate. Its history is full of enchantments and dancing fairies, and it's even been mentioned in more than a few plays and poems."

"That sounds exactly like what I'm looking for," Kat said, delighted. She asked for directions and headed downstairs. Taking time to talk with the museum employees was one of things that Daniel always groused about and now, thinking back, it was one of the reasons she'd kept doing it. God. How childish. She was almost embarrassed for herself. She remembered that time at the Getty in L.A. and how strange it had all been.

The getaway had been going about as well as a trip with Daniel could go until they happened upon a painting by Peter Lely of a woman in a green dress, painted in the mid 1600s. "I had a dress just like that," Kat remarked out of the blue, and Daniel cut her one of his exasperated, here-we-go-again looks that just served to piss her off.

She'd stepped closer, peering at the painting. "Only mine was velvet and that looks like silk." She'd said it in a flippant tone, but something inside her seemed to be shining and pulsing, like a strobe lighting up her soul. Daniel, of course, just rolled his eyes. Until she said, "I was wearing it the night I met Elias."

"What the hell are you talking about?" he demanded, but she had no answer. Later that night, she woke to find Daniel staring at her from a chair across the room. "Who the hell is Elias? You called out to him *in your sleep.*"

She'd had no answer for that, but had stayed clear of portrait galleries ever since. Now, she was going to see a piece of glass. No chance of seeing strange portraits in the Middle Eastern gallery. It'd be full of glass and pottery, books and rugs, mosaics and tapestries. She'd be perfectly safe.

By the time she hit the landing, the air seemed to take shape around her, vibrating and shimmering like the aura hugging a streetlamp on a foggy evening. She reached out and steadied herself with a hand against the wall. *Maybe she should have had that cup of tea after all.* The place had gone quiet, as if her ears were plugged from a rapid change in air pressure. She shook her head, stuck a finger in one ear like when she had water in it from swimming. *Maybe she hadn't eaten enough.* She hadn't stayed around for lunch at the conference and was probably just hungry. Or dehydrated. *I'll get something in the café before heading back to the hotel.*

Blinking back the viscous feelings, she wended her way through the maze of displays toward her destination, hoping for a bench in one of the galleries.

As she went, something took shape in her belly. As if on a snug tether, she followed the pull toward the next gallery. Her vision swam and her skin went cold and damp, like she was walking through a morning mist. Her fingers flew to her temples, kneading hard, trying to focus, keep herself upright. Her breath came in shallow gasps as the room spun around her in lazy circles. *Oh god, I'm going to be sick.*

She swayed and gripped the purse strap draped across her shoulder as if clutching it could keep her upright. *Had she stepped through some magical portal like Alice falling down the rabbit hole or the kids climbing through the back of the wardrobe into Narnia? Did she have food poisoning? Was she having a lucid dream?* No. Because this was real. *This was real!* Right there in front of her, close enough to touch, was a piece of her dreams.

A dream, yet not a dream. A memory, yet not a memory. That was the first thing that popped into her mind. Then: *What the hell?* She stepped forward to read the information.

The Luck of Edenhall
Goblet about 1350
Case 1400–1500

This superb example of luxury Syrian glass, in pristine condition, is one of the most famous objects in the V&A. Possibly a souvenir from a pilgrimage to the Holy Land, it belonged to the Musgrave family of Edenhall in Cumbria and became their talisman. Traditionally, the cup is said to have belonged to the fairies. When disturbed, they fled and left it behind, crying "If this cup should break or fall/Farewell the luck of Edenhall."

*How is this happening?* How could something she'd seen and touched in her dreams be real, be right in front of her, displayed under glass in a London museum for the whole world to see as if it were just another pretty artifact. *Impossible.*

Even as her thoughts wavered between the underwater sensation of dreams remembered and the solidity of the here and now, she became aware of a presence at her side. "Miss, you are white as a ghost." A man's voice. The words came at her from a distance, like whispers bubbling up from the bottom of the sea. "There's a bench on the other side of the case." A touch at her elbow sent a shockwave through her. Her knees buckled and two strong hands gripped her arms, keeping her upright.

"No." she jerked away.

"Please, let me help or Security is going to have to scrape you off the floor." His hand took hers—skin to skin—and just as quickly dropped it. She stumbled and reached out blindly. A mumbled curse and the hands gripped her again as he stepped closer and wrapped an arm around her waist. "I've got you," he whispered. "I'm here. Let me help."

She dragged her eyes away from the case and toward the man trying to steady her and *oh my god*. She swallowed back a cry as she met the dark, knowing gaze of one of the most striking men she'd ever seen.

∞

When Michael was about four years old, he'd stuck fork tines in an electrical socket. It was one of his earliest memories, not just because of the shock, but because of the look of horror and fear on his mother's face. Now, he was reliving that moment. Only this time, the fork tines were his own fingers and the electrical socket was the woman collapsing into him. The one whose beautiful face stared up at him in horror.

He tried to appear calm, even as his hands shook. He was amazed his lungs could push air up through his larynx to form words, and it wouldn't have surprised him if his hair was standing on end.

"You need to sit," he managed, pulse thudding in his ears. *Who is this woman?* "You're about to faint." Gingerly, he guided her to the wooden bench beyond the display case. She sunk down on it, put her head between her knees, hands over her face and shook her head back and forth. He crouched at her side, watching. Waiting. Not wanting to alarm her. Not wanting to tell her he knew what she'd experienced. That he'd experienced it too.

"Better?" he asked finally.

She shook her head slightly. Michael looked around the gallery to see if anyone else had witnessed the encounter. He didn't know what to do. His instinct was to press his lips to her hair, pull her into his arms, and hold her close until she felt better. Clearly, that would not go over well. "Shall I locate a guard and let them know you're not feeling well?" After a moment, she raised her head and gradually straightened. Her gaze caught and held his.

"No." It was a barely there word that contained a universe of meaning.

"At least let me get you some water. There's a water fountain upstairs." He looked around again as if the gallery itself would tell him what to do.

She shook her head again.

"But you almost passed out!" He stood and ran both hands through his hair, frustration, confusion, and the need to do something—*anything*—for this woman.

"I can't have a drink down here."

"Then let me help you to the café. We'll get you some water or tea, juice. Something to eat or…"

She turned to look at him, her gaze cutting through to the core of his soul. "Who are you?"

Michael angled his head toward her. How to answer that? At that moment, he wasn't sure he knew the answer. But whoever he was, he was connected to her. She was connected to him. And they were, he knew in his bones, both connected to the Luck. "I'm a frequent visitor. An art historian. They all know me here."

Her eyes searched his face as if looking for something. Trying to place him from a different context. Or remembering.

"Please, let me do something for you." He could feel the panic rising in his chest and he held himself still so he wouldn't frighten her.

She nodded slowly. "Water, then."

"Right. Don't go anywhere. I'll be back in a jiffy." He turned on his heel, heading for the stairs. On the main floor, he rushed to the information desk and caught Dayo's eye. The girl was friendly and kind to everyone and they'd exchanged many a flirtatious conversation over the years.

"Hey," he said. "You've a visitor downstairs by the Luck who's had a dizzy spell. I'd like to get her some water before she faints dead away."

Dayo's eyes went wide. "Oh, no! Shall I summon help?"

"No need. She's just a bit unsteady on her feet. I think some water will put her to rights."

"We keep paper cups squirreled away back here." Dayo bent to pull out a stack of cups and handed him one. Just use the drinking fountain."

"You're the best."

Dayo smiled up at him, but he was already heading down the hall for the fountain. When he returned moments later, Dayo called out. "Michael, is your visitor wearing a blue jacket and white V-neck?"

"Maybe," he said, impatient to head downstairs. The truth was, he hadn't even noticed what she was wearing.

"I think it's the woman who asked about my favorite exhibit, and I told her about the Luck. But she must be feeling better." Michael's eyes narrowed as Dayo went on. "Because she just left."

For a heartbeat, he just stared at Dayo, a wave of nausea sweeping over him as if he'd been driving over a hill too fast and had gone airborne. She can't be gone. *She can't be gone.*

Dayo's expression, soft and sympathetic, made Michael want to scream. "Sorry," she said. "She left as soon you went to the water fountain. She's probably still out front, couldn't have gone far."

He was pushing through the front door and running toward the street when the woman closed the door to her taxi. He watched her turn toward him. Watched as she placed her hand against the window, and then quickly removed it. Watched as the taxi pulled away from the curb and disappeared down the street.

# EIGHT

The cabbie's face was expressionless as Michael paid her. *Thanks for nothing,* he thought as he shut the door and dragged himself up the steps to his flat. As one of only a handful of female drivers, she had obviously been unhappy about a crazed man scrambling into her taxi and shouting *Follow that cab!* Like someone from a BBC crime drama. Especially when she had to have seen the woman get into the cab parked at the curb in front of her. Even as the words came out of his own mouth, Michael had been appalled at how they sounded. At how desperate they seemed. Then they'd lost sight of the woman's cab. Of course. His driver slowed at every intersection, paused to let pedestrians cross, and generally did everything she could to lose the woman they were supposedly tailing.

And now she was gone. The woman he'd been waiting for his entire life. Of course, he hadn't known he'd been waiting for her until she appeared on the staircase landing. She'd swayed and braced herself on the wall, and the air in the room shifted, thickened, taking on that viscous quality he experienced whenever he got too close to the display case. He'd been reluctant to approach her, instead waiting to see what she did, how she reacted to the Luck. That was why she was at the V&A. It had to be. Even if she hadn't yet realized it. He knew it as surely as he knew his own name.

He went straight to the kitchen for an ale, ignoring Sal's whining for attention. He was parched. Wrung out. After a moment spent staring into the distance at everything and nothing, he headed out to his little postage stamp of a backyard and sat on the steps as Sal leapt past him to chase some bird that had the audacity to violate the perimeter of his territory.

She would return to the V&A, of that he was certain. She'd been scared—of the Luck, of herself, and, especially, of him. The jolt of recognition in her eyes when she'd first laid eyes on the display case was obvious, and when she'd looked up at him…well, he'd never forget the expression on her face. Just like he'd never forget the first time he'd seen the Luck.

The strangest thing was that he only had a vague idea of what she looked like. Attractive, yes. Well, *he'd* been attracted to her immediately. *Viscerally*. On a cellular level. Her eyes had been a mossy, inviting green when she'd stared up at him in shock. Her hair…what color was it? It'd been pulled back in a ponytail, and he hadn't paid it a bit of attention. He wouldn't have even known what she'd been wearing, except that Dayo had noticed: a blue jacket and white V-neck shirt. But somehow, she was as familiar to him as his own face.

Yes, she'd go back. Clearly, the Luck called to her the same way it called to him. And when she returned, he'd be there. Ready to find out exactly who she was and why she seemed like the answer he'd been searching for.

∞

Kat closed her hotel room door and leaned against it as if it were a barrier that could keep the questions and confusion at bay. Her head pounded. Her stomach roiled. *What the hell happened back there? Who was that man and how could that thing, that glass goblet, be real? Pulsating with energy? Calling to her?* It was just a pretty prop in her dreams, wasn't it? Maybe this entire day had been a dream. The whole trip to London, the conference, all of it, just some hallucinatory episode. A lucid dream from which she'd soon wake. Lord knew she'd had plenty of bizarre lucid dreams before. She just needed to burrow into it, acknowledge the dream state, take control of it, and then climb her way back out. Back to reality.

She stumbled into the bathroom, rustled through her toiletries bag, and extracted a couple of ibuprofen. She threw them back and downed them with a glass of water, aimed herself toward the bed, stripped off her clothes, and climbed in. Pulling the covers over her head, she curled into a tight ball, the faint silvery birthmark tracing down her midsection throbbed with every heartbeat. Stress pains, her doctors told her when they'd made her wear a Holter monitor to test for an arrhythmia. Maybe she should've taken more than two ibuprofen. Maybe she needed a shot or two—or three—of good old fashioned bacanora.

She thought about getting back up, but instead, curled tighter around herself. She squeezed her eyes shut. But there, lurking behind her lids, was the man from the museum, staring at her in, what? Wonder? Incredulity? Awe? Desire? Dreams aren't meant to be intelligible or fair. She knew that. She'd lived it. They were not explanatory reviews of the day's events. But why did hers have to be so fucked up? How could they intrude into her reality? How was that even possible? It wasn't. It couldn't be. And yet… the thing she saw before falling into a deep sleep was the look in the man's eyes—deep understanding and unbridled desire—as he held out his hands and offered the Luck of the Edenhall to her. *For us,* he whispered. *I made it for us.*

# NINE

"Three things."

Sergei Badawi looked up from the laptop open on his desk as Carson strode into the room. "Good evening to you too."

Carson waved away the greeting with a smile. "First," he said, sitting heavily in the chair facing Sergei's desk, "it turns out the Corning Fellow is Canadian and she's an art historian like your man, Michael Samaan. Her name is Celeste Simpson. She specializes in old glass, pieces associated with religious rituals, purification rites, rites of passage and, get this, medicinal and alchemical practices. Chalices, censers, ampullae, and the like. Kinkaid's sending over her information. Curricula vitae. Family history. Everything you asked for."

Sergei's breath caught and he dropped his head into his hands. After a moment, he exhaled slowly, breathing through the hope. Through the eviscerating pain. After a long moment, he looked up. "What else?"

"There was an incident today at the V&A, next to the display."

"What kind of incident?"

"A visitor—a woman, maybe American—nearly faints and Michael, who was there because he's always there, catches her. He goes upstairs to get some water and she takes off. And get this," Carson leaned forward, "Lindhurst, saw it from outside. Says Michael ran down the steps, hailed a cab and went after her, like a chase scene in a movie."

Sergei snapped his laptop shut and stood, adrenalin flooding his body. "Was Lindhurst able to follow?"

Carson shook his head and sat back. "Happened too fast."

Sergei couldn't stand still after hearing news like this. He moved around his desk. Leaned against it, crossed his arms, uncrossed them, put his hands in his pockets, looked expectantly at Carson.

"But, according to Lindhurst who immediately went in to talk to Dayo Otieno—that cheery girl with the dreadlocks at the information desk?—Michael looked like he'd been hit upside the head with a wrecking ball when she told him the woman was gone. Dayo said, and I quote, 'He spun around and ran out the door as if the devil himself were snapping at his heels.'"

"All right," Sergei said. "It's 24/7 on Michael now."

"We're already 24/7."

Sergei's eyes went wide in surprise as Carson shrugged. "Which leads to the third thing. Remember the break-ins? Right after the hit and run?"

Oh, he remembered. He hated that he'd not been able to do anything about the accident that had killed Michael's father and sent his mother to the hospital. Hated that the family had been vulnerable in the weeks after the accident. Most of all, hated that he suspected he knew who was behind it but couldn't prove a damn thing. "What about them?"

"Carys Samaan's security system has been hacked again. We were able to kick them out almost as soon as they got in, but—"

Sergei crossed his arms. "There shouldn't be a way to hack that system."

Carson gave him a narrow-eyed look. "There's always a way. You know that. Anyway, Kinkaid put a man on her."

"Christ."

"So, we've got her and her place surveilled, but they also report that someone has been tailing Michael. Someone besides us, I mean. We checked his system and there's no evidence of a breach."

"So," Sergei let out a grim sigh, "the woman who murdered Michael's father is back."

"Are you sure it was a woman? Even if you're positive, no one could prove first-degree murder."

Sergei shot him a dark glance. "Even if the police couldn't tell from the CCTV footage, it was a woman. I'm sure of it. And even if she just meant to get Michael's attention, his father died as a result. Not two weeks later, there was the attempted break-in at his mother's house. While she was still in hospital, for god's sake. A month after that, Michael's terrace was ransacked."

Carson nodded. He remembered all of it. Remembered how fucking out of his mind Sergei had been. "Who is she and what is she after? You know, don't you?"

"As to the who, I'm pretty sure I know. Unfortunately, she's notoriously hard to pin down. There's never been many of us around at the same time." Sergei rubbed a hand over his face. "As to the what, it's the same thing I'm after. The glass spheres the Alchemist made, the ones tied to the Luck of Edenhall and to each of the couples he 'helped.'" He put air quotes around the word.

"But why harm Michael? Doesn't that defeat the purpose?"

"Not if the purpose is revenge. Not if the purpose is to end it all."

Carson raised an eyebrow.

"Don't look at me like that," Sergei said. "I tried revenge. It didn't help."

"Has anything like this happened before?"

"Over and over again."

"Why is it that you remember everything, and he doesn't?"

"I have no idea. It's a curse, maybe. A fluke in the magic. A flaw in the alchemical process. I've always wondered why Michael's genetic line goes straight back to the Alchemist while I am just…a floater. Some sort of mongrel adopted over and over again or just left to roam the streets. I remember everything but am reborn without roots. Always just…suddenly appearing. Suddenly existing, with a memory of all my former lives, but without a sense of any current family connections."

There were times Sergei thought he'd go mad with the sheer exhaustion of it all. The repetition. The failure. The loneliness. He had gone mad. Before. But not this time. Not now. Marie was the wildcard. Her and her murderous tosser of a husband. Marie Scarpa. That had been her name back in the past. When Michael had been in grad school, she'd resurfaced. Or at least Sergei was convinced she'd resurfaced. At the time, he had his chief of security search for her. He came up blank. There wasn't a single record in all of Europe for a woman by that name with any chance of being the one he was searching for.

"So, it's all related. The terrible hit and run, the sailing accident in Scotland, the broken arm..." Carson studied Sergei.

"Don't forget last Christmas when Michael had to get his stomach pumped."

"Right. The belladonna. And the poor bloke has no idea?"

"Oh, I think Michael has an idea," Sergei said. "Or at least a growing awareness. He certainly suspects I'm connected but doesn't know what it all means. Not yet."

"But soon?"

"I think so. I feel it." He paused in his pacing to stare down at the pattern on his carpet for a long moment, then looked up. "This time it feels different."

Carson stood. "For your sake, I hope you're right."

"I have no idea why you don't call the authorities and have me locked away in a padded room."

Carson laughed. "I'd miss the perks that come with the job. And your sparkling sense of humor."

The muscle in Sergei's jaw clenched and unclenched. "You know, I've not always found someone I could trust. Too often, it's been..."

Carson shrugged and strode back to the door. "This time around you got lucky."

# TEN

Michael looked up from his book and met her gaze. Slowly, he marked his page, closed the cover, and stood. His destiny had just walked in. *Destiny.* Was that cliché? No. It was the only word that made sense, and it resonated now like an echo in his head, as if someone had shouted it over and over again into the previously bleak cavern of his life.

For two days, Michael had wandered between the museum's café, art library, study rooms, and the Luck's display case, trying to work and doing a piss-poor job of it. Good thing he was a known quantity, or someone on staff would have already called Metropolitan Police. He pictured helicopters hovering and sirens blaring. He'd asked Dayo to keep an eye out from her position at the information desk and to text him if "the woman" showed up again, insisting he just wanted to make sure she was okay. Dayo had rolled her eyes and had not texted him. But it didn't matter. The woman had come looking for him.

He didn't have to glance at his watch to know they had only thirty minutes before the place closed; he'd been watching the clock since the museum opened that morning. Now, he watched as she wound her way through the tables toward him. *Who was she? What had she done since she'd run from him? What was going through her mind? What had her life been like before she'd set eyes on the Luck? Before she set eyes on him.*

She took in the room hesitantly, eyes widening at the ornate ceiling, extravagantly tiled and painted walls, tall stained-glass windows, and large globes of light illuminating the space like harvest moons. The café was one of Michael's favorite places in London and he was unaccountably pleased that she appeared to like it too. After what seemed like an eternity during which he dared not breathe, she arrived at his table.

"May I join you?" A barely-there tremor in her voice. Was it just nerves or was she still afraid of him?

"Of course." He motioned to a chair and waited until she sat before taking his seat again.

"I wanted to thank you for helping me the other day," she said.

"It was my pleasure. I'm only sorry you…felt you had to leave so quickly." He heard himself speak and wondered what made him sound so damn formal?

"I may have had a panic attack."

He nodded. There were a thousand things he wanted to say, wanted to know, but he waited. Let her lead the conversation.

She shrugged. "Although for the life of me, I don't understand why."

Michael willed a smile. He suspected he knew why.

"I went to the display case again," she said. "Just now."

"And?"

"Well, I didn't have another episode, if that's what you're asking. But that doesn't mean I'm okay, either."

"I understand."

"Yes." She nodded slowly. "I think maybe you do." It was an enigmatic reply and as soon as she'd said it, her eyes drifted away as if she couldn't hold his gaze.

"Would you like a cup of tea? The café closes soon, but I feel compelled to offer."

"Thanks, but no." She picked at the cuff of her jacket. "Do you work here?"

"Sometimes it seems like it, but no. I do spend a lot of time here, though." He reached into his back pocket and pulled out his wallet, extracting a card. He put it on the table and cautiously pushed it toward her, afraid of crossing her boundaries, of touching her and sending her running again. "I'm an art historian. On sabbatical right now, doing research for a book on the history of Syrian glassmaking. The Luck of Edenhall has long been a favorite of mine. I was in primary school, on a field trip, when I first saw it. I've been coming back ever since."

She leaned forward and scanned the card. "Michael Samaan. University College London." Her gaze flicked back up to his. "Did I pronounce that correctly?"

"Samaan?" He nodded. "Perfectly."

"Well, it's nice to meet you, Michael. I'm Katherine. Kat, for short."

He noted she didn't offer her last name and he didn't press. "Your accent sounds American."

"I'm from Tucson. In Arizona."

The corner of his mouth tipped up in a smile. "Ah, I've heard of Tucson. And Arizona. Famous for stolen de Koonings and large holes in the ground."

She smiled, and it was like lightning *zinging* through his bloodstream. His reaction was immediate. Increased heart rate. Increased blood flow. Straight to the groin.

"As an art historian," she said, "you must know the de Kooning was returned and restored and, I believe, the large hole you speak of is actually quite *grand*. With a magnificent river at the bottom."

He nodded, as if giving deep consideration to the subject. "One might even call it a canyon, I suppose."

"One might indeed." She glanced down at his card again, lightly touched a fingertip to one corner. "And what about you? Are you from London, Dr. Samaan?"

"Are you asking where I live or about my ethnicity?"

She offered him a one-shouldered shrug. "Sorry, I just…Samaan doesn't sound very British."

"No apology necessary. I was born and grew up about an hour outside of London. My mother is Welsh, blue-eyed and black-headed as the devil himself, as she likes to say. Her forefathers were likely among the locals who hauled the bluestones from the quarry and stood them on end at Stonehenge. But my father is a newcomer. He immigrated from Aleppo for university and ended up staying." He offered her a smile. "That's in Syria. In the Middle East."

"Touché." She smiled again. I'm not a world traveler, but I do watch the news."

"So, Kat from Arizona, what brings you to London?"

"A conference. I'm a geneticist."

One dark eyebrow lifted. "Did you present a paper?"

"No, but I was on a panel. My first international conference."

"Impressive. A panel on…?"

A woman with a V&A nametag appeared beside them. "Sorry to disturb, Dr. Samaan," she said, "but the museum closes in fifteen minutes." She gave them an expectant nod and moved toward the only other occupied table in the room.

Michael swore under his breath. "We're about to be expelled. I don't suppose you'd let me buy you a drink. Or take you to dinner." His heart skipped a beat as her expression went flat. *I've been too forward. She's going to disappear again, and I don't even have a last name!* "I'm sorry. Of course. I'm being presumptuous. It's just that—"

"No. It's fine…I mean, I could meet you somewhere, but I don't want—"

"You're right. I don't have a car here anyway. We could go somewhere close enough to walk. Take the Tube." *What is wrong with me? I can't stop babbling.* "Or we could share a cab." *She's going to think I'm a complete nutter.*

She looked at him from under a fringe of thick lashes. "Or you could charge after me in a separate cab."

"Bloody hell." He groaned and rubbed his temples. "I am sorry about that. It was rash and impulsive, and I know how it must've appeared, but I needed to make sure you were okay." She gave him a skeptical look and he raised his hands in surrender. "I was—"

"Having a panic attack?"

He laughed. "God, yes. That's exactly what I was having."

She pushed back her chair and stood. "I could eat something," she said with as much nonchalance as she could muster.

His gaze held hers for a moment as if to make sure she wasn't going to vanish, then he stood, stuffed his book in his messenger bag, and slung it across his shoulder. "Do you like Greek food?"

# ELEVEN

Elias craned his neck yet again to try to catch sight of their destination. After two months on the road, he was weary of travel, although he loathed to admit that to Roland. His buttocks ached from sitting, his back was stiff, and he was bored. He would have preferred to ride instead of sitting in the carriage, but a thick mist had been hanging in the air since mid-morning and he'd rather be uncomfortable and dry than uncomfortable, cold, wet, and susceptible to catching a chill.

The plan was to spend a week at Hartley Castle to pay respects to Roland's aunt and, hopefully meet the cousins of whom he'd spoken so fondly—especially the lively Emmaline. Since Roland's own mother had died delivering him into the world, Roland had spent a good deal of time at Hartley Castle under his mother's sister's supervision and roistering with the Musgrave boys—and with Sir Philip's bastard daughter.

Emmaline.

Since landing on British shores, Roland had talked incessantly of Emmaline, the girl he'd romped with as a child, the girl who'd done her best to keep up with her brothers. Although she'd been tutored like the daughter of a baron must be, she'd apparently cultivated a wild side, taking advantage of a father too often away from home and a stepmother who had no interest in cosseting another woman's child.

"I have a feeling about you two," Roland had said. Repeatedly. "I'm going to get you two in a room together, sit back, and watch the alchemy work its magic."

The idea of Roland's rebellious cousin had caught burr-like in Elias's consciousness. So much so that his mind kept wandering back to his brother's admonition that he return home to marry, settle down, and become the man he was meant to be. Of all the women his family had paraded before him as potential wives, none had captured his attention as much as Emmaline Musgrave, and he hadn't even met the girl yet. It was absurd. Thus far, he'd managed his thoughts of her with a tight grip and an imagination rife with images of her disrobed and writhing beneath him or bent over the edge of a bed, his fingers wet and frenzied, her breasts swinging, his hips thrusting into her over and over and over again. He'd taken the matter in hand last night. And the night before that.

God's bones. He was hard just thinking about her.

He'd certainly not lacked for female companionship these last few months. In fact, during their travels, Roland had introduced him to a world that had been beyond his wildest fantasies. The man was acquainted with people from all walks of life, but he gravitated toward a more adventuresome sort and had dragged Elias along with him, taking part in debaucheries he hadn't even had the vocabulary to describe. These escapades kept his demons at bay, but not for long. Too often they returned with renewed vengeance as soon as his hangover passed and the visions of drunken orgies in opulent salons or whipping posts in dark cellars with masked men and women wielding velvet ropes and leather thongs came back into focus. Thinking now of the things he'd done—and the things done to him—filled him with equal parts humiliating shame and rampant lust. He shifted uncomfortably in his seat and tried to concentrate on the passing scenery.

In recent weeks, Elias recognized a chasm opening inside him. He wanted to attribute it to weariness, but the fact was he was lonely. He needed a stopping place. He thought again of Boutros and smiled. His brother doted on his wife, likely now plump with child, and had never wanted another woman. Good thing too as they'd been promised to each other since an early age. Eldest son of a successful tradesman and eldest daughter of a wealthy wool merchant. The match was made while the two were still toddling about and their delight at the prospect of spending their lives together never wavered.

For Elias, there had never been such a woman. Maybe there never would be. Maybe it was the ever-present darkness in his soul that kept him from forming an attachment. What woman would want to be saddled with such a man? What kind of man would saddle any woman with the shadows he carried around with him?

Outside, carriage wheels slid in and out of muddy ruts as the horses pulled them inexorably closer to Hartley

Castle. From there, they would go north to their final stop in Carlisle where they would winter at the empty estate on which Roland had spent so many lonely hours while his father, an earl, and much older brothers attended to the king. The carriage bounced, Roland grunted, and Elias's thoughts turned again to Emmaline.

After leaving Aleppo, Elias and Roland had reveled their way by land and sea—lingering in Constantinople, Venice, Genoa, Marseilles, Cadiz, Lisbon, and London. In London, Elias had met Roland's fearsome father and sycophantic brothers. Now, traveling in one of the earl's plush coaches, they were within throwing distance—almost—of Roland's aunt's home in Cumberland where they could rid themselves of this ever-present English chill before the roaring fires of Hartley Castle. Elias could not wait. Just getting out of the carriage would temper his anxious mood.

Roland cleared his throat, rubbed his eyes, and leaned forward to look out the window. "Almost there," he mumbled, leaning against the plush cushions of the coach his father had given him for the trip to Carlisle.

"Are we very close to the border?"

"Close enough."

"Growing up so close to Scotland must have been interesting," Elias said, hoping conversation would keep Roland awake.

"Aye, one becomes particularly attuned to the currents."

"The weather, you mean?" Elias peered out the window.

"The political currents." Roland licked a finger and stuck it in the air. "One must know which way the winds are blowing. From the north? Scotland has the upper hand.

From the south? England is on the march." He shrugged. "Politics. It'll get us all killed one day."

"Being a merchant is a much better choice than being cannon fodder."

"Not like I have much of a choice. I'm not fit for the church and haven't the temperament to lay my life down for some liege lord I've never met."

"Your father never presented you at court?"

"I've never met a king or a queen or even a princeling. I'm certain my august father would rather shove a dagger through his eye than present me to a princess. I was the unexpected child whose arrival in the world accompanied my mother's departure from it, and my father has never let me forget it."

"That's why you spent so much time at Hartley?"

Roland grunted. "It was more fun to be amongst people my own age rather than ancient tutors and greying nannies. I enjoyed testing my mettle against my cousins—sword play, riding, boxing, hunting and fishing, inventing ways to get into trouble. Of course, we all delighted in teasing Emmaline." He chuckled. "Did I tell you about the time I told her she was overtaxing her female brain by reading a history of Richard the Lionheart and the Third Crusade?"

"What did she say to that?"

Roland reached up and touched the bone under his right eye. "Say? I don't remember. She threw the book at my head. Gave me a little scar. Still have it."

Elias laughed. "I'll be on guard for flying books."

"See that you do. One never knows with Emmaline."

# TWELVE

"I am unsettled tonight, Mary, and I've no notion why." Mary twisted Emmaline's hair into a braided coronet and worked to pin it high on the crown of her head, leaving crimped curls hanging down to frame her face.

"It's not one of your headaches, I hope. Have you been having nightmares again?"

"No. I must have outgrown those," Emmaline said. She'd regretted confiding to Mary as soon as she'd done it, so even when she suffered from restless nights spent in darkness and agony or woke from a frenzied dream with her body covered in sweat and her fingers wet and still buried between her legs, she kept it to herself.

"The prospect of seeing your cousin again?"

"I am eager to see him, but there's something else. Something about the air. Do you think it will storm? I feel buzzing, as if lightning is about to strike."

Mary looked to the window. "There's not a cloud in the sky."

"Well, something is making my skin prickle." Emmaline sighed. "Aren't you done yet? How do I look?"

"No, I am not done yet and you will look lovely as always. As well you know it," Mary said with a smile. "The green velvet suits you, but you'd look lovely dressed as a stable boy."

Emmaline laughed. "But I have dressed as a stable boy! Before I acquired these." She waved a hand at her generous bosom. "I do love a beautiful gown but, oh, I wish we could dress like men sometimes. Riding in skirts is bothersome." She swiveled in her chair. "Maybe we could—"

Mary held up a hand. "Whatever mischief you're dreaming up, don't get me or Giles involved. We cannot afford to lose our positions."

"Hartley would crumble about our feet without you, and Giles would never be let go. All the horses would follow him home. The Pied Piper of Hartley."

"Only to be caught and flogged as a horse thief. Your wild ideas will cause trouble for all of us."

"I'll keep you and Giles out of it, but I need adventure before my impending doom, or betrothal, or however one must properly speak of the prospect of marriage to a kindly old toad or a malevolent young rooster. Enslavement seems apt."

"Oh, Emmaline. I do wish you'd speak to your father."

"He won't listen. My fate is in Lady Musgrave's hands. She had a talk with me this afternoon after my ride, by the by." She cast her voice up an octave in imitation. "Roland has sent word that he is accompanied by a gentleman from the Holy Land. You are to treat him with the utmost respect as I have reason to believe he is a rich trader and my nephew's fortune is tied to his. Must I remind you that your prospects for marriage depend on your proper behavior?"

Mary giggled. "You sound just like her."

"Of course, I asked if he was from Jerusalem itself and she said he hailed from some place called Aleppo."

"Wherever is that?" Mary said.

"Nowhere near the Holy Land! I read about it in a book on the Crusades. Oh, Mary, Roland is so lucky to be able to travel to exotic lands! How I dream of such places. The scents and the food and the bustle of the marketplace. Handsome gentlemen in exotic dress, all dark-eyed and mysterious, daggers stuck in their belts. I can close my eyes and imagine the narrow lanes, donkeys pulling carts on cobbled streets, living in a small house with a tidy garden, fruit trees growing right outside my door."

"At least you get to read about them," Mary said with a frown.

"You are learning your letters quickly, and soon you'll be reading too."

"Lady Musgrave will never allow me access to the library."

Emmaline waved the concern away. "I will."

"But what about when you're gone?" Mary lamented, brows drawn together. "I will miss you terribly and I will miss our lessons too. I never dreamed I would learn to read."

Emmaline reached up to squeeze her friend's hand. "Shall I tell you more about our visitor?" Emmaline didn't wait for an answer. "I inquired as to the man's age, but our esteemed Lady Musgrave didn't know. Apparently Roland has not been forthcoming in his missives. It is typical of their relationship. Lady Musgrave pries, her nephew parries.”

“And you vex.”

“Me?” Emmaline’s hand flew to her bosom in a demure, put-upon gesture. “I am the very embodiment of the demure, docile daughter. Or stepdaughter. Or bastard daughter. Whatever. In any account, I then inquired whether, since he’s supposedly from the Holy Land, Roland’s friend is a good Christian or if he might instead be a Jew or even a Mohammedan. I swear neither of those prospects had so much as roamed in the vicinity of her mind, and I promptly lost sight of her eyebrows when they fled north to hide beneath the hedgerow of her hairline. She turned beet red and nearly toppled over.”

“Goodness! How did she reply?” Mary pulled on one of Emmaline’s curls just to watch it bounce.

“Once she reinflated her lungs and rediscovered her voice, she said,” Emmaline imitated her stepmother once again, ‘It does not signify what the poor man is, you are to behave like a lady.’ So naturally I said, ‘But I thought you said he was a rich trader and not poor at all.’”

Mary covered her mouth in astonishment. “You are wicked indeed!”

Emmaline went on taking Lady Musgrave’s voice up another scandalized note or two. “‘Do you wish to sup with us tonight or not?’ I was gentle and contrite as a dove after that.”

“I wish I’d been there,” Mary said. “But you mustn’t provoke her so or you’ll end up married to the first available man who walks in the door so eager will she be to be rid of you.”

"As eager as I am to be rid of her," Emmaline said. "She went on and on until my pulse nearly slowed to a stop from sheer boredom. I wonder if she would have noticed." She drew in a breath and cast her voice higher. "Do not broach any topics inappropriate for females. Do not talk over much. Do not annoy our guests with questions. Do not sneak any spirits from the servants. And, for mercy's sake, do not cling to your cousin like a monkey!" She let out a healthy snort. "The whole list of do nots is worthy of a bound law book suitable for collecting dust on a library shelf."

"And naturally you promised to be on your best behavior?"

The two women locked eyes in the looking glass. Emmaline smiled. "Naturally."

# THIRTEEN

After a short cab ride and a banal conversation about the weather and various tourist sites around London, bells jangled as Kat stepped into Mt. Olympus, Michael holding the door and ushering her inside. She'd spent much of the day moving like an automaton from conference room to conference room paying little attention to the presentations she'd flown across a continent and an ocean to hear. Instead, her mind had buzzed all day with snippets of the conversation she'd had with researchers during her visit to Cambridge the day before and with memories of her body's shocking reaction to the Luck of Edenhall.

And, of course, to the penetrating gaze of the man from whom she'd fled. The man whose hand now rested lightly at the small of her back as the door to the restaurant closed behind them.

Mt. Olympus was a deep, narrow space with tables set snug along walls decorated with murals of the Athenian Acropolis and lofty mountaintop monasteries on one side and remote temple ruins, inviting beaches, and brilliant seascapes on the other. A booming voice caught Kat's attention and garnered a smile from Michael. She turned to take in the sounds and smells of a busy kitchen in the back and a woman striding toward them wearing a dark expression.

"Why you never come see us anymore?" The plump woman frowned and crossed her arms over her generous bosom.

"Why do you always sound like my mother?" Michael said with an exaggerated eyeroll. He turned to Kat, his hand still resting lightly—possessively—on the small of her back. "This is Aphrodite Galatas. Aphro and her husband Dorian, the loudmouth in the back, serve the best Greek food in London."

Aphro shook a finger in Michael's face "Not best Greek food in London. Best food, period." Aphro turned to Kat and opened her arms wide in an expansive gesture. "Welcome to Mt. Olympus, Miss…"

"Kat," Michael said, biting back the alarming realization that he still had no idea what her last name was. "She's from the States. Be nice so she'll come back."

Aphro gave her an appraising look, "For you, I bring a bottle of wine on the house. You prefer white or red?"

"How about some Retsina?"

Aphro wrinkled her nose. "Pah. We have good wine from the family vineyard in Nemea. You know story of Herakles and Nemean lion?" She didn't wait for an answer. "Michael will tell you while I get your menus." She waved at the table set up on a riser near the front window. "Your favorite table."

Kat glanced at Michael and then back to Aphro. "Can you direct me to the ladies' room first?"

"Follow me." Aphro marched with purpose toward the kitchen. "Loo's this way."

Kat shut and locked the bathroom door and then leaned back against it, pulled out her phone, and started Googling. She typed in "Michael Samaan art history" and clicked through to his departmental page at the university. Her pulse raced as she read his bio. Unless he was leading some nefarious secret life, he looked totally legit. She skimmed through his list of publications then went back and scrolled through other links.

She clicked on a *London Times* link for a Michael Daoud Samaan and read the obituary of a man who'd come to England to complete a doctorate in chemistry, founded a prosperous business that developed tests and testing equipment for medical and industrial applications, and who had been killed in a hit and run car accident. He was survived by his wife, his son Michael, and daughter Leila. She checked the date. Five years ago. So, Michael had suffered loss too. How had it changed him? *If* it had changed him.

She went back and clicked on the Images search. She studied his features as she scrolled through photos of him in his doctoral robe and hood, then a younger man with teammates on the Cambridge rowing team, broad shoulders, strong legs that went on forever, and those dark eyes that seemed to bore holes straight through her soul. Why did he feel so familiar? Like she could smell him on her skin? She closed her eyes and swore. *Damn, Kat! Get a freaking grip.*

She opened her eyes and turned to glare at herself in the bathroom mirror. "You don't need this in your life right now," she told her reflection. She didn't want the complication of some woo-woo connection to a man whose inner life was as muddied and messy as her own. A man who may very well not be playing with a full deck—and what did that say about her own deck? And she certainly didn't need a long-distance relationship with a man who lived clear across a continent and an entire ocean. She'd gotten used to being alone and was fine with it. Honestly.

Yes, the idea of sharing her life with someone special was nice, but it wasn't *necessary*. It wasn't a *requirement* for happiness. Her career was taking off. She had friends. She had a snug little house, a cranky cat, a doting mother, a meddling sister-in-law, a stalwart brother, and adorable nieces and nephews. She was *fine*. She straightened her shoulders and leaned forward to look deep into the eyes staring back at her. "Do not let this…whatever it is…get away from you. Manage it. Control it. No matter how it wants to suck you in, remember that you are in charge of your destiny. Wrestle it to the ground and stomp on it if you have to, but for god's sake, do not let the *romance* of it carry you away. There. Good. Done."

She brushed a hand over her hair and tugged at her sleeves. Slipped her phone back in her bag, wiped her sweaty palms on her pants, and yanked the bathroom door open.

∞

Michael, surreptitiously wiping his own palms on his trousers, stood courteously as Kat approached the table and moved to pull out her chair even as she waved him off. "We can move to another table if you want, he said lowering himself back into his seat. "My sister and I meet here for lunch once a month. We usually sit here, although she calls it the aquarium. She's been known to make blowfish faces at people who stare too long as they walk by."

Kat smiled, draping the strap of her bag over the back of her chair and trying to act casual. "It's perfect. I'll refrain from making fish faces."

He laughed at that and motioned to the two wine bottles on the table. "Aphro brought us a white and a red so you can take your pick. I took the liberty of ordering the mezza platter to get us started."

"White, I suppose." Kat watched as Michael poured the wine and offered her a glass. She turned the bottle so she could read the label. "I've had this before. My local wine store carries it."

"If you mention that to Aphro, you'll have a friend for life." Michael said. "Her cousin runs the family business back home where they make wine and olive oil. Once she gets started, she can talk the hind legs off a donkey."

Kat laughed. "Hind legs off a donkey? I've never heard that expression, and I certainly don't want that. A few years ago, my mother adopted the sweetest little donkey and he's always following us around. Dapple. My nieces and nephews treat him like a pet—one that's not allowed in the house, of course."

"Dapple. As in Sancho Panza's donkey?"

"Are you a *Don Quixote* fan?"

"It was the first full novel I read through in another language."

Kat's eyebrows went up. "Impressive. When I was little, I learned to ride on my dad's old horse. Rocinante. *Don Quixote* was his favorite novel. Well, that and *The Count of Monte Cristo*." She laughed. "And, of course, *Catch-22*."

"He had good taste in his reading material," Michael said with an appreciative smile. "Did you grow up in the country, then?"

She savored a sip of wine. Michael got the distinct impression she was gathering her thoughts, carefully choosing her words. He casually ran a finger along the rim of his glass. Under the table, his leg joggled up and down with nervous tension.

"I grew up on a small ranch south of Tucson," she said. "Surrounded by horses, dogs, cats, and coyotes. Javelinas. The occasional mountain lion. Rattlesnakes." She shrugged. "It was idyllic."

He raised a brow. "Mountain lions and rattlesnakes? I'm not sure that sounds quite as idyllic as the fluffy sheep frolicking in the pasture behind the house where I grew up."

"Depends on your definition of idyllic."

"And, um, *javelinas?*"

"They look like wild pigs, but hairier. And they're not pigs."

"Right. Hairy non-pigs. Were there brothers or sisters on this idyllic rattlesnake-infested ranch?"

She smiled again, this time with her whole face in on the action—her lips curving up, her eyes raying out like sunbursts from the edges—and the force of it hit Michael in the solar plexus. "One brother," she said. "Craig. My father died of a heart attack a few years ago, but my mother still lives on the ranch, in a little casita. Craig, his wife, and their kids live in the main house."

A server arrived and set a large mezza platter on the table. "Do you wish to order now?"

Kat looked to Michael. "This looks like plenty to me. Go ahead and order something, but I'm fine."

"Why don't you check on us in a bit," Michael told the server. "See how we do with all this." The young woman nodded and left them alone again, and Michael watched as Kat quietly spread her napkin on her lap and carefully arranged her cutlery. Was he going to have to draw every word out of her like a fisherman repeatedly casting and pulling in his line?

"You said you're a geneticist…"

"I work in a lab at the University of Arizona. I'm interested in epigenetics and heritability."

"And a genetics conference is what brought you to London…"

"That and a need for a change of scenery." She shrugged, wondering how far to go, how much to reveal. "My mother's a bit of a meddler, especially now that my dad's gone. She's been pushing me to take a break from work. Get out of Dodge, so to speak."

"Dodge?"

"An American cliché, from the Old West. Means leave town or get away from where you are."

Michael dipped a cucumber into the hummus and hoped his hand wasn't shaking. "So, you took a break from work to go to a work conference."

The corner of her mouth tipped up and a pretty parenthesis curved around her lips. "Sounds pretty sad when you put it like that." She rolled an olive around in her mouth and then plucked out the pit. Stared at it for a long moment, then set it on the edge of her plate and looked up at him. "You said you're working on a book on Syrian glassmaking and that the Luck of Edenhall is a favorite piece of yours."

"That's right." Under the table, Michael's leg stopped moving.

"Is that why you were there the other day?"

"I spend a lot of time in that gallery, but that day…I just had a feeling, you know how that happens?" A muscle in his jaw clenched and unclenched. "I don't know, I just felt like something momentous was going to happen and I need to be there. In that spot."

Kat nodded. "And I was just sightseeing. I picked the V&A for the glass collection because…I mean…." She chewed on her bottom lip, took a long look at Michael, and continued. "Has it ever…have you ever had a reaction to it?"

"Has the Luck ever stolen my breath?" She held his gaze as he went on. "Has the room ever tilted and swirled around me as if the Earth's axis had shifted and the whole world had been knocked off balance? Yes. Not every time, but many times. And for a long time. Since the first time I laid eyes on it."

"What does it mean?" Her voice was barely a whisper.

"I'm not sure."

She looked away, licked her lips. Her hand reached up to play with one of her dangly earrings. A nervous tic. Michael waited, heart ricocheting around his ribcage, every cell on fire, every nerve taut, poised, like the proverbial deer in the headlights.

Then she turned back to him, slowly, and said, "I've seen the Luck in my dreams. Felt it pulse like a living thing in my hands. Traced a fingertip around the gold rim. I had no idea it was a real thing. And, Michael, my last name is Musgrave."

# FOURTEEN

Michael blinked. *Musgrave?* His field of vision exploded with stars, like he'd taken a blow to the head. He shook his head to clear it and leaned forward. "As in the Luck of Edenhall Musgrave?"

She'd brought a business card of her own and now slid it across the table. Michael picked it up and read: Katherine S. Musgrave, PhD, Associate Research Professor, James R. W. Bryant Genomics Institute, University of Arizona.

"My father loved genealogy. He traced his ancestors back to when they emigrated to America sometime in the late 1600s. But yeah. There's a connection. Ancient. Tenuous, but it's there." Michael swore under his breath as she went on. "You may be the one person who understands what I've been going through." She wetted her lips and looked away. "You see, I started having disturbing dreams around the onset of puberty. Something in my body turned on—besides my hormones—and I became this other person. Still me, but with multiple realities. Not multiple personalities, although there was one doctor who…well, it's not that. It's hard to explain."

"You don't have to explain."

"I do, though. Talking things through is how I think. I rattle around my office and my house having entire conversations out loud with myself. Another reason I live alone."

Michael hung on every word. *Another reason? What was the first reason?*

"Somehow," she continued, "we're both connected to the Luck and that means we're connected to each other, and there should be a perfectly rational explanation for all this so, I need to talk this through with someone who won't think I'm—"

"No," Michael interrupted. "I mean you don't have to explain because I already understand. I went through the same thing, only my multiple realities—that term is great, by the way—began the first time I saw it. I hadn't even hit puberty. Ever since, I've been having dreams in which the Luck belongs to me. I *made* it. It's *mine.* It's always me in the dreams, but there are different *me's* in different times and places. And it gets weirder. You've got this Musgrave connection, but my father's family, back in Syria, has owned a glassmaking studio for hundreds of years, and sometimes I wake up in the middle of the night and imagine…" He ran a hand down over his face and waited for her to say something. But she remained silent, now staring down at her hands playing with the stem of her glass.

"Look," he went on when the silence got too much for him. "From the outside, I seem like a normal, run-of-the-mill bloke. I've got friends, family, a career. A ridiculously misbehaved mutt. But when I first saw it all those years ago, this dark thing inside me woke up. It's a haunting," he said, the pitch of his voice dropping," but it's *me, me* haunting *myself.*" He paused to gauge her reaction, but she just kept twirling her glass, as if she was afraid to meet his eyes lest she reveal her thoughts.

"My mum is into all sorts of mystical stuff and one night I got up the nerve to tell her about the Luck. She took me out of school the next day and we went on a 'field trip' to the V&A so she could see it for herself. We sat in that gallery for what seemed like hours as I tried to describe what I was feeling, trying to put into words these visions and feelings that made no sense." He snorted in frustration. Embarrassed at his outpouring. "What boy is good at talking about feelings at that age?"

Daring to look up at him again, she smiled. "What did your mother say?"

"What's a loving mum who believes in the tylwyth teg, in Welsh fairies, going to say? She told me I should trust my instincts and believe in myself," he said with a one-shouldered shrug. "But how can I believe in myself if I'm comprised of many selves? What does that even mean?"

Kat's lips parted as if she were going to speak, but then said nothing.

"You're the scientist. You tell me." His voice was more demanding than he intended. "How can you and I, on opposite sides of an ocean, both dream about a goblet made hundreds of years ago, that you didn't even know existed?"

Kat stopped twirling her wine and looked out the window. "I spent the afternoon in Cambridge yesterday," she said slowly, as if carefully choosing her words, "at the lab of one of the foremost experts in epigenetics and inheritance."

The statement was so unexpected that all Michael could do was stare.

"One of her postdocs," Kat continued, "made an offhand comment about how he'd dragged himself to work that morning because he'd stayed up all night playing Verdun, an online multiplayer wargame based on a battle in World War I."

*Where the hell is she going with this?*

"He said he's one of the top players in the world although he's never studied military strategy, doesn't have any military training, and has never even read a book about the battle. All he knew was that his great-grandfather had been an officer in the French army and that he'd fought there. That's it." Her teeth scraped back and forth on her bottom lip. "It's just one anecdote about one man who happens to be good at a game set in a time and a place he knows nothing about."

She leaned forward, both elbows on the table, encouraging him to bend toward her as though pulled on a string, their heads nearly meeting above the mezza platter as if they were sharing secrets.

"But all I could think about was that stanza in *Leaves of Grass*—my father's favorite book of poetry."

"Whitman?"

Kat nodded. Her voice was quiet, almost as if she didn't want to say the words aloud. "'*Do I contradict myself? Very well then, I contradict myself; I am large, I contain multitudes.*'"

She paused and looked into his eyes, her gaze gripping and holding his as if they were enclosed in a magnetic field.

"Scientists understand how physical traits are passed down one generation to the next, but the more important question is whether *lived experiences* that epigenetically change the *expression* of a gene during one person's lifetime can be passed down and whether those changes can impact the lived experiences of their descendants. It sounds outlandish, but think about it. Could epigenetically encoded memories of one man's traumatic experiences in battle have been passed down to his grandson so that knowledge of the battlefield seems almost instinctual?"

"What are you saying?" Michael asked.

She gave her head a little shake. "I'm not sure. That we've both inherited…that our ancestors were…" Her voice caught and she bit her lip in that way that sent a bolt of desire surging through his veins. "That in the past we've been…"

She swallowed, her eyes going dark as he reached across the table to touch a fingertip to the back of her hand, and then they both watched, mesmerized, as her hand turned over, as their fingers curled together, as shared warmth suffused through their skin, comforting, like the answer to an unspoken prayer.

They both stared down at their clasped hands, riveted. Reverential. The feeling of completeness overwhelming their emotional lifeboats, as if a circuit breaker had been flipped and emotions were set free to flow through their systems like electrons surging down a wire. Tears pricked at her eyes and nose.

After a moment, she looked up to see deep pools of understanding staring back at her. One part of her brain screamed out at her to remember the little lecture she'd given herself in the bathroom—*Do not get swept up in whatever this is, you fool!*—as he squeezed her hand in reassurance, and she whispered, "That somehow you are already a part of me."

*Tap. Tap. Tap.* They jumped, tore their hands apart, and turned at the sound of someone on the street rapping on the window next to them. *Tap. Tap. Tap.*

Michael buried his face in his hands as a striking young woman with big eyes, bright pink lips and fuchsia-streaked black hair stood just outside the window puffing her cheeks in and out and waggling her eyebrows at Michael.

"Bugger all," Michael looked up at Kat through his fingers. "My sister."

# FIFTEEN

The bells on the door rang out gaily as Leila Samaan pushed through and came to stand beside the raised platform. Michael groaned. "Maybe sitting in the aquarium wasn't the best idea."

Leila tapped one finger against her chin. "Let me think…what was the last thing you said to me as we were sitting in this very restaurant last week?"

Ignoring her, Michael looked to Kat. "Kat, this is my sister, Leila. Leila, Kat Musgrave, an American geneticist in town for a conference. We met a couple of days ago when she was sightseeing and ran into each other again today."

Leila held out a hand and Kat took it, giving it a shake. "It's a pleasure to meet you," Kat said.

"Oh, the pleasure is all mine, I assure you. And—"

Before Leila could go on, Michael interrupted.

"And now that introductions are out of the way and before this goes any further, let me apologize for anything my sister might say. Or do."

"Pish posh, Michael." Leila turned, motioned to a waiter. "Can you bring two more glasses? There will be one more joining us."

Michael gaped at her. "You cannot be serious."

"Indeed, I am, dear brother." Leila stepped up onto the platform, moved around the table and took the seat that backed up to the window. "George should be here any minute. If you wanted to avoid company, why'd you sit in the aquarium? You know George and I often meet here for dinner on Thursdays. The gods know you've joined us often enough."

"Difficult as it might be to believe, your dining schedule is not always top of mind."

Leila set an elbow on the table and leaned forward, chin resting on a beautifully manicured hand. "So, you two met while you were sightseeing and then randomly ran into each other again. How fortuitous."

The undercurrent to the siblings' interactions was obvious, but Kat had no idea what it meant. "This is my first time in London, unless you consider layovers at Heathrow, so running into an art historian did seem fortuitous. The city is so full of history with so many museums and sites to explore."

"And did you initially meet at one of our museums?"

Kat glanced at Michael. "At the V&A. I was interested in the glass collection."

One of Leila's eyebrows rose in a delicate arch. "How lucky you are then that you met an expert in glassmaking. I suppose Michael told you that he's writing a book on it." The bells jangled again, and Leila looked toward the sidewalk and then back to Kat. "That'll be my fiancé."

Michael caught Kat's gaze. "I'm channeling Dante here, wondering which level of hell this is."

"Michael," a rich voice said. "I didn't know you were joining us."

Kat's eyes widened as she turned to see the man who'd just entered the restaurant. A soft *Oh!* escaped her mouth.

"Well well well," said George Hempstead, III, Faculty of English, Clare College, Cambridge and Kat's erstwhile flight seatmate, looking her up and down with an intrigued smile. "Fancy meeting you here." He turned to Michael. "Hmm. So, you're the knight in shining armor."

"What? Wait." Michael looked back and forth between Kat and George. "You two know each other?"

"I had the honor of being her seatmate on my flight back from the States," George said, setting his backpack beside the riser and stepping around Michael to press a kiss to Leila's upturned lips before taking his seat at the table.

"Are you serious?" Leila said, now wide-eyed, at the same time Kat breathed out, "This can*not* be happening."

"I think that's my line," Michael muttered.

"We both mostly dozed, but we managed a fascinating chat at the end." George leaned away as the server delivered two more wine glasses to the table along with menus.

Kat pinned her gaze on George, hoping for some semblance of mercy, like a heretic pleading to be spared the torture rack. He raised one intrigued brow and gave her a noncommittal smile in return, then turned to Leila. "White or red, darling?"

"I'm in the mood for lamb," Leila said, "so red tonight."

Each a bit stunned at the strange coincidence, they all watched in silence as George poured two glasses of red and carefully slid one across the table. With the corner of his mouth tipped up in a self-satisfied smirk, he held Leila's gaze with a knowing look, picked up his glass and held it high in a toast.

"To serendipity."

∞

Serendipity my ass, Kat thought. This was farce writ large. She glared at George as he set his glass on the table and looked between Michael and Kat. "So…?"

Rarely had a two-letter word embodied so much portent—or suppressed amusement. Kat wanted to wipe the stupid smirk of the man's face.

"They met at the V&A, darling," Leila said. "Apparently Kat, here, shares Michael's interest in glassmaking."

"Is that so?"

Again with the raised eyebrow. Gah! Kat was tempted to flick wine in George's face. From Michael's expression, he was tempted to do much more than that.

"Quite fortuitous, wouldn't you say?" Leila's smile was incandescent. "One might almost say, foreordained."

Kat pressed a knuckle to her temple with a groan.

"Foreordained." George's lips curled around the word as if relishing a spoonful of gelato on a hot summer day. He winked—*winked!*—at Kat. "FYI, Michael is quite the equestrian. I thought you might be interested in knowing that considering all the murmuring about thundering hooves and midnight rides."

"Oh. My. God. That's not fair." Bright red flags painted Kat's cheekbones as she raised both hands in the air in surrender and gave Michael a pleading look. "To my abject horror, I must've talked in my sleep on the flight."

Michael glowered at George. "You heard a stranger talking in her sleep and you *listened*? Did you take notes too?"

George shrugged. "You know me. I'm a curious sort and I'm always looking for interesting tidbits to incorporate into my work in progress. Besides, I've a very good memory. No need for notes."

"Curious sort," Michael said with a snort. "Nosey bastard is more like it. And don't think about including any of Kat's 'tidbits' in your book."

Leila leaned toward Kat. "He's working on his fourth novel," she whispered sotto voce. "Gothic mysteries, all very spooky and atmospheric. A bit of romance with star-crossed lovers and bad endings. Of course, he writes under a pen name, so not very many people know." She mimed zipping her lips together.

George shrugged. "Like many English majors, my real dream was to be a novelist, not to teach sentence structure to seventeen-year-olds. By the by, do you know you called out to someone in your dream?"

Kat gave him a blank look. "How could I? I. Was. Asleep."

"I believe the name was," he looked across at Leila, "Elias."

Michael choked.

"Strange," George went on, "but isn't Elias a common name in the Samaan family?"

"Bloody hell," Michael ground out.

"In point of fact," Leila said, a flawlessly manicured fingertip tapping at her chin "Elias's and Michael's are scattered far and wide amongst our family tree. There should be a word for them. Like a murder of crows or a conspiracy of ravens."

George's face brightened. "Well, we already have a convocation of eagles, a parliament of owls, a wake of buzzards, and a flamboyance of flamingos, so how about—"

"An exasperation of Eliases and a magisterium of Michaels!" Leila offered and she and George clinked their wine glasses together, smug smiles painting their faces.

"For Christ's sake," Kat said, drawing in a long breath as Michael pinched the bridge of his nose and squeezed his eyes shut. "I feel like Alice. I've hit rock bottom of the freaking rabbit hole." As soon as the words were out, she went still, recognizing the words she'd used with her father years ago, that she couldn't go to London for fear of tumbling down a rabbit hole. Was this the rabbit hole? Was this what she'd feared?

George sent a glance toward Leila. "Interesting that you bring up *Alice in Wonderland* as Leila's quite taken with Lewis Carroll. In fact—"

"In fact..." Leila leaned forward. "How long are you here?"

"I took extra time off to do some sightseeing. I've got ten days left."

"Excellent! You should come to my show tomorrow night. I'm graduating with a Masters in Fine Arts—I do videography and performance art. Our thesis exhibition opens tomorrow. And serendipity strikes again as my thesis centers on the Mad Hatter's tea party. It's all about time and how it's always 6:00, always time for tea, and how time itself is a riddle. A bit of fractured physics, relativity, and a touch of whimsy."

"That sounds fascinating," Kat said.

"Much of my work is inspired by our mum." Leila cast a glance at Michael. "She writes and illustrates the retellings of Welsh myths and fairytales. She's into all sorts of things that make my all-too-grounded brother's hair curl. Tarot, runes, divination, augury. Reincarnation and time travel. The whole bit. In fact, just the other day she was saying—"

"Leila." Michael said, a low warning in his big-brother voice.

"Anyway, Kat. Consider yourself officially invited. You'll meet Carys Samaan herself. She's a hoot."

Michael grimaced. "Has it occurred to you that she might have already made plans?"

"Have you already made plans?" Leila asked.

"Well, the conference is over, but I don't want to intrude."

"Nonsense," George said, that damn smirk just barely curving the corners of his mouth. "I feel like we're already old friends. You must join us for dinner afterwards. I promised Leila a celebration and Michael was planning on coming along. Now he won't have to feel like a third wheel."

Another low groan from Michael. "I'm sorry. These two are so completely insufferable."

"Insufferable?" George feigned affront. "It's my duty as a future peer of the realm to make welcome visitors to our fair land. We could even recommend some good spots for sightseeing. Perhaps we could find some destriers and take a moonlight ride over the moors."

"Hilarious." Kat glared at him. "I begin to wonder if you were listening to a lecture in flight or busy invading my privacy."

"Ah, well, I'm a master at multitasking."

"Ignore the boors," Michael said, cutting a look at George. "If you haven't had enough of them already, I'd love for you to join us tomorrow. We could at least recommend some places to see while you're here. Did you have any particular places in mind?"

"The usual tourist spots, I suppose. I already saw the Tower of London and the British Museum. And obviously, the V&A. Not sure what else I'll have time for on this trip, but I'd like to see the Stonehenge, Hadrian's Wall maybe. And, if there's time, explore a bit around Carlisle."

"There's a fort along Hadrian's Wall right outside Carlisle," George said. "You could easily hit both on the same trip. But, can I ask what's so special about Carlisle?"

Kat glanced at Michael. "That's the area the Musgrave side of my family came from. A long time ago—mid 1600s, I think—but my father dragged my mother on trips to the area several times, and I thought it might be interesting to visit someday. He was really into the history of Hartley Castle and Eden Hall. Unfortunately, both are gone now, but it could be fun to poke around." She caught and held Michael's gaze. "Look for connections to the past."

# SIXTEEN

*Connections to the past.* He couldn't stop thinking about Kat Musgrave in the here and now. Every word. Every glance. Every smile and laugh and frown of concentration put down roots in Michael's mind. The way she'd taken in everything he'd said without thinking he'd lost his mind. The way she'd told him about her dreams. Confided in him, as if she trusted him. The way the searching look in her eyes called to the need in the deepest recesses of his soul. Every fired synapse and rush of blood through his veins told him that this woman, Katherine Musgrave, was the answer he'd been searching for.

Now, if he could only figure out the question.

He'd offered to escort her back to her hotel, but she'd said no. She needed time to think, to process everything. To think through the ramifications. "As I said, I talk to myself when I need to work on a problem." She'd shrugged. "One time my mom was at my place, and I was carrying on such a long conversation with myself, my mom thought I had someone in the shower with me." She laughed and shook her head. "She was more than a bit disappointed when I emerged alone."

So, he'd chuckled softly and raised a hand to brush a tendril of hair from her face. Then he hailed her a taxi and sent her on her way, saying, "You have my number. We'll talk more later."

He'd remained on the sidewalk, watching as the driver pulled into traffic and disappeared around the next corner. As soon as the cab was out of sight, he rubbed absently at his breastbone, like he was soothing an ache. A bruise. He felt her absence like it was a physical injury.

Dazed and reeling from his reaction to Kat, Michael had wandered distractedly to the Tube where he leaned against the tiled wall of his platform stop, waiting for his train and thumbing through the half dozen text messages from his mum without really seeing them.

*I'm sure you're busy, but pls ring me right away…I've found something*

*If you're not out saving the world, pls give me a ring*

*Text me back…I'll be up late, waiting*

*I hope you're on a date bc otherwise you should not be ignoring your mum*

*I just tried to call and it went straight to voicemail…where are you?*

*Helllooooo. It's your one and only beloved mum who hates to be a pest but PLS RING ME ASAP. I'm starting to worry.*

He shook his head and chuckled. Carys Samaan did not countenance being ignored. It couldn't be a real emergency, though. She would've said. He typed out a message and pressed send. *Waiting for the tube. Will ring when I get home*

The little dots indicating Carys was typing started moving.

*Pick up Sal and come out tonight…there's something you need to see*

"Christ, Mum," he mumbled, typing: *It'll be after 8 before I'm home. Can't it wait till tomorrow?*

*No. I'll explain when you call*

With an annoyed exhale, he sent her a thumbs up and slipped his phone back into his pocket. Moments later, his mind had already dismissed his mother's texts and returned to Kat Musgrave and the look on her face when she'd first set eyes on the Luck. When she'd curled her fingers into his and whispered, "That somehow you are already a part of me."

∞

He emerged up from the tube station into the soft twilight of a cool London evening, already breaking the promise he'd made to himself not to text or call Kat. He didn't want to appear too…too forward, too needy. Too aggressive. Too persistent. But the connection between them seemed so right, that it seemed natural to check in on her. He typed out a quick note and pressed send before he could stop himself.

*This is Michael. Hope you made it back safe & sound. Can't wait to pick up the convo where we left off. Pls don't hold Leila/George against me. They're not always so obnoxious and nosy.*

*Wait. Yes they are*

*Sorry*

He made himself put his phone back in his pocket as he headed home to feed the dog—and to call his mum.

∞

"You need to come out tonight and see what I found," Carys said as soon as she picked up Michael's call.

"A little context would help, Mum. It's after 8, so it'd be 9:30 before I could get there."

"All right. So, this afternoon I'm sitting out in the garden having tea, maybe around 4:30 or so, and I had this, oh, I don't know, *compulsion* to do something. But I couldn't figure out what. I was…*itchy*, for lack of a better word. Like something happened to set me off—"

"Slow down. You're talking so fast, I can  barely keep up."

He heard his mum suck in a breath.

"So, I wandered around the garden for a bit and then found myself out in the carriage house opening the containers your father's cousins sent to him for safekeeping."

"The ones in the storage room off the garage."

"Right. Remember they'd gone through the house in the Old City and packed things for safekeeping before the war took a dangerous turn in Aleppo."

"I remember."

"Well, your father had planned to go through them when they first arrived, but one thing led to another, and he didn't get far. A dozen crates and none with any sort of packing list. We assumed it was all from the house. We opened a couple of crates and found the typical heirlooms. A couple of old rugs. Embroidered table linens. Silver service and jewelry. That sort of thing. And then there was the accident."

Michael could almost see her bite her lip, straighten her shoulders, and will herself to go on, will herself to be strong now for him.

"And I didn't have the energy or the interest to go through them after he was gone."

"Of course not, Mum. It wasn't a priority."

"And there wasn't any hurry," Carys continued. "The war was going from bad to worse. Then the glassworks was bombed…"

"Yeah. I understand. It's okay." He let the silence draw out for a moment, then said, "So, Mum, what did you find that won't wait until tomorrow?"

"Michael, they didn't only pack things from the old house. Two of the containers are full of stuff from the glassworks. Lots of photos, some smaller finished pieces, some computer disks and a random assortment of office supplies including what appear to be old record books. And when I say old, I mean museum old."

Michael dropped into a chair at his kitchen table. "Go on."

"The photos are mostly staged as if they were taken to showcase pieces for a catalog, or to identify a piece for inventory, but it's the books, Michael. Ledgers, account books. With illustrations from way before photography was invented. Maybe from the beginning. It's a treasure trove. Think what it could mean for your research."

After seeing Kat again and then Leila and George interrupting their conversation and now this, his central nervous system was lighting off fireworks in his blood stream. But before he could say a word, his mother continued.

"Darling, there's something else. You'll see when you get here, but remember all those years ago when we went together to the V&A to see that piece you couldn't stop thinking about, the Luck of Edenhall?"

He went still.

"Even when you were young, you cycled through periods where you'd be morose and withdrawn or you'd be like a whirling dervish. Pushing yourself academically. Trying every sport. A regular little daredevil. Then finally, one night you came to me and told me about your dreams, about your obsession with that piece. You were so scared to tell me. Do you remember?"

Throat thick with emotion, he nodded as if she could see him, remembering how relieved he'd been to finally tell someone.

"And do you remember what I told you at the museum?"

He swallowed hard. "You told me to trust myself."

"That's right." Her voice carried a mother's tenderness, and he choked back a sob, as if he knew what was coming next. "You're going to need that trust, Michael. Always remember that I believe in you. I always have and always will." She was quiet for a moment, as if she knew he needed time to collect himself. "Now, pack up that pup of yours and come on out. I'll have a pot of coffee waiting."

# SEVENTEEN

Scowling, he dipped the tip of his quill into the black ink and with a practiced, steady hand began to trace the outline of the goblet onto the fine paper of the ledger. The mere act of drawing the thing that had taken hold of his soul, that had haunted the last few years of his life, was almost more than he could bear. He swallowed back a sudden craving for the poppy that had sustained and comforted him and bent his head to his work. Years of practice kept his hold light and his lines sure and smooth when he wanted nothing more than to snap the quill in two.

When Yaqub had first seen the goblet, he'd gasped. "My god, brother! With your talent and my determination, we will make the Samaan family rich!"

"It can never be sold," Micah had protested. "Never. Do not ask me why and do not attempt to change my mind. You must swear it. Your sons must swear it. It can *never ever* be sold, Yaqub. Never!"

At the desperate pleading in his eyes, his brother had relented, but he still wanted a record of it.

"I'm willing to swear to your terms, but this is the most beautiful piece you've ever created," Yaqub, always thinking like a merchant, said. "If we're to keep it locked away, at least give me a record of it, if nothing more than to show potential customers the quality of our work. You're the most talented craftsman I know. I'm pleading with you to capture the beauty of this piece on paper so I can show the world what Samaan Glassworks can do."

Micah did not want to show the world what he was capable of. It was horror enough for him to know the monster he'd become. That he could cut flesh, draw blood, grind bone. That he could conjure the darkest of magiks to deliver the deepest desires of the human heart. He'd done it again and again until it had driven him mad. He didn't want anyone else to know that dark side of him. But he would do this for Yaqub. He owed him this much for saving him. And for caring for Rose when he had neither the strength nor the sanity to do so.

He dipped the nib into the ink again and studied the goblet sitting on the table before him. He would gladly destroy it a thousand times over if he could. But that was impossible. The unholy thing must be protected or the pain would be for naught and the promise he'd made to his wife—and to the others—would be a lie.

It had been five years since that day he'd held Yasmine and felt the life ebb out of her body. Five years since they'd last walked through their garden together, inhaling the scent of jasmine, checking the ripeness of the figs and olives, holding each other close and making love under the boughs of the old pine tree. Five years of torment of waking and wondering how it was he still lived while she slumbered.

He'd promised her the world. A second chance. A third. Who knew how the strength of their love and the power of his magiks could change the world? He still wanted it all. Needed it like his lungs needed air. But then she'd extracted a different promise. One he'd agreed to her in her last moments, one that he'd tried his best and done his worst to fulfill. One that had nearly killed him.

He grimaced and watched, detached, as his pen seemed to move across the page on its own, recreating the flourishes of leaves and petals Yasmine had designed. How bold he'd been. How audacious. How ignorant and foolish. Micah Samaan the Alchemist of Aleppo. That's what they'd called him when desperate lovers had sought him out as though he had the right to decide who deserved a second chance and who did not.

He stopped and listened to the laughter filtering in through the open window. The children were playing in the courtyard. If it weren't for his brother's stubbornness and the familiar smile of the auburn-haired daughter of Yasmine's blood, the little girl who trailed after him like a puppy, he would have welcomed death's dark embrace. But that was another promise Yasmine had extracted from him. *While I sleep, you must live on.*

And so, he lived and dreamt of death.

He'd spent the morning mixing the colors—red for the power of memory, cobalt for the color of her eyes, gold for desire and contentment, green for rebirth and renewal— and tried to forget the other times he'd mixed these same colors and drawn these same designs. The times he'd taken blood and bone from those other fools, so willing to place their hopes and dreams in his unworthy hands, and he'd given of himself only to be drawn deeper and deeper into the nightmare world no mortal could control.

He'd loved too hard. Learned too late. Paid too high a price for daring to alter the natural order. Now, he wondered how long he would pay. Lifetimes, he suspected. And so would the others. Lifetimes. With no way out.

# EIGHTEEN

Kat arrived at Goldsmiths Centre for Contemporary Art for Leila's graduation show, her body buzzing with excitement. A morning spent at the Tower of London and an afternoon at the British Museum hadn't distracted her from dwelling on Michael Samaan and the Luck of Edenhall, and she'd spent more time thinking about the puzzle they presented then paying attention to the tour guide or the museum artifacts. She'd managed to drag her imagination away from the pull of Michael's dark eyes long enough to wonder about the two little princes likely murdered in the Tower and to appreciate the Rosetta Stone, the Elgin Marbles, and the Sutton Hoo display. But much of the rest of the day was spent in a fog of anticipation, confusion, and frustration.

She pulled open the door and was met with soft jazz played over invisible speakers as guests gathered amidst high-top tables, plucking appetizers off trays offered by wandering servers dressed in black. Michael had wanted to pick her up, saying he had something to tell her, but despite her visceral attraction and her gut instinct to trust him, she insisted on making her own way to the gallery. It was a date, yes. But still, things were spiraling so fast that managing her mode of transportation seemed at least a small way to maintain some semblance of control. Silly, maybe. But comforting.

At the reception desk, Kat gave her name to the flame-haired student marking arrivals on the guest list and accepted an exhibit program. She checked her coat, slipped her purse across her shoulder, made sure her hair clip was still snug at the nape of her neck, and glanced around. No sign of Michael.

With a glass of white wine from the open bar, Kat took up residence at one of the cocktail tables, assessing the guests as they arrived. Such a fashionable crowd. She wished she'd packed something a bit more…expressive. She wished she *owned* something more expressive. Her wardrobe was functional at best, dreary at worst. After she and Daniel broke up, Isabella had begged her to go shopping with her in L.A. Or Phoenix, at least. "You dress like a lab rat," her sister-in-law had said. "A gorgeous lab rat, but still. You're not going to catch anyone's eye wearing khakis, a university-branded pullover, and a ponytail."

Amidst a flamboyant crowd of artists and their friends and family, Kat was glad she'd brought the cashmere, blood-red, V-neck, the neckline cut low enough to reveal plenty of cleavage, and matching drop earrings that Isabella had given her for Christmas. God, it annoyed her when Isabella was right. Channeling her relentless sister-in-law, Kat had even gone so far as to stop in at a shop down the street from her hotel to buy a couple of new bra and panty sets. Just in case.

She started flipping through the program when a group of six or seven talkative middle-aged women swept up toward the reception desk. Their apparent leader, wearing an outrageous knit cap with a plump bouquet of knit daffodils poking up from the crown, was a diminutive woman who scanned the room with bright, perceptive eyes as if she were 007 searching for enemy agents and potential escape routes. Kat smiled as the woman's gaze swept over her. Although slimmer, with her close-cropped steel grey hair and sun-washed skin marked with deep laugh lines, Kat couldn't help but think the woman looked alarmingly like Judi Dench in her role as M.

Moments later, she looked up from her program to find the woman, now stuffing her knit cap in her bag, striding toward her with a self-satisfied, I'm-the-cat-that-ate-all-the-cream look on her face.

"You must be Kat."

"Pardon?"

"Katherine Musgrave? Michael's date?"

"Goodness, yes, I guess that's me," Kat laughed. With Leila's distinctive eyes, prominent cheekbones, and almost otherworldly presence and Michael's brooding good looks, this striking woman had to be their mother. Kat wondered what their father had looked like. Some mashup of Henry Caville and Omar Sharif? "And you must be Mrs. Samaan."

"Carys, please."

"Carys, then." Kat looked over Carys's shoulder at the women she'd arrived with. "Leila said you were bringing your book club. You must be very proud of your daughter."

"Exceedingly so. I'm proud of my son too, but his clock always runs five minutes late," Carys said. "You'll get used to it, dear."

Kat blinked.

"He's already told me all about you so, naturally, I looked up your bio on your university website. That's how I recognized you. From your photo."

What could she say to that? She'd Googled Michael in the Mt. Olympus bathroom, but maybe she should have Googled the whole family.

"You are quite an accomplished young woman, obviously beautiful, and most certainly brilliant, just as Michael described. Yes, I think you'll rub along well together."

Rub along?

"And imagine," Carys went on, "meeting at the V&A. As if it was foreordained."

"Oh, yes, well..." Kat gave her head a little shake. Maybe she'd wake up and discover this encounter was part of a totally new kind of dream. She'd call it *dumbfounded* and add it to her *desolation*, *danger*, *desire*, and *death* dream classifications.

"And here we are now," Carys declared with a soft pat on Kat's hand as she turned toward the door to see...nothing.

A moment later, two tall figures appeared in the doorway as Michael and George strode in, one dark and one blond, and both looking as if they could grace the cover of a men's magazine. Good lord. Michael was so.... His gaze locked on hers as he approached and a flush spread through her, hot and delicious. She couldn't look away.

"Kat." Michael's throat worked as if he was going to say more, but nothing else came out. After an awkward silence, he turned to his mother who was holding a program out to him. He took the program and bent to give his mother a kiss on the cheek. "I would do the introductions, but I see you two have already met."

A muscle twitched along his jaw. Of course, Kat didn't know the tenor of his relationship with his mother, but she could sense his frustration. "I hope she didn't already regale you with any wild tales."

"Such dramatics." Carys waved away Michael's comment. "We were just getting acquainted."

"Beware," George stage-whispered to Kat, "Carys loves to adopt strays like us, Ms. Musgrave."

"You're hardly a stray." Carys swatted his arm.

"Soon, she'll have you wearing ridiculous knitwear and playing cards till all hours." George bent down to kiss Carys on the other cheek. "By the way, her knitwear is atrocious." He peeked at the cap not quite tucked into Carys's bag and grimaced. "Daffodils?"

"Why not? They're the official flower of—"

"Wales. I know." George rolled his eyes. "Let's go find that brilliant fiancé of mine," George said, taking Carys's arm.

As they headed into the main gallery, Michael extended his arm and Kat took it as if she'd done it before. Then a bizarre thought flitted through her mind: *maybe she had.*

# NINETEEN

George led them to a small gallery with a long bench. The lights were dimmed for viewing the expansive wall-mounted monitor set up for Leila's video. They donned 3D glasses and sat through it twice. Developed with help from a fellow student working in augmented and virtual reality technologies, the project featured Leila and several of her friends wearing a variety of period costumes while enjoying a formal English tea while a video constructed from cut up and reassembled clips from old newsreels and movies played in the background. Armies marched in reverse. Cavalries charged upside down. Time went forward and backward and nothing made sense. It was absurdist and jarring, but strangely compelling. Especially with Michael sitting beside her as if they'd always been side by side.

Leila's thesis advisor appeared. Carys and George both whipped out their phones to take photos, and Michael suggested he and Kat tour the rest of the exhibit. As they wandered, he introduced her to several of Leila's friends and they fell into an easy conversation about art and museums. Then, abruptly, Michael stopped. "So, what did my mother say to you before I arrived?"

"She told me she'd looked me up on the university website. That's how she recognized me."

"Anything else?"

He seemed overly serious all the sudden. "No, why?"

Michael cocked one eyebrow at her. Damn, she wished she could do that eyebrow thing. "Nothing else?"

"Well, she said we'll 'rub along well' together.'" She gave the phrase air quotes.

He looked off into the distance and then brought his gaze back to her. "Let's find somewhere quiet to talk."

"What's happened?"

He hesitated a long moment, studying her face as options and repercussions sorted themselves. "Nothing's wrong," he said finally. "But we need to talk."

He could easily convince himself to wait until tomorrow. To enjoy dinner out tonight with Leila and George as if it were a regular date between regular people. But he'd never been regular and that felt disingenuous. Like he was hiding something. It was important that he be transparent about what he knew—and what he didn't. The problem was that telling her now meant that she might feel bound to him because of the past, not because she chose him freely. Not because she liked him or wanted to be with him now, but because of who they'd been to each other long ago. And damn it all, he wanted her to choose him now.

"I don't want any distractions."

"Okay," she said, her voice full of worry. *Whatever is going on, he's tied himself into knots over it,* Kat thought.

She took his arm again, her touch gentle, caring, and it felt so right he nearly bent down to kiss her in the middle of the gallery. Instead, he led her back toward the lobby where she retrieved her jacket and then he ushered her outside to a bench in a little copse of trees near the entrance. It was chilly outside, but an earlier rain had rinsed the humidity away leaving the air smelling fresh.

"So, my mother," he started once they were settled. "Yesterday, after I put you in a taxi, I checked my phone only to find a string of texts from her. Once I got home, I rang her, and she was insistent that I drive out to her house. She'd found something, she said." He looked up at the evening sky and then back at Kat.

"Let me back up. Remember I told you I'm doing research for a book on Syrian glassmaking and that my father's family, back in Aleppo, were craftsmen who ran a glassmaking business for years. Centuries, in fact. It was founded in 1350 by two brothers and, although it never grew very big, it stayed in the family right up until the building was destroyed during the civil war. Three of my cousins and their wives, the ones who ran the business, were in the building, cleaning the place out. None of them survived. It was a fucking barrel bomb." He was quiet for a long moment and when he finally spoke, his voice was thick, raw. Angry. "Six hundred years. All gone."

"Oh, Michael."

"Fucking war," he growled, and then was silent for a long moment. "Did you know there's a Japanese construction company founded in 570 or something. Can you imagine? It's been around for over 1400 years. Still going."

"Maybe your family will rebuild."

"I don't know." He shrugged. "Many have emigrated. Those who stayed are accountants or dentists or engineers. Lots of engineers. Like my dad. Still there was always someone who wanted to keep it going. An artisan in the true sense of the word. I guess I inherited an appreciation of the art without the desire to create it myself. Still the work was beautiful. There was even a glassmaking school. Students could go in and make their own pieces, learn the old craft. I tried my hand every time I visited." He shrugged. "Reuben, one of the cousins who was killed, said I had the Samaan touch. A gift for glass, he said." Michael tried but failed to suppress a shudder.

"Do you have any pieces that you made?"

"I brought home a few. Usually gave them to my parents or to Leila." He didn't say he couldn't stand to keep them in his own house or that working over the furnace almost wrecked him. Didn't say anything about the visions that nearly blinded him while he worked. Visions he craved, that appalled him, that haunted him still. He didn't tell her that one time he'd fainted dead away and had to be hospitalized. Dehydration, the doctors had said. Sheer terror, Michael knew.

"Anyway, before things got too dangerous in Aleppo, the cousins packed up the house our grandfathers grew up in—it was in the Old City, which has now mostly been destroyed—and they sent a bunch of crates to my father for safekeeping. We thought it was just stuff from the house: rugs and keepsakes, silver coffee sets and old jewelry, and the like. It was a big house with a lovely central courtyard. Steps down to an old tunnel that originally led to the Citadel. No one lived there anymore, but it was maintained for guests and family gatherings. I loved staying there. Like living in a museum."

"And now it's gone too?"

Michael nodded, turned his body toward her so his knee pressed against hers, as if the physical connection could tether him to the present. "Well, it turns out not all of it was from the house. There are two crates full of material from the glassworks." He shifted to face her. "And, Kat, there are old photos and accounting books. Ledgers that appear to go all the way back to the beginning. Paper folios, parchment covers, hand sewn bindings. Books full of illustrations. Like an inventory. Maybe records of clients and sales. I don't read Arabic, so I can't be sure, but this could make all the difference for my research. I could shift my focus from a general history of glassmaking in Syria to the history of one family's business. My family's business."

"And to think it's all been right there waiting for you. Like it's meant to be."

"It doesn't belong just to me, of course. Cousins in Syria still have an interest in the business, even though, like me, they didn't have the running of the place."

"I'm sure they'll want you to do what's best to take care of everything sent to your father."

"I called the curator at the V&A—"

"You said you're a regular there," Kat said with a smile.

He chuckled. "Yeah, I spend an inordinate amount of time at the National Art Library located there. Anyway Liz Bridewell—she curates the glass collection—has agreed to contact a colleague, a rare book archivist, and meet us at Mum's to look through the crates, give us a preliminary sense of what it's all worth and what needs to be done to protect it."

"When is that going to happen?"

"Tomorrow morning. Ten o'clock. I'd like you to be there."

Kat held his gaze. "All right. Can I ask why?"

He took a deep breath and continued. "There's more. The oldest books, despite their age, are in beautiful condition. Reuben, the cousin I was closest to, managed the business side of the glassworks. He would've kept all their records in a safe. Climate controlled, if I know him. Knew him. He was really into family history. I've been thinking of him all day. I went to his wedding. He'd been so happy. I think he would've wanted me to have the glassworks stuff. You know, as an art historian."

His voice caught and Kat scooted closer, her thigh against his.

"But it's more than me being an art historian." He pulled his hand from Kat's, closed his eyes and bent over, propping his elbows on his knees. He drew in a long breath and let it out slowly.

"Remember how you felt when you first saw it? the Luck?"

"How can I forget?" Kat said, her voice low. "That moment was like…an awakening. A rebirth."

"Yeah. Well, seeing these old books, it was like that first time. I felt…"

"Felt what?"

"I didn't want to touch the pages, get oils from my fingers on them, so Mum found a pair of Pop's old gloves. Kid leather, so soft." He laughed. "Not that that has anything to do with anything except that it was strange wearing his gloves while…and even with the gloves on…"

"What did you feel?" Her voice was still soft, but urgent now. Impatient.

"Naturally, I went to what looked like the oldest books. Mum already had them set out for me. The crates had been kept in the carriage house storage room, and she'd taken several books to the guest flat upstairs. She had on a pair of her knit gloves and opened one of the books to a page she'd bookmarked with a piece of scrap paper. I was already feeling lightheaded, almost feverish. Just being near the books made me break out in a sweat. Then I saw it. My vision swam. Everything went dark. Mum had to pull out a chair for me and push me down into it. It was a good five minutes before I could even move. When I came back to myself, I realized I'd been crying, for god's sake." He huffed out a soft laugh. "Sobbing like a bloody baby. She'd brought out a box of tissues and I had a wet wad in my hand with no memory of how they got there." He pressed his palms into his eye sockets, as if he had a raging headache.

"I had a vision, Kat. A waking dream, whatever you want to call it. I saw my hands, holding a quill pen. Drawing. And it wasn't like I was seeing them from a distance, like in those dreams, you know, when you're floating above yourself, watching from the outside? This was me, putting ink on the page in smooth, practiced lines. I was in the man's head. I knew what he was thinking. God, Kat, it was…" He stopped and stared at her, eyes bleak, haunted.

"Was what? Were you drawing? Writing?"

He reached into his back pocket and pulled out his phone. "At Mt. Olympus yesterday, you mentioned some sort of epigenetic inheritance, that maybe our ancestors were somehow connected to one another through the Luck itself and that we inherited that sense of recognition, that somehow we're already a part of each other."

"Yes…?"

"Well, how do you feel about reincarnation?"

"Reincarnation?" She squeaked out. She cleared her throat and tried again. "What do you mean reincarnation?"

He thumbed in his passcode, went to the photo app, and handed the phone to Kat.

Her hand shook so she almost fumbled the phone. She used her fingers to zoom in on the image and peered closer. She could see the texture of the page. The dark ink. The vibrant colors. The smooth, practiced lines of a craftsman. The illustration a perfect rendering of the piece she now knew as the Luck of Edenhall. Drawn over six hundred years ago.

# TWENTY

With a glass of Spanish sherry from Cadiz in one hand—one of Roland's several gifts to his aunt—Elias wandered about the sitting room, examining the tapestries and furnishings with a now-practiced merchant's eye. Roland, meanwhile, was flattering his aunt with such subtleties as *Aunt, you've put the lie to the work of Father Time as you are as lovely as last I saw you*, and *You have made us feel more welcome than even the finest hostesses in Lisbon, Le Havre, or London.*

Elias thought his friend was, as he'd heard Roland himself say, laying it on with a trowel, but he was content to be amused rather than embarrassed. So, apparently, was Aunt Julia, as he'd come to think of her from all Roland's talk of the woman. After having soaked until he was nearly pickled in a steaming hot bath, Elias was more than happy to prove a gracious guest, generous to his hostess and her neighbors. He half listened to conversation and made appropriate comments when called upon, smiling and answering questions as needed. After months in Roland's company, his English was quite good, even if his accent still betrayed his origins.

She'd invited a few of her neighbors to Hartley to welcome her itinerant nephew home, including a pleasantly non-descript looking young couple, newly married and settled nearby and an elderly man named Sir Gregory and his wife, their morose, grey-clad widowed daughter, and Gerard, their handsome grandson who had declared himself anxious to be off to Cambridge to study the Ancient Greeks as soon as possible. Preferably before dinner, if the young man had his way. Although, the gleam in Roland's eye told Elias that the young man had become his friend's latest mark. Likely Cambridge would wait a few days.

The conversation turned to the vicissitudes of travel in these dangerous times yet none, save Roland and himself, had traveled farther north than Edinburgh nor south than London. Still, they were a roomful of experts on the best coaches, the finest inns, the risks of brigands, and even shipboard fare, though he'd wager none could discern the difference between a single-masted sloop or a fully loaded frigate. He listened to it all with a smile on his face, but the truth was that he was not only growing hungry, he was growing impatient.

For all Roland's talk of Emmaline, Elias was surprised the girl hadn't met them at the gates, flinging herself at her cousin like a long-lost brother. Roland, Elias knew, was surprised too. And disappointed. Maybe even worried.

"The Mistress has her sequestered to keep her out of trouble before dinner," the groom, a man named Giles, told Roland as they were disembarking from the carriage and seeing to the storage of their trunks and baggage. "Me own woman—ye remember Mary?—is with her. Helping with her gown, fussing with her hair, and the like."

"Are you certain my aunt doesn't have her mucking out the stables or doing the laundry?" Roland shot back.

Giles grinned at that. "Oh, the Mistress would like that now, wouldn't she? Trouble is, I'm not sure Emmaline would mind spending more time with the horses, and that would defeat the purpose."

"And has Aunt Julia sold the girl to the highest bidder yet? Is there a marriage in the works?"

*Marriage?* The idea of Emmaline betrothed before he'd even met her sent a dull pang through Elias's limbs. He'd set out on this journey with Roland to conduct business on behalf of the glassworks and to expand their trading partners, but his growing preoccupation with this as-yet-unseen girl was taking alarming precedence in his thoughts.

"Nah, she's no betrothed yet, but that scoundrel Will Beacham has been sniffing about and Sir Neville is bound to make an offer sooner or later."

"Beacham? He's an idiot and a brute and Neville is older than her father." Roland shuddered even as ice formed in Elias's veins. "Last time I saw Beacham, he'd nearly ridden a prize mare to death, poor thing foaming and heaving, eyes rolling in the back of her head. The last time I set eyes on Neville, the man had more hair in his ears than on his head and spent all the air in his lungs complaining about his gout. Neither will do for our Emmaline."

"Agreed, but there's naught a groomsman and a maid can do about it. We're the only ones around who seem to care."

"Well, I'm here now," Roland had said and then turned and strode to the main house with Elias following close on his heels.

And still, as conversation dragged on in the sitting room, there was no sign of Emmaline.

Elias watched as Roland set out to charm the Cambridge-bound youth and his family all the while keeping an eye on the door. Finally, Elias felt a shift in the air. As if a storm was brewing in the rafters. He turned toward the doorway and the room tilted, like when a carriage careens too fast around a tight corner, throwing the occupants sideways. His fingers clenched around his glass, and he grasped the back of a chair to steady himself.

"Emmaline! Finally." Roland crossed the room to his cousin. He bent, kissed her hand and then stepped back as her perfect mouth opened on a soft, round "*Oh!*" He turned, followed Emmaline's stunned gaze toward Elias who now stared back, pale and wide-eyed, as if he beheld a ghost.

Emmaline's throat worked as she tried to swallow. Tears welled in her wide eyes. And Elias, along with a roomful of startled onlookers, watched as she stepped toward him and whispered, "You found me."

# TWENTY-ONE

"There you are."

Michael and Kat jumped and looked up from Michael's phone to see George approaching, a strange look on his face. "Damn," Michael groaned at the interruption.

George stopped, brows drawn down in a worried frown. "Everything okay out here?"

"Yeah, you just startled us."

"You sure? Seems like I interrupted something. Apologies, if so."

"No, no," Michael said. "We'll tell you later."

George studied the two a moment longer, then let that explanation go. "Did you know Sergei Badawi was going to be here?"

"What? No." Michael stood and held his hand out to Kat as if to help her up.

George waved a hand back toward the building. "He's in there chatting up your mum. He's with his man Friday."

"You mean Carson?"

"Yeah, him. They've both watched Leila's video and are singing her praises to whomever will listen. Not that I mind, she's bloody brilliant, but the half dozen goons with him acting like art lovers aren't fooling anybody. The staff's all aflutter and instructors and students are coming out of the woodwork to meet him."

"Jesus. I had no idea."

George glanced at Kat. "I think the man is positively besotted with Michael. And if he weren't twenty years younger than Carys, I'd swear he was besotted with her too."

"Who are you talking about?" Kat asked.

"Only one of England's richest men," George said. "Self-made, if you believe his mythology. Came out of nowhere. My father's a member of his investment group, so I've known him for years, but he seems to harbor a particular interest in a certain art historian's career. Appears at his public lectures, supports his research. Says it's because he's interested in Near Eastern glass. All a bit suspect to me."

"His father was Lebanese, so it makes some sense," Michael said, using the same justification he used for himself. "Still, he does turn up at the oddest times. Like this past Monday." He glanced at Kat. "I ran into him at the V&A. He offered me a ride home. The museum was about to close, but he was heading in. Claimed he was after some papers or something. He's on the board so who am I to argue? Anyway, I told him I was heading off to have dinner with a friend and declined the ride."

"I mean, he's fine, I suppose," George said. "Dignified. Wealthy. Destined for knighthood. Just a bit odd. Brutally brilliant, though. Has made the Hempsteads an immense amount of money, so my father's a big fan. But still, turning up here—"

"Yeah, I'm not in the mood for Badawi right now," Michael cut in sharply.

"I texted to warn you, but you didn't respond, so I came looking. Our dinner reservations are for 8:30 and it'll take 20 or 30 minutes to get there, depending on traffic. I was thinking you two could go on ahead. No reason for you to go back in and see the bloke if you don't want to. I'll cover for you. I'll say goodbye to Carys for you as well."

"Thanks, bruv. Just make sure he doesn't show up at the restaurant."

"Thank god I didn't let on where we were going. Leila would go ballistic."

Kat's eyes went wide, appalled. "Surely, he wouldn't—"

"No," Michael assured her. "I'm kidding. He's not that much of a stalker." He turned to George. "Go on in and we'll see you at the restaurant in a few."

"On it," George said, turning and striding back to the door.

After George was out of earshot, Kat said, "Will you tell Leila and George about the Luck and the illustration?"

"I imagine we'll have to, sooner or later." Michael caught something in her voice. "Why? Do you think it's a bad idea?"

"No, it's just that…I'd like to wait a bit. I think we need time to process this first. Just us."

"Just us and my mother, you mean. After the vision, after touching the ledger, I told her that you'd had the same reaction to the Luck that I'd had."

Kat smiled. "And she went straight to Google to find out what kind of person is getting mixed up with her son."

"She's convinced the whole thing—you and me meeting—is fate."

"As much as my scientific training and rational mind wants to convince me otherwise, I'm not sure she's wrong." He put a hand at the small of her back, guiding her toward New Cross Road to hail a taxi. "What about Leila and George? What will they think?"

Michael laughed. "Mum already told Leila that a big change was in store for me. Runes, auguries, Tarot, whatever. Mum's into it and that's why Leila was so obnoxious at Mt. Olympus last night. And George? Well, he's a mostly rational bloke, but as a novelist, he loves a flight of fancy. His imagination is in excellent working order, and he adores both Leila and my mother, even with all their barmy ideas."

"Tell me about this Badawi person. Is he really obsessed with you like George said?"

"Honestly, I don't mind Badawi, but sometimes I can't help feeling, I don't know, exposed around him, like he's caught me with my hand in the proverbial cookie jar. The way he looks at me, as if he's waiting on tenterhooks for me to say or do something. It's unnerving. Sometimes..." He gave his head a shake.

"Sometimes what?"

"Nothing."

"Michael, sometimes what?"

He bowed his head and ran both hands through his hair. "Sometimes I wonder if he isn't somehow connected to the Luck too." He let out a sigh. "He just seems too damn familiar. Too interested in me and my work. He's like an old acquaintance you think you recognize but can't remember their name. Or they've changed so much, you're not sure they're the same person."

Kat chuckled. "I know that feeling. The people you avoid by crossing the street or ducking down a different aisle in the grocery store. I once abandoned a cart full of groceries to avoid the minister from my mother's church."

He laughed. "Exactly."

She turned serious again, still shaken by the photo he had shown her. "Have you ever talked with him about the Luck?"

Michael nodded. "He's on the board of the V&A and is a constant presence at their events. I've even run into him down in the gallery. Sitting there looking at it, always with his sidekick, Carson, standing sentry nearby."

"How does he explain it?"

"Oh well, he's a great patron of the arts, isn't he? I'm an art historian. We're both thoroughly enchanted by the piece's history and craftsmanship." His voice was laced with sarcasm. "We're both intrigued by the delightful story about fairies and how it was made somewhere in the Middle East and mysteriously ended up in the north of England. How our fathers both hailed from the same general area and how now we both live here and isn't that such a coincidence. We dance around it well enough, but there's always something left unsaid and since I have no earthly idea what that unsaid thing is, I can't very well say it. And if he knows, he's not saying it either. It's like he's waiting for me to…I don't know."

That last part came out harsher than he intended. He rubbed the back of his neck to erase some of the tension.

"Still, although his presence can be disconcerting, I don't get malevolent vibes from him."

Kat's brows shot up. "You get malevolent vibes from other people?"

Damn. "I shouldn't have said that. "Never mind."

"You brought it up," Kat protested. "What do you mean?"

"It's hard to explain. More than a few times, I've felt like someone really is stalking me. Usually, it's a general skin-crawling feeling, you know? I turn around and no one's there. But..." He cleared his throat and looked away. "I don't want to scare you."

God, sometimes his thoughts were so tangled up in...everything. He didn't want to scare *her* because *he* was scared of losing her. Of her turning away from him because he was, what? A madman who dreamed of doing unspeakable things? Desperate to keep her near now that he'd found her? Greedy for the sight and smell of her, the feel of her? *She's the only thing that makes sense right now*, he thought, *and if I tell her, what then? Yet, she deserves to know, and I can't lie to her. If she's with me, she might be in danger. But if she knows, she might leave me. If she knows, she might decide I'm not worth the trouble.*

She gripped his bicep and pulled him to a stop. "Too late now."

He frowned and looked away. For years, he'd tried to shrug things off with a *well, I must be accident prone* or *it was just bad luck* or *I was at wrong place at the wrong time.* But not anymore. Not since last Christmas when he'd had to have his stomach pumped. Now he knew better. Now, everything strange that happened took on amplified meaning. He'd even second-guessed the random hit-and-run that had killed his father. And that the fact that his parent's house was broken into and his own terrace was ransacked not long after. Now, there was Kat's safety to consider. She deserved to know.

He cleared his throat. "Once," he said as they started walking toward the street again, "I was skiing Glencoe Mountain, up in the Highlands, when I swear someone came barreling down the slope and ran right into me. Pushed me into a tree. Broke my arm. Seemed like it had to be on purpose because otherwise they would've stopped to help."

"Did you report it."

"Yeah, but Ski Patrol was too busy getting me to hospital to do anything other than call it in to police. Besides, accidents happen on the slopes. Nothing ever came of it. Then there was last December. I hadn't eaten anything all day and ended up meeting Leila and George at a gallery opening after my last class. Had two beers and next thing I know I'm getting my stomach pumped. According to the toxicology report, someone added belladonna—otherwise known as deadly nightshade—to my drink."

Kat's voice shot up an octave. "Someone poisoned you?"

He reached out to smooth a wayward tendril of hair and push it behind her ear. "It wasn't enough to kill me. Just made me miserable for a few days. But that's not the worst."

"What the hell? Getting poisoned isn't the worst?"

He shook his head and plowed on with the story. "It was my second summer of grad school, and one of my mates was studying archaeology. His family kept a sailboat up in John o' Groats, in northern Scotland, and five of us decided to sail up to Orkney for a few days. See the standing stones, Skara Brae, sail around the islands. While we were getting the boat ready, I noticed a woman standing on the pier watching us. I sensed something familiar about her, but she never approached us, so I ignored her. Or tried to. She was staring daggers at me."

A vision of jilted lovers and jealous girlfriends blazed through Kat's mind, but she kept her mouth shut, afraid that if she interrupted, he'd stop talking.

"Anyway, we were about twenty nautical miles from Burwick when the stove in the galley exploded. We tried to put out the fire, but there was too much smoke and it must have blown a hole right though the hull. We were able to radio for help and luckily the ferryman of one of the regular ferries also saw it happen and radioed in our location. It didn't take long for the boat to sink, and we spent a good fifteen, twenty minutes bobbing about in the North Sea before the Coastguard pulled us from the water. The whole lot of us ended up in hospital in Kirkwall. Smoke inhalation and hypothermia. When I was released, I could've sworn the same woman was standing across the street, watching as Mum and Dad picked me up."

"Did you report her?"

"I told the detectives investigating the accident."

"Detectives? So they suspected foul play?"

He couldn't hold back a smile at that. "Foul play. Sounds so dramatic. Downright Sherlockian."

She stopped again, her face a shifting montage of anger, fear, incredulity. "Holy shit, Michael! It *is* dramatic. Someone tried to murder you and your friends!"

His heart was near to bursting at the thought that she was so concerned for his safety.

"We all had time to don our life preservers and to radio for help. And, it turns out galley explosions are not that rare. Butane and propane are both used for on-board stoves and if there's a leak, it can get dangerous fast. The boat had recently been refurbished so who knows if a valve was not tightened properly or—" He shrugged, trying to sound nonchalant about the whole thing which, remembering the moment the boat slipped under the water and they were left floating in the freezing waves was quite a feat. "No one could prove anything since the boat was at the bottom of the North Sea. And besides, it happened a long time ago."

"Getting poisoned in December is not a long time ago." Now she couldn't help herself. "Are you sure it wasn't a woman from your past? A jilted lover or something? Why else would someone want to harm you?"

He almost barked out a laugh. A woman from his past was exactly what he suspected, but not an ex-lover. And not from the recent past. He could never pin down *why* he suspected this, so he never told anyone. That and he would sound like a lunatic.

"Kat, I promise you I don't have any jilted lovers who'd care enough to want to do me in."

"What if—?" She rubbed her arms, suddenly cold to the marrow. "What if you hadn't made it and we'd never met?"

He wanted to pull her into his arms and hold her close, but he sensed that would be too much, too soon. Instead, he jammed his hands in his pockets and smiled at her. "Don't think like that. I did make it. We did meet. And now, we've plenty to think about besides Sergei Badawi or bad things that happened in the past." He hoped like hell that nothing about his past would put her in danger. He'd do anything to keep her safe from the darkness that too often claimed him.

"I'm sorry." She shivered. "All this is making me a bit crazy. Especially thinking of you bobbing around in the North Sea waiting to be rescued."

"Well, I was rescued and I'm here now." He cleared his throat. "Do you still want to go to dinner with George and Leila? It's a lot to take in and still pretend all is well."

"It's way too much to take in and all *isn't* well. We need to acknowledge that. But it seems like there are three options for tonight: I can go back to the hotel and drive myself crazy brooding and second guessing everything that's ever happened in my life. We can go to your mother's and look at the books so I can see that illustration for myself. Or we can proceed as planned."

She thought of her lecture to herself back in the bathroom at Mt. Olympus. *This is me being in control, taking charge*, she told herself. *I'm not going to let this pull me under.*

"We aren't going to solve this mystery tonight," she went on, "so we might as well celebrate Leila's accomplishments. We both know what it's like to hit that finish line and get that terminal degree. Let's give your sister the party she deserves. Tomorrow will take care of itself."

# TWENTY-TWO

Kat had nodded and smiled when Michael warned her in the cab to the restaurant that Leila had few inhibitions and that she really *really* enjoyed good food, especially when washed down with expensive Champagne. But nothing had prepared her for watching Leila Samaan eat. Kat had simply never realized the act of eating could be quite so sensuous. Or that public displays of affection—and Leila and George were not shy about those—could feel so…*freeing*.

"Now you understand why I had to make reservations over a month ago," George said as he watched Leila moan, eyes closed, pink tongue darting out between red lips to lick the backside of her dessert spoon.

Leila had so far compared the relative merits of each of their seven courses to the frisson of a spectacularly brilliant first kiss, stepping into a hot house full of hyacinth and mock orange, a hot bubble bath, a hot bubble bath with someone else, the sweet smell of puppy breath, and the adrenalin rush of galloping at full speed across the moors—apparently George's family had horses and they had all indeed galloped across the moors, whatever moors were. Kat still wasn't sure. As Kat had not experienced any of those things, except the puppy breath, she had nothing comparable to say about the food. She felt lacking. And utterly enthralled.

Kat's past was no help for the situation she found herself in. Her feelings toward Michael were exponentially different than anything she'd ever felt before. The heat of his presence beside her, coupled with the knowledge of the illustration he'd discovered in the old book, had unlatched something in her that had been completely battened down and was only now slowly unwinding. *Do not give up control*, she kept repeating to herself. Still, that illustration of the Luck was like a permission slip, giving her leave to let go with a man for the first time in her life.

Her natural inclination, up until this very moment, had been to carefully back away from any precipice she came near. She was an expert at treading carefully, maintaining control. Now she wanted to run headlong at the feeling, to charge the edge of the cliff, fling her arms wide, and leap. Soar into the unknown. She hardly recognized herself. Every time she caught Michael's hot gaze on her, her breath hitched, her blood warmed, and the feeling of being so thoroughly seen nearly swamped her senses. Every time his dark eyes landed on her, she felt as if lightning was about to strike, as if she would burst into flames like dry buffelgrass in the high heat of a Sonoran summer.

George motioned to the server, whispered something and stood. "That's all sorted. Now the real fun begins."

Leila took Kat by the arm as they walked to the door. "I sincerely hope you like to dance, because my brother is an excellent dancer."

"It's been a while."

"Be prepared. As a dancer friend of mine says, Michael doesn't dance to the music, he moves through it." Leila leaned in closer. "Just so you know, Michael has never wanted for admirers—both female and male. He's always had that dark, broody thing going on. Half my friends would cut off a limb for a tumble, but he's always been quite the monk. Don't know when the last time was he had an actual date, let alone a good shag, so—"

Kat glanced over her shoulder at Michael and George and whispered. "Why are you telling me this?"

"Because I like you and I love him. I think you're exactly what he needs. Whether he knows it yet or not."

"I don't know what Leila is whispering about, but it's best to ignore her when she's up to no good," Michael said, taking Leila's place at Kat's side as the doorman ushered them into the now blustery night air.

"She was just telling me what a good dancer you are."

"Really?" Michael cast a skeptical glance at his sister who was now walking arm in arm with George.

"So, where're we off to?" Kat asked.

"The Parliament Club. It has a great sound system and George always springs for a VIP booth. But we don't have to stay as long as they do. Just because they'll likely close the place down, doesn't mean we have to. You say the word and we'll call it a night."

Kat slipped her arm through his. "Let's see how it goes. Right now, I feel like I'm up for anything."

∞

Michael held Kat's hand as George led them through the crowd to a private booth on the VIP balcony, otherwise known as the "House of Lords," and rolled his eyes as George ordered more Champagne. Before they'd even settled into the booth, friends of George's and Leila's joined them. Soon the booth was crowded with well-wishers and fellow partiers.

"What do you think?" He asked Kat, raising his voice over the thundering bass of whatever the DJ was spinning.

"I've never been to a club like this!" She leaned into him. "Let alone hang out in a VIP booth." She motioned to the dance floor. "Dance with me?"

Michael smiled. "I thought you'd never ask."

Kat turned to see if Leila and George were following, but found them locked in an embrace that, just a few hours earlier, she would have considered inappropriate. Now, it made the blood thrum in her veins.

Michael took her hand again and led her down to the dance floor where bodies jumped and twisted and twirled. He loved the freedom of the dance floor, where the air shimmered as neon colors pulsed, turning the whole place into a fantasyland of sound and movement, a place where he could, for a while at least, turn off the insistent voices in his head.

He ushered her into the throng, pulled her to him and then expertly pushed her out into a spin and pulled her back up against him. With Kat in his arms, the blood pounded in his veins, a syncopation of desire as if they were made of music. As if together, they made up a full symphony of sound. It was euphoric. A lump caught in his throat, and he blinked back tears. He knew with a soul-searing clarity that he'd waited lifetimes for this woman. Before Kat could say a word, he let go, raised his hands above his head and began to move.

At first, Kat just stared. Leila's friend was right. She'd never seen anything as beautiful—as sensuous—as this man moving through the music as though the muscle and sinew, blood and bone of his body were generating oscillating waves tuned for her ears alone, reverberating in synch through her own body. The man was fluidity and grace personified, and Kat's body began to move on its own, a call and response to his every turn and twist. Heat pooled at her core. Her toes nearly curled in her boots. Sensation and awareness spooled through her as her skin seemed to scream out for his touch. They moved together, gazes held, knowing. Expecting. Anticipating. Their bodies creating a new language, intimate, unspoken, evolving with every beat and change of tempo.

The floor was packed, but Kat and Michael danced song after song as if they were alone in the world and music was invented just for them, until finally, he looked down at her through shining eyes and put his lips to her ear, warm breath sending shivers down to her toes.

"Come home with me."

# TWENTY-THREE

Michael wanted to make love to her in the cab. On the steps leading up to his front door. Against the front door. Fuck the cabbie, the neighbors, or any unlucky—or lucky—asshole who happened to be out past two a.m. Instead, he led her up the sidewalk, slid the key into the lock, opened the door, and then stood aside as Kat stepped over the threshold. The air was heavy with anticipation, but the house was quiet. Neither of them said a word. He wanted to slam the door shut, push her up against it, and press himself into her. But he also wanted everything to be perfect, to discover her slowly, deliberately. *Christ*. He just wanted. Her. This. Everything.

For as long as he could remember, there'd been something dark haunting him. Now, the idea that there was someone who might understand him, who might help shine a light on his darkness and help chase away the shadows, was intoxicating. He bent his head intending to brush his lips across hers and…*Shit*.

Saladin tore down the stairs, leapt from the second step, slid across the parquet entryway, and slammed into his legs.

"Bollocks," he whispered on a ragged exhale, then "Down, Sal," he commanded. Ever obedient, Sal stood on his back legs and put his front paws on Kat's knee, his entire backend vibrating like a coiled-spring door stop. *Someone new someone new someone new!* "Did I tell you I have a dog?"

"I think you mentioned something about a ridiculously misbehaved mutt."

Michael pulled at Sal's collar to get him off Kat's leg. "I'm sorry I didn't warn you, but I was a bit distracted."

"It's fine. I love dogs."

"He must have been having one incredible doggie dream as he usually greets me at the door."

Kat crouched to ruffle the dog's fur and massage behind his ears as Sal's big caramel-colored eyes looked up at her adoringly.

Relieved, he shook his head and laughed. "Look at the poor sod. Already smitten."

"His name is Sal?"

"Sultan Saladin, actually. Beware. He's very fierce."

Kat laughed as she stood. "Oh, I can tell."

"This way." Michael led her through the front room and back toward the kitchen. "Let me get him a treat and check his water bowl."

Kat's gaze took in the foyer where a mirror hung above a mid-century modern console table with one bowl for keys and another for a leash and plastic doggie bags. In the front room, beautiful rugs in deep reds and blues covered the wood floor and played host to a long, low-slung leather couch, a stone-topped table with Savonarola-type forged metal legs, and two facing upholstered chairs, all arranged in front of a white brick fireplace. The mood was mostly modern with an antique added here and there.

As she passed through the dining room, she noted the dark, oversized but intricately carved sideboard and matching wooden table piled with books scattered around a closed laptop. Both pieces were scratched and scuffed and looked like they could have been salvaged from ruins of a Medieval castle. The kitchen, on the other hand, was bright and clean with white countertops, grey cabinets, and a small breakfast table next to a bay window overlooking the dark expanse of the backyard. But what caught Kat's attention was the art. Every available space on the walls was filled with paintings, prints, or wall hangings, every surface adorned with glasswork, pottery or sculpture.

After refilling Sal's water bowl and setting a new flavored bone in his food dish, Michael noticed Kat's gaze fixed on the tapestry hanging over the dining room sideboard.

She nodded toward it. "That looks familiar."

"It's a scene from the Bayeux Tapestry. The Battle of Hastings. An old girlfriend gave it to me after I picked up the dining room furniture at auction. She thought it fit the mood. My mood, specifically." He snorted in derision. "She bought it as a joke. I loved it. We didn't last long."

"Some of these pieces are stunning."

"Art historian." He shrugged. "What can I say? It's why my savings account is not what it should be." He held out his hand. "Can I take your coat? Get you a drink?" *Pull that sweater over your head and bury my face between your breasts?*

Kat shrugged off her jacket and glanced at the clock on the wall near the breakfast table. "It's 2:30. Water would be nice."

"Still or sparkling?"

"Still is fine," she said.

He took her coat and laid it over the back of a chair with his, then poured two glasses of water from the tap. Kat watched his throat move while he drained his glass, licked his lips, and then set it on the counter with a decisive thud. He waited until she finished, took her glass, set it aside and stepped toward her. He reached for her hand and drew it up to his mouth, watching her face as he pressed the tip of each finger to his lips, drawing them one by one into the warmth of his mouth with a gentle nip and a slow suck. His voice was low, full of want. "Will you come to bed with me?"

A surge of desire flooded through her, hot and liquid as if she'd just bolted a double shot of mezcal. She *felt* more than she thought she could stand, a marrow-deep emotion welling up and over her like a tidal wave. Thrilling. Familiar. *Forever*. She'd never felt anything like this. Didn't even know this *engulfing* of emotion was possible. She cupped his face with her hands, held his dark gaze, then slid her fingers down along his jaw, around the back of his neck where the hair curled against his nape. Softly, carefully, she let her fingertips play there as if caressing a precious piece of art, like the ones displayed around them. Then gently, slowly, she pulled him down until his lips met hers.

And that's when everything changed. That's when light bloomed behind her eyes and the sound in her ears went quiet, muffled, like she had entered a deep tunnel. That's when time seemed to stutter and then restart, stutter and restart, sending her equilibrium and sense of being in her own skin, here and now, reeling sideways like some carnival ride loosed into the midnight sky. And that's when she knew that whatever this was, controlling it was going to be nigh impossible. She couldn't control her breathing. Couldn't control her hands, appendages that seemed to have grown an entire new layer of nerve endings. Her skin was alight, an electric current pulsing across its surface.

The kiss deepened. He took what she gave and pressed for more, running his hands up and down over the shape of her, tucking his thumbs under the hem of her sweater and lifting it slowly, slowly, slowly until she raised her arms, and he dragged it off and tossed it toward the kitchen table.

"Christ," he breathed the words. "You're more beautiful than I even imagined." He dragged his mouth along her hairline and down her neck as his fingers slipped the bra straps off her shoulders. He slid his hands to her back and unclasped her bra, then pulled it down and let it fall to the floor between them. With a touch as light as breeze, he rubbed his palms over her breasts, his warm exhale causing shivers to ripple over her skin. She thought she might spontaneously combust. He bent and swirled his tongue around one point and she felt as if her knees were going to buckle. She held on to his shoulders and arched back on a low moan.

And then the doorbell rang.

∞

Sal was barking and clawing at the door by the time Michael got there. Braless and with her sweater on inside out, Kat appeared a moment later.

"Michael Samaan?" The constable standing on the steps asked before Michael had even fully opened the door.

"Yes, I'm Michael Samaan." His pulse raced, sweat beaded on his forehead, his mind going back to the day two constables showed up at the door to his lecture hall to tell him his parents had been in a car accident, that his mother was in the hospital and his father was…gone. "What's happened?" *Please please please don't let this be happening again. Don't let anyone hurt Mum. Or Leila. Or George. Please.*

"Officer Martina Searcy, Metropolitan Police." She held up a badge for Michael to inspect. "Wallingford Police have been trying to ring you, but all the calls have gone to voicemail."

Michael felt Kat's hand squeeze his and tried to keep the panic from his voice. He braced his other hand on the doorframe to steady himself. "What's going on? We just returned from a club; it was loud."

"No one has been seriously hurt. But there's been a break-in at the carriage house on your mother's property. Sir, Mrs. Samaan apparently took after the burglar with a cricket bat and sustained a minor head injury from the scuffle."

"Jesus Christ." Michael's fingers were white on the door frame. "Is she in hospital?"

The officer looked down at her mobile phone. "No. The detective sergeant who responded, a DS Rao of the Wallingford Police, said paramedics recommended she be taken to hospital for observation, but she refused. Insists it's just a small bump and she's survived worse. She's asking for you, though. Been texting and calling."

Michael pinched the bridge of his nose and groaned. "She does that."

"Paramedic says there's a chance of concussion and would prefer to be certain but—"

"Bloody hell. Tell me everything you know." Michael peered out at the police car double parked in the street. "You want to come in?"

"No need. Okay, according to our information, it looks like a run-of-the-mill attempted burglary. It's a posh area, so it's certainly not out of the realm of possibilities. But DS Rao says your mother keeps talking like she knows what the intruder was after. Keeps insisting she was 'after the books.'"

Michael sucked in a breath and cast a glance at Kat.

"One thing to note," Officer Searcy said, "the security system was bypassed somehow and your mother's alarm never went off. Rao's got someone looking at it. Still the security company noted the breach and called it into police. Even sent someone out in person, apparently. Constables were patrolling the area and were able to respond within minutes. It appears that as soon as the intruder heard the siren, she took off. There's quite a bit of woods behind the house and open field beyond that, so they managed to get away."

"You keep saying 'she.' The intruder was a woman?"

"That's what your mum says.'

"And you sure my mother's okay?"

"Paramedic says she'll need to be careful for the next 24–48 hours, but she insists she's fine."

"Of course, she does. The house could be burning down around her, and she'd insist she was fine." He drew in a long breath. "Thank you, Officer. I appreciate you coming to the house and am sorry to cause you any trouble."

"Part of the job, sir." The officer turned to join her partner, waiting in the car. She stopped and looked back over her shoulder. "By the way, DS Rao says your mother specifically asked you not to bother your sister. She just wants you."

"Understood." Michael already had his phone in his hand and was calling his mother. "I'll be there within the hour," he said as soon as Carys answered. "Do not, under any circumstances, go to sleep. I'm bringing Sal to stay with you." He ended the call, exhaled, and stared down at his phone as if wondering what it was and how it appeared in his hand.

"I'm going with you," Kat said. She didn't know what she was getting into but seeing the panic-stricken look on his face, she didn't care. Yes, the last few days had been a whirlwind. Yes, things appeared to be spiraling out of control. Yes, she was confused about a lot of things. But not this. Not about wanting to be with this man in this moment. Not about wanting to be by his side when he needed someone. Not about needing to be with him because it was what *she* needed too.

His throat thick with emotion, he nodded and reached for his keys.

# TWENTY-FOUR

Sergei Badawi rolled over and grabbed the phone off his nightstand. "What?"

"There's been a break-in at Carys Samaan's place." Carson's voice filtered in through the fog of sleep.

Sergei pushed himself up to a sitting position and reached over to switch on the nightstand lamp. "When? Is she okay?"

"Happened about 1:30."

Sergei held his phone out to see the time. "It's 2:45!"

"I wanted to get more details before I woke you."

"Fine," he groused. "Tell me."

"Remember I reported that her security system had been hacked and that we put a man on her? Rollings. Retired Special Forces. He's staying in Wallingford and hadn't gone back to his hotel yet."

"Where was he?"

"Parked just down the lane. The system was tripped at 1:27 a.m. when an intruder bypassed the security code and entered the carriage house. Our security team immediately alerted Rollings and Wallingford Police. Apparently, whoever is behind this would've been in and out undetected except for the fact that we were already onto them, monitoring all activity that wasn't coming from our own team."

"Damn good thing you picked up that system breach." Sergei reached for the water he always kept on his nightstand and drained the glass.

"Yeah. So, anyway, Rollings immediately headed toward the carriage house and saw Carys slip through the door, obviously sneaking in behind the intruder. He followed her lead and approached the building, intending to stay close to monitor the situation. Then everything went sideways. He heard yelling upstairs and rushed inside, only to be nearly bowled over when the intruder barreled down the stairs and out the door. He managed to grab an arm, but got a knee to the groin, an elbow to the throat, and about 500,000 volts to the chest for his troubles."

Sergei's hand gripped the edge of the mattress. "Jesus."

"It'll take more than a Taser to take him down. The man's built like a fucking prize bull."

Carson paused and Sergei heard him take another call. He wanted as patiently as possible, fingers white as they gripped the edge of the bed.

"That was Rollings. He's back at the hotel now."

"Okay, go on. He just got tased…"

"He managed to drag himself around the back of the carriage house and get his arse into the woods where he heaved himself back into his car. After the police arrived and he was somewhat recovered, he made his way to the driveway to talk to the constables, presenting his Citadel I.D. Passed his presence off as personal service for a privileged client and all that. Fortunately, he didn't get any pushback. Unfortunately," Carson went on, "we're dealing with Carys Samaan here."

"Good lord, what did she do?"

"She told Wallingford police that she'd had a 'premonition' about the whole thing and that that was why she'd grabbed an old cricket bat from Michael's room and had gone out to confront the perpetrator."

"For fuck's sake, bloody woman is no bigger than a minute! What did she hope to accomplish?"

"Said she wanted to see the intruder so she could identify him later, but that once she got upstairs, she got mad and started swinging."

"Carys Samaan *is* mad. The whole damn family. Stubborn as a godforsaken clan of badgers. Did she get a good look? Wait. Was she hurt?"

"The intruder picked up a brass coffee grinder and hit her over the head with it before she fled. Might be a concussion. But get this, Carys says the intruder was a woman."

Sergei swung his feet over to sit on the edge of the bed. If it was a woman, he could guess who it was. Marie Scarpa. Damn bitch had been haunting Michael almost since the beginning, always threatening disaster, never quite succeeding.

"What about Michael?"

"Metropolitan Police went to his house. I guess he hadn't been answering his calls. Probably preoccupied because get this, Lindhurst says the woman with him at his sister's exhibit was at his house when the police arrived. The same woman that tore out of the V&A earlier in the week and had Michael jumping into a cab in pursuit."

"He's certain?"

"Lindhurst was Michael's tail tonight and he was the one outside the V&A that day. It's definitely the same woman. They were standing in the doorway together. Middle of the night."

"My god. Maybe it's really happening. Maybe it's finally all coming together."

He took a deep breath, the palm of his free hand pressed against his chest. His heart thudded so hard he could hear it in his ears. He didn't know what to do if it was really finally happening. How should he act? What should he say? And what if it was another wild goose chase? Another dead end? He didn't know if he could take it.

He found his voice. "What about the Canadian? The V&A Fellow?"

"Didn't you get the file Kinkaid sent?"

"I got it." *I've got the damned thing memorized and can't get the woman out of my head.* "Is there anything new?"

"She's not in London. She flew back to Toronto three days ago for a funeral. Apparently, she's taking time off to deal with family issues."

"Let me know as soon as you find out when she's returning. What flight she's on. And the moment her flight touches down."

"Got it."

"Is that all?"

"Not by a long shot," Carson said. "I saved the best for last."

"Jesus, man. Spit it out!"

"Carys insists that the burglary wasn't random."

If it was Marie Scarpa, Sergei thought, it most definitely was not random. That woman lived by a twisted logic, but she always had a singular purpose. Taunt and torment Michael. Ruin his life. Make him pay for what he did to her. Make him hand over the glass spheres the Alchemist had crafted six hundred years ago and end it all. *Once and for all.*

"She told the police," Carson was saying, "that her sixth sense premonition or third eye or whatever she claims to have showed her the intruder was after 'the books.'"

"The books? What books?" Sergei somehow managed to get the words out.

"She said her husband's cousins sent crates of family keepsakes to London in the early days of the Syrian civil war. Among the crates were records from Samaan Glassworks. Apparently dating back hundreds of years."

*Holy Mother of God.* Sergei's heart skipped a beat. Skipped several beats. Maybe he'd suddenly developed an arrhythmia because it felt like his heart was a rabid dog trying to claw its way out of a cage. He closed his eyes and let himself fall back onto the bed. It'd been a long time since he'd felt like this. Scratch that. He'd *never* felt like this. *Never* had this kind of hope.

"Still there?" Carson asked.

After a long moment, Sergei marshaled the air in his lungs. "Yeah."

"You okay?"

"Never better."

# TWENTY-FIVE

Forty-five minutes after the police officer interrupted what Michael was certain would be one of the most memorable nights of his life, he pulled into his mother's driveway, triggering the motion-activated lights along the side of the house. Conversation had been limited and the mood tense as they drove from Michael's terrace in Bloomsbury Square to his childhood home in Wallingford, the picturesque market town between Oxford and Reading where his father had founded his company and where Michael and Leila had grown up.

"When the doorbell rang tonight," he told Kat once they'd passed Windsor, "all I could think of was the day the police came to campus to tell me about the accident. When my father was killed. I was in class, and they rapped at the door. I stepped out into the hall and, Christ. Mum had contusions to her face, a concussion, a serious case of whiplash, and a dislocated shoulder. But Pop…he…it was his spine. The other car clipped them from behind and their car—*my* car, they'd borrowed my little roadster for their anniversary weekend—spun, hit the guardrail, and flipped. The other car didn't stop."

Kat took his hand in hers and let him talk.

"Tonight, seeing that officer on my doorstep, it all came rushing back. Leila arrived at the hospital not long after me and she was so distraught she had to be sedated. I was the one who told Mum that Pop was gone. Truthfully, she already knew. She just gripped the blanket in her fists and stared out the window. After a while, she closed her eyes and curled in on herself. She was on pain meds and slept on and off for the next few days. Existed in a fog for months."

Kat nodded and stared out the window at the passing shadows. "I watched my mom go through it. Watched her struggle to make sense of it all. The hardest thing is to know someone you love is missing their other half, to watch someone be lonely and not be able to fill up that space. How do you go on when you lose the person you love most in the world?"

"You rearrange the world." The words were out, hanging in the air and he couldn't take them back. Didn't want to. He thought of his vision, the man's hands—*his* hands—tracing the outline of the goblet, pressing the pen nib against the paper while thinking of the woman who'd inspired him. Filling in the floral design on the page even as he felt emptied out. Body and soul. Because the wife he'd loved beyond reason had died and there'd been nothing he could do to save her. The emptiness he'd felt when she was gone squeezed in around him even now. He gripped Kat's hand as the darkness that overwhelmed him so long ago threatened to creep back into his consciousness.

"My father dropped dead on the golf course," Kat was saying. "Heart attack. He'd just made a bad putt and had joked with his friends. 'Think I'll take a mulligan.' A do-over. He was dead before he hit the ground."

"So, how'd your mother go on?"

"Like she deals with everything. She planned. She planned the funeral and the funeral dinner and travel and hotel arrangements for everyone coming in from out of town and then, when that was all over, she worked with the lawyer on the will and trust and then when that was over, she started planning everyone's lives. Mine, included."

Michael held up their clasped hands. "She couldn't have planned for this."

"No one could." Kat drew his hand to her mouth and pressed a soft kiss to his skin. And then they'd lapsed into silence for the rest of the drive.

∞

He turned off the car as the back door to the main house opened and his mother, a shawl draped around her shoulders and a mug in her hand, made her way down the sidewalk to the driveway.

"Michael. And Kat! Goodness. I'm so glad you're here."

Michael climbed out of the car. "Mother—"

"Before you start in on me, I'm fine. Truly." Michael frowned at her. "I promise!"

"Let me see your head."

Carys lifted the hair off her forehead to reveal a nasty bump, purplish red around the swollen edges. "It's not that bad, darling. Besides, I gave as good as I got."

"A case of 'you should see the other guy?'" Michael scowled as he held his mother's chin, tilting her face toward the light for a better view.

"I'm sorry I interrupted your evening," Carys said, swatting Michael's hand away.

Not nearly as sorry as I am, Michael thought.

"We're just relieved you're safe." Kat said, breathing in the scent of flowers—roses, hyacinth, maybe lilac?—hanging in the night air as she joined them with Sal on his leash. "Are you certain you don't need to go to the hospital?"

"No, no. An ambulance came and paramedics gave me the once over. I assured them I've lived through worse." She cocked her head toward the carriage house.

Carys reached down to pet Sal who'd been sitting patiently as if sensing something important had happened. "Come on, boy. Your nemesis is nowhere to be found."

As Michael grabbed a hastily packed overnight bag from the back seat, Kat asked, "Nemesis?"

"My cat, Pooka. Black as night with eyes as gold and round as a harvest moon. She has a tendency to sneak up on people, so don't be surprised if you find her on the end of your bed staring at you. She hid when the police showed up, so who knows when we'll see her again."

"Forget about your bloody cat," Michael said. "I want to know what possessed you to head toward the scene of a break-in instead of staying inside and calling 999? The constable said you ran the intruder off with my cricket bat?"

"She wasn't going to hurt me."

"How did you know it was a she," Michael's voice rose, "and how the bloody hell did you know *she* wasn't going to hurt you?"

"I can't explain it. I just knew. Besides, I saw her coming"—she tapped the center of her forehead—"and knew exactly what she was after." She looked at Kat to explain. "I had a premonition, you see. It happens sometimes."

"Oh, for god's sake," he muttered.

Carys lifted her chin in a stubborn gesture. "I knew what I was in for, darling. I'm not a complete idiot."

"Sometimes I wonder." he glared at his mother. "What would Pop have thought about you running headlong into danger, taking risks you know better to avoid? Did you even think about the consequences of confronting an intruder? What if this person had been armed? Christ, Mum!"

"The carriage house alarm didn't go off, but it's wired to the system in the main house. I couldn't get to sleep— it was the premonition keeping me awake, of course—so I was watching the telly and saw the system panel light up and knew someone had opened the door up to the carriage house flat. I assumed something was wrong with the alarm, but that the security company would still be monitoring the system. It's what we pay them for, and you'll be happy to know they called the police and sent out a local Citadel representative as soon as the alarm was triggered. A very nice man. Mr. Rollings."

"That's all well and good, Mum, but you should have stayed in the house."

She waved the notion away. "Mr. Rollings said he'd find out why the alarm didn't go off and call in the morning to report what he'd discovered. Plus, I told him we'd need a new safe for the books we found, and he said he'd said he'd handle it himself. He'd make sure we get priority, expedited service because of the alarm and because we're 'such valued customers' and all that blarney."

"He better have a damned good excuse for why the system didn't work. They're supposed to be one of the best security agencies in the whole blasted country, and I want to know what went wrong. Still, you should never have gone to the carriage house in the first place. What the hell were you thinking?"

"That she might take the books and get away before the police arrived!"

"What makes you think she was after the books?"

"She *was* after the books, Michael. I could feel it. Or maybe not the books specifically, but something that has to do with them. Either way, I wanted to know why and to get a good look at her." She frowned. "Turns out she was wearing one of those masks—balaclavas or something?—so I didn't see her face. But she spoke to me."

"She spoke to you? What the hell?" Michael held open the door and then followed his mother, the dog, and Kat up the stairs to the carriage house flat. "Did the two of you have a little chat before or after she gave you a concussion?"

Carys didn't say anything else until they were all inside the guest flat. "You two want tea? Coffee?"

"For Chrissake, Mum! Sit down and stop stalling. Tell me what she said."

"All right. Just after she koshed me over the head with the coffee grinder, she leaned over me and spoke in a very slow, clear voice with perfect enunciation. I'm quoting now: 'You tell him I'm always watching. This is the last time. You tell him that Micah Samaan is finally going to pay for playing god.'"

Michael went still. The color drained drained from his face. He swallowed hard and managed to croak out, "Did she say Michael or—?"

"Micah. She said Micah Samaan."

# TWENTY-SIX

Everyone in the room turned and stared. For a long moment, no one said a word. Roland gaped at how Emmaline and Elias gazed at each other, oblivious to their surroundings. As if everyone and everything else had simply fallen away, leaving the two of them as the only people left standing. He'd suspected the two would find each other attractive, but he hadn't anticipated *this*. Whatever *this* was. Out of the corner of his eye, he saw his aunt raise her eyebrows and the flush on her cheeks forced him into action to defuse the situation before she made an inappropriate comment.

"My dearest cousin," he positioned himself between Emmaline and Elias. "I am happy to bring yet another admirer to your doorstep. I have sung your praises daily as we traveled, like a veritable chorus of twittering birdsong."

Emmaline blinked and looked up at him. "What? I'm…yes…thank you," she murmured as he took her trembling hand and tucked it in his arm. She gave her head a little shake, darted a glance at her stepmother, and forced herself back to the present moment. Following Roland's lead, she said, "It is good to see you after so long. I am delighted that you and your companion have finally arrived. You must know I've been anxious for your visit for weeks."

"Before I introduce my friend, let me accompany you as you pay your respects to the other guests."

To give her time to collect herself, Roland guided her first to Lord and Lady Palmer and then to their daughter and her son, a doe-eyed young man who gazed admiringly at Roland and Elias, and then to the others in the room, watching as Emmaline curtseyed and greeted them all in turn. Her hand tightened on his arm as he guided her toward the fireplace where Elias stood stock still, as if hewn from the same stone as the mantle.

"Cousin, I am delighted for you to make the acquaintance of Mr. Elias Samaan of Aleppo, my companion these past months and an esteemed friend for longer than that." He turned to  Elias. "I could not be happier to present to you my cousin, Miss Emmaline Musgrave."

Conscious of everyone in the room watching with avid attention, Elias fought to keep his voice from quavering as he offered his most courteous bow. "Miss Musgrave, I hope I am not too forward in remarking that making your acquaintance has quickly become the high point of my entire journey."

The sound of his voice sent a thrill up Emmaline's spine. His English was lovely, flavored with an accent that seemed to add spice to each word. She fought to keep the heat from her face as she could feel her stepmother's eyes on her and knew that her outburst upon first seeing Mr. Samaan had been unseemly. *You must act the proper lady, Emmaline, or Julia will never let you out of her sight.* So, she curtsied and allowed her years of training in courtly manners—behavior she would never practice at any actual court—guide her every look, gesture, and word.

"With some slight knowledge of the course of your travels, that is a most generous compliment, indeed, sir. Now that you have seen our beautiful countryside, I hope you will come to know and love it as I do. Pray tell, how long do you and Cousin Roland plan to tarry with us here at Hartley?"

Elias looked mutely to Roland to answer as he was too busy absorbing the wonders of the woman in front of him. *He knew her!* But how? It made no sense. She stood before him as if all his dreams had been answered, and as if he were a man dying of thirst, his eyes drank in the rich browns and golds of her hair, the elegant curve of her neck, the blush of sun on her cheeks, but above all, the gleam of recognition in her eyes. The lips that parted ever so slightly as her tongue darted out to wet them.

"We expect to stay a fortnight before traveling on to Carlisle where we will spend the winter," Roland said. "It is my hope that we all celebrate the holidays together, if not at Hartley, then certainly at Naworth." He ushered Emmaline to a chair and addressed his aunt. "It is likely my father will remain in London, but I would welcome your help in showing my friend what a joy an English Christmas can be."

"So, Mr. Samaan," Julia said, shooting a glance at Emmaline, "you *do* celebrate Christmas then?"

Despite the tumultuous roar of emotions and impressions and memories—indeed, *memories!*—rushing and receding through her brain and blood like storm-tossed waves crashing against cliffs, Emmaline could almost hear Julia's exhalation of relief that Mr. Samaan's family was of the Christian faith.

"Indeed, Madam," Elias forced his attention back to the present and offered Julia a wide smile. "My family's devotion to the Church likely predates the first cornerstone laid in the first chapel in the whole of the British Isles."

Roland laughed inwardly at Elias's little dig at his aunt's prejudicial presumptiveness. The woman truly had no concept of the world outside her castle walls. No wonder his uncle had been tempted to take Emmaline's mother—whoever she was—to his bed.

"Aunt, the Samaan family is a highly respected one among many old and distinguished families in what is, arguably, the oldest city in the world."

"Arguably?" Elias tsked. "My friend, on that point there can be no argument."

"Try telling that to a Damascene," Roland quipped. He turned to the other guests. "It is common among those from the great lands of the Near East to claim their city as the oldest of them all."

"And have you been to the Holy City?" Lord Palmer inquired. "I have long dreamed of visiting Jerusalem."

"Several times, Milord," Roland said.

"I had the privilege of visiting the Church of the Holy Sepulcher and describing it to my beloved mother and my grandmother, blind these many years from tragic injury," Elias said gravely, knowing that anything that had to do with mothers, grandmothers, and Jesus Christ would go far toward winning the hearts of the women in this room.

"My goodness," Lady Palmer's daughter whispered, her hand fluttering about her neck, her voice thick with awe.

Elias smiled at the woman and wondered what she'd say if he told her his grandmother was very likely an opium-addicted witch who believed she chatted regularly with a long-dead ancestor who claimed to be a powerful magus who could conjure the philosopher's stone to bring people back to life.

"We have seen the glories of Constantinople and Rome too," Roland was saying. "While Mr. Samaan was curious to travel west to see the British Isles, my dream has always been to travel the Silk Road and see the Great Wall of China. Alas, that must be my next journey."

"Quite the adventurers, you young men!" Lady Palmer exclaimed. "I trust you will entertain us this evening with stories of your journeys. I am sure Gerard will be in raptures with your tales. Won't you, Gerard?"

Besides tracking Elias and Roland's movements around the room, and speaking only when spoken to, Gerard had thus far spent his evening leaning against the harpsichord in a bored, insouciant pose. He ignored his grandmother's cue.

"He sets off for Cambridge soon," Lady Palmer continued, delighted to do the talking for him. "It is the farthest from home he will have ever been." She cast her doting gaze at the striking young man.

Roland turned toward Gerard. "Are you interested in traveling to the Holy Land? Perhaps you dream of tracing Our Savior's footsteps along the Via Doloroso?"

Gerard held Roland's gaze and gave his head a tiny shake. "Greece. I want to walk the Agora, climb the Acropolis, sail the wine-dark sea. Meet other men interested in the classical studies."

One eyebrow ticked up as Roland ambled toward Gerard, looking him over head to foot. "An admirer of the Greeks, are you," he asked with an enigmatic smile, then leaned closer to whisper in Gerard's ear. "Come riding tomorrow, and I will share tales of my adventures there that cannot be recounted in the company of ladies."

After an almost imperceptible pause, Gerard gave a short nod. "Tell me what time and I'll be there."

Lady Palmer turned to her daughter. "I don't know what the gentlemen are whispering about, but I do believe our Gerard has finally heard something that has captured his interest."

Roland gifted Lady Palmer with a wide smile. "I was just inquiring as to whether your grandson would like to accompany us on a ride tomorrow morning." He turned back to the young man. "Shall we say seven? Meet us at the Hartley stables and I promise a ride to remember."

At the slight twitch of muscle in Gerard's jaw, Roland flashed him a knowing smile and then turned back to Emmaline. "Are you still going for your morning rides? Last time I was here, you could outrace us all." He glanced at his aunt. "I'm sure you won't mind if my cousin joins us."

Lady Palmer's eyes went wide, and Julia sputtered. "I'm not sure that's appropriate, Roland. Riding alone with three gentlemen?"

"I—" Emmaline started, but clamped her mouth shut when Julia sent her a warning look.

"Nonsense," Roland said, waving away his aunt's objection. "I am perfectly capable of keeping my cousin safe. But if you have concerns, Giles can accompany us as her protector. I assume he still escorts her every morning?"

"Yes, but—"

"Lovely!" Roland's broad smile lit up the room. "Then it's settled."

Emmaline considered the exchange, her mind whirling. She could feel Elias Samaan's eyes on her. God, she swore she could feel his *hands* on her! A trickle of sweat rolled down her spine as a desperate heat spooled through her, settling in her most private places. She could hardly wait for the dawn.

# TWENTY-SEVEN

He leaned back against the sofa cushions, eyes distant. "Micah." He turned the word over in his mouth again and again. Then he rose and went into the kitchen, pulled open a drawer and grabbed a pen and a notepad.

"Does it mean something to you?" Kat asked.

"Yeah." He went back to the living room, set the notepad on the coffee table and perched at the edge of the sofa. He paused a moment, and then put pen to paper. Kat and Carys watched as he carefully drew the rounded swoops and elegant ascenders of his name. In Arabic.

مايكل

He stared at the paper, glancing up only to acknowledge Kat as she settled into the sofa beside him.

"Is that Arabic? What's it say?"

"It's my name, Michael. Pop taught me."

Carys touched a finger to the paper. "The instruder didn't say Michael. She said, Micah. She was very clear about that. Almost insistent."

He wrote in Arabic again.

ميخا

"Micah," he whispered the name. "That was my name too. A long time ago."

"How long?" Kat asked.

He turned to her, his eyes dark. "From the time of the first Samaan Glassworks record book. It's the name of the man who made that illustration. It's the name of the man who *made* the Luck."

"*Ah.*" One word that encompassed so much—understanding, recognition, fear. She chewed on her lip and studied her reflection in the black pools of his eyes. "Can I see it now? The illustration? I saw it on your phone, but—"

Carys stood. "It's time for Sal and me to go back to the house. Kat, we're set up for guests, so you'll find everything you need for the night. Extra toothbrush. Shampoo and the like." As she passed Michael on the way to the stairwell, Sal's leash in her hand, she stooped to cup her son's face and whisper in his ear, "You're a good man, Michael. Trust me on this. And remember what I said. You trust yourself."

∞

Once the door closed behind his mother, Michael began moving, his body as agitated as his mind. "The crates are still locked in the storage room downstairs, but we brought a few of the books up here last night."

He opened the door to one of the built-in bookshelf cabinets surrounding the fireplace and pulled out a shoebox along with a pair of men's kid leather gloves and a smaller pair of multi-colored knit gloves.

He continued, "If Mum is right and the intruder was after the books, the question is how did she know about them? The only other person I've told besides you is Liz Bridewell at the V&A and she certainly wouldn't try to steal the damn things. No matter how much they may be worth."

Kat moved a decorative centerpiece to a side table so he could place the bundle on the coffee table and begin unwrapping the scarf.

"These first two books date back to the mid fourteenth century. One is a bookkeeping ledger, and one is, I'm guessing, more of a catalog. Perhaps to show customers or to keep an inventory of pieces made or available to customers. It's the one with the illustration I showed you. This one," he held up a leather journal, "is much more recent. Mid twentieth century."

"Looks like a journal I could buy in a bookshop today. I've got half a dozen just like it and always keep one by my bed so I can record my dreams."

He flashed her a smile. "So, you're one of those?"

"Those what?"

"You have a journal obsession. Don't worry, we're kindred spirits on that front. There's nothing quite so fine as a brand-new journal, pages smooth to the touch, so pristine I don't want to spoil it by using it. It's a common affliction."

He set three books in front of them, a slight tremor in his hands. "Let's start with this one. Antiquarian books are definitely not my area of expertise, but I did take a summer seminar in book binding as an undergrad and yesterday I did some frantic Googling."

She raised an eyebrow. "The sure sign of a Cambridge-educated researcher, frantic Googling."

"Desperate times and all that." He picked up the first book and turned it over so Kat could see the cover. "This is what is known as a stationery binding. Books like this were constructed to withstand daily use and were intended to be written in. Like a business ledger, which is what we have here. The folios are sewn together with coarse thread and attached to a couple of pliable leather straps which are then sewn to a wraparound parchment cover. Then, the cover can be fitted with a buckle and strap or a loop and toggle closure to protect the interior pages. And they could date the covers of each ledger to make record keeping easy. This one reads: Samaan Glassworks, 1350 to 1360."

سمعان للزجاج

١٣٥٠

١٣٦٠

Slowly, he turned a few pages so Kat could get a sense of how the book was laid out. "And, look at this—" he pointed to pages filled with columns of Arabic numbers "—they used double-entry bookkeeping from the very beginning. I looked it up. The earliest evidence of this method—using debits and credits that must balance out—comes from a Florentine merchant around the end of the 13th century."

"Impressive," Kat said. "Your ancestors were sophisticated businessmen."

He set the book back on the table. "This one"—he tapped the cover of the other book—"is the one you want to see."

He started to open it, but Kat stopped him with a hand on his arm. "Wait. Tell me what you're feeling right now. You said when you first touched it, you—"

He tried but failed to suppress a shudder. "It was like when I first saw the Luck, only worse. *Exponentially* worse. I've never touched the Luck, of course. Not sure I'd want to." He sucked in a breath. "I can't even imagine it. But my first response to this was, well, I already told you about the man's hands drawing the goblet, the Luck. That jolt of recognition and wash of alarm has eased, though, replaced with a sort of magnetic pull. What I feel right now is a sharp prickle of awareness on my skin, a sort of pulsing in my ears as if I can hear my blood flow, and a low buzz at the base of my skull. Have you ever stood near an electricity transformer?"

Kat gave him a blank look.

"They give off a sort of hum caused by the alternating current flowing through the transformer's coils." He huffed out a soft laugh. "Pop was an engineer and he loved explaining how things worked. That was his idea of a good time, posing questions like that to Leila and me, even when we were quite young. What causes the tides? Why is the sky blue? How do animals know how to migrate?" He sighed.

"You miss him."

"More than I can say. Even though we often clashed. Oil and water, you know? He wanted me to be an engineer, take over his business, and I just..." He shook his head. "My brain didn't work like his. I wish I could ask him about this now, though, it's his family, his bloody legacy." He blew out an exasperated breath. "After Mum took me to the V&A, she encouraged me to tell Pop. I tried. Once. You know what his response was?"

"What?" Kat said, figuring she probably would've gotten along with Michael's father. Like Daoud Samaan, she certainly thought more like an engineer than an art historian.

"'For Christ's sake!'" Michael frowned and shifted his voice into a lower register laced with a thick accent. "'You sound just like my Uncle Michael, your namesake, always hinting at some mysterious knowledge about the past. Growing up, he drove us all crazy.'"

Michael drew in a deep breath. "That was his response. Needless to say, I didn't try again. Maybe I was afraid that admitting to bad dreams wasn't very manly. Or that he'd be too damned logical to understand why I didn't just decide to not have nightmares any longer and be done with the whole mess. Besides, it was easier to talk to Mum since she already believed in all sorts of superstitious nonsense. But if he were still here, maybe he would have some answers. There's no one else left from his generation who would care. A couple of elderly aunts, but one has always been barmy and the other has Alzheimer's. No help there."

"We're going to figure this out. We already have our observation—it's us, our dreams, our connection, the Luck itself and now, the illustration in this obviously centuries-old book. The next step in the scientific process is to ask a question and after that, we formulate a hypothesis."

"The question is, obviously, *What the fuck is going on.*"

She huffed out a soft laugh. "That's a bit vague for a research question, but it'll do for a start. Next, we make predictions and design an experiment—which is, I guess, find out more about us—gather data, analyze the data, and then draw conclusions."

He let out a low laugh and snapped his fingers. "Nothing to it."

Her lips curved up in a smile. "I didn't say it'd be easy. Let's start back at the beginning. Tell me again about the founders of Samaan Glassworks."

"Two brothers—one an artisan, the other a merchant. It was the artisan who achieved notoriety in family lore. He was the one referred to as the Alchemist. Tradition has it that he immersed himself in magic and the occult and eventually went mad."

Kat tapped a finger against her lips, thinking back to her undergrad class on the history of science. "This was in the middle of the 14th century, right? So, alchemy wasn't so strange then. It was just early chemistry. More haphazard to be sure. There were no universally accepted standardized measurements, so it was way less precise. Certainly, the ideas of reproducible results and documentation wouldn't have been prevalent as many alchemists wrote in code and considered their experiments and processes part of a whole set of mysteries. Almost like secret religious rituals. Or even a competition. The first one to the philosopher's stone wins sort of thing. As for the occult, anything inexplicable back then could be interpreted as magic. Or a miracle. Saints, superstitions, and divine intervention made more sense than rational scientific explanations."

"Yeah, well, I don't think saints or divine intervention feature here. More like madness. Or melancholia, as one of my uncles called it. Family lore has it that the Alchemist died with a quill in his hand and ink on his tongue, obsessed with alchemical formulas, lost treasure, and bad poetry. And that every few generations, one of his descendants goes mad searching for his treasure. Seems like the crazy is baked into our gene pool." He snorted. "I always assumed

I was one of the lucky ones to inherit it and that's what accounted for my dark moods and dramatic dreams."

"Michael, there isn't a clear pattern of inheritance for depression." Her heart ached for the boy who, like her, had come of age haunted by bizarre dreams and disturbing nightmares. "There is a greater risk for those with a first-degree, immediate family member, but it's not clear cut. Many people with a family history never develop it. Still, an alchemist with a lost treasure is certainly an intriguing story to pass down."

"Intriguing. That's a nice way to put it." He picked up the book of illustrations and flipped to the page where he'd inserted the bookmark. "Here. This is what you want to see."

And there it was. A 650-year-old illustration of the glass piece that had appeared in her dreams since she'd been in her teens. Beautifully illustrated. In pen and ink. Vibrant colours that could be analyzed and dated through chemical analysis. This was it. Evidence. *Evidence of what, though?* Their past connection? Their reincarnated selves? Their supposed true love? *What did it all mean?* And how could she rationally be using the word reincarnation in a sentence to describe what was going on in her life?

The muscles in her body seized up. Her pulse raced. She had the sudden impulse to squeeze her eyes shut and turn away. Run screaming from the room just as she'd run from the V&A on that first day. But the fact that she didn't want this in her life wouldn't make it go away. The fact that she didn't want complications that could threaten her career and her reputation as a scientist didn't make any of this less real. She couldn't ignore it. As a woman or as a scientist.

So, she drew in a long breath, let it out slowly, and leaned forward to peer more closely at the page. She'd wanted proof. Now she had it. Proof she could reach out and touch.

She looked up at him, searched his face, winced as the pain and worry in his eyes sliced open her soul. His hands trembled as he held the book out to her and she took it, expecting it to swamp her senses. It was uncanny and unbelievable, but touching the book itself did not set off alarm bells in her body. Not like seeing the Luck for the first time. Not like seeing Michael. It was almost as if she had no direct relationship to this book. This had to do with *his* past. Not *hers*.

"Tell me what's going on in your mind right now," she said. "Do you see glimpses of the vision? Of hands drawing on the page?"

He tapped his temple. "I can conjure it at will and access the feelings associated with it as if it's encoded in here, but it's not overwhelming. It's feels like a part of me now."

She set the book on the coffee table, still opened to the illustration of the Luck. "Before the curator from the V&A comes, why don't we do an experiment. We're researchers, remember?" Her voice sounded preternaturally upbeat even to her own ears. "We need experiential data." She picked up his right hand and tugged at the fingertips of the glove until his hand came free. "I think you should touch it."

"I don't think that's a good idea. My hand could have oils and dirt on it. I could damage the illustration."

"Then go wash your hands."

He stared at her, not moving. "I'm not sure I can handle it."

"You said the worst was already over. The initial shock has passed. We're not going to know what this really means until you do this, you know that don't you?"

He went still. Eyes boring into hers, his voice low. "I'm afraid of what I'll see."

"You know you're not the same man you were then, Michael. This is a different time. You're a different you. A trained academic. An art historian, not a Medieval alchemist. You need to do this."

He nodded, drawing in a ragged breath. And then he abruptly stood, went to the kitchen, and scrubbed his hands with soap and water. He dried them thoroughly on a linen dish towel and returned to sit beside Kat. A muscle twitched in his jaw. He looked down at the page and gently, slowly, lowered his hand until it rested flat on the illustration. Kat watched as he stared down at the page, his expression moving from sadness to anger to horror.

"Can you tell me what you see?"

His lashes lowered, he bent his head as if in prayer. "I am dipping my quill into an ink well, drawing a smooth line, down the paper, thinking of…No." He shook his head as if to rid himself of the vision. "I'm working at the furnace, using a blowpipe. Now, I'm rolling the glass into…" He shuddered. "My hands move on their own, muscle memory, rote actions. But my mind is elsewhere, thinking about why I'm making the piece. Who I'm making it for." His eyes snapped open, and he snatched his hand back like he'd just pulled it from the heat of the open furnace.

"What is it? What happened?"

He shook his head and kneaded one hand with the other, as if injured. "I get these flashes. Then the drawbridge is yanked up, a portcullis slams down, and the memories remain locked behind impenetrable mental walls." He slumped back against the couch cushions and closed his eyes, his knuckles digging deep circles at his temples. "I'm doing unspeakable things, Kat." His voice dropped to a whisper. "Unforgiveable."

"What do you mean?" Kat pressed.

"It's…it's too much." He leaned forward again, elbows propped on his knees, restless.

"Whatever it is, it wasn't you. Not the Michael Samaan sitting here right now with me."

"It *was* a different time," his voice was vehement, as if convincing himself of a truth long denied. "We *believed* in the alchemy, the magic, the power of words and rituals and blood and bone and, my god, Kat. We *believed* in the promise of the philosopher's stone and resurrection and reincarnation and second chances." He ran his fingernails hard along his jawline, back and forth until Kat gently took his hands in hers and pulled him back beside her.

"Does this have to do with what the intruder told your mother? About Micah Samaan 'playing god'? You know why she said that, don't you?"

"Unfortunately, I think I do." He blew out a breath.

"Tell me."

"I can't."

"Michael, you have to let me in."

His eyes were bleak pools of dread as he shook his head. "You don't understand—"

"I don't understand because you won't tell me!" She was frustrated now. Angry. "This is my life too. If we're going to figure this out and find a way forward, a way we can both live with, you can't protect me from this. Why the hell would you want to? We're in this together, whether we like it or not."

*Whether we like it or not.* The words landed like a kick to the ribs. He knew she *felt* their connection, but did she *want* it? Did she want him? Would she want him if she knew what he was. What he'd done. He shifted on the couch. "Maybe you were smart to run away from me the day we met at the V&A. Maybe you should run now too."

"Yeah, well, believe me, I've thought of that." Her voice was harsh. "It would certainly make my life easier. Just go back to London. Pack up. Head home. Forget I ever saw the Luck. I've made it this far dealing with fucked-up dreams, I figure I can keep right on going. Ignore it all. Keep working in my little corner of epigenetics research and pretend none of this ever happened. Build my career. Live with my cranky cat. Forget I ever met you. Simple, right?"

His face went white. "Is that what you want?" His voice was barely a whisper. "Because I wouldn't blame you."

"For god's sake, Michael!" She threw herself back against the sofa cushion and rubbed her eyes as if they were on fire and kneading them hard was the only way to quench the flames. Finally, she let her head fall back and her eyes slitted open to study him. The man looked so forlorn. Lonely. Bereft. It totally pissed her off. It made her want to shake some sense into him, and it made her want to wrap her arms around him and hold him close. Forever. "It doesn't matter if I want that or not because running away isn't going to make any of this go away! And you think I want to forget you? Jesus."

"Kat," he looked up at her, his eyes glistening. "I don't know what to do."

"Well, welcome to the real world, bucko. Neither do I. I'm still trying to wrap my head around the fact that this is truly happening. I've had some outlandish theories about epigenetics and inheritance swarming around in my head for years, like so many angry bees, but I can't make sense of them—of any of this—without you." She pulled herself back up to a sitting position and laid a hand on his arm. "You can't shut me out. We need each other."

There was a long moment when they just looked at each other, a kaleidoscope of feelings pouring into the space between them.

"I'm afraid you'll be disgusted with me. That you'll turn away."

"I know."

"I don't think I can survive that."

"I won't turn away," she said. "I promise."

He studied her face for a long moment and then drew in a deep breath. "Sometimes I tell myself it's all about love, but I'm not so sure. The more I think about it, the more I think it's about obsession. The selfish refusal to let go. The lengths people will go to for a second chance. It's the things the Alchemist did to draw this power to him, to harness it, to wield it." He cleared his throat. "It's blood and bone. Fire and ash." He swallowed. "It's dark magic, Kat, and once you go down that path, you're never the same."

# TWENTY-EIGHT

They'd stayed up talking until the sky turned grey on the horizon, then brightened with slashes of vermillion, lavender and violet as the new day dawned with both peril and promise. Kat had listened mostly, knowing that Michael had to work through his fears in his own way, learn how to live with the sort of low-level fever of lingering remorse and revulsion that plagued him like an ever-present shadow. Whatever he'd done in the past, he was the one who had to make peace with it. And whatever he'd done, she now knew with a certainty that his story—*their story*—had touched more lives than he'd been willing to admit. Maybe even than he knew or remembered.

"Many of the entries in this journal aren't relevant to our story," he'd said when he picked up the third book, the journal he said dated to the twentieth century. "But look at these doodles." He untied the leather thong and opened the first bookmarked page.

"Those are like the designs on the Luck," Kat said, tracing a finger along the edge of one page.

"Yeah. It's variations of the same basic design of intersecting arches, vines, and split palmettes that we see on the Luck of Edenhall." He tapped a finger on the lines and loops filling up the corner of the page. "That's what these leaves are called. Palmettes. They're all over the place. Almost as if the owner of the journal couldn't stop himself from using these motifs. Then there's this."

He opened to another page where the bookmark turned out to be a piece of old newsprint. He took it out and handed it to her.

"It's the Luck of Edenhall." She turned and held it more closely to read the fading print. "A notice from the V&A Museum announcing the addition of the goblet to its collection, on loan from the Musgrave family."

"And look." He took back the newsprint and handed her the journal. "The journal is written in a hodgepodge of Arabic, French, and English, but these last entries are in English. Read it aloud, if you want."

"You have no idea whose journal this was?"

"None." Michael slumped against the couch cushions and rubbed at his temples while Kat pulled a knee up under her to get comfortable. She cleared her throat, glanced back up at him, and thought, *Here goes.* Then she began to read.

*7, March – 1928 - London*
*I found it. As of 1926, the Luck of Edenhall, circa*
*1350, has been on loan from the Musgrave family*
*to the Victoria & Albert Museum. This morning, I*
*went to to see it for myself and was nearly brought*

*to my knees. There is no question. I can feel its power. It's exactly as Michael always described it. But where is my piece? My life sphere? I fear I may never find it. How many times must I go through this torment? Will it never end?*

*16, May – 1928 – Aleppo*
*After much prodding and not a few threats, Michael has finally admitted he knows who I am and what I am after. And so, history repeats itself.*

*I have heard the story before, of course, each man recalling the details either in bits and pieces or all at once. Each man confronting the past in his own way even as I am cursed to remember in exquisitely gruesome detail, as if repeatedly experiencing a blow to the head and waking up a different man.*

*Michael confirmed that Micah, the Alchemist, suffered a period of madness after his wife's death. And that the madness held him in its sway until Yaqub, his brother, intervened. It was during this period that the work was done. I remember him kneeling over me, feeling the agony of his hands on my broken body. I do not hate him any longer. He suffers enough.*

*But why can he not tell me where my sphere is? The lodestone—the Luck of Edenhall—still exits, so can it be that the glass sphere made with the same magic, the very thing that ties me to my wife, has been lost? Could he have been that careless? Is it all in vain?*

*Michael confirmed again that Yasmine had a daughter from a previous marriage, and that the Alchemist—for I must continue to call him that*

*to keep the generations straight in my mind—
remarried several years after his wife's death, the sole
purpose being to produce an heir in order to maintain
some semblance of control over and connection to
the glassworks. Upon his and his brother's death,
Samaan Glassworks did indeed pass to his eldest son
by his second wife and to Yaqub's sons. There is no
record as to what happened to Yasmine's daughter.
Could she have ended up in England somehow, with
the lodestone? Is that how the Luck arrived on such
distant shores?*

*How does all this work anyway? How am I here,
generation after generation with no ties to a family,
no sense of being bound together like all the Samaans
I have known? Does my soul simply take flight until
it finds a suitable vessel to occupy? The thoughts that
whirl through my head are enough to drive one mad.*

*22, June – 1936 - Beirut*
*The specter of evil rises in Europe and I am once
again consumed by thoughts of ending this journey.
I have lived through war too many times to suffer
again through the blathering of idiots repeating
the same old justifications for murder, for rape, for
pillaging. For self-aggrandizement and greed. For the
Fuhrer! For the Thousand Year Reich! For the Pope!
For the Sultan! For God and King and Country! I
was one of the blathering idiots. I called men to arms.
I have wielded the sword and shield, the musket and
bayonet, the bomb and the blade, and am sick to death
of it.*

*Still, how can I shutter my soul once again when there is a chance she will be caught up in the evil that is now on the march. What if I could find her this time? Protect her? Save her as she once tried to save me? If I go now and sleep through this horror, I am taking the coward's way out, and no matter what crimes I have committed, I am no coward.*

*So, I sit on my balcony overlooking the sea and remove the bullets from my pistol. I hear the clattering of a tea tray as my housekeeper approaches. Housekeeper. What a mundane word for the woman who forgives my rages and comforts me in the aftermath. For the woman who claims to love me even as she knows I love another. The hopeful look on her face each time she gives her body over to me is like a knife to the heart. Still, I have always been honest. I cannot give my heart to her when it belongs to another.*

*The question of Yasmine's daughter remains unanswered. Before I last left him, Michael admitted that in 1639, the lodestone was included in an inventory of goods taken by Elias Samaan on a trip to Britain. Michael says Elias traveled with an English merchant named Roland. I was just a boy then, not yet awakened to the horrors of my past or I might have contrived to accompany them. Michael was less than forthcoming, unable or refusing even to give me Roland's full name. He did say that a letter sent by Elias was posted from Carlisle, a city near historic Eden Hall in Cumberland. Michael has this letter still, but he refused to show it to me. This is, I presume, how the lodestone ended up in England. How it came into the possession of the Musgraves is still a mystery to me. Michael revealed that he has memories of this trip, but refuses to relate any additional details, saying it has nothing to do with my search. I dread the day he dies, and I am forced once more to carry on alone. Waiting. Until the cycle begins again. It is no wonder we both have been driven to madness. Each time, I tell myself this time will be different. And each time…*

*22, January – 1959 – London*
*Last year the V&A formally acquired the Luck of Edenhall. I am no closer to discovering the whereabouts of my sphere. I have been living in London since the end of the war as my work with the Joint Intelligence Community brought me here often. Being multilingual has its advantages, and I have found a home of sorts here. It is here that I will find her. Whether in this life or the next. The lodestone is here and so must I be too. Eventually, we will all end up here. I know this as well as I know anything.*

*Michael writes that time is closing in on him, and so I will make one more trip to Aleppo to see him. As for me, as in the past, I must think ahead, store up goods here on earth as certainly storing up treasure in heaven is a fool's errand. As always, I continue to watch and wait. As I have been doing all these years. As I will do, I fear, forever.*

Kat choked out the last line and looked up at Michael who'd been gripping and releasing the arm of the sofa, like a cat kneading a pillow for comfort. "My god. It's so sad. Like a lamentation. I don't understand what it really means, but the hopelessness…the futility…" She chewed on her lip, momentarily unable to speak. "And yet, he carries on."

"He doesn't have a choice," Michael said quietly.

She wiped her nose on her sleeve and turned back to the March 7, 1928, entry. "So, this lodestone this man had been searching for is obviously the Luck of Edenhall. But what is the sphere he is referring to? And who is this Michael?"

"Remember that first night at the restaurant? Mt. Olympus. Leila and George talking about the name Elias? Michael is a family name like that. Samaans use it over and over again, generation after generation. Along with David—or Daoud, which was my father's first name—Reuben, Jacob. Micah. All very Biblical. I'm thinking this Michael was maybe the uncle my father referred to and was, I don't know, some version of me?"

"Jeez, okay." She glanced at the clock. "Can you spell it all out for me because, my circuits are overloaded and I can't think clearly."

He picked up the old book with the beautifully illustrated goblet and stared down at the painted page. "What if the hypothesis for our scientific puzzle is this. One man, an alchemist, working over 650 years ago, created a sort of philosopher's stone, an object imbued with the magic to reunite him with his wife in a future incarnation, and after her death, this man went on to create similar objects, all tied to the original, for the reunification of other lovers in their own future incarnations."

She closed her eyes for a moment, isolating herself from his gaze, allowing the words to sink into her mind, weighing the truth of them. Finally, she looked at him and gave him a short nod. "You believe *you* are the Alchemist and *I* am your deceased wife. That through the alchemy of the lodestone—the Luck—we have finally been reunited. And that others are waiting to be reunited as well. Others, like the man who wrote this journal and who is looking for his 'sphere.'"

He replaced the book on the table and clasped her hands in his. "This is not the first time for us, Kat. We've been reunited before. Think about your dreams. Think about what you've experienced and how real it all felt. It seemed real because it wasn't a dream. It's a memory."

She pulled her hands from his and ran them over her face. "God, it sounds so ridiculous."

"But you *feel* the truth of it."

"I can't deny my reaction to the Luck, and I can't deny my reaction to you." She let out an exasperated breath. "But still, my mind is over here throwing up roadblocks even though I'm seeing the evidence with my own eyes. I'm so steeped in the idea of a rational world, of the existence of a scientific explanation for everything that this whole idea of reincarnation—or even my private theories about the inheritance of genetically encoded memories—seem too much like pseudoscience to take seriously. So, I'm sitting here processing all this and all I can think is that my life has split into two parallel versions: one in which I'm a regular, rational scientist, and the other in which I'm living some gothic tale with a sci-fi twist."

"Reincarnation and the notion of the transmigration of souls, has been part of countless belief systems and artistic representations from time immemorial."

"This is not a *belief system*, Michael. This is our lives!"

"Believe me, I know that. His throat constricted and he couldn't get any more words out. Her eyes were bleary with exhaustion. They both were on their last legs for the day and it was just beginning. But they had to get this sorted tonight so that they were on the same page before Liz Bridewell showed up.

He swallowed and continued. "We both agree something otherworldly is going on between us, correct? It's more than two people meeting and being attracted to each other. It's more than just you and me in the here and now. It's about this other Michael and the Elias he remembers and the woman in your dreams and the man who kept this journal. It's about the woman that man loved. The woman he was searching for. And all the others he said will eventually end up in London seeking the lodestone, seeking the Luck. And for the first time in my life, I'm close to understanding who I am and remembering what I did that has tortured me all these years." He gave his head a little shake to dislodge those visions. "What I did then drove the Alchemist mad and has haunted me ever since. But everything is different now. As long as you don't turn away…"

Kat hoped he was right, that she could keep her head on straight through all this. Whatever she'd gone through, she knew it wasn't anything like what he'd been living with. She brushed her thumb against his bottom lip. "What a burden you've carried all these years. All these lifetimes."

He wrapped a hand around her wrist and held her thumb in place against his mouth. "In the car you asked how you go on when you lose the person you love most in all the world."

"Michael—"

His eyes shone as he looked at her. "Most people would accept the natural order of things, but I possessed the knowledge and the arrogance to change it. We were young, you were dying, and I was desperate. So, I rearranged the natural order of things. Kat, I rearranged the world. For you."

# TWENTY-NINE

Michael woke with a start to the sound of his phone buzzing. He reached out to silence the text or call or whatever the hell it was and stared blearily at the screen. Bloody hell! It was the reminder for his meeting with Liz Bridewell. That meant it was 8:45. He pulled himself to a sitting position and nearly knocked Kat to the floor. Then he remembered. They were still on the couch. She'd fallen asleep nestled in his arms, head resting against his chest, fully clothed, and he'd been too exhausted to do anything more than pull a woolen tartan blanket over them. He even still had his shoes on.

"What time is it?" Kat said, sitting up beside him, clearing her throat and rubbing her eyes.

"It's 8:45 and Liz is going to be here in fifteen minutes. Earlier, probably. She's annoyingly punctual."

Kat sat bolt upright. "Shit, is it really almost 9:00?"

"Unfortunately, yes. How about you take the bathroom first and I'll make coffee."

"Deal." When she emerged a few minutes later, teeth and hair brushed, face washed, bladder emptied, she felt like a new woman. And when she was greeted by the aroma of fresh-ground coffee in a paper filter atop a Chemex coffeemaker and Michael reaching up to pull down two coffee cups, something flip-flopped in her chest and left her warm all over.

He turned and caught the intensity of her gaze. Carefully, he set the mugs on the counter and stepped toward her, reached out to smooth a tendril of hair on her forehead, to trace the line of her neck down to the curve of her shoulder, and then stopped as he heard a car door shut.

"Damn. I'll be quick," he stepped back, turned and hurried down the hall toward the bathroom.

∞

"Remarkable." Liz Bridewell used a gloved finger to turn another page in the old ledger. "Truly remarkable. So far, you've shown me just five ledgers, a dozen photos, a bowl, a vase, and a paper weight, and I'm ready to call my boss and put together a proposal. All this belongs at the V&A. Good god. I can't believe it."

"I know. Me either."

"I feel like a broken record here, but these are…well, you know as well as I do what this means. Discovering the glassmaker responsible for the Luck of Edenhall will be all over the news. It's one of the most popular pieces in our entire collection. But combine that with a supporting collection of photos and these books—once we get them translated and if they are what we think they are—and just imagine the special exhibition we could put on. 'A History of Glass Making from the Middle Ages to the Present.' We'll be inundated with doctoral students hoping to make a name for themselves." She looked up at him. "I cannot believe these have been sitting in a storage room off your garage and you didn't even know it."

"That part is, admittedly, quite embarrassing." Michael cast a glance at his mother. "But we figured it was all just knickknacks and keepsakes from the old house. As long as the war was going on, there was no urgency."

"You should be ashamed of yourself," Liz said with a teasing tone that belied her very real frustration. "No blaming your mother on this. Any art historian worth their salt would've jumped at the chance to go through the knickknacks and keepsakes from a house purportedly a thousand years old."

"I'll hand over my diploma in shame."

"I may need to suggest Cambridge rescind it." She let out an exasperated laugh and waved a hand at the coffee table.

"Oh no you don't," Carys said. "Not without a tuition refund."

Kat sipped her second cup of coffee as she and Carys watched Liz Bridewell examine the items Michael had laid out for her. She noted that the twentieth century journal was not among those items. That one was personal. It was never going to be available for public inspection.

"I'm sorry Lionel couldn't join us today. He and his wife were on babysitting duty when his granddaughter fell out of a tree and broke her arm. He'll be kicking himself when he hears about these books."

"I hope his granddaughter is okay. I've had a broken arm," Michael said with a laugh. "It's not fun."

"We spent more time in hospital getting Michael stitched up and encased in plaster than I care to remember," Carys offered with a rueful smile. "He was a right terror, courting danger as if he had no fear of the consequences."

"I've got one of my own," Liz said. "Texted from uni this morning to say she's off hang gliding with her boyfriend today. Sometimes it's better to not know what they're up to." She and Carys exchanged commiserating smiles. "Okay, back to business. How do you want to proceed?"

"We've got a climate-controlled safe that will be connected into our security system on its way as we speak." Carys said. "I talked to our security company first thing this morning and they're handling everything. They assured me it will be delivered and installed this morning."

Michael looked at his watch. "I want to keep everything here for now, but you and Lionel are welcome to come back Monday to take a closer look."

"Monday is jampacked, but I can do Tuesday."

"All right. Do you mind contacting Lionel to see if he's free? If you'd like to take one of the ledgers back with you then, we can figure that out at the time."

"Let's say Tuesday late afternoon to be on the safe side. I don't like the idea of all this remaining here since you just had a break-in, but it's your property and with the new safe arriving shortly, I guess I'll have to live with it."

"Speaking of the break-in," Michael said. "We don't have anything else of real value out here, and it seems more than coincidental that we'd have an attempted burglary right after we've discovered what was in those crates."

Liz's eyebrows shot toward her hairline. "You're not suggesting—"

"No, no. Not you. God, no. But maybe someone you talked to? Someone who overheard your conversation with Lionel?"

"I don't know. Lionel is above reproach, and it seems impossible that anyone associated with the V&A would be implicated in this. We're all family there and everyone is dedicated to the museum's mission. And our background checks are very rigorous."

Michael drew in a long breath. "I've certainly spent enough time there to know it's a dedicated group of professionals. But still…give it some thought?"

Liz pulled off her gloves, stuffed them in her purse, and stood. "I will. I promise. I'm still worried about—"

"Don't be," Carys said. "Citadel Security is bending over backward to be helpful and they're coordinating with Wallingford Police to make sure they keep an eye on the place. This is going to be one of the safest places in England, at least for the next few days."

# THIRTY

"I just got off the line with Wallingford Police," Michael told Ethan Rollings, the representative from Citadel Security who'd shown up at the house not long after the break-in and who was now supervising the delivery and installation of the new safe. "I'm trusting you and DS Rao to keep an eye on the place while I'm not here. We're going to head back to London this afternoon."

"We're on it, sir. You have my word," Rollings said with a sage nod, watching as the delivery truck's hydraulic lift settled onto the driveway. "To say we were unhappy to learn that someone was able to bypass the alarm and gain entry to the premises would be a gross understatement. But rest assured, our system has multiple layers of redundancy and, like last night, notice of any breach will automatically be transmitted immediately to our operations center, to Wallingford Police, and, simultaneously, to me as your mother's local agent."

Agent. The word certainly seemed to apply to Rollings, Michael thought. The man was built like a prize bull and had the steely-eyed gaze associated with hardened spies in action movies.

Michael stepped back as the team of three equally burly men maneuvered the 900-pound safe onto an industrial-looking automated dolly and guided it into the garage and toward the storage room tucked under the stairwell.

"How long is it going to take to get this set up?"

"They'll have it in place momentarily, but it will take a little longer to get it linked into the system and to test it."

"How about your men get it in position and we'll get everything loaded inside. Then Ms. Musgrave and I can return to town. I understand you're going to do a room-by-room inspection of the whole house."

"That'll work. We've already done a remote system check, but I'd like to have eyes on the hardware as well."

"Good. I'm especially concerned about how the intruder knew we had something worth stealing," Michael said. "So, when you're doing your review…" He hesitated. "Well, I don't want to sound paranoid, but can you do—what do you call it—a sweep? To see if there are any listening devices anywhere on the premises?"

"Of course. I'll call in a couple of my colleagues to bring the appropriate equipment. I know it might sound trite, Mr. Samaan, but trust me when I say that our number one goal is to make sure your family is safe and secure."

"I'm sure that's what you say to all your clients, but I do appreciate it." They were paying good money for Citadel's premium service, and he wanted to make damn sure his mother was safe. "And I'm going to hold you to it."

"I expect nothing less," Rollings cut in. "Let's go get your items into the safe so you can be on your way."

∞

Over the next hour and a half, Michael and Carys unloaded the two crates and carefully arranged each item on the safe's built-in-shelves while Kat took photos and created a written inventory. Meanwhile, Rollings sent the three men from the delivery and installation crew out to walk the perimeter of the property, noting and photographing anything they thought might be anomalous. By two in the afternoon, the crates were empty, Michael had a photographic and written inventory stored on his phone, Kat's phone, and in the cloud, the passcode had been set, and the colleagues Rollings had sent for had arrived and were busy doing the electronic sweep.

"You've got my mobile now, so feel free to text or call 24/7." Rollings said as Michael and Kat prepared to leave. "If I'm not available, another representative will return your call immediately."

Michael extended his hand and Rollings took it firmly, then he opened the car door for Kat and turned to envelop his mother in a hug. He stepped back and held her at arm's length. "Promise me that you'll text me immediately if you get one of your"—he waved a hand around his head—"premonitions. Or let Rollings know if you sense anything wrong. And for god's sake, do not, under any circumstances, go after any intruders with a cricket bat or any other object."

"There won't be any intruders," Rollings said. "No one will be able to get near the place without Citadel knowing about it."

"See?" Carys said. "Don't you worry about me. Besides, Sal will bark like a maniac if anyone gets near."

They all turned to see the dog scuttle around, tongue wagging and back-end wiggling, trying to get the attention of every member of the Citadel Security team as if they were long-lost friends.

"Rest assured, Mr. Samaan, we won't be relying on the dog," Rollings said, a faint smile on his lips. He nodded to Kat before she shut the car door. "It was a pleasure to meet you, Ms. Musgrave."

# THIRTY-ONE

Kat's first reaction to the invitation was to say no. "I don't want to be a burden," she told Michael when Leila had called during their drive back to London with an offer to accompany her and George on an quick visit to see George's parents. Apparently, she and George had officially set a date for their wedding and Leila wanted Michael there when they broke the news. "It'll be a lovely private family celebration," she'd said when Michael had put Leila on speaker phone. "George's parents adore Michael, and Kat, they will welcome you with open arms."

To Kat, it all seemed too soon. It'd barely been a week and she'd met Michael's sister, his future brother-in-law, and his mother. And now she was going to meet George's parents? Her family back in Tucson had no idea she'd even met someone. And if she'd sprung extra people on her mother with barely a 24-hour warning, she'd be thrown in the doghouse. Literally. To clean it. Bea loved to entertain but company required an organized assault on Costco, a full dusting and sweeping of the house, making sure all the dogs had been bathed and hadn't hidden anything dead under the furniture recently, scrubbing all the bathrooms on her hands and knees, and changing all the sheets—even if they'd just been changed.

But Leila had practically begged, and Kat didn't have anything else to do but go back to her hotel and brood and worry and pace and worry some more or brood, worry, and pace at Michael's—he was pushing for her to check out of her hotel and just stay with him for the rest of her stay and she was pretty sure she wasn't quite ready for that—so she'd finally agreed to the visit. It would be short. Just dinner and an overnight. Back to London the next morning.

So, once they got to London, they'd driven straight to her hotel where she packed an overnight bag, and then they'd gone back to Michael's terrace so he could pack a bag while they waited for George and Leila to pick them up. Now, they were driving down a one-lane country road shaded by tall hedgerows and George was warning her about meeting his parents.

"Point is," George said over his shoulder, "you shouldn't be intimidated. They wouldn't want it."

Kat shook her head. "So, you're telling me your father is an earl and you are a viscount? Like Anthony in Bridgerton?"

George glanced at Leila. "Who's Anthony and what's a Bridgerton?"

"Viscount Bridgerton. From a television show on Netflix. Regency romance." Leila gave Kat a conspiratorial smile. "Anthony is quite handsome and the show is very sexy."

George brightened. "Oh yes, then. I'm just like that. Quite handsome and very sexy."

Leila leaned over and gave him a kiss on the cheek.

"Anyway, the whole idea of title and privilege in the 21st century makes me uncomfortable," George went on. "And there are hundreds of earls roaming the countryside since the bloody bastards insist on reproducing. It might sound impressive, but it's not like dear old dad did anything noble to earn the title, nor did I do anything to become a viscount. I hate to disappoint you, but there was no slaying of dragons or fighting off Viking hordes necessary to win the title. All I had to do was be born."

He glanced in the rearview mirror. "Leila and Michael's father came to this country and reinvented himself through intelligence, pluck, and perseverance. He started a company and became a successful entrepreneur. My father can't simply reinvent himself. He's an earl and that's that. Yes, he can be more than that, but he can't truly escape the title. And unless the whole bloody system is disassembled piece by piece, his title is a part of my heritage, shaping expectations and responsibilities."

Kat nodded thoughtfully. "Well, titles may not be inherited in the States, but money and privilege certainly is. We've got our own aristocracy—political dynasties, tech billionaires, movie stars, musicians."

"Oh, we've got those too," Michael said with a laugh. "A couple of these tech types are even decent blokes, but one or two are right nasty bastards. Crazy as loons. Completely lost the plot after they made their first hundred million and believe themselves to be brilliant in all things just because they made money at one thing."

"Like your Mr. Badawi?" Kat said.

"He's not *my* Mr. Badawi," Michael said, immediately wondering if he was wrong. Perhaps Sergei Badawi was, in some way, his. Part of him. Part of his past.

"He might as well be," George countered. "My father is one of his investment partners, but the man sometimes seems more interested in you than in the latest trades on the London Stock Exchange."

Leila turned in her seat. "I know he sometimes seems too intense, but he was quite sweet at the gallery the other night. Wouldn't stop going on about my work, and high praise from him certainly won't hurt my career. He even told a group of undergrads about Mum's children's books. Did Michael tell you she does illustrated retellings of Welsh fairytales? Oh, look!" she exclaimed as the narrow lane lined by hedges gave way to an expansive lawn and a long drive ending at a house that looked, to Kat's mind, like it belonged in a period drama on Masterpiece Theater. "Here we are! Now Michael, don't say a word until George makes the announcement. Abby, that's George's mother," she told Kat, "has been absolutely dying for us to set a date and we want it to be a surprise."

"I won't give it away." Michael reached up and squeezed Leila's shoulder. "But I do reserve the right to make a toast for my little sister."

"They'll be plenty of toasting if my father has anything to say about it," George said with a laugh.

# THIRTY-TWO

Sergei Badawi stood at the window of his home office staring out at the gardens, not seeing the lush grounds, flowering trees, or colorful spring blooms that comprised the grounds around his London estate. Though calm on the outside, his heart pounded like a kettle drum, and he wondered if, after all this time, the sheer anticipation might kill him. His body was hot and cold at the same time. He heard the rush of blood in his ears and the creak of bone against bone in the slightest movement of his neck. His senses were acutely attuned to the slightest tremors of his hand even as his mind was wholly consumed with wondering if everything he'd hoped for over too many lifetimes was finally, maybe, possibly happening. He didn't know how to be, what to think. He just didn't know.

When Carson strode into the room and repeated what Rollings had reported on the phone, Sergei's mind had blanked. "Tell him to come directly here," he remembered saying. Now, he braced one hand on the window frame and opened and closed the other as if the act could discharge some of the current arcing through his body.

Carson ushered Rollings into the office and Badawi turned to greet him, pinning the man with a forceful gaze. He strode away from the window to grip Rollings' hand in a firm shake and then motioned to a sofa and chairs arranged before a cold fireplace decorated with an antique screen that should probably be on display in a museum. "Please have a seat. We've got coffee, tea, or water. Make yourself comfortable. Carson's already told me about the break-in, so start with what you know about the woman Michael Samaan was with last night."

"Her name is Katherine Musgrave," Rollings reported. She's a researcher at the University of Arizona in Tucson. A geneticist. In London for a conference. She met Dr. Samaan in the V&A gallery where she had some sort of fainting spell. As you already know, when he went to get her some water, she bolted. Now, apparently, they're together. She was with him when the police informed him about the break in and she accompanied him to Wallingford. After the two of them returned to London, they were picked up by Dr. Samaan's sister and George Hempstead. Lindhurst is off, but his backup is tracking them. It appears they are headed toward Hempstead House.

"Second, Liz Bridewell from the V&A was in Wallingford this morning before our team showed up with the safe. Apparently, she and Lionel Millhaven, an antiquarian, are going back out Tuesday.

Sergei held himself very still as Rollings spoke.

"Third," Rollings continued, "Dr. Samaan asked me to conduct a sweep of the property, for listening devices, and the team found two, both in the main house: one in the kitchen and one in the sitting room. And finally, I was able to hover about, supposedly fiddling with climate settings for the new safe, while Dr. Samaan, his mother, and Katherine Musgrave made an inventory of the items to go in the safe. There are approximately twenty pieces of glass of various types, all relatively small. Several portfolios of photos, some dating back to late 1800s, three external hard drives, a box of old computer disks, and books. Lots of books. Dating from mid-1980 to mid-1300. Hence the antiquarian and involvement by the V&A. It seems that prior to the advent of photography and computers, the Samaans kept two books for each five-or ten-year period, give or take. I guess it depended on the volume of business. A ledger of accounts and a sort of illustrated inventory or catalog for each period."

"And the set is complete?"

"As far as I understand it, sir. I don't have the exact number but last I heard, they were up to 250 volumes."

Sergei reached out and poured himself a glass of water, immensely proud that his hand didn't shake. "I know this was a long way to come for such a short report, and I won't keep you much longer. If my team hired you, I have confidence in you, but I wanted to meet you in person. To emphasize that the job you've taken lead on, watching over Carys Samaan and her property, is of the utmost importance to me. Carson always knows where I am and can always reach me, so if there is ever a need to go directly to us instead of through the Citadel team, call Carson directly."

"Certainly, sir. Thank you for your confidence."

"Now." Sergei stood. "Carson, why don't you see if Rollings needs something to eat before he heads back to Wallingford. And make sure we've got back-up personnel in place whenever Rollings needs them."

And then the two men were gone, and Sergei was alone. He made himself stroll casually back to the window where he rested his hand against the frame, and, once again, stared blindly out at his lavishly manicured gardens. Finally, after who knows how long of standing there not moving, he turned to his desk, picked up his phone and called his pilot.

# THIRTY-THREE

"Gerard drew it this morning."

They were in Emmaline's bedchamber so Mary could help her out of her riding clothes and brush out her hair after she'd returned from the morning ride her stepmother had forbidden. "He is extraordinarily talented, don't you think?" Emmaline said. "He sketched it while we were picnicking under the old yew down by the river."

Mary took the paper and looked from the drawing to Emmaline and back again. "Why, it looks just like you! And Mr. Samaan. Look how he captured your expressions. It's so lifelike. I can imagine it as a painting hanging on a wall. It's magical." She raised an eyebrow. "And very intimate."

"It *is* magical, isn't it? I feel like I've been caught up in a fairy tale! As if I just woke up to realize I have known Mr. Samaan my whole life."

Mary handed the paper back to Emmaline. "You both have the look of love."

"Oh, Mary, I didn't even know feelings like this existed. When I look at Mr. Samaan, I just…I just know we belong together."

"How can you be so sure of him? Or of your feelings toward him? You only met last night."

"He's Roland's dear friend. He must be a fine man."

"Or a wicked rogue," Mary muttered. "Does he return your affections?"

Emmaline held the sketch out again. "What do you think? Would a wicked rogue gaze at me so?"

Mary thought that a wicked rogue would do exactly that very thing. "Well, you'd best not let the Mistress hear of it. She'll have you packed off and married to Will Beachem or Sir Neville before you can blink."

"Why wouldn't she let me marry Mr. Samaan?"

"Has he asked you?"

"No, but—"

"If he does, would he whisk you away to the Holy Land?"

"It's not the Holy Land, it's Aleppo. But, maybe. And I would be glad to go." Emmaline hesitated. "I would miss you, of course, but yes. I would go to the ends of the earth with him."

"But see, it don't matter what you or Mr. Samaan want. Your father will decide who you marry. As much as the Mistress may want you out of the house, Sir Musgrave would not allow you to go so far away. He does care for you, you know."

"I could run away."

"Oh, Emmaline." Mary set the hairbrush aside and knelt beside her friend. "Your father's men would catch you. You'd never get far, and it would not end well."

Emmaline looked down at the sketch again, marveling at how Gerard had captured their likenesses in so few lines. With the picnic hamper in the foreground, she was drawn in the act of handing a cup of ale to Elias who leaned on one elbow and gazed at her as if he'd never seen anything so captivating in his life. The lines were confident, sensuous and finely drawn. It was an intimate scene. As if she and Elias had been the only people in the world, lounging in a private pleasure garden designed just for them. And tonight...tonight, they would go further than kissing. Tonight, she would give herself to him completely.

But this morning! Oh, what a morning it had been. After Roland told Giles he wasn't needed as an escort— after all, who could better protect Emmaline than her own dear cousin!—the foursome had set a sedate pace down the still-misty lane. They rode two abreast until Roland veered off on a well-worn path through the wood and kicked his mount into a canter and then a gallop and they had flown out across the moor as if the very devil himself was snapping at their heels. With Elias beside her, she had never felt so full of life. So free. When they'd finally stopped to rest the horses under the ancient yew that had been a favorite of her childhood, she discovered that Roland had brought blankets on which they could lounge while partaking of the light repast he'd stuffed in his saddlebags. If ever there was heaven on earth...

At first, Elias had been very serious and far more subdued than Roland—or even Gerard, who seemed to have found his voice—but he eventually relaxed, and the three men teased and delighted in scandalizing her.

Roland told stories of their travels and probed Gerard about his interest in Greece. Elias described his home and told them about his family, especially his brother Boutros and his little sister Rania, the one who carried a wooden sword and fancied herself Zenobia, Queen of the Palmyrene Empire, foe to all things Roman. But then! As if that had not been enough, Roland jumped to his feet and suggested he show Gerard his favorite fishing spot along the bank of the Eden River and the two were off together, hooves pounding, and she and Elias were alone.

Inexplicably, she'd felt shy. She'd never been alone with a man before. Not like this, with such wanton desire unraveling within her, spooling out from the very core of her body to the tips of her toes and the tingling skin of her scalp. Although she'd never lain with a man, she knew how it would be with Elias's body pressing into hers. She could feel the warmth of his breath on her neck, her breasts, between her thighs. Over every inch of her.

He stretched out his legs on the blanket and propped himself up on one elbow, his eyes blazing into hers. Ardent. Knowing. A single finger reached out to trace the graceful line of her neck, catching a tendril of hair, twisting it around his knuckle, letting it spring free. The air was heavy with anticipation, weighing them down and she did the only thing she knew to do. As if she'd done it a thousand times, she lay back next to him, reached her arm up around his neck and pulled him to her. His lips found hers and with the heat of his tongue probing her mouth, it was as if the layers of time unfolded and they'd been transported back to a walled garden where they lay naked, entwined under a bower fragrant with orange blossoms and jasmine and enveloped by a velvety moonless night, lit only by the blanket of stars spread across the heavens.

And so that morning, under the thick branches of that old yew, desperate hands explored the contours and swells of their bodies, they kissed until their lips were swollen. But there were too many layers between them. Her gown and bodice and petticoat and chemise. His breeches and shirt and doublet and boots. Panting and covered with a sheen of sweat, she wanted more. They both did. But who knew when Roland and Gerard would return? No matter when, it would be too soon.

So, they had held themselves back and then Roland and Gerard had returned, flushed from their ride, and from his panier, Gerard had taken out a slim portable drawing table containing paper and small bottles of ink and had begun to draw. Watching the lines take shape—first the boughs of the yew, then the picnic hamper, then Roland's hand, then his face, and then, finally, he'd turned his attention to her and Elias. Now, she could not stop staring at the drawing, seeing herself in a new light. As a woman desired. A woman desiring. Desperate for the night when Elias Samaan, this man who had traveled from so far away and yet who she knew intimately, would take her, mold her, shape her into the woman she was meant to be.

# THIRTY-FOUR

The sound of whirling rotors cut through the cool, evening air as Sergei Badawi's helicopter settled on an open area of the Hempstead House lawn. The expanse of flowering gardens and green grass undulating toward the surrounding woodlands seemed to give off a soft glow, as if reflecting the crystalline blue sky, now deepening on the western horizon. The scene was marred only by one fluffy cloud, a single lamb drifting away from a distant flock.

"I know, I know. But I could hardly tell him to bugger off," Richard Hempstead groused, holding a Champagne flute in one hand and a half-empty bottle of Roederer Cristal in the other. Kat would have recognized him anywhere, he looked so much like his eldest son. He was tall and broad shouldered with sandy blond hair streaked with salt and pepper, and tanned laugh lines raying out from the corners of his mouth and eyes. Wearing dark slacks and a white button down, complete with monogramed cuff links, he was still imposing, even well into his sixties.

"I told him we were celebrating your forthcoming nuptials," Richard said. "He insisted his stay would be brief. He was just 'in the neighborhood' and wanted to drop off information on some startup The Badawi Fund is considering as an investment. Said he'd be 'delighted' to extend his congratulations and then be on his way." Richard tried to make air quotes despite having his hands full.

"Hmm." George watched Michael's grim-faced reaction to Sergei's imminent arrival. "The odds of him 'being on his way' before dinner are about as good as me winning the Booker Prize."

Abby Hempstead gave her son a sympathetic smile. "It's not that I necessarily mind Sergei," she said, her mouth pursed in a frown that seemed foreign on a face that appeared to be designed for happy smiles. "It's just that now we have no choice but to extend an invitation for him to dine with us." She sighed. A tall, full-figured woman with soft features and intelligent grey eyes, Abby was dressed in a flowing white linen skirt and daffodil yellow sweater set. She gestured beyond the terrace to the south lawn where a large man dressed in dark trousers and matching sweater opened the helicopter's passenger door and lowered a set of steps. "I so wanted the evening to be just family."

Family, thought Kat. How strange was it to be considered family when she'd just met George's parents not even an hour earlier. When they'd had no idea she'd even existed before George had informed them she was coming to stay the night.

Richard and Abby Hempstead had been out for the afternoon when they'd arrived at the house, so they'd decided to take advantage of the good weather and go for a ride. As Kat had stepped up onto the mounting block in her black leggings and borrowed knee-high boots, she'd thought of the last time she'd gone riding. From the back of the barn, she'd taken the trail down through the wash and then up the rise where she had a 360-degree view of miles of undulating rangeland dotted with palo verde, mesquite, creosote, ocotillo, and yucca, prickly pear and agave all surrounded by distant, saguaro-studded mountains. Some days, depending on where she rode, she could see down into Mexico and up toward Tucson.

That day she'd worn her dusty cowboy boots, jeans with a hole in one knee, a faded University of Arizona long-sleeved T-shirt, and the sweat-stained, straw cowboy hat she'd had since high school. The one that had spent time in the dirt, been stuck on a cactus, and stepped on—by herself and her horse—more times than she could count. This afternoon, she'd climbed into an English saddle—something she hadn't done since middle school formal riding lessons—with a velvet helmet cinched snug under her chin and had explored the grounds of a centuries-old estate with a viscount, his betrothed, and the man who had—through magic or alchemy or whatever—snuck around her defenses to become... *imperative* to her. Now a billionaire was joining them for dinner. Kat was being swept along on a river studded with rapids, dangerous eddies, and unforeseen shoals that she could never have predicted and could barely fathom.

"How is it that he's here?" Michael said under his breath.

She slipped an arm around his waist, studying the distinct deer-in-the-headlights look on his face. "Are you okay."

They watched Badawi, tall, lean, and ruggedly handsome, casually take the steps and start toward the back terrace of the sprawling mansion. With a portfolio in one hand and a confident stride, he looked as if he owned the place. "He's fucking following me," Michael growled out. "I mean, it's one thing for him to turn up at lectures and conferences, but this? He's crossed a line, and I feel like..."

"Like what?"

"Like he's taunting me. Like a boarding school bully who stole my favorite book and is dangling it in front of me, daring me to grasp it."

"Maybe it doesn't have anything to do with you at all. Maybe it really is a coincidence."

He shot her a dark glance. "No. He's here for me. I know it." He pressed a fist against his heart. "I can't explain it away any longer. It's all coming to a head. Finding you. The books. That journal. Badawi always lurking nearby. The break-in. These are the pieces. I just don't know how they all fit together. It's right there on the edge of my consciousness, but I can't grab it." He shook his head as if weary. "It's so fucking frustrating."

"And you're convinced he's tied to all of it?"

"After this stunt? More than ever. But...*Christ.* He wants something from me. It's like he's constantly in my face because he's pushing me..." He turned and held her gaze. "To remember something."

"Whatever it is, I'm here with you," Kat said and turned, catching Sergei's gaze before it slid away from her and Michael and toward Richard.

"Sergei! Welcome to our little gathering." Richard met the billionaire at the edge of the terrace, took the portfolio, tossed it to a nearby table, and gestured for Sergei to join the others.

"Richard, Abby," Sergei said with a slight bow. "Please forgive my intrusion."

"Nonsense," Richard said with a genuine smile. "I believe you know everyone but the newest member of our little tribe. I'm pleased to introduce Michael's friend, Dr. Katherine Musgrave, joining us all the way from Arizona."

"What a delight to meet you," he stepped forward and offered his hand to Kat. "Any friend of the estimable Dr. Samaan's is a friend of mine."

Conscious of Michael at her side, she took his hand and gave it a firm shake. "A pleasure, Mr. Badawi."

"Champagne?" Richard asked, holding up an empty glass.

"Only if I may toast to the happy couple." Sergei turned to Abby, who held out her hand to him, and said, "I am sorry to disrupt what is obviously a joyous family occasion, but I'm also delighted to be among the first to be able to offer my felicitations on the coming marriage of your eldest."

"Even though we just saw you Friday night at the museum, old man?" George reached out for a handshake, trying to keep the edge out of his voice.

"Even though," Sergei said, turning toward Leila. "As I've already told you, Ms. Samaan, your thesis was imaginative and thought-provoking, but now I wonder if your most challenging project will be managing Lord George."

"George is first and foremost a gentleman, Mr. Badawi. I fear I'm the one who is the challenge."

"Were you at the opening, then?" Abby asked, brows raised. "We were taking our youngest to Heathrow for her summer program in Athens, so we missed it. We're going on Wednesday."

"I was indeed. As a major donor, I enjoy going to as many exhibits and presentations as possible. Having met Ms. Samaan several times and knowing George, it was an event I did not want to miss. And, as expected, it was a lovely evening. Indeed, all the students in the show were impressive."

Richard handed a Champagne flute to Sergei who then held it aloft. "To the soon-to-be-newlyweds," he said. "Remember that time is ephemeral, always slipping through our fingers. Love, however, lasts forever."

Michael went still. His ears buzzed as if his head was a hive of angry bees. His vision narrowed and spangled, a spattering of stars against a field of black, and he had to reach out and press a fingertip to the terrace railing to maintain his balance. He'd heard that before. Was it a line from a poem? A book he'd forgotten? Or was it something he'd once said. A long time ago? In a very different time and place. As his vision cleared, he heard Sergei go on, "Make the most of every day you share, and you will be rewarded beyond measure."

"To George and Leila," Michael heard Richard say the toast and, like a distant echo, he saw his hand raise his glass and heard his own voice parrot the line. "To George and Leila."

"What's wrong?" Kat whispered. "You went…quiet."

But Michael didn't hear her. His gaze was locked on Sergei who was staring straight at him, eyes bright. Waiting.

"Ah, it looks like dinner is ready," Abby said, nodding to a young woman who appeared in the open terrace doorway. "I do hope you'll join us, Sergei."

Sergei's throat worked as he swallowed hard and turned away. After a few polite protests in the *thou doth protest too much* vein, Sergei was persuaded to stay.

Of course.

# THIRTY-FIVE

Meals hosted by Richard and Abby Hempstead were always sumptuous and understated, and this one was no different. Richard's doctor had recently informed him that his blood pressure was too high, so the chef had been preparing heart-healthy dinners, this one featuring an entrée of grilled salmon atop a bed of fresh spinach, roasted pine nuts, sweet potatoes, and roasted Brussels sprouts, and plenty of olive oil with a variety of fruit ice sorbets for dessert. Everything was delicious, the wine was well paired with each course, the presentation Michelin quality.

Michael registered none of it.

He knew Sergei had come for him, to get something from him, and it was clear the man wasn't about to give up until he had it. Whatever it was. And by the time dinner was over and they'd moved to the sitting room—Michael's favorite room at the house, a comforting space decorated in pale blues and creamy whites, thick carpets and soft lighting, paintings of dreamlike landscapes and horses and hounds on the walls—he found himself wanting to give it to him.

Needing to give it to him.

If he could just figure out what it was.

Amidst the plush carpets, casually elegant furniture, and soft lighting from artfully arranged lamps set on brightly polished tables, the sitting room was at once comfortable enough for a family gathering and formal enough for entertaining guests. Once everyone was settled in around the cold fireplace, Sergei steered the conversation toward the new startup he was considering funding.

"Like several other biotech companies," he was saying, "the idea is to use CRISPR to develop more robust crops able to withstand the vagaries of climate change and improve yield, especially in arid lands. And by using AI and big data sets, researchers can identify which genes drive which desired traits for increasing resilience and minimizing plant stress levels."

"Someone remind me again what CRISPR is," Abby said, looking around the room.

Kat spoke up. "It's a relatively new but game-changing gene editing technique. Sort of like using genetic scissors to cut into a cell's genome at a particular location in order to add or remove genes in vivo."

"In vivo…?" Abby went on. "Within the living?"

Kat nodded. "As opposed to in vitro. Within the glass. Think petri dishes and test tubes. CRISPR can be used for germline editing within living organisms."

Abby let out an exasperated laugh and glanced up at Richard, "I need a glossary for this discussion."

Kat's mouth tipped up at one corner. "I had to create color-coded flashcards as an undergrad to keep all the terminology straight."

Abby laughed. "Next question," "What do you mean by 'germline'?"

"Germline refers to the cells that pass on genetic material to the next generation. Like eggs and sperm. If you use CRISPR to make edits in the germline of a living organism, those changes are passed on to the next generation. And the next and on down the line."

Leila frowned. "And they do this in humans?"

"That's where it gets morally and ethically muddy. It would be great to edit out the genes that cause inherited diseases, like Huntington's, for instance. Or to create mosquitos that cannot transmit diseases like malaria and West Nile. But, of course, the worry is that some Hitlerian researcher like Josef Mengele could come along and use CRISPR to design a particular type of human. Or to introduce a deadly disease into the germline of your political enemies."

"On my trip to L.A.," George cut in, "I read a paperback about the owner of a fertility clinic who was doing exactly that, altering the genomes of in vitro fertilized eggs so that the children of people he didn't like died of terrible diseases shortly after they were born. Made for a good murder mystery, but Jesus…"

"Exactly," Sergei spoke up. "The technology is very exciting, but like so many things in life, it is a double-edged sword. For developing more resilient crops able to withstand, or even thrive, in rising temperatures and dwindling water supplies, however, it might very well be a godsend." He turned to Kat. "I know several researchers at your institution are working in this area to improve agricultural output in the face of climate change."

"I'm sure my colleagues would be delighted to hear they've caught Sergei Badawi's attention," Kat said, glancing at Michael, pride for her hometown university leaking into her voice.

Sergei nodded and went on. "For humanitarian and financial reasons, I'm committed to supporting this line of research, but my personal interests go deeper."

"Deeper how?" Abby asked.

"While CRISPR editing used to eliminate disease is promising and laudable, it is—as Dr. Musgrave pointed out—"

"Kat." She interrupted. "Just Kat is fine."

Sergei tipped his head toward her. "As Kat pointed out, using such powerful techniques on humans is ethically and morally muddy. Thus, scientists experiment on other species as human stand-ins."

"The proverbial guinea pig," Leila cut in.

"Exactly," Sergei said with a nod. "Take, for instance, the tiny fruit fly. *Drosophila melanogaster* is often used because of its ability to breed quickly and because it shares 75% of the genes that cause disease in humans. They're perfect canvases for genetic manipulation, hybridization, and experimentation. In many ways, plants are similar. You can experiment on them in the lab and manipulate growing seasons and genetic traits to get results quickly. But because of environmental degradation, climate change, pollution, and deforestation, we're also experimenting on plants at a global scale."

Leila nodded along. "What we've learned about trees in recent years beggars belief. How they cooperate and communicate via these vast mycorrhizal networks. The Wood Wide Web." She looked to George, her lips curled in a mischievous smile. "Makes me believe Tolkien really knew what he was talking about. Like Treebeard and Fangorn Forest really exist."

Sergei's face brightened. "Ah, a Tolkien fan, are you?"

"Avid. You?"

Sergei cast a quick glance at Michael and gave an almost embarrassed half-shouldered shrug. It was at times like these that he wished he could tell of meeting Tolkien in an Oxford pub and hearing him and C.S. Lewis talk about the worlds they were conjuring. "It's my 'go-to' escapist read," he admitted. "I have no idea how many times I've read him. Or watched the movies." He offered the room a self-deprecating smile.

"I like to think of his description of Eru Ilúvatar's creation of the world through the Music of the Ainur as the first description of string theory. All those voices, all those notes, vibrating in harmony to bring the world into being." He huffed out a breath. "It's fanciful, yes, but perhaps the world needs more whimsy. Perhaps we would all be better off if everyone believed in Treebeard."

"How whimsical you are, Mr. Badawi," Leila said, her eyes wide as if seeing Sergei for the first time.

George snorted. "We'd certainly take better care of the trees if we thought a forest would show up on our doorstep to devour us."

"Indeed." Sergei leaned forward, elbows on knees, warming to the topic. "What do you think? Do trees have inner lives? Do they hurt when we cut them down to build houses or make paper on which we ink our stories? Do they pass on knowledge to their seedlings? Do they 'talk' to each other about climate change and the threat it poses to their survival? What do they think about the humans around them?"

"That we're a bunch of murderous, buggering bastards?" George suggested with a shrug.

"No doubt." Sergei chuckled, picked up and set down his coffee cup without taking a drink. "But is it true? Are we simply a bunch of murderous, buggering bastards? If so, why? What is our *purpose*? Why is it so hard for us to learn such simple truths like war is bad and caring for our environment is good? Why do we keep repeating the mistakes of the past?"

"You've become a philosopher in your old age, my friend," Richard said with a laugh.

Abby rolled her eyes. "If forty-three is dotage, my dear, then what are we? I hardly have one foot in the grave."

"Christ, I hope not." George let out an appalled gasp. "Who else would help plan the wedding?" He winced at Leila's light slap on the arm.

"Sometimes I feel I have both feet in the grave," Sergei quipped, a dark frown passing across his features. He picked up his coffee cup again, this time taking a sip, and then stood, moving to lean against the mantlepiece above the empty fireplace. "Anyway, without getting too maudlin, all this is to explain why I am particularly interested in both the potential and the dangers of CRISPR. What are the ethical and medical implications of manipulating the human genome?" His fingers drummed on the mantel. "Who would we be if we could change who we are?"

Michael ran a finger around the rim of his coffee cup. "That's no small question. To understand that we need to understand evolutionary processes, the heritability of genetic traits, and, ultimately, who we are as a species."

Sergei turned toward him. "Along with the why and the how we became who we are, it's the ultimate question. I admire those who set their sights on the stars, but my interest is in exploring what's in here." He pressed his fist to his chest. "What does it mean to be alive? To think? To create? To learn?" He glanced at George and Leila. "To love?"

"As a researcher fascinated by epigenetics, I applaud your interest in heritability," Kat said, holding her coffee cup up in a mock toast. "But aren't we all made of star stuff, as Carl Sagan famously said? Those who study the origins of the universe might argue that to understand what's in the human heart, we need to understand where we came from. How we got here. Certainly, imaging the cosmos—as the James Webb Space Telescope is doing, led by University of Arizona researchers, by the way—is awe-inspiring. Some of the images almost make me weep with the wonder of it all."

Leila spoke up. "Wasn't it one of the first astronauts who said seeing Earth from space made him realize there are no borders, that we are one people, and that we should try harder to live together and understand each other?"

"Seems like seeing the pale blue dot from space would be an amazing thing to experience before one dies," George added. "We're getting close to the point where anyone with a big enough bank account can be a space tourist."

If that was intended to be a dig at billionaires, Sergei ignored it even as a grimace of pain flashed across his features. "Before one dies…"

Michael abruptly set his cup in the saucer on the coffee table, causing it to rattle. Standing, he went to the sidebar to pour himself a dram of whisky. He stared at the rich amber liquid for a moment, then bolted the whole thing.

Sergei glanced out the window toward the darkness and went on, "Death is…"

Michael cleared his throat, forced himself to turn, to face Sergei. "Death is…what?"

Sergei held his gaze. The room seemed to collapse in on them, like a tunnel deep underground, barely lit, with each man standing at opposite ends. A confrontation. A reckoning. "Memento mori." Sergei said finally, his voice soft, almost pleading.

Michael didn't blink. "Remember you must die," he whispered.

The moment stretched between them, and Michael watched Sergei move toward one of the tall windows facing out to where his helicopter sat waiting. He watched the man run a hand over his thick dark hair and brace the other on the window frame.

"Death seems such a waste of energy," Sergei said quietly, tapping a finger against the window frame as if to emphasize his point. "In my more fanciful moments, I think of great scientists—Democritus, Archimedes, Galileo, Einstein—and wonder what the world would be like if genius was not snuffed out by the inexorable decay of biology or the tragedies of starvation, war, and disease." He huffed out a soft breath. "What is it called when golfers take a do-over?"

"A mulligan," Kat said, instantly thinking of her father's last words.

"Yes." Sergei smiled at her. "Seems a pity we don't all get a mulligan on life."

A rivulet of sweat ran down Michael's back as he settled back into his chair, another dram of whisky clutched in his trembling hand.

Kat sat on the arm of his chair and casually leaned into his shoulder. Maybe she sensed his inner turmoil. "Maybe you should invest in a company that studies *Turritopsis dohrnii*."

Sergei's focus settled on her. "And what do you know of *T. dohrnii*?"

Abby laughed. "What in heaven's name is *T. dohrnii*?"

"It's a jellyfish," Kat answered. "Through a process called transdifferentiation, they basically live forever. That's why it's known as the 'immortal jellyfish.'"

"It's actually immortal? As in *lives forever*?" Leila's eyes went wide with disbelief.

"Yes and no." Kat turned to her. "Transdifferentiation is basically the transformation of one cell type to a different cell type. For T. dohrnii, it means that when an adult encounters environmental stress, physical injury, or becomes diseased, it has the ability to flip a cellular switch and reprogram its cells to restart the growth and maturation process. When the switch is triggered, the jellyfish sinks to the ocean floor and transforms itself into a blob of baby polyp cells which then regrow into a genetically identical, mature jellyfish. Theoretically, it can do this forever."

"And do you believe other species could be genetically programmed to perform a similar transformation, Dr. Musgrave?" Sergei said, moving back to his place near the mantlepiece. "Could homo sapiens sapiens use an advanced form of CRISPR technology to engineer and trigger such a process? Or perhaps learn to reconstitute themselves by passing their genetic code unaltered to a direct descendant or someone else in their bloodline?"

Kat was aware of everyone now watching her. She pondered the question a moment, then said, "Considering that over millions of years of natural selection very few species have been able to get close to such a process, it seems improbable."

Sergei nodded thoughtfully, moving to lean against the back of an empty chair, trying to contain his restless energy. "Improbable, but not impossible?"

"Many things our ancestors believed impossible are commonplace today, so who's to say?" Kat shrugged and brushed a wisp of hair from her face. "A newt can regenerate its eye lens and several types of salamanders and amphibians use stem cells that appear at the site of an amputated limb to regrow it—bone, muscle, blood vessels and all. But tiny little *T. dohrnii* is unique in its ability to regenerate its entire self."

"Unique as far as we know," Sergei said.

"As far as we know," Kat agreed. "Let's talk about heritability. Obviously, children inherit DNA from both parents, so how would the genetics work? Would the descendent be a unique individual or some sort of clone of the ancestor? Or would the ancestor somehow *inhabit* the descendant's genetic code? A proverbial ghost in the machine?"

"A ghost in the machine." Sergei smiled at that, absently rubbing the palm of his hand over the soft nap of the upholstery. "Could that be another way of describing the soul? The idea of an eternal soul is a foundational principle of most belief systems." He waved a hand in the air as if to encompass everything in the room and beyond. "There are hints of the survival of the soul in the Torah wherein the souls of the fathers of the faith were gathered to their kin. In Christianity and Islam, the soul lives on for eternity and life after death—whether in heaven or hell—is a given. In Hinduism, Jainism, Buddhism, Sikhism, and many other faiths, the soul lives on through the cycles of life and reincarnation is a given. Why is that?"

"People are afraid to die," Abby said with a shrug, "and are looking for comfort and assurance. It's hard to accept the finality of death." She glanced at Richard, seated on the sofa beside her, and at her son. "I am not afraid of dying, per se, but the idea of never again seeing or touching or holding the people I love, especially my children, is heartbreaking."

"I always liked that Robert Browning quote, '*My sun sets to rise again.*' It's widely interpreted as some positivity pablum, but I like to think it's more than that." George said, giving his mother a soft smile, knowing she'd recognize it as the theme of his first published novel, a gothic ghost story about a mother who haunts her children's nursery in a long-abandoned and crumbling castle, always dreaming of another chance to hold her long-lost babies.

Looking across to Kat and Michael, Leila reached out and curled her fingers into George's. "We all pay the ferryman to cross the river Styx, but maybe some of us are lucky enough to get a round-trip ticket."

"Or cursed, as the case may be," Sergei said, his voice low and full of frustration as he turned a dark look on Michael.

Kat felt Michael flinch at Sergei's words, his muscles tightening as if to ward off a blow, and suddenly she was angry. Angry at Sergei for playing games with Michael—with all of them—for that was most assuredly what he was doing. Angry, even, at Michael for not standing up to him, for not forcing his hand, for not making him just say whatever it was he so obviously wanted to say. *What the hell was the man up to?"*

"Cursed?" She couldn't stop herself from challenging Sergei. "Wouldn't it be a gift to be able to take that mulligan and have a second chance at life? A second chance to hold and touch and talk with the people you love?"

There and gone so quickly, Kat wondered if she'd imagined the dark glance Michael gave her before turning the full force of his own frustrated gaze on Sergei.

"Curse or gift," Michael ground out through clenched teeth. "Perhaps they are one and the same."

Sergei's piercing gaze darkened. "How are you to know the difference if you refuse to remember the past?"

Kat felt the air in the room shift, like a breath held or a moment suspended in time just before the guillotine falls. She studied Sergei's expression, watched as he drew up to his full height, eyes dark, mouth tight as he stared at Michael from across the room, demanding an answer to his question. Even as the others in the room said nothing, looking between Michael and Sergei as if watching a tennis ball sail over the net, volley after volley after volley.

The evening had started weird and was getting weirder by the second, Kat thought. Given everything Michael had told her about Sergei—and how he'd reacted to the man's appearance tonight—she was acutely aware and suspicious of everything the billionaire said and did. Her mind raced through the conversational threads, trying to find meaning in his words and gestures. Michael was right. She was sure of it now. Sergei was pushing him toward … something. Some realization. Some memory. But of what? Was he from Michael's past? Had they known each other before? A prickly feeling crept up her spine. *What were these two men to each other?*

Whatever the truth was, she had the feeling that the entire evening had been leading up to the moment Sergei could oh-so-casually bring up the idea of reincarnation. It seemed too bizarre to be a coincidence. She tried to mask her anger with humor.

"I certainly share your fascination with *T. dohrnii*, Mr. Badawi," she said. "And since you said you're looking to fund research into these questions, remind me to give you my card in case you want to throw some money my way. As a geneticist, perhaps I can help figure out a way to bioengineer humans to be immortal."

Sergei pulled out his wallet, opened it, and riffled through some bills. "I suppose you'll need more than 85 quid." He smiled and held the wallet open to Kat. "I'm a little short today, but it's an intriguing idea, is it not?" He slipped the wallet back into his pocket. "I read somewhere that all the species able to regrow their limbs shared a common ancestor around 400 million years ago. Since we all share a common ancestor if we go back far enough, what if we have that capability too? And it just needs to be switched on."

"A triggering event." Kat said, holding his gaze.

"Something to wake up the ghost."

Another silent moment. Like a breath held. And then George slapped his hands on his thighs, making everyone jump.

"Well," he said, standing and pulling Leila to her feet. "This has certainly been an uplifting conversation. At our engagement soiree, we'll discuss death masks, funeral pyres, and comparative burial practices." He pulled Leila to him and planted a kiss on her lips. "For now, I think I need a large dram of whisky. Pop, you pouring?"

# THIRTY-SIX

Michael stood in the middle of the room with a dazed look on his face. His brain registered the helicopter rotors speeding up outside and the sound of people talking in the room, but it all seemed to be filtering in from a different dimension, like he was experiencing everything through a wormhole.

"Anyone have a clue as to what the hell that was all about?" Richard reappeared in the doorway after having escorted Sergei and Carson back out to the terrace where they went on across the lawn to the waiting helicopter. "I mean that was one of the more bizarre evenings I've ever spent, and I've dropped acid with Keith Richards." He crossed over to the sideboard.

George coughed out a laugh. "Wow, Pop. That might be in the realm of way too much information."

Richard laughed and held up the bottle of whisky in query. George gave him a nod and he turned to Michael who just stood there, staring into space. "Another dram?"

"What?" Michael shook his head and looked at Richard. "No, no thank you." And then suddenly Michael was on the move. He took Kat by the elbow and steered her toward the door. "Dinner was lovely, Abby," he said as he walked by her chair, his manner robotic, but polite. "Richard, thank you, as always, for your hospitality. Leila, George, I'm glad we could be here to celebrate with you. We'll see you in the morning. Good night." Then he practically dragged Kat out the door and disappeared up the stairs.

Richard pinned George with a stare. "Looks like he's in shock."

"There's obviously some … something … going on with Badawi and Michael we don't understand." George shot a Leila a pointed look. "But we need to let them sort it out."

Given all the woo-woo stuff Carys had been feeding Leila—about Michael's true love and danger and big changes—George was starting to think Badawi and Kat and the break-in were all related somehow. His novelist's radar for ferreting out the threads of a story and linking clues together to unravel a mystery were making his nose twitch. Seriously. He could almost *smell* it.

∞

Michael leaned heavily against the door in their guest room, hands scrubbing up and down his face until Kat took his wrists and held them still. "Talk to me," she said.

Her voice was a soothing salve to his agitated mind, but he just shook his head and slid down until he was sitting on the floor, back to the door, knees drawn up before him. Kat lowered herself to sit cross-legged next to him.

"Did you hear him? At the end? What he said?"

Kat shook her head. "No. His voice was too low."

"'When you wake up,' he said. 'I'll be waiting.'"

Kat bit back a curse. "Nothing like being cryptic. For god's sake, why doesn't he just come out and confront you if he wants something from you?"

A muscle twitched along his clenched jaw. His dark eyes glittered as if trying not to cry. "He's turning himself inside out to get me to remember something, but I can't. It's there, but I can't reach it."

"If he won't tell you, why don't you force the issue? Ask him what he's all about?"

"I tried that once. Had a few too many at a gallery opening and turned around to find the man standing right next to me. I held my glass up in a mock salute and said, 'What is it you want from me, old man? Seems like every time I turn around, you're there.'"

"What did he say?"

"For the longest time, he said nothing at all. We just stood there staring at this sculpture that was really quite hideous. I almost gave up and went to get another drink. Then, without even turning to look at me, he said, 'You'll know exactly what I want as soon as you stop acting like a frightened child and put some effort into remembering what's important.'"

"God! What an unmitigated asshole." Kat rubbed her temples in exasperation. "I feel like the two of you need couples therapy. What was that even supposed to mean?"

"Hell, if I know. I did ask him. I think my exact response was, "What the bloody hell does that mean?"

"And…?"

"And he said, "If I told you, you'd think I was insane. No, Michael, you have to figure it out on your own.""

"Are you sure he's not insane?"

Michael sighed. "I'm afraid he's exactly as sane as I am."

"Maybe you should try hypnosis. Or magic mushrooms or something. Try to step outside yourself, break down whatever is holding you back, preventing you from remembering."

He barked out a laugh. "Oh, I've done the whole mushroom thing. My history of psychedelic drug use is quite impressive, probably should be in a police blotter. But I always used it as an *escape* from my dreams, not to try to fucking remember them more clearly."

"Did it work? Were you able to escape?"

"If by escape you mean hellscape. Dantesque circles of hell. Bosch, van Eyck, Fra Giovanni. I used to be obsessed with their paintings because that's what my dreams were like. Not all the time, but way too often." He looked over at her, his expression softening. "Sometimes I dreamt of you. Those were the best dreams. And the worst because then I'd wake up and you'd be gone."

"I'm here now," she whispered and laid a hand on his knee. "Have you ever tried hypnosis?"

He shook his head.

"I've got a friend who swears by it as a treatment for anxiety. A clinical psychologist. She says it helps patients with PTSD too."

He let out a long sigh. "I'm willing to try anything after tonight. I felt awful. Like Badawi is trying so damned hard to prompt me, to get me to remember, and I just can't get there." He huffed out a sad laugh and ran his fingers through his hair. "I felt like I disappointed him."

"No." With a hand framing his jaw, Kat turned his face toward hers. "You don't owe him anything. Don't do this for him. Do this for you."

"But that's just it. Tonight, the way he looked at me, the way he directed the conversation…something shifted loose. I *do* feel like I owe him. I don't know what it is he wants from me, but I know I want to give it to him."

"Try the hypnosis. Maybe everything else will fall in place. Maybe Badawi and the intruder at the carriage house and all these things you're feeling will finally make sense."

"The only thing in all this that makes sense is you."

She studied his face for a long moment, then got to her feet and reached a hand down to him. "It's time, Michael."

"Time for what?" He took her hand and stood.

"Time for us to forget about Sergei Badawi. Set aside thoughts of the Luck and old books and supposed past lives. It's time for us to concentrate on us in the here and now."

She reached behind him and flipped off the light. "I don't want to wonder about what that man wants from you. I want to concentrate on what we can give to each other. Not what we were to each other in the past, but what we are to each other right now."

She slid her hand down his arm, twined her fingers with his, and led him toward the bed.

# THIRTY-SEVEN

By the time they got back to London, Kat had called half a dozen clinical psychologists with expertise in PTSD and that used hypnosis in their practice. A couple weren't taking new patients, and several were taking appointments two or three months out. They settled on Dr. James Tully, a veteran who'd served in both Iraq and Afghanistan and who had specialized in treating trauma. He'd recently retired from the NIH and had just opened a private practice in Greenwich. With a little more digging, they were able to discover that he had a stellar record, was highly regarded by his peers, and, just as importantly, was able to see them that very day.

Instead of navigating the surface streets to get there, Michael decided to surprise Kat with a river cruise, and by the time they reached their destination, she'd fallen in love with London. Or at least set aside her previous anxiety. Seeing the Tower of London and Traitor's Gate from the water, spotting a few scattered mudlarkers combing the riverbank, and gliding past old warehouses, inns, and taverns dotting the shore, all chockfull of tales of pirates and pilgrims, made her feel like she was floating through history.

There was no rational reason why she'd always had that bone-deep reluctance to accompany her parents on their trips or to visit England on her own. But as she'd discovered in the past week, rationality didn't always rule the day. Besides, maybe it wasn't London, per se, that had made her shy away from a trip to England with her parents. Maybe it was something about the whole country that had made her gut clench, like a warning ache slithering up and down her birthmark, wrapping itself around her insides and squeezing. Maybe it was that somehow her body knew what was waiting for her here even if her mind refused to see it.

Once they'd disembarked and made their way through town and up a narrow, cobbled lane, they found the psychologist's townhouse with a pristine plaque—Dr. James T. Tull, Clinical Psychology—affixed to the wall beside the front door. After ringing the bell and waiting a few moments, the door swung open to reveal a giant of a man with shoulders, biceps, and a weight-room-worthy chest wide enough to fill the doorway. He wore a blue blazer, white button-down, and trim beige slacks, and sported closely-cropped greying hair and a dashing white goatee that seemed to glow against his dark complexion. Stepping back to let them in, he greeted them in a business-like manner.

"Dr. Samaan, my office is in the back." He looked to Kat. "Would you like to wait in the drawing room? I can make you some tea."

Michael shook his head. "Dr. Tull, this is Dr. Kat Musgrave. The reason I'm here impacts her so I'd like her to join us. And as this is just a consultation...."

Dr. Tull hesitated a moment before leading them back to his first-floor office. "So, Dr. Samaan," Dr. Tull said as he gestured for Kat and Michael to take the couch and then settled into what was obviously a much-loved old brown leather wing back chair, "you are interested in hypnosis. Why don't you tell me about yourself, your treatment goals, and why you think hypnosis might be a good option for you."

They'd settled on their approach but had no idea if Dr. Tull would swallow it or how hard he might press for an explanation. Depending on the vibe they got from him, they were prepared to tell him why they were really seeking his help. After all, doctor-patient confidentiality guaranteed that he wouldn't go traipsing around town telling their story without jeopardizing his reputation.

"I brought Dr. Musgrave because my situation, and the reason I'm interested in hypnosis, is inextricably intertwined with her presence in London. If hypnosis is a viable option, she might be interested in a session as well."

"We're not certain it *is* appropriate for us," Kat jumped in. She certainly wasn't sure it was right for *her*. "But our situation is unique and we're grasping at straws. Hypnosis is one of those straws." Dr. Tull nodded gravely. "As I told you on the phone, we are looking for someone familiar with trauma and PTSD and your background stood out."

"I'm a lecturer in art history at City University," Michael said, picking up the story. "Dr. Musgrave works in a lab at the University of Arizona in Tucson."

"I'm a geneticist," Kat said, "interested in how trauma may be passed down epigenetically from one generation to the next."

"Fascinating topic, indeed. Some may say fantastical," Dr. Tull said, nodding for him to continue.

"Fantastical or not, the idea of trauma or, dare we say, past trauma from past lives, is at the heart of our … situation."

Dr. Tull's eyebrows hitched up a millimeter or so, barely registering the outrageous claim.

"Here's the gist of it." Michael leaned forward. "We just met last week here in London for the first time, and yet we have been known to each other in the past. The distant past."

They watched Dr. Tull's face for his reaction. But all the man did was temple his fingers together and nod slowly. As if he was holding himself very still so as not to betray his thoughts. It was no wonder, Kat thought. He'd probably heard all sort of outrageous tales over the years.

"However bizarre or unbelievable this may sound," Michael went on, "this is something we are very confident about and for which we have rather incontrovertible evidence. At least incontrovertible to us. Additionally, there may be someone else—or more than one person, in fact—with whom I have been acquainted in the past. It is a particular person and my previous relationship with him that brings us here today. I believe I am missing memories of this person, and he seems to be prodding me to recover them. After an encounter over the weekend, I can no longer wait for the memories to come back in their own time."

"What does this other person have to say? Have you spoken to him about this?"

"Yes and he responds in riddles. He's forever dropping hints and waiting for me to pick them up, but they keep eluding me. I need to get past whatever mental block is preventing me from remembering. I mean, it's just right there. Under the surface."

"First," Dr. Tull said, "memory is malleable and the idea that memories are repressed and that they can be uncovered through hypnosis is, well, it's not good science. Even the way a hypnotherapist phrases a question can shape the way a patient comes to understand the past. Further, memory is not only malleable; it can be dangerous. You mentioned trauma and PTSD. However, you must understand that most of the traumatic things that happen to us, things we'd most likely want to suppress, if that were possible, such as sexual abuse or horrific experiences on the battlefield, are locked down in the amygdala as part of our fight or flight survival mechanism. The brain doesn't bury such memories; it keeps them primed and ready for reactivation at even the slightest suggestion of the event that triggered the memory in the first place. These types of memories are hyper intense and can be so vivid that the past feels as though it's happening in the present."

He crossed his legs and considered Kat and Michael for a long moment. "So, you are seeking therapy because you see no other way of dealing with this man? Is he threatening you in some way?"

"No, no. It's nothing like that. On the contrary. It's just that…" Michael tapped his fingers on the arm of the couch, considering what to say next. He shot a glance at Kat and she gave him a short nod in return. "Dr. Tull, I fully recognize there is likely some sort of trauma associated with this person. This is why I need to remember. In the past decade or so, I have experienced a few, shall we say, strange accidents. A broken arm on the ski slopes after I was pushed into a tree. A sailing accident that nearly killed me and four of my close friends. A dose of belladonna in my ale that resulted in me having my stomach pumped. Even a hit-and-run accident that claimed my father's life. Just this past weekend, my mother's house was broken into, and she was assaulted."

"That is quite a litany of 'accidents' and it does add urgency to your request. Do you believe this man is behind these incidents?"

"No. It's not him. He's not that kind of person, but I have a feeling he may know who it is."

"Are you sure you know him well enough to make that judgment? That he's 'not that kind of person?'"

Kat watched Michael, just as anxious as Dr. Tull to see how he'd answer.

Michael drew in a breath and looked down at the rug for a moment. "I just know he would never harm me. There's a…" Michael waved his hand back and forth. "A bond between us." He cast an almost guilty glance up at Kat and then leaned back into the sofa cushion.

Again, Dr. Tull raised his eyebrows. He uncrossed his legs and leaned forward, elbows on his thighs, hands clasped under his chin, index fingers pressed to his lips. He looked like the psychotherapists' version of Rodin's *The Thinker*. And nearly as big. "You do know that nothing you say leaves this room. I hold patient confidentiality as a sacred trust. In all my years as a clinician, I've heard stories far more outlandish than yours and do not like turning away patients who truly want help. If you give me more context into this relationship, I might be able to suggest a way forward. If you're unwilling to do that, I'm uncertain hypnosis is the answer or that I can assist you without inadvertently causing harm."

"Before you show us the door," Michael said, scooting forward on the couch, "I'd like to show you a few photos and tell you a story. Once you hear what we have to say, you may change your mind. And, of course, you're welcome to do any due diligence on us that you feel necessary. To verify who we are and that we're not the kind of people to go around making up stories like this."

"All right," Tully said, taking the phone and sitting back in his chair.

"This photo," Michael began, moving to stand beside Tully's chair, "is of an illustration from a 600-plus year-old book belonging to my family. The book is being authenticated by a curator at the V&A Museum."

Tully nodded and Michael talked him through one photo after another and told his improbable story of past lives and alchemy and love lost and found. When the story was over, Michael returned to his seat on the couch beside Ms. Musgrave.

"That's quite a story," Dr. Tull said with a shake of his head.

Michael huffed out a laugh. "Believe me, of that, we're well aware. The problem is that we believe others are searching for this goblet right now—or, rather, searching for other pieces somehow associated with it. And I'm convinced that the man with whom I share some past relationship is one of these people. That the person behind my so-called accidents might be another." Michael took Kat's hand in his own. "I need to remember how this is all connected before the next 'accident' happens and before anyone else is hurt."

"I'm not a stranger to the idea of past lives and reincarnation," Dr. Tull said carefully, not wanting to admit that it was a topic that had long fascinated him, especially now that he'd lost his wife. "I've had a number of patients tell me all sorts of tales about who they were in the past—usually some great conqueror—Leonidas of Sparta, Alexander the Great, or even Admiral Nelson—and what great things they achieved. Most of them were obvious cases of self-delusion. But there were one or two situations that were … inexplicable." He paused and drew in a breath. "I never offered, nor would I have recommended hypnosis to try to reconnect any of these men or women to a past life—if such things exist. But I admit I am intrigued by your story. Before I agree to help, however, would it be possible to see this evidence myself?"

Kat and Michael exchanged a glance. "I don't see why not," Michael said. "The books are being stored at my mother's place and we've got others coming to see them tomorrow. I don't see why you can't come too."

"If, after that, I'm convinced that what you say has no other ready explanation, I'll assist you in any way I can. Still, I must caution you again that hypnosis may not be the solution you're looking for. Perhaps giving yourself permission to remember is all you need."

"I would be ecstatic it could be that easy. Maybe, it will be like making a dentist appointment when you've got a toothache, but by the time the appointment rolls around, it no longer aches. Maybe, I'll just magically remember. But even if that happens, I doubt the magic will happen before tomorrow."

Dr. Tull laughed. "Well, if your toothache resolves itself before tomorrow, let me know."

"Will do," Michael said. "Now, if you've got pen and paper, I'll give you my mother's address. Can you be there by, say, 1:00?"

"I'll be there."

# THIRTY-EIGHT

Elias paced back and forth in his room, running his hands over his face and through his hair. He lowered himself to the chair by the fire and then, as if launched by catapult, was back up on his feet. After what must have been thirty minutes or more of trodding a path across the thick carpet, he gave up, grabbed his cloak, flung open his door, and took himself outside to pace in the cold, damp evening.

His mind was in a tumult. He couldn't seem to form a coherent thought. Snippets of conversations rang in his ears. Nonsensical images swam before his eyes. He strode out through the gardens, nodded to the drowsy young man supposedly keeping watch at the inner wall, and then practically ran across the outer courtyard.

"Better to stay inside the castle walls," a gravelly voice said from the shadows.

Startled, Elias backed away.

"No need to fear me, sir," a burly guard stepped forward. "Just warning ye that if you canna sleep, take a turn about the gardens. A stroll in the woods this time of night is not a good idea as poachers and brigands prowl hereabouts in the dark."

Elias mumbled his thanks and turned back toward the gardens. He couldn't go back to his room. Not yet. The idea of it felt like a vise around his throat. His face felt hot, flushed, as if fevered. Temples throbbed, stars danced before his eyes. Was he sick? Had he eaten something bad? Had too much to drink? He stumbled forward blindly and soon found himself pulling a torch from a wall sconce and heading toward the small room near the stables where Roland had arranged to have the several Samaan Glassworks crates stored after being unloaded from the carriage. He held the torch high to illuminate the cramped space before securing it in a bracket by the door.

At first, he didn't know what he was looking for, but soon, he watched, as if from a distance, as frantic hands pried open a crate and tore through the straw packing to find the sturdy box he wanted. Fingers trembling, he fumbled at the latch, then removed the finely decorated leather case. Carefully, he set it on top of one of the other crates and settled down on his haunches to study it. Then, breath held, he reached out to grasp it. Despite the chill in the air, the leather was warm to the touch. Slowly, he opened the clasp and slid the enameled glass vessel from its snug, protective home.

His heart pounded. He could hear the blood whoosh through his veins. The flickering light of the torch reflected dancing flames amidst the traceries, vines, and leaves, as if the fire burned within the vessel itself. The glass grew hot to the touch but instead of setting it away from himself or replacing it in its case, he gripped it tighter, one finger outlining the delicate design wrapping around its slender form. It hummed in his hands, calling to him. Recognizing him.

He backed up against the wall and slid down to sit, legs splayed, goblet held tight against his chest, eyes staring into the past. *The fates are aligned…Grandmother says the goblet was still waiting.* Boutros's voice echoed in his ears. *The Alchemist insists the vessel is tied to you, that it is your destiny…that you feel the call of the magic.*

This was *his*. He had *made* it. Had labored over *his* furnace, had mixed blood and ground bone into the glass. *Holy Mother of God.*

And in that moment, he knew himself. As if he'd been struck by lightning, all the hairs on his body stood on end, his heart stuttered, his vision blacked, and he was transported back to the moment in time in which he pressed the hand of his dying wife to his heart, tenderly stroked a strand of dark hair back from her cold brow, and kissed her lips one last time as if to capture her final exhalation and store it in his lungs like a dragon hoards treasure. There were rose petals on her pillow. He had scattered them there. A reminder of the garden she loved, of the garden in which they had made love under a radiant arc of stars and beneath the branches of fragrant fruit trees when their bodies spoke more elegantly than words ever could.

As if standing before the heat of his furnace, sweat beaded on his skin, the wonder of it all truly penetrating his understanding of who he was and why he was here. He choked back a sob, then another, then it was no use. The dam of emotions broke free and he wept. *He had done it. It had worked.* He wiped his face with his sleeve, tilted his head back against the wall as the coils of self-doubt and uncertainty, the sense of not belonging that had held him in his grip for so long began to ease. How long had his grandmother known? Witch indeed. She must have been communicating with some essence of his past self all along. With Micah Samaan, the Alchemist of Aleppo. Did Grandfather know too? Boutros? Did they know what he would find at the end of his journey? *Who he would find?*

In some corner of his mind, he wondered how the magic had worked. He closed his eyes and conjured memories of the furnace in his workshop, of the opium he'd smoked before snipping off his smallest toe, boiling off the flesh, and grinding the bone, of tending his wife's foot after he'd done the same to her. Of bleeding her, of taking the knife and slicing into his own vein. Of shaping the vessel that would forever bind his soul to his wife's. But what of the rest of it? The incantations? The alchemical combinations? How long did he fire the glass? How did he apply the design? In this life, he'd not followed the impulse to work with glass. Why? Because he'd feared it? Or because, as he'd always told himself, he preferred to be out in the world. But he remembered now that he had made a record of his work, as all good alchemists did. In a small book he'd never shown anyone. Where was that book now? Maybe Grandmother knew. Maybe it mattered. Maybe it didn't.

All he knew was that Grandmother was home in Aleppo and he was here, in England, and at the moment, he didn't much care where his secret book was because his love was alive. He had found her. And in the morning, he would see her again, would reach for her and sweep her into his arms.

Oh, how he longed for daybreak. No man had wished for the rising sun more than he. He swallowed hard and licked his lips as if he were parched. All that would soon change. His thirst would be quenched. He would send Roland away with Gerard and then lay Emmaline down beneath the spreading branches of a sheltering tree and with his hands, his mouth, his tongue, with his whole body, he would know her again. He would know her as Emmaline and as Yasmine. He would take her as a husband takes a wife. As he had done so many times before, when she had been his. And he had been hers.

# THIRTY-NINE

Liz Bridewell found Michael and Kat sitting on the wooden bench next to the Luck of Edenhall display case. A few other visitors ambled around the gallery, a few stopping to admire the stunning goblet and its leather tooled case. "I was going to call you," Liz said, "but Dayo said she saw you arrive and head down here."

Michael looked up with a sheepish smile. "I can't seem to stay away."

"I'm glad you're here." She checked her watch. "Can you come by my office before you leave? I know I'm going to see you tomorrow at your mother's place, but I have something you'll want to see before then."

Liz's voice was even, but Michael and Kat glanced at each other, hearing something in her tone. "Now?" Michael asked.

"Give us fifteen minutes?" Kat said.

"I'll be waiting." Liz gave them a perfunctory nod and headed back upstairs.

Michael leaned back on his hands, staring at the display case in front of them. "Wonder what that's all about."

"We'll know soon enough," Kat said. "In the meantime, tell me why we're here now."

Michael shrugged. "I need to be near it every once in a while. And after seeing Dr. Tull earlier and knowing we're going to show the books tomorrow, I…." He sighed. "It's weird. What it does to me is both oddly comforting and wildly disturbing. But either way, it calls to me. Do you feel it?"

"I do," Kat said, squeezing his leg to reassure him. "But not, I suspect, to the extent that you do. You're—I mean, Micah—is the one who made it. Not Yasmine. Not me."

Michael sat forward and took Kat's hand in his. They sat in silence for a few moments, soaking in the energy of the Luck, each feeling its otherworldly pull. Finally, he took in a long breath and let it out slowly. "Okay. Ready?"

"I'll follow you."

∞

Liz shut the door to her office behind them and gestured toward the small conference table in the corner where an archival folder sat on the polished wood surface. "This morning, I decided to go back to the archives," she said, "to see if there were any additional materials or papers relating to the Luck of Edenhall from when the family first loaned it to the museum. Or from when it was purchased. Maybe there was something we'd overlooked that could tell us how the Luck traveled from Syria to Cumbria."

Kat stopped, her gaze sharp. "You found something?"

Liz nodded. "Stuck in a file with information on Edenhall, the house, the legend of the Luck, and a copy of Baron Philip Musgrave's will, which, as you know, contains the first historical mention of the piece itself."

She put on a pair of white cotton gloves then slowly, carefully, pulled a piece of parchment, browned with age, from the folder and laid it on the desk. She stepped back as the sharp intake of breath from Michael and the choked sob from Kat filled the room.

"I know," Liz said. "And it's titled, signed, and dated. The writing is small, but precise. Here," she pulled a magnifying glass out of her purse and handed it to Michael. He bent over the sketch.

"*Emmaline Musgrave and Elias Samaan by Gerard Palmer Sinclair, 1640.*" Michael's hand shook as he handed the magnifying glass to Kat, and she bent over the drawing.

"I remember this," Kat whispered, her voice barely audible over the cacophony of sounds in Michael's ears, like a full orchestra tuning up inside his brain.

"I had to sit down when I saw it," Liz said. "Nearly had a panic attack. The likenesses are unmistakable."

Michael held himself still, watching the emotions play over Kat's face.

"And the execution is remarkable," Liz went on. "The intensity of the shared gaze...well. This Gerard Palmer Sinclair was very talented indeed to capture the intimacy of the moment with such economy of line. I'm going to have one of our summer interns see if they can find out who this man was."

"Have the intern start at Cambridge," Kat murmured. "He went to Cambridge."

Liz's eyes went wide. "You're sure?"

Without taking her eyes off the drawing, she nodded. "He wanted to study the Classics. Travel to Greece. He talked about walking the Agora, seeing the Parthenon."

Liz swallowed and used her fingertips to brace herself on the table. "All right." She looked from Kat to Michael and back again. "I'd just like to say for the record that I am a rational person, a trained researcher. And I've been doing this work for over two decades, but I cannot explain or ignore what is staring me in the face. I can only guess at what this means, but…"

She shook her head and blew out an astonished breath. "Listen, there is no record of this drawing in our system. It must have been overlooked, although the prospect of such a thing happening—from an archivist's point of view—is distressing." She glanced back at the closed door. "What I'm trying to say is that although this is V&A property, I thought you should see it before I show it to anyone else."

Michael gave her a sharp look. "No one else knows it exists?"

"Not to my knowledge. I'm reluctant to give you the original, but I don't feel the need to run down the hall and alert my team. Or my boss."

He swallowed and when the words came out, his voice was rough. "Thank you."

"I need to check in with a colleague before she leaves for the day," Liz said. "I'll be back in ten." She didn't wait for an answer, instead stepping out into the hall and leaving Michael and Kat alone.

Kat's vision swam and her hand trembled as she touched a fingertip to the corner of drawing. *Emmaline and Elias by Gerard Palmer Sinclair, 1640.* Seeing the Luck for the first time was like having an asteroid knock the Earth off its axis. Everything went sideways, but the Earth was still spinning. Looking up and seeing Michael? That was worse. Or better. It was like the Earth stopped rotating for a long moment, long enough for eons and epochs to come and go, and then it started up again, still off kilter, somehow in a different plane of existence. Now, this drawing…this was like a jagged blade slashing through the remaining excuses for denying the reality of everything that had happened since she first set eyes on the Luck. Since she'd had her first dream all those years ago.

"It was the morning after we met. We rode out to the old yew tree near the river. Elias, Emmaline, Roland, and Gerard. Do you remember?"

"No," Michael shook his head. "I'm sorry." He let out a coarse laugh. "Must be something else my subconscious doesn't want me to remember."

"Gerard, the grandson of some neighbors, drew it. We had a picnic. Emmaline poured the ale and Elias took and drank from the cup. Your eyes never left my face." She wet her lips and swallowed. "I felt so … so *cherished.*"

"What happened to us?" Michael whispered. "Do you know?" He pulled her to him, wrapped his arms around her, running a soothing hand up and down her back as her breath hitched and she choked back a sob.

He wiped away a tear with his thumb. "Whatever it is, remember it's like you keep telling me. We're not those people. We're not Emmaline and Elias. We're Kat and Michael. That was then, this is now. And we're here, together, in the 21st century."

"But for us to really understand—"

"Yes, I know we said we'd approach this like a research project but think about it. It's important for me to remember these things, not only for my own sanity, but because other people are involved. The Alchemist tampered with forces that should not be tampered with and 600 years later people are still living with the consequences. Intellectually, I know I'm not that same man, but what if someone is hurt because I can't—or won't—remember?"

Kat stepped out of his arms. "As a scientist, I want to understand. But as a woman who has loved and lost and who *remembers the pain*, I just want to forget. Live my life forward."

Michael glanced at the drawing. "Of course, we have to go forward, but this drawing validates our story. We've got the books and illustrations and now this. Something we didn't know existed and that Liz brought to us, not the other way around. It proves we're not nuts, Kat. It proves we're connected."

Kat nodded and shot him a smile. "As if we needed proof."

"We may not need it, but others do." He pulled his phone out and opened his photo app. Leaning over the drawing, he took a number of photos, zooming in on the faces and the signature in the corner just as there was a soft knock on the door.

"Can I come in?" Liz opened the door and peeked in.

"We're done, yes," Michael said.

"Did you take some photos?"

"Yeah. And thanks for giving us a few minutes to process this."

Liz gave them both a sympathetic smile. "How about I make copies of everything in the file and bring it tomorrow?"

"Thanks, Liz," Michael said. "For everything."

∞

As they approached the information desk, Dayo, holding a phone to her ear, held a finger up indicating Michael should wait a moment. The rotunda was filled with the soft hum of visitors talking as they headed out at the end of the day.

"This," Michael told Kat as they waited for her to disconnect her call, "is one of my favorite V&A employees. She knows everything about everything."

Dayo cut the call and laughed. "Not everything, but certainly a lot of things. For instance, I knew to advise your new friend to go see the Luck the other day."

"One of your more brilliant pieces of advice. Dayo, meet Kat Musgrave."

"Happy to see you again, Dayo." Kat extended her hand. "You certainly sent me in the right direction that day."

"And here you two are, together. You are a very popular man today, Michael," Dayo said. "There was another woman here asking about you. Not even ten minutes ago. She left you a note, but she's probably still around."

"Asking about me?" He frowned and turned to Kat. "No one knows we're here."

"Maybe it's Leila?" Kat said.

"Black hair, pink tips, slim build even though she seems larger than life? It could've been my sister. But she would've said."

Dayo shook her head. "Said she was a colleague. And she has short sandy brown hair, cut in a severe bob. And I hate to criticize, but she didn't seem like anyone I'd like to have a cuppa with." She picked up a small envelope from her desk and gave it to Michael.

He opened it and pulled out a note card, something obviously purchased in the V&A gift shop. He held it so Kat could read along with him.

*I'm out of patience. Give me what's mine or the people you love will pay for your sins. Your choice. I'm coming for you, and this time you better be ready. I don't want there to be a next time.*

"What the hell?" He looked around, frantic. "How long ago was it?"

"Not ten minutes. She came from the gift shop, and asked if I knew if you were still here. I told her you were in a meeting with Dr. Bridewell, so she asked me to give you this note."

"Did you see which way she went?"

Dayo shook her head, her brows drawn down in worry. "No. A school group was leaving, and the rotunda was teeming with teachers and children. I just took the card and she melted away." She looked between Michael and Kat. "Is this woman a problem? Should I look out for her?"

"Definitely look out for her and text me if you see her." Michael gripped Kat's arm. "Stay here. I'm going back down to the Luck."

"I'm coming with you."

"Kat, no. This might be her. The woman who—"

"I know. The woman who slipped the belladonna in your beer and almost sunk you in the North Sea."

Dayo's eyes went wide. "Should I call Security? Or the police?"

Michael shook his head. "No, but if you see her, text me immediately. She could be dangerous."

Dayo's eyes went wider. "Bloody hell, Dr. Samaan."

"Exactly. Dayo. Bloody fucking hell." And then, he took Kat by the hand and hurried toward the stairs.

But when they got downstairs, there was no one in the gallery around the Luck's display case. Michael prowled around the other rooms as if the mysterious woman would magically appear. He supposed it was too much to hope that he could lay his hands on her. Still, he kept looking.

"Michael!" Kat called to him. "She left you another note."

He hurried to the bench where they'd been sitting thirty minutes earlier and where another notecard was propped up like a little pyramid. He grabbed it and opened it so they both could see. The only thing written inside was:

*Be ready. You'll hear from me soon.*

# FORTY

Sergei pulled himself up out of the water and sat on the edge of his indoor lap pool, waiting as Carson handed him a towel. "Get me everything you can find on this psychologist, James Tull."

"We're on it. What I can tell you now is that his reputation is first class. After he left the navy, he attended Kings College London for his undergraduate and his Doctorate in Clinical Psychology. He is well-liked and respected. Rollings said he knew him by reputation before he left the service. Helped many a lad back from Iraq or Afghanistan. His specialty is PTSD and anxiety disorder, and he's known for using hypnosis in his practice."

"Hypnosis." Sergei sighed. "I think that dinner at Hempstead House pushed Michael over the edge."

"Wasn't that what you wanted?"

"Yes…*no.* Christ, I just wish he would remember without all this goddamn subterfuge. Last time, the first time I approached him, he was sitting in a coffee shop near the Citadel in Aleppo. He took one look at me, beckoned me to join him, and said, 'How is it you never change?' And I'd shot back, 'How is it I always come back a mongrel abandoned on the street and you're always a Samaan?'"

"I've never asked before, but how does it work," Carson said. "I mean, do you remember each time? How you looked? Who you were?"

Sergei shook his head and gazed off into the middle distance. "I'm always me. I look the same, to me at least, but my appearance probably changes because of the style and fashion of the period. My childhoods are always murky. Sometimes I'm taken in by someone, a family or a tradesman. Sometimes, I make my own way. I don't understand it. But once I hit that trigger point, always around twelve or thirteen, I remember. I remember every damn thing."

"But Michael Samaan—or whatever name he is using at the time—doesn't remember the same way you do?"

"You'd think he'd be the one locked into the memories, but no. I think it's because back when all this started, he was … damaged. Mentally. The things he experienced through the alchemy he practiced—the dark magic, as he calls it—drove him over the edge. And then he piled on with the opium. The way he tells it, when he remembers who he was as Micah, is that he was barely sane, barely able to walk or see or think straight before his brother and his second wife pulled him back from the edge."

"He remarried?"

Sergei nodded. "Apparently. Although he's never really spoken of it. I've always gotten the sense it was simply a marriage of convenience."

"Sounds like he has PTSD from it all. From what he went through and from what he did to people like you."

Sergei nodded. "He knows at some basic level—maybe even at the cellular level, for lack of a better term—but he pushes it all away. Closes his mind to the memories because it was so traumatizing. Something inside him shuts down. Sometimes the memories break through; sometimes they don't. For me, ignorance and forgetting would be a blessing, but it's always the same. It may take a few weeks or months to fully manifest, but one day, I just know. Then…" He looked off into the distance. "Then I start searching and the descent into madness begins."

"Does it always end in madness?"

Sergei considered the question, then shook his head. "No, but the mere act of remembering is a kind of madness. No wonder Michael tries so hard to avoid it."

# FORTY-ONE

Tuesday morning turned out to be sunny and mild, with the heady scent of flowers, cut grass, and complete incredulity filling Carys Samaan's backyard where they'd gathered over an early lunch. Leila hadn't said a word in nearly ten minutes, which might have been a world record, while the generally laconic George peppered Michael and Kat with questions like he was repeatedly hurling cricket balls at their heads. Carys, meanwhile, sat back watching and listening with an I-told-you-so grin on her face.

Since Liz Bridewell and Lionel Millhaven were expected at one o'clock, and since they'd invited Dr. Tull to see the books at that time too, they'd decided to see if Leila and George could come to Wallingford as well. Michael insisted that it was time to tell them what was going on, especially after the bizarre dinner with Sergei Badawi at Hempstead House. Kat hadn't been so sure, though.

"I know we said we'd have to tell Leila and George sometime," she'd said in the car after he'd picked her up at her hotel—which she refused to give up even though he'd practically begged her to stay with him—"but it seems so, I don't know. Intimate. I feel exposed."

He'd glanced over and started to reply, but she'd looked away, staring out the window as the landscape rolled by. And now she sat quietly with her hands gripped around her mug. Holding herself close.

"Now you know everything we know," Michael said finally, checking his watch. Recounting everything they'd experienced had taken longer than he expected. He'd left out the notes the mysterious woman had left him at the V&A the day before, but it still felt like a weight had been lifted from his shoulders. The question now was how would the revelations change their relationships. How would it change the way Leila and George saw him? Saw Kat's presence in his life?

And of course, he was anxious about Bridewell, Millhaven, and Dr. Tull arriving soon. While Millhaven would have no idea about what the books meant beyond revealing the connection between the maker of the Luck of Edenhall and Samaan Glassworks, Liz Bridewell had already seen evidence of Michael and Kat's past connection and Dr. Tull was coming to see hard evidence of their past lives. Showing the evidence in real life—beyond photos on an iPhone—seemed to make the whole thing more real. More consequential.

He glanced at Kat again. He understood her reluctance to tell Leila and George. Of course, his mother already knew, but maybe she thought there was no going back after telling anyone else. *Did she want to go back?* The question gutted him. Did she want to go back to the

States and put all this behind her? Forget about him? Was that why she was keeping her distance, refusing to give up her hotel room? He wiped his hands on his jeans as a bead of sweat tracked down his spine.

"And this little gathering," George said, "Bridewell and Millhaven and this psychologist, are coming to do what? Verify that the books are what you say they are?"

"Bridewell and Millhaven are coming to give us their input on the age, authenticity, and value of the books and on how to preserve and protect the collection of photos and records. Liz is bringing some materials from the V&A archives, but Millhaven knows nothing about a connection to our pasts and we want to keep it that way. So no big *ooohs* and *aahhs* or inadvertent comments that would reveal anything connecting me to the books or the Luck." He pinned his sister with a look. "Understand?"

"I understand," Leila said, holding her brother's gaze. "I don't think I'll ever be able to look at you in the same way, though. I'm not sure I can hide that."

"And as for Dr. Tull," Michael went on, "he wants proof we're not completely barmy before he agrees to hypnosis. I think it's a first-do-no-harm kind of thing."

Kat piped up. "Honestly, I think he's more intrigued than he was willing to show when we met with him."

They all looked up at the sound of first one and then another car turning into the driveway.

Michael reached for Kat's hand. "Looks like the show's about to begin."

# FORTY-TWO

By the time Michael and Kat made it down to the carriage house, Lionel Millhaven, Liz, and Dr. Tull had all arrived. Everyone was talking about what they were about to see. Liz took him aside and handed him the file she'd promised, the one with copies of everything the museum had on the Luck, including the drawing. He gave her a nod of acknowledgement and set it aside.

"I trust all the introductions have been made," he said, "I want to thank you all for coming, especially you, Lionel. Since discovering the contents of the crates sent to us from Aleppo, my mother and I have talked about what we should do with the collection. We have to clear everything with family back in Syria, of course, but before we make any decisions, I wanted to have you take a look at the books, and I wanted Liz to have the opportunity to see what else we have. But I didn't want to pack it up and transport it somewhere else. Hence," Michael swept his arm out to indicate their surroundings, "the carriage house garage."

"I'm sorry to disappoint, but I have a family obligation this afternoon," Lionel said. "Based on what Liz told me, I wanted to make the drive, but I can't stay long. Still, if it is what Liz says it is, I would gladly drive across the country to see it."

"We'll let you have a first crack then, and you can be on your way."

Michael turned and entered the code to open the safe and then he and Kat donned gloves and began laying the oldest books out on one of the tables. "We've got cotton gloves for everyone, just to be on the safe side."

"Oh, my," Lionel exclaimed, pulling on a pair of gloves and examining the first page of the oldest ledger. Dressed in a tweed jacket, rumpled trousers, and with a shock of white hair, he looked every bit the book-obsessed antiquarian used to spending time hunched over old volumes in dusty rooms. "This is in excellent condition, indeed."

Everyone watched as he held the page up to the light and then brought out his own magnifying glass. After a moment, he looked up. "It's paper, you know. Not vellum or parchment. Papermaking was prevalent in the Middle East well before it became commonplace here or in Europe."

He turned another page and bent over the book. "In fact, we have reports of river-mounted paper mills located in modern-day Iraq and Syria dating as far back as the 800s. Linen-rag paper made books more inexpensive and accessible which led to relatively high literacy rates. One library in 12th-century Damascus had as many as 2,000 books."

He picked up the ledger and turned it over in his hands, examining the cover and spine. "And this is an excellent example of superior book binding. The cover is a sturdy parchment, and coupled with this toggle closing, it has done an excellent job of protecting the paper folios all these years." He looked across the table at Michael. "These were obviously well cared for. I suspect they were stored in a climate-controlled safe."

"My cousin," Michael said. "He was into preserving family history."

"Liz told me about what happened," Lionel said. "Condolences, of course, to your family. War is always the enemy of scholarship." He shook his head in disgust. "Now where is this illustration Liz told me about?"

"Here." Michael's fingertips vibrated, sending a ripple of awareness through the rest of his body as he opened the other volume to the bookmarked page, the one on which the Alchemist of Aleppo had inked his lodestone. "Recognize this?"

Lionel sucked in a breath. "*Mother of God.* There's no doubt as to what this is." He looked to Michael and then Liz. "This will set the art world on its ear! To be part of such a discovery!" Lovingly, he ran a gloved finger over the illustration, hovering just above the page, not touching the ink. "Of course, to verify the age of the books, an analysis of the ink and paper will have to be done."

"The V&A is prepared to do that as soon as Michael gives the word," Liz spoke up.

"My understanding," George said, "is that it doesn't take much of a sample to do the job. So, the books won't be harmed, correct?"

Lionel nodded and continued to examine the illustration, holding the book this way and that in the light.

"Understanding the composition of the ink will also go a long way toward determining how to preserve the books. The use of iron gall ink, can, over time, damage the paper substrate."

"I wondered about that. Does this look like iron gall?" Liz asked.

"I'm afraid it does. Fortunately, I believe the colors will be more stable. I'm particularly interested in whether this blue is from lapis or azurite. Whether the artist used cinnabar or vermillion for the red. Both were toxic, so sometimes the root of the Madder plant was used." Lionel set the book down. "Truly, this is a magnificent find. The artist's rendering of what we know today as the Luck of Edenhall is, well, absolutely astonishing. It's almost otherwordly. Magical."

Michael swallowed. "We understand the importance of dating and analyzing the paper and ink, but I don't want this illustration touched," Michael said. "There are plenty of others to choose from."

"Agreed," Lionel said, looking at Liz. "This page must remain pristine. It is critical to establishing provenance and for the museum to showcase in any unveiling or ongoing exhibit."

He stepped back, shaking his head. "Thank you, Michael, for including me in this. I'm honored to have gotten a first look at such an astonishing discovery. Honestly, I don't believe I know enough adjectives to describe the importance of such a find. It was well worth the drive out, and I'm sorry this is such a short visit, but I must be going." He peeled off his gloves. "Adolescents can be quite demanding, and I am bade not to miss my granddaughter's end-of-year orchestra performance else I suffer punishments worse than death."

"I thought your granddaughter broke her arm falling out of a tree." Carys said.

Lionel laughed. "Twins. They are our greatest joy and the very bane of my existence. And they could not be more different. One with an obsession with the cello, and the other who goes from football to horses to rock collecting to…who knows what comes next." He gave them all a brilliant smile. "It's exhausting." He bid everyone a short goodbye and within moments, his Audi was backing out of the driveway.

Something about the mention of twins stuck in Michael's mind, but he couldn't pin it down. He waited until Lionel's car disappeared down the lane and then picked up the folder Liz had brought him. He cleared his throat.

"You all now know about the Luck of Edenhall displayed in the V&A as well as the old ledger and the illustration from Samaan Glassmakers. Yesterday, Liz brought something else to our attention. A drawing she found in the V&A archives attached to a copy of Baronet Sir Philip Musgrave's last will and testament. It is in Sir Philip's will that we have the first mention of the Luck in the historical record, and it was his home, Eden Hall, for which the piece is now named." He paused. Cleared his throat again.

"Get on with it, bruv," George said, his tone gentle, encouraging.

Michael bit his lip, held his friend's gaze. "Sir Philip died in 1677." He held up the folder. "Liz just found this.

Unrecorded in V&A files. And she hasn't shown anyone else. What I'm about to show you is from 1640. It's signed and dated. I have no memory of it, but Kat does."

Kat nodded, clasped her arms across her chest, rubbing her hands up and down as if she were freezing. "I remember the day it was made. And the man who drew it." She shuddered. Cleared her throat. "There's a lot I remember, but much more that I don't. And even more that I never *ever* want to think about again."

Michael opened the folder, found the copy of the drawing, slid it onto the table and watched as everyone's mouths dropped open on a collective *Oh My God*.

# FORTY-THREE

*Whoosh!* The air in the garage seemed to evaporate, vacuumed up instantaneously into some invisible black hole. Michael and Kat faced the shocked and questioning looks of everyone gaping at the sketch Liz had found in the archives, gaping at the all-but-impossible likenesses between the two people picnicking nearly four hundred years ago and the two people standing before them. Then Michael's phone buzzed in his pocket. Absently, he pulled it out, intending to silence it. Then his brows drew together in confusion. He turned away from the group and answered.

"This is Michael. What can I do for you, sir?" Two minutes later, he dragged George out to the yard, out of earshot of the others.

"That was your father."

George raised an eyebrow. "What'd he want?"

"Remember when we got to Hempstead House, and I told your folks about the break-in? And that Citadel

Security had really been on top of things? Helping with the safe and sending a rep to the property right away?"

"Yeah. So?"

"Guess who owns Citadel Security."

George's face went blank and then, in a rush of understanding, went dark. "Badawi? Holy shit!"

"Your father thought the name sounded familiar, so he did some digging."

"That man is fucking obsessed with you."

"Michael," Kat said, striding toward them. "What's happened?"

Michael pushed his fingers through his hair. "George'll tell you. I need to talk to Dr. Tull."

"Wait!" She grabbed his arm. "I want *you* to tell me."

Michael glanced at George and then cupped Kat's face with his palm. "I'll talk to you after. It's all coming together, and I need to do this *now*. Before I fucking detonate." He turned away from Kat just as George stepped up to her side and wrapped an arm around her shoulders. She shrugged George's arm off and started after Michael, but George caught her hand.

"Hold up," he said. "Please. Michael just got some news and he's seriously about to go nuclear."

"What news and why can't he tell me?" She was still stomping back toward the group in the garage, right on Michael's heels.

"My father just called him."

She stopped. "Your father?"

"Turns out he did a bit of digging after Michael told my parents about the break-in the other night. Remember? He was talking about how well Citadel Security was handling everything. Pop just called to let Michael know he found out who owns Citadel."

"Who?"

"Sergei Badawi."

Her stomach lurched. Her throat closed up. She looked up at George. "I don't understand."

"The company that manages the security system for this property *and* for Michael's terrace is owned by Sergei Badawi. It's his private security company. The man has been watching Michael and his family for years."

Kat felt nauseous. "But…why?" She thought of how upset Michael was after the dinner at Hempstead House. How disappointed he was that he couldn't interpret the signals Badawi was so obviously sending. And how frustrated it had made her that Michael seemed more concerned about Badawi's feelings than his own. And now this? She'd suspected that Michael and Badawi had a past connection, but what the hell? *Exactly what kind of connection was it?*

"That's what Michael has to find out," George said. "On his own. That's why he's dragging Tully across the lawn right now." George motioned to where Michael was marching toward the main house with Tully by his side. "My guess is he wants to do the hypnosis right now. That he feels like everything is bubbling up and he's ready to make a breakthrough. That drawing of the two of you and now this news? Maybe he thinks the agitated state he's in right now will help him remember. I'm not sure, but he's not in a good place. Let him do this on his own. Please."

∞

Michael punched his fist into the pillows on the bed upstairs in the room he grew up in. "You can use my desk chair," he told Dr. Tull. "Pretend I'm your latest homework project."

Tully pulled out the chair and folded himself into it, trying to get comfortable. "Hypnosis is not some parlor trick, you know, and some people are not susceptible at all. I realize this has been an eventful day and that now you're livid about something, but there's no chance it will work if you don't relax. You can start by not attempting to beat your pillows into submission."

Michael ignored the jibe, trying to force himself into a state of relaxation. He failed. The muscles in his jaw clenched and unclenched, his fingers flexed and unflexed, and his foot jiggled, shaking the bed.

"This process is dependent upon your state of mind," Tully went on. "As I said, if you're ready to remember, if it's all just right there on the tip of your tongue, so to speak, you likely don't need me at all. You may just need to give yourself permission to *open up* to what you already know."

"It *is* right there, damnit. So close, I can almost reach out and touch it. Sometimes I can even smell it. Taste it. Like exotic flavors from a favorite cuisine. Foreign but familiar. But for some reason, I…" He scrubbed his hands over his face. "But today is different. Today, I am ready to face this. In the past, I've always pulled back and turned away at the last minute. It's like if I know this *one* thing, the floodgates will open, and a tsunami of understanding will flow through. I'm afraid I'll drown in it." His voice caught. "I'm afraid there are things I've done in the past that I…the conscious part of me does not want to face."

"Things in the past you don't want to face," Tully repeated Michael's words back to him. "Then why are we doing this?"

"*Because I have to face them!* Whether I want to or not. Jesus."

Unfazed by the outburst, Tully went on. "I asked you before, are you in danger? Is someone threatening you? Because if that's what this is about—"

"No, I haven't received any specific threats, but there is someone...someone from my past who wants tomething from me. And there's just something in the air. It sounds insane, but I feel like things are converging around me and I need to know why. I feel caught in a whirlwind. In the eye of a hurricane that's out of control. Spinning. Ripping me apart. There's a darkness at the center and...I think...I feel like...that darkness is me." He tipped his head back. "I need to understand before someone else gets hurt."

"Are *you* in danger of hurting someone, Michael?" Tully's voice was low, but steady.

"Me?" Michael shook his head. "No. Not anymore. Not in this lifetime."

Tully said nothing for a moment. Michael's breathing, his sharp inhale and exhale, as if he'd been running and was just now trying to catch his breath, was the only sound in the room."

"Fine," Tully said finally. "Are you ready to do this?"

"I'm ready," Michael told Tully after his pillows had been sufficiently pummeled into submission. "More than ready. This is it. Right now. Let's go."

"Okay," Tully said, patiently. "Tell me very specifically; what do you want to accomplish today?"

"I need to get past whatever mental block is preventing me from understanding who Sergei Badawi is to me." Tully's eyes widened at the name. "I have these flashes of insight or memory, a sense of a shadowy presence beckoning me, something fleeting in my peripheral vision," Michael went on. "I should be able to reach out, grab, and hold it. Embrace it. But it always eludes me. And I need to know. I need to know Sergei. For both our sakes."

"You feel like understanding your relationship to Mr. Badawi will open your proverbial floodgates?" Tully said.

"I know it."

"All right. Remember, you won't feel any different," Tully said. "This is about you letting go, not me guiding you."

Michael nodded and focused on the glow-in-the-dark stars he and his father had stuck on the ceiling when he was a nine-year-old dreaming of being an astronaut. He counted to ten, took a deep breath, then closed his eyes.

"Being in a hypnotic state is simply a matter of heightened awareness," Tully went on. "I promise I won't ask you to hop on one foot or howl at the moon."

"Good. I fear if I start howling, I won't be able to stop."

"Sink into the pillows at your back, remember that you're in a safe space." Tully's voice was naturally low and resonant. Comforting. "Think of those fleeting shadows in your peripheral vision. Instead of trying to move your eyes to see them or reach out to catch hold of them, imagine widening the scope of your gaze, enabling your mind's eye to see more comprehensively. Now, take a deep breath. Let it out. Allow your heart rate to settle. Allow yourself to ease into a state of peaceful awareness. Give yourself permission to remove the barriers you've erected in your mind. Deconstruct them. Brick by brick if necessary."

"If you've ever gone stargazing," he said, "you may have found that if you concentrate on an object—a star or even a constellation—while averting your vision just slightly, you can see the object more clearly. Think of Mr. Badawi in this way. Imagine him as an object in your peripheral vision. Then fix your gaze beside or beyond where he stands. Think of your interactions with him, but don't try to see him. Let him come into focus."

Michael shifted on the bed, crossing his legs at the ankles.

"Or think of a camera. The lens you're most familiar with is the one that encompasses who you are today, the close-up. Think of your most recent interaction with Mr. Badawi. What he said to you. How he looked at you. How you felt when you were around him."

After a few quiet moments, Tully said, "Now pull back a bit, to the landscape in the middle distance. Imagine Mr. Badawi in a previous encounter. An incident that struck you as strange or that made you consider him in a different way. Was he trying to tell you something? Was he signaling something through his behavior?"

Again a pause. "Now, take a few moments and think about the first time you met him. That's your horizon line. That's as far as your mind wants you to go. Think of how you might see past that line. Imagine climbing a hill so that you can see further. Driving a boat into the distance so that the horizon line is always receding, so that you're pushing further, going farther. Widen the gaze in your mind's eye and, again, think of those focal lengths: close-up, the middle distance, and the horizon line. Think of others you might see at these various points in your life. Family members. Friends. Associates. Lovers. Enemies. Where does Sergei Badawi fit in? At the different focal lengths. Amongst the people you know. Try to *feel* who he is to you. Give yourself *permission* to see him."

Michael felt the tension ease and let his internal gaze wander further and further afield. Soon the only sounds in the room came from birdsong outside the window. In his mind's eye, the images flickered in and out—the first time he met Sergei, the times they had laughed together, when he was discovered wounded on the battlefield, when the man grabbed his hand and begged him to do the impossible, and when he had, finally, acquiesced and done it. He took a deep breath and spoke.

"He claims it's a curse that he always remembers everything. Even when the past is a muddied mess for me, he remembers. When our lives overlap, he finds me. We've been friends. Lovers. Enemies. We're bound together. Blood and bone. Like Kat and me. He was dying and Cyrine, his wife and Yasmine's closest friend, begged me to do something. I refused. But he'd do anything for Cyrine. Walk through fire for her. God, he worshipped her. And she ruled that house like a queen in her castle. And when she threatened…my god, when she threatened to kill herself and their son, he begged me. And I gave in. I thought, what could it hurt? I don't even know if the alchemy works. They were our friends. And they were my first." Michael opened his eyes, sat up, and pinned Tully with a dark gaze. "They called me the Alchemist of Aleppo and I was there when Sergei Badawi died the very first time. I tried to—"

The crack of a gunshot. A scream. Michael shot to his feet. Yanked the bedroom door open and tore down the hall, down the stairs, Tully right behind him. He started to yank the back door open when Tully grabbed him from behind.

"Wait," Tully said. "We can't just—"

Michael's phone buzzed with an incoming call and George was already talking when he answered. "What the hell did you conjure in there? Someone is fucking shooting at us out here!"

"Where are you? Where's Kat?"

"We're all crowded in the storage room, wishing we were inside your hulking 900-pound safe. You're mom's got Sal and Leila's ringing 999."

"Ask him where the shot came from." Tully said.

Michael put the call on speaker. "Can you tell—?"

"I think it came from the woods across the lane. Straight down the drive and into the back wall of the garage."

A splintering crash. Bullets tearing through metal and glass.

"What the hell was that?" George hissed. "I can't see from here."

"That was the back window of my car," Michael growled.

"Good excuse to upgrade," George said and then yelled. "Leila, Carys, get the fuck down!"

Michael heard voices in the background. Kat telling Liz Bridewell to stay calm, that everything would be okay. More voices, then, another shot rang out. And another. Again and again, the barrage of bullets kept flying.

"Jesus. Are those hitting anything?" Michael asked.

"No," George said, breathing heavily. "This asshole seems intent on murdering the garage."

Another shot.

A bark. A curse. George growled into the phone. "It's like fucking Christmas in here. The bullets are tearing up the drywall, spraying it about like snowflakes. Jesus, Leila! Stay down. Liz scoot back. Goddammit."

"I'm going out the front," Michael said, shoving his phone at Tully and heading back through the house before Tully's beefy hand grabbed his arm and stopped him.

"What the hell are you doing? You're not armed, and someone is shredding your garage with automatic gunfire."

"She's sending a message, and I need to let her know message received. Loud and clear. And that she needs to stay away from my family." He wrenched his arm away and kept striding toward the front door.

"You know who's doing this?" Tully grabbed him again. Michael turned on him.

"*Yes!* No. I'm not certain, but—"

"Do you hear that?" Kat's voice caught their attention. Michael's phone was still in Tully's hand.

"Sirens. Don't go out there," Tully urged. "Not yet."

Leila spoke up. "I'm still on the line with the police. They're almost here."

Everything went quiet. No more gunshots. Everyone held their breath, waiting. A few more seconds ticked by, and all was quiet except for the wail of approaching sirens.

Tully cautiously handed the phone back to Michael and stepped back. Michael pivoted and headed back to the kitchen door, flinging it open, and stepping outside. He switched the phone off speaker. "George?"

"I'm still here."

"Take care of Kat and call your father back. Ask him to contact Badawi and tell him to get his ass out here. Today."

"You remembered?"

"Not everything. But enough."

"You coming down here now?"

"No. I'm going after the shooter."

# FORTY-FOUR

"**W**ait!" Tully called after Michael just as several police cars squealed to a stop in the lane fronting Carys's house. Uniformed officers spilled out, one heading toward Michael and Tully and three, crouching low, heading into the woods across the street.

"Get down!" The officer yelled as she ran across the lawn toward them.

Michael obeyed even though his whole body vibrated with the need to confront the shooter. *It was the woman who left the note at the V&A.* It had to be. How many other people out there wanted to hurt him? Or hurt the people he loved? And this had to be what she meant by *Be ready. You'll hear from me soon.*

He knew she was from his past. From Micah's past. *What had the Alchemist done to her?* Nothing good. Whatever it was, she was still here, still paying the price of his actions.

The officer knelt beside him. "Is everyone safe? Where's the woman who called 999?"

"They're all in the garage."

A voice came over the officer's radio: *All clear over here. Looks like the shooter's taken off.* "Okay," she said, getting to her feet. "Let's go see how everyone is doing."

Michael stood and headed toward the carriage house with the officer and Tully beside him. "It's all clear," he called out when they reached the threshold, and when he finally pulled Kat into his arms, he couldn't talk around the emotion clogging his throat. All he wanted was to hold her. Feel the warmth of her body, the beat of her heart, know she was still with him. Still alive. *Because if he lost her again...*

"I'm okay," Kat murmured against his chest. "We're all okay." Her voice was a thready quaver.

"She's gonna pay. I promise."

"The notes yesterday...the gunfire...she's gonna keep at it until she gets what she wants."

His phone buzzed with an incoming call, and he pulled it from his pocket, keeping his other arm tight around Kat's shoulders. "Did you get through to him?" he said as Kat craned her neck to look up at him, watch his face.

After a moment, he turned to face the backyard. "How much space does he need?" He nodded again and looked over the property. "I think that'll work. As long as they don't ruin the flower beds." A pause. "Okay. Text me his number so I'll know it's him if he calls." He was silent a moment more, then, "Thank you, Richard. For everything."

"What's going on?" Kat asked.

"I remembered." And then he said nothing more until he steered her into the garage where the old books still sat on a folding table. Liz was on the phone, pacing and gesticulating wildly. George, Leila, Carys and Tully were talking to the officer, trying to piece together what happened. Michael cleared his throat, and they all turned.

"Sergei Badawi will be here within the hour. He's coming by helicopter." He gestured toward the expansive but well-tended backyard and looked to his mother. "I hope your flower beds survive. I'm not sure I'm going to, but maybe they're made of hardier stock."

"Excuse me," a voice cut in, and they all turned to see a tall, thin man with salt and pepper hair and an impressive mustache walking toward them. "I'm Detective Sergeant Rao. Is one of you Michael Samaan?"

"That's me. I'm Michael."

"We've found something you need to see. Can you come with me for a moment?"

DS Rao turned and headed back up the drive to where a cluster of uniformed officers were standing. Michael squeezed Kat's hand and then followed him. When they reached the top of the drive, Rao took a clear plastic evidence bag from an officer and handed it to him. "Ever seen this before?"

Michael's throat was dry, but his hands were steady. He held it up and turned the bag this way and that to examine the hunting knife inside, as if the curve of the blade, the pattern of whorls on the gleaming steel, or the elegant arc of the bone handle could reveal its secrets.

"No." Michael said, handing the bag back.

"They found that knife," Rao said, "pegged to a tree with this note."

An officer held out another bag with a piece of paper inside.

Michael took it and smoothed the plastic over the note. *To Michael Samaan. Remember Latakia. No man should have the power to resurrect the dead. Give me what's mine or I'll start taking what's yours.*

Michael's vision spangled. His face went hot. His body seemed to disassociate, as if part of him—*one version of him*—existed outside of time. The cool breeze and bright afternoon sky faded away and then, like opening the first page of a new book, he was there.

Latakia.

And yet he was still acutely aware of the detective's piercing gaze, as sharp as the knife he'd used to spill the blood and slice through the flesh of the young woman who'd been pulled from the water. Drowned. Not dead yet, but soon. She'd been under too long. No one could possibly survive it.

After she'd been pulled from the sea by a sailor strolling nearby, her husband sent for Micah, the Alchemist of Aleppo. And when the Alchemist refused to leave the falling-down hovel of a house and workshop in which he'd found some semblance of sanity, the man sent two giants with shoulders like walls and arms like tree trunks to retrieve him. They'd dragged him into a room and dropped him at the feet of a dark-haired man with black eyes as dark as bottomless pools and dressed as fine as any Micah had ever known.

"I am *Nicolo Scarpa*," the man declared, as if that was supposed to mean something. When it became apparent Micah had no idea of the name Scarpa, the man went on. "From Venice. We trade in oil and wine and spices and silks, and this woman is my wife." Scarpa gestured toward a young woman laid out on a bed in the corner of the room. "She suffered a fall yesterday, not long after we disembarked from our ship. We'd taken a stroll along the quay. She tripped. Tumbled into the water. After some difficulty, she was pulled from the depths, unconscious. She has not stirred since."

"What does this have to do with me?"

Scarpa ignored Micah's question and cast a dark glance at the woman lying as still and pale as death on the bed. "My lady's sisters are traveling with us, and the youngest has heard fantastical tales of your mysterious talents. She insisted I seek you out to heal my wife. The 'famed Alchemist of Aleppo.' She says you can defeat death, so surely you must know something of life. Heal her and you will be rich."

Micah shook his head in astonishment. *How had word of his work reached as far as Venice? And how had this man found him in his hidden refuge?* "She was misinformed," he managed to croak, struggling to his feet.

Scarpa grabbed Micah's arm and dragged him toward the bed, hissing as they went. "Do something so I can placate the little one. She is obsessed with the occult and suffers from hysteria. I would have her confined but my wife refuses. Of course, if my wife dies...."

"Get a physician to treat them both," Micah mumbled, trying to wrest his arm away from the man. "I can save no one." *Least of all myself.*

He'd left Aleppo weeks ago to clear his mind of the suffocating darkness and rid himself of his demons. To take refuge in the ebb and flow of the calming sea and escape the opium fog that circled his mind like a goshawk on the hunt. And if his demons refused to leave, if his mind refused to clear, he'd promised himself a swift end. If the sea could not calm him, it could claim him.

Scarpa scowled. "I do not want a physician."

"Then give your wife peace and let her die."

"But the sound of her sisters' weeping!" Scarpa clapped his hands over his ears as if the sound was driving him insane. "Do you not hear it? Do you not have pity?"

In fact, Micah did not hear any women weeping. He did hear a woman screeching. Shrill. Angry. Cruel even. Directing some servant to do something. His head pounded and the world around him spun and wavered, so far gone was he on the opium still warping his mind. But his ears still worked. There was no weeping.

"I will pay a king's ransom," Scarpa went on, his voice hot and wet in Micah's ear. "The little one will chatter like a magpie to her parents, and the servants will talk if I do nothing."

Micah sank down into the chair at the edge of the bed as dread washed over him. The way Scarpa spoke. The way he looked at the woman in the bed. The timbre of his voice. His movements. All of it made the hair on the back of his neck stand on end.

Not so long ago, Micah had been a robust man in the prime of his life who could have easily knocked the trim, elegantly dressed Scarpa to the ground and taken his leave without a second thought. But now, two years of grief, dark magic, drink, and opium had turned him into a shadow of his former self. A shadow of the exuberant and inquisitive husband. Brother. Artist. Craftsman. Now, he could barely rise from the floor unaided.

He turned to the woman in bed. He did know something of healing, did he not? He'd cared for Yasmine throughout her illness. He could at least examine her. He took a long breath to steady himself and then studied her face. Eyes closed, she looked as if she were already dead, but the rise and fall of her chest was discernable. He put a finger under her nose and waited until the slightest hint of a breath brushed his skin. With his ear to the woman's breast, he heard the faint, shallow beat of her heart.

Scarpa, looking over his shoulder, said, "I watched her sink beneath the waves. But then a passing sailor dove in and dragged her to the surface. Such a hero, this man. Jumping headlong into someone else's business."

Micah's skin prickled. Gently, he turned the woman's head to examine her skull. Thick hair, damp and tangled. Sticky with blood. Even though the opium had seeped so deep into his mind that his power to discern truth from lie had dissipated like so much morning mist, he knew that this was no injury sustained from tripping on the quay. This was a bludgeoning. *This was a murder.*

"She hit her head hard when she fell," Scarpa said with a shrug of his shoulders. "There was nothing I could do."

"Your wife will not survive much longer," Micah said in answer. "And if she does recover, she will not be the same woman you knew. You should let her go. If her sisters wish to say a final farewell, they ought to do it now."

"Stay here," Scarpa commanded. He went to the door, opened it a crack, said something to a servant, and waited a moment. Then the door swung wide and a woman stepped inside followed by a young girl. Scarpa closed the door behind her.

"This is my wife's sister, Marthe. Her twin. And her young sister, Miriam. She has a great interest in alchemy and has heard of your talents. She insisted we send for you"

Marthe was a replica of her dying sister, except for the piercing gaze filled with icy malice, while Miriam, probably no more than twelve or thirteen, was willow-thin and as pale as the woman lying in the bed.

"So, I am face-to-face with the Alchemist of Aleppo at last," Marthe said, her voice as sharp as her gaze. "Miriam is obsessed with rumors of your accomplishments, and yet you look as if you can barely stand on your own. You are filthy. You smell worse than a dung heap. And when was the last time you thought to wash your hair?" She looked him up and down. "Your beard is revolting and your breath is worse."

The Alchemist stared up at Marthe as if she were an invention of the opium clouding his brain. He had nothing to say in response to her little speech. About his condition, she was only stating the truth.

But then she kept talking. "You will perform the ritual that has brought you to Miriam's attention, thereby alleviating the sorrow of our tragic loss and providing some comfort to our bereaved family."

*What?* Micah's stomach revolted. "No." His voice was flat as he struggled to his feet. "Your sister is nearly dead. I will not cut her."

Scarpa pushed him back down into the chair as Marthe placed an elegant, bejeweled hand on her abdomen and rubbed it lovingly, sending a message even Micah in his muddled state could not misinterpret. Then she looked to Miriam who sniffed the air in disgust and said, "Force him."

Scarpa growled in frustration and glared at Miriam. "Force him to do what? Sending for him was your idea."

"Murdering her on the quay was your idea," Miriam said. "Make him perform the ritual or I will tell Mother and Father what the two of you have done and will watch happily while the executioner has his way with you. Both of you."

Scarpa turned to Micah. "Alchemist, you heard her. You will perform this ritual, whatever it is, now. Before it is too late."

"She will die no matter what I do," Micah protested.

Scarpa fixed Micah with a hard stare. "And if you do nothing, this young witch will make sure I go to the gallows along with the woman carrying my child. But first, I will cut out your tongue and your heart and feed them to my dogs."

*Perhaps it would be for the best*, Micah thought. It would save him the trouble of loading his garments with rocks and wading into the waves. Yasmine was gone. He'd walked in the darkness where no mortal should ever tread. His mind and body were broken, and his purpose was...*I have no purpose. Not anymore.* No one did. A man was born. He lived. He lost. And then he died. There was no purpose in life but inevitable death.

He thought of Yasmine's cancer and the pain wracking her frail body before she slipped away. Of Sergei, Cyrine's brave husband, who had been gutted by a stranger's sword while he fought another man's war for another man's power, another man's profit. Sergei had been a good and honorable man, quick to laugh, generous to his friends. What purpose did his life serve? What purpose did his death serve? Leaving behind a beautiful wife and a newborn son? What purpose does the loss of hope and the stink of decay offer any man or woman. He had no idea if the magic even worked.

And then he thought of Yasmine's daughter. He could suddenly hear her laughter. See her fat cheeks and merry eyes and dark curls. He'd promised to care for her. He had loved Yasmine with all his heart, and he loved her still. He could not fail her. He must live and fulfill his pledge. For if there was even the smallest chance the alchemy *did* work, someday he would face her again and have to account to her for his sins. He dragged his gaze from the dying woman to her husband and her sisters.

"You have a choice, Master Alchemist," Scarpa said. "Do this and you live. You become a rich man. Otherwise, I have a dozen guards waiting just outside. My sources say you've been away from home for weeks. It is likely no one will wonder when an opium eater turns up dead, washed up on the shore."

Micah's skin went cold even as he broke out in a sweat. *So, I am to be a party to murder.* "I will need a knife and a piece of cloth."

Scarpa slipped his blade from the sheath on his belt and handed it over. "Will silk do?" he said with a laughing sneer, pulling an embroidered piece of fabric from his sleeve.

Blade in one hand, Micah took in a deep breath and set aside the grieving man, taking up the mantle of Alchemist. He laid the fabric on the bed and turned to Scarpa. "And I must know her name."

"Marie," Miriam said. "Her name is Marie."

With a nod at the young woman, he turned to Scarpa. "You first."

"Fine. What does this ridiculous ritual require that I do?"

Miriam stepped forward to watch, her eyes gleaming with interest and fascination as the Alchemist of Aleppo pulled himself to his feet, finding strength in his growing anger. He pointed to the wooden seat of the chair. "Place your hand on the chair."

"Why?" Scarpa asked even as he placed his right hand flat on the surface.

Without answering, the Alchemist brought the knife down on the knuckle of Scarpa's smallest finger as if he were cutting beef from the bone. A curse echoed through the house even as the Alchemist grabbed Scarpa's wrist, turned the hand over, palm up, and dug the blade deep into his flesh until blood poured forth, staining the chair red. As Scarpa continued cursing and demanding that Marthe and Miriam help him, the Alchemist turned to Marie. He moved the chair next to the bed and gently placed her hand on it knowing that the pop and snap of this woman's bone would haunt him forever. The tip of Marie's finger rolled away from her pale, lax hand, and he lifted the silk from the bed and pressed it to her finger, soaking up the blood seeping from her wound. Then he gathered the two fingertips and dipped the silk into Scarpa's blood, now pooled on the chair.

He tasted salt on his lips. *Never again. Never again. Never again,* he swore as he sliced open his own scarred arm and held the cloth to his flesh, mingling his blood with theirs to cement the unholy bond. Why he continued the ritual, he would never understand. He should have walked away as soon as he realized Scarpa and Marthe had left the room leaving only young Miriam to watch him with a look of fascinated awe painting her fine-boned features.

Scarpa's voice rang out from elsewhere in the house, angry and confused. The candles guttered as he recited the essential words, compelled by a force stronger than his own. As if from a far distant shore, he realized Miriam was saying the words with him:

*Bind Marie and Nicolo one to the other now and forever. Feed the Earth from that which is subtle, with the greatest power. It ascends from the Earth to the heaven and becomes ruler over that which is above and that which is below. Feed the Earth with blood and bone for time is ephemeral and only love is everlasting.*

The last thing he heard before he took his leave was young Miriam kneeling beside her sister's bed, whispering as if in prayer. "*Make them pay for your murder, Marie. Make them pay for all eternity.*"

In the night, as Micah stood before his furnace, he prayed for Marie and cursed Scarpa and Marthe—and even Miriam—for all time. Cursed himself for his weakness. His arrogance. His overweening hope in the power and salvation of love.

And by morning it was done. Like a wraith in the mist, Michael went to the house to deliver the glass sphere encapsulating the very essence of Marie and Nicolo's futures. Knocking on the door, a servant opened it to report that the Scarpa party had left for their ship well before daybreak. She handed him a heavy purse and told him the galley was leaving on the morning tide.

Michael ran toward the quay only to see Scarpa and Marthe standing at the rail of a handsome vessel moving slowly toward the open sea. Two murderers dressed in raiment fit for the finest of merchants and with eyes only for each other. When at last they disappeared over the horizon, Michael reached into the purse, filled his fist with silver coins, and threw them into the sea.

Now, the rhythmic lapping of waves against the quay was disrupted by a man's voice. Michael blinked. Swallowed. Looked down at his hand to see if he was still holding the empty purse. But no. He held a plastic bag. With a note in it. Then his ears were ringing, and he wanted to clamp his hands over them and turn away from the noise.

"I said, do you know what this note means?"

Michael swallowed again and looked at the detective. *What was his name?* Rao. D.S. Rao. "I'm sorry. I have no idea."

He handed the evidence bag to Rao, turned, and strode purposefully back toward the carriage house garage.

# FORTY-FIVE

Kat nearly jumped out of her skin when Michael flung open the back door to the main house and stormed into the kitchen. The expression on his face was one she'd never seen before. She carefully set aside the knife she'd been using to cut apple slices and braced herself, as if expecting bad news. "What's happened now?"

"You aren't in the garage."

"No." Kat gestured toward Leila and Carys who stood with her around the kitchen island full of half-made sandwiches, chunks of various cheeses, bags of crisps, and fruit waiting to be sliced. "George, Liz, and Tully are still there, but we decided to make lunch. And we needed something to do to keep busy."

"I need you."

Everything about him was tense. Strung tight and as prickly as barbed wire caught on a cactus. More tense, even, than when he'd held her just after the gunfire had stopped. More tense than any time since she'd known him. *And god, what a short time that had been.* She had to keep reminding herself that she hardly knew this man.

Michael's gaze flickered over his mother and sister and returned to Kat. "I need to show you something."

He stuck out his hand and waited. Kat wiped her hands on a dishtowel and placed her hand in his. Without a backward glance, Michael pulled her toward the interior of the house, up the stairs, and then down the hall to his childhood bedroom.

When she stepped into his room, she took it all in. She didn't know what Michael wanted to show her, but she couldn't pass up a chance to look for clues as to what he'd been like as a boy. There was a double bed covered by a plain white duvet and what looked like an antique wooden headboard, a matching dresser topped by a few framed photos of him and Leila playing in the yard—both adorable dark-haired, mischievous-looking children—and a painted desk and office chair for homework.

Decorating the walls were photos of Michael as a teenager wearing his school uniform, posing with teammates on a soccer pitch, sitting in a stone courtyard surrounded by a large group of men who looked like extended Samaan family members, and a photo of him in full academic dress with his parents after what must have been his PhD graduation ceremony. There were several framed sketches of landscapes, each with his name scrawled in the corner. So, Kat thought, he hadn't become a professional artist, but he still harbored the artistic talent of the Samaans of the past.

Kat waited as he turned on his closet light and fished around on a top shelf until he pulled down a shoe box. He held it for a moment and then brushed past her to set it on his desk. He tapped a single fingertip on the lid.

"I haven't opened this since the day I left for university. Haven't even thought about it. Maybe my subconscious refused to allow me to think about it."

"What's in it?"

"Cricket and football player cards, a list of books I read each summer, a wish list of places I wanted to go, old coins from Syria." He shrugged. "Childhood treasures, otherwise known as junk." He slowly lifted the lid. "And this."

Kat slipped her arm around his waist and gave him a reassuring squeeze as he picked up a small, folded piece of paper sitting right on top of the rest of the treasures.

"What is it?"

"A combination." His hand was unsteady as he unfolded it and read aloud: "One Three Five Zero."

"1350. That's the first year of Samaan Glassworks."

"Easy enough to remember." Michael put the paper back in the box.

"But what's it a combination to?"

He turned to her and cupped her face in his hands. "I remembered. I know who Sergei is to me."

Her eyes went wide, questioning.

"He was a friend. A confidant and…."

She sensed he wanted to say more, so she waited.

"I think I already knew. My body recognized him before my brain did. No 'malevolent vibes,' remember? I likely didn't need Tully at all. Everything is converging and I think it was the illusion of the hypnosis that gave me permission to remember things from the past that were… problematic."

She searched his face, wanted to ask him to explain exactly who Sergei was to him and why he was problematic, but knew his story had to be told on his terms. "What about me?" She whispered. "I'm from your past."

He smiled down at her. "Ah, but you're hardly a problem. You are my heart. You are my joy and hope and love and possibility, not the darkness that came after."

"After the Alchemist's wife died. After Yasmine."

He nodded. "But now, it's time to remember everything. Past time. George told you about Citadel Security?"

"That it's Badawi's company?"

"He's been looking over my family all these years." He shook his head and looked out the window at the green expanse of the backyard, probably thinking, Kat guessed, about what would happen when Badawi's helicopter landed amid his mother's flower bed.

"What happened when you went off with the detective?"

He turned back to look at her. She could see the fine lines raying out from the edges of his eyes, the parenthesis around his mouth that deepened when he smiled. This was a man who, despite the darkness, had learned how to laugh. To build a life. A life that, she supposed, now included her. What that life would look like was yet to be determined.

"The police found a note from the shooter. Pinned to a tree across the lane with a bone-handled hunting knife. Spent shells littered the ground."

She tensed, gripped his arm. "What did it say?"

He closed his eyes, picturing the note. *To Michael Samaan. Remember Latakia. No man should have the power to resurrect the dead. Give me what's mine or I'll start taking what's yours.*

Holy hell. *Give me what's mine or I'll start taking what's yours.* That was a threat if Kat had ever heard one, and she'd watched *a lot* of crime dramas. "Clearly that's a threat to life and limb," she said. "Two questions: What is Latakia, and what are the police going to do about this crazy woman who keeps threatening you?"

"First, come with me. There's more." He took her hand again and led her back downstairs, to his father's office. Her mind was spinning, but her attention pinioned back to him when she felt a shudder ripple through his body as they crossed the threshold and he shut the door behind them.

"This room always gave me a dark, unsettled feeling," Michael said. "I thought it was because, as a young man, I was afraid I would never live up to my father's expectations. That I could never fill his shoes and so felt insecure and inadequate. But Pop never made me feel that way, so it didn't make sense. Turns out, it was the room all along. It was what was hidden in here."

Kat watched in silence as Michael pushed his father's chair away from the desk, lowered himself to the floor, and then laid back so his head and shoulders were under the desk.

"There's a latch." He ran his fingers along the seams of the wood, pressing until a piece louvered out like a little hinge. After pulling it back, a drawer dropped open and out slid a rectangular metal box.

"Here." He handed the box up to her as he scooted from under the desk and stood. Kat set it on the desk and they both stared at it, then jumped, startled, as Pooka, Carys's black cat, appeared out of nowhere to leap up on the desk.

"Damn cat," Michael groaned as Kat stroked a hand down the cat's sleek back. "Probably smells the magic."

It was Kat's turn to shudder. "I still can't believe we're casually talking about magic," she said as she and Pooka watched Michael run a finger over the box's dusty lid and tilt it up to see the four-digit combination lock set into the front where the top and bottom met.

"To answer your question, Latakia is a port city in Syria. On the Mediterranean. The day I left for university," he said, setting the box back down, "my father asked me to come in here, said he had something to show me. He told me he'd had this box for years but that he'd never opened it. That he'd sworn not to. His job, he said, was to keep it safe for me until I needed it."

"Where'd he get it?"

"His uncle, also named Michael—I know that's confusing, especially since I suspect many of the old Samaan Michaels were me in some previous incarnation—gave it to him just before he died. Before my father even came to the UK. Anyway, apparently, this Uncle Michael made my father swear to keep it safe for his son and to never open it. Said it was a family heirloom to pass from generation to generation."

"If this was before your father came to the UK, how did this guy know your father would have a son?"

Michael snorted out a laugh. "Good question, right? Logically, none of this makes sense, so we must suspend logic. Especially for this next part. Anyway, at the time, I asked my father how the hell I was supposed to know when I'd need it, and Pop shrugged. Said Uncle Michael was certain I would know. Then he told me the box was fireproof, showed me the hidden compartment in his desk, wrote down the combination, and that was that."

He raked trembling fingers through his hair, and Kat felt the tension radiating off his body in waves. She pressed a hand to his back and rubbed gentle circles between his shoulder blades. He dropped his head forward and let out a low groan.

"God, that feels good." He rolled his shoulders and let himself revel in the soothing pressure, just for a moment, before straightening back up. "You have to understand that back then, I was a mess. I was in denial about everything and didn't want to think about my crazy dreams or how the Luck made me feel or the dark places through which my imagination too often traveled. I'd been on a bender with friends for weeks and could barely see a hole in a ladder, let alone think coherently. I just wanted to get out of the house, get to Cambridge, get stoned, and get laid." He huffed out a soft laugh. "And not necessarily in that order."

"Like most young men setting out for college."

He shot her a glance. "At least in that, I was not out of the ordinary." He moved his head back and forth as if to work out the kinks in his neck. "Ready?"

"If you are."

He thumbed in the combination, then opened the lid. "Christ Almighty. Another fucking box."

Kat traced a finger over the polished wood, engraved with a familiar design. "Look at the design. It's the same as the leaves on the Luck. As the doodles in the journal."

He drew in a long breath and nodded, as if giving himself permission. He lifted the lid to reveal an interior covered in tufted black velvet topped with a plain white envelope. He picked up the envelope, opened it, and pulled out a card written in an elegant script. In English.

*To my successor:*

*The contents of this box have been handed down to a Samaan son for generations. I am its current caretaker. If you are reading this, you are its current caretaker—and you have remembered. To bind Yasmine to me through the ages, I made a vessel of transference for our souls. (Have you already seen this? Remembered this?) And then, to fulfill a promise she demanded on her on her deathbed, I used this magic on behalf of others, creating talismans for lovers who sought my help. Through this process, I tied these talismans to our vessel and to us—Yasmine and Micah—through blood and bone and magic.*

*Now, our vessel—you know it now as the Luck of Edenhall—is a beacon calling to those whose bodies and souls have been bound together through this powerful alchemy. The process was sound, but not perfect, and I have spent many lonely lifetimes during which the one I sought was never found. (Including this one. Have you found your love? I hope your journey will be different from mine.) And what, you wonder, about the other lovers? Well, they are searching too. Some harbor romantic dreams of past and future love and others harbor dreams of murder and revenge.*

*I have written this note in the first person, as if I was the Alchemist. And I am. And am not. As you are. And are not. Time is ephemeral. It is easy to turn away from the past, even as our former selves live within us.*

*The decisions we made and the things we did haunt us, but as bleak as that may sound, you are your own man. A new man. In a new age. You have choices.*

*Make them wisely. But most importantly, make them with love. Because even though time is ephemeral, love is everlasting.*

*As always,*
*— Michael Samaan, Aleppo, 1977*

# FORTY-SIX

Kat took the note from his trembling fingers. She scanned the lines until she found what she wanted. She read aloud, "And then, to fulfill a promise she demanded of me on her on her deathbed, I used this magic on behalf of others, creating talismans for lovers who sought my help."

She looked up at Michael. "So, these other lovers. These are the same people the man who wrote the twentieth-century journal talked about. People who would eventually congregate in London where the Luck is. Is this Uncle Michael saying everything was set in motion because Yasmine demanded a terrible promise from the Alchemist? Oh, god! Is Yasmine behind everything you've gone through? Is this what haunts me?"

He brushed the backs of his fingers against her cheek. "No. It is *not* because of Yasmine. The Alchemist had free will. He made the decision to—"

She pulled away. "But she *demanded* he keep his promise! What did he think would happen if he ignored her deathbed request? How could someone be so selfish and cruel to demand such a thing."

"Kat, stop. He didn't even know if the alchemy would work. And he didn't give a flying fuck! At that moment, as she was taking her last breaths, as he was holding her for the last time, he would have promised her the moon and the stars and dealt with the consequences later."

Kat clasped her hands over her ears as if she could prevent his words from entering her brain.

"She was dying, for Christ's sake!" Michael went on. "She couldn't have been in her right mind. And Yasmine would never have asked for anything that was cruel or selfish. She believed the Alchemist's talents were a gift from god and that he should share them. Once she was gone, I—Micah—could have gone back on his promise. Or once he started, he could have stopped. But he didn't. The power in the process was intoxicating. Addicting. He couldn't get enough of it. It wasn't Yasmine's fault. It was Micah's."

She shook her head, but he put a fingertip to her lips. "Sweetheart, no. Imagine realizing you've discovered the power of resurrection. That you can bring people back to life. That you've looked into the dark maw of death and conquered it. That was the power Micah discovered. That was the power he learned to wield. Once he tasted it, he wanted more—even as he knew he couldn't control it. Knew it would eventually control him. And haunt him through the ages."

"God, Michael. What if I'd never—"

"Listen to me. You keep telling me I'm not the same man I was in the past, and you're right. And that means you're not the same woman. You are not Yasmine." He gestured toward the note on the desk. "And just as that Michael Samaan said, I am my own man. I have choices. But I must *own* this. I must finally confront the past. Do you understand? This is on me. Not you."

He held her gaze for a long minute until she finally gave him a reluctant nod. Then he turned back to the wooden box. "Now, let's see if everything is here."

She pinched the bridge of her nose and watched as he lifted the top velvet pad and there, sitting snug and surrounded by more tufted velvet, sat a small volume bound in parchment and clasped with a leather and bone toggle. Michael sucked in a breath and reached out and touched a trembling fingertip to the cover, then drew back quickly.

"The Alchemist's book. Like a modern chemist's lab notes. It's all in here. What he did. How he did it."

Kat could feel the heat pouring from Michael's body, sense him pulse with energy like a struck tuning fork. As a scientist, she was fascinated. As a woman whose life had been turned upside down, she was appalled. "Are you okay?"

"Honestly?" Michael snorted out a coarse laugh. "Far from it. But I'm prepared. I know what to expect now."

Kat saw sweat beading on his forehead and upper lip. His breathing was shallow. He bit his lip and stuck his fingers down between the black pad and the sides of the wooden box, lifted the book and its velvet bed up and out and set it on the desk only to reveal another thin velvet pad.

"This is it," he said. Steeling himself with a fortifying breath, he reached out to pluck up the pad and then drew his hand back as if he'd been burned. He cleared his throat and wiped a sleeve across his face. With a look of chagrin, he said, "Can you do it? Pick up the velvet pad?"

Kat held his gaze for a moment, then pinched the velvet between her fingers and lifted it. Even Kat sensed the change in the air as Michael staggered back, sank into his father's chair, and dug his fingertips into his temples.

"I said I knew what to expect, but still, seeing them again after all these years is..." He shook his head as they both looked down at six glass balls—like beautifully crafted paperweights—sitting snug in their recessed beds of black velvet padding.

She dug her fingers into his shoulder. "This is what the man who wrote the journal was looking for."

"The life spheres," Michael whispered. "And that journal?" He swallowed, his voice thick. "That journal was Sergei's. It's part of what I remembered today. He and I have known each other since—"

She took a step back. "He was there at the beginning?"

He nodded toward the collection of spheres and reached out to point to one. "This is his. The very first one the Alchemist made. This is what he wants from me."

"But that can't be all of it. He seems so…invested in you. As a person. I mean, you said he's been using his own security service to watch over your and your mom."

"Oh, the life sphere is not all he wants." He ran a hand over his face and tried again. "What I mean to say is that it's complicated. Our relationship. Obviously, we have a lot of history and we've been many things to each other over the years. But ultimately, it's always been about these spheres and his search for his wife."

Kat nodded, trying to adjust to this new knowledge. "And the shooter? The woman who put the belladonna in your beer and tried to drown you?"

He pointed to another glass ball sitting snug in its velvet cushion. "This is the one I made for her and her husband. The last one I ever made. I remembered that today too and, believe me, it was not a good memory. Once, in an opium-induced haze, I decided to destroy them all, but I couldn't bring myself to do it." He shrugged. "So, I hid them. And then I forgot. Or I made myself forget. But obviously someone knew. Maybe it was the old woman. Elias's grandmother? She was a witch, I think."

Kat stared, mesmerized, at the six perfectly formed glass spheres about two inches in diameter, the perfect size to fit snug in the palm of her hand. Each sphere was different, a unique world enveloped by the moving swirls and streaks of red, green, yellow, and blue clouds eddying and flowing as if a strong wind moved across the surface of a small planet. "It looks like what's inside the glass is moving. They look alive."

It took a long while for Michael to answer. Finally, in a voice that sounded as if it had been scraped from the bottom of a deep well, he choked out, "They are."

"How? What exactly are they?"

"The Alchemist's life spheres. The hopes and dreams—*the eternal souls*—of lovers who wanted a second chance."

# FORTY-SEVEN

Michael stood alone on the stone terrace, arm up to shield his face from the buffeting wind of the helicopter's rotors. As it settled into the grass, a door opened, and a short ladder extended out to the ground. For a moment, Sergei Badawi stood in the doorway, not moving. Then, his shoulders rose and fell as if he had drawn in a long breath and let it out again slowly. Preparing himself.

Michael moved first, walking down the terrace steps and toward the man with whom he'd shared so much, the man who knew him better than anyone. Better even than the woman he'd loved for so long. He stopped in the middle of the yard and waited. And then Sergei walked forward deliberately until he stood an arm's length from Michael. They stayed that way a moment, not saying a word, the air around them charged with anticipation. Michael stepped forward and pulled the older man to him. Sergei's arms went around him and, in the middle of the yard for everyone to see, they held onto each other as if they were clinging to a life raft in a raging river. For over six hundred years, they had cared for, resented, and tormented each other, had come to understand each other, and finally, grown to love each other. Had even, in their darkest moments of despair, taken comfort in each other's arms. And in each other's bodies.

After a long moment, they stepped back. Michael swiped a forearm across his face and Sergei pulled a pressed handkerchief from a pocket and wiped at his nose, dabbed at his eyes. An awkward silence enveloped them once again until Michael spoke up.

"So, Citadel Security. How long have you—"

"Since before you went to Cambridge."

"You know about the 'accidents' then." He started back toward the terrace. "Will you sit with me a moment before we go in?"

"I know about the accidents, and I've had people looking into them, to the extent possible. The broken arm, the blown-up boat, the belladonna. The hit-and-run." Sergei gripped Michael's arm. "Jesus Christ, I felt so useless. I wanted to be there for you. To tell you everything. But, you know..." He looked away for a moment. "I've done everything I can think of to find her, but the woman is slippery as a bloody eel."

Michael nodded, motioned for Sergei to sit at the outdoor dining table, and pulled out a seat for himself. "And today's shooting?"

"It's got to be her."

"Christ," Michael blew out a breath and looked past Sergei, off into the distance. "How many times do I have to go through this?"

"There's only one way to stop Marie Scarpa. And for you, with the Luck on display and under guard, an enchanting and beloved part of England's past, stopping it would be almost impossible even if that's what you truly wanted. But for the rest of us? For Marie who, if the story you always told me is true, never had a choice? You can end it."

Michael cut him off. "Once, I had the hubris to make life and death decisions, but now? Now, I know better."

"People make life and death decisions every day."

"I have your journal. The one you gave me the last time you visited Aleppo. After the War. I showed it to Kat."

"Ah. Does she know who I am?"

"She does now. But, bloody hell, that stunt you pulled the other night at Hempstead House? Jesus, that was ballsy. And fucking aggravating as all hell. Parading in there and orchestrating that conversation like—"

"I was at my wit's end." Sergei pinched the bridge of his nose. "I couldn't find a way to get through to you."

Michael cut him a sharp glance. "And today when I found out Citadel is your security firm? That was the tipping point for me. I was both blindingly furious and extraordinarily grateful. And I want to thank you for that, for trying to look after my family."

Sergei sat back into his seat and gave Michael a rueful smile. "I have an ulterior motive, as you well know."

"All these years…Jesus, you should've pushed me, made me understand."

"Pushed you?" Sergei raised an eyebrow. "I've dropped so many hints on you, I'm surprised you're not permanently concussed. You've been amazingly obtuse. Almost like you didn't want to know."

Michael laughed, the tension ebbing. "Of course, I didn't want to know. This time was different. Growing up here with the lodestone—the Luck—on display for everyone to see. My god, I first saw it on a primary school field trip and felt like I'd been stripped naked and put on a pedestal for everyone to see my most private thoughts—and my private parts! I didn't even know what those thoughts were and barely knew what those parts were for." He shook his head. "I just knew there was something dark and disturbing deep within my soul. I haven't been quite right since."

Sergei sighed. "We neither one are quite right. Our pasts, the things we've done—to each other and for each other—will always haunt us. Arrogance. Guilt. Regret. Loneliness. Rinse and repeat over and over again." He shook his head. "The first time I saw you this time—I went to one of your sixth form rugby matches—I was already a man grown and could not wait any longer for you to… to know me." He looked away, swallowed hard, and then turned back to Michael. "I had this crazy idea that you'd look up and see me on the sidelines and just know. What a ridiculous fantasy."

"It's not a fantasy. It's happened before." Michael laughed. "Well, not in the midst of a rugby match."

"For some reason, maybe it's part of the curse, I've never been as fortunate as you on the family front, but I've been lucky in that I found a friend this time, Carson." He glanced over his shoulder at the man now standing, waiting, on the grass beside the helicopter's steps. "But bloody hell, I've missed you."

"Look at you," Michael said, a touch of awe in his voice. "I'm always the same old Michael or Elias or Micah or whatever the fuck Samaan family name I inherit, always an artist or scholar, and you're what? Soldier. Merchant. Spy. Diplomat. Billionaire. By god, what's next?"

Sergei's expression sobered and his eyes glittered. "Someday, I hope to be a husband again." His voice caught in his throat. "Maybe even a father."

# FORTY-EIGHT

"Liz went back to town," George said when Michael and Sergei finally made it inside to find Kat and George in the kitchen nursing cups of tea. "The police took our statements and left. DS Rao will be in touch about taking your statement later. For now, Ethan Rollings of Citadel Security is talking with Carys and is taking the situation in hand." George shot Sergei a glance. "Everything's still laid out like we left it in the garage if you want to—"

"I don't need to see some old books to know who Michael is."

"Ah…" George looked between the two men, understanding washing over him. "I take it your interest in art and glassmaking isn't the only reason you've supported Michael's career."

"No." Sergei let his gaze fall on Kat. "I'm sorry if I made you uncomfortable at dinner the other evening. My approach was, well, born of desperation. If you're willing to listen, I'd like the opportunity to explain why."

Michael shot him a look. "Explain?" To Michael's knowledge, Sergei had never told his story to anyone but him.

Sergei plucked an almond out of a bowl on the counter and played with it between his fingers. "People look at me and see what they expect: a wealthy, decent-looking man in the prime of his life. A man with the world at his feet. But living with my history is not easy." He looked at Michael. "I've told Carson a good bit of my story, and he has yet to consign me to Bedlam." He smiled and gave a one-shouldered shrug. "He says he'd miss the perks of employment if I were locked away in a padded cell. But seriously, going through life without ever being truly known by anyone is, quite frankly, lonely."

He cleared his throat again and looked down at his hands, the nut resting in one palm. "I've come to understand that the tales we tell ourselves blur around the edges over time. Some say truth is relative and while I don't subscribe to that point of view, I do know that humans are apt to lie to themselves when it suits them. And to believe their lies. For some reason, I feel the need to be held accountable for the truth of the story I've been telling myself." He looked to Michael. "Obviously, you're the only one who can help me fact check my memory, so...." He looked around. "Aren't Carys and Leila here?"

"They took a lunch tray down to the carriage house flat. Dr. Tull is there and they're having lunch. Rollings is with them too. I was just getting ready to join them." George pushed away from the counter.

"Dr. James Tull?" Sergei said. "He's here?"

Michael gave him a sardonic look. "You didn't know?"

"I'm not omniscient," Sergei said with a laugh. "Even though I was aware you two had gone to see him."

"So, I wasn't crazy!" Michael slapped a hand on the kitchen counter. "I knew I was being followed."

"Round-the-clock surveillance for weeks," Sergei admitted. "Ever since we first detected someone trying to breach your mother's security system. The break-in the other night wasn't the first attempt."

"And that's why Rollings is on the job? What is he? Retired special forces or something?"

"Or something," Sergei shrugged. "At any rate," he turned to Kat, "it is true that I've had Michael followed for months for his own protection, so news of your reaction to the Luck and your…mutual attachment reached me almost immediately. Of course, I don't know you well, but the *idea* of you has played a part in my life for a very long time."

"Six hundred years or so?" Kat said.

Sergei studied her. "Or thereabouts."

Michael turned to George. "Do you mind going down to the carriage house and keeping Leila, Mum, and Tully occupied until we give the all clear?"

"No problem. Let me make another cup of tea and I'll be on my way."

Michael glanced at Kat. "We'll be in the front room. Give us a few minutes first, please." He waited for a nod of agreement then turned back to Sergei. "Follow me."

∞

As George waited for the kettle to heat up, he pinned Kat with a look. "Ready for Sergei's 'explanation'?" She was staring out the windows onto the yard where the helicopter sat. "Kat," George's voice took on a soft, comforting tone. "Are you feeling jealous of Sergei?"

Kat let out a long exhale. "Not jealous, per se, but this connection of theirs…my mind keeps conjuring the most—"

He turned to face her, one hip resting against the counter. "I'm a novelist, Kat. I've put the most outrageous and murderous and lascivious and lurid thoughts into my characters' heads, which is to say that I've had all those thoughts in my own head. After hearing Michael's story— *your story*—nothing you say will shock me."

"Okay. Maybe I am a bit jealous of all the time they had together in the past. But what little Michael's said about it, I know it wasn't all coming up roses. Our own time together was, I fear, too short and too"—she suppressed a shiver as her hand drifted to her stomach where her birthmark seemed to let out a little thrum— "fraught."

"Fraught. What a fine word that is."

She laughed. "Fraught. Short. Sad."

"Is that all it was? Your time together?"

A wistful smile tipped up the corner of her mouth. "I remember feeling loved. Cherished." A slight pink tinged her cheeks. "Worshipped." She picked up her cup again. "But I think our times together were short. And not necessarily sweet."

"Have you remembered more?"

"No. It's more vague feelings. Shadows of feelings."

"Do you want to remember? Do you want to do the hypnosis like Michael did?"

"No." Her fingers drifted up and down along her birthmark. "I don't think it would do anyone any good."

∞

Armed with a cup of tea, Sergei sat facing Michael and Kat across a low, marble-topped table situated in front of the now cold, painted brick fireplace. In any other circumstance, he thought, it would feel as if they were getting ready to enjoy a relaxed cocktail hour of drinks and conversation. Golden sun from two nearly floor-to-ceiling windows splashed bright blocks of light on the furnishings, brightening the room and giving it a warm, welcoming feeling. What he had to say next was not, he would wager, going to be welcomed by Dr. Katherine Musgrave.

He took a sip, set his teacup in the saucer with a soft rattle, and touched his fingertips to the old journal Michael had just given him. He looked directly at Kat and began.

"So you understand our history and can put our relationship in context, I'd like to tell you what happened, how it all started with Michael and me."

"Okay," Kat said. "I'm listening."

"A long time ago, a prosperous man, a soldier and a merchant, lived in a grand house with a beautiful wife and a newborn son, their first and only, one they had tried for years to conceive."

Sergei thought it sounded very much like a 'Once upon a time' beginning to a Brothers Grimm fairy tale. Only this story didn't have an ending. Not yet, at least. Maybe it never would.

The truth was, Sergei hadn't told this story to anyone except Michael. His mind flashed back to a drafty room over a coffee house on a back street in Beirut. 1833. Sergei had been stunned when Michael turned up at his door, a ragged, half-starved man with empty eyes who had walked all the way from Aleppo through a war zone. As soon as the door closed behind them Michael collapsed in his arms. *I have nothing to lose*, he said, his eyes too dry for tears. *Nothing to live for.* He held up his shaking hands as if offering proof. *I can barely hold a pen let alone work at the furnace. My uncle...*Michael peeled off his shirt to reveal the welts and scars crisscrossing his skin...*he cast me out for being an opium eater, and I have no hope of ever finding her again. My Yasmine, my Emmaline...she's beyond my reach. You're all I have.* Sergei wondered if Michael remembered their time in Beirut. Lying in each other's arms. Seeking and finding solace in each other's bodies.

"The year was 1351," he went on, "and like every other year, someone was fighting someone else somewhere. It was this man's job to lead men into battle. He was a mercenary, and he was well paid for putting his life on the line. Over and over again, he rode headlong into the fight and over and over again, he returned home unscathed. Until one day, he didn't."

He took another sip of his tea, licked his lips, and for a moment, stared into his cup. Again, his eyes flicked to Michael who sat with his elbows resting on his knees, head in his hands, staring down at the pattern on the rug for which his parents had once paid a small fortune on one of their trips to Syria.

"This soldier," Sergei said now, his attention focused back on Kat, "let's call him Sergius, for, in truth, that was his name, had been nearly disemboweled by someone whose job it was to kill him and others like him. Which war it was, who was fighting whom, doesn't matter to the story. Suffice it to say that Sergius lay dying on the field of battle until one of his servants found him, bound his wound, and somehow dragged him home. By turns delirious or unconscious, he woke to find a man bending over him and his beautiful wife, Cyrine, weeping and begging—no, *demanding*—for the man to save him.

'I can't,' the man said. 'I am no surgeon.' The man was familiar to Sergius, but as feverish as he was, he could not remember his name.

'You may not be able to save him now, but we can still have a future together.' Cyrine's voice was ragged from crying. 'Yasmine told me what you made, what your alchemy can do.'

The man glared at Cyrine and turned away. 'She should not have told you.'

'But she *did* tell me! She told me how you did it, what it takes, and I'm willing to go through it for another chance with the man I love. Just like Yasmine was willing to go through with it for another chance with you. I will not go on without hope, Micah. I can't.'

'Cyrine, please,' the man, Micah, said. 'You cannot abandon your son just because war will claim your husband. He is a soldier. He always knew this day could come. In marrying him, you accepted this fate, and now, you must live with it. For your son. For *his* son.'

'Why must I live with it? Why must I become a poor widow cast out on the world's mercy?'

'But Sergius is a wealthy man!'

'And you think this house will be mine when he is gone? His snake of a brother will claim everything in it, including me!'

'I will help you. I can give you money and you can go away from here, but please don't ask me to do this one thing.'

'I don't want your money, I want my husband! If not now, in the future."

"Cyrene, stop. I will not do this."

"Then take my son when you go. Have him raised up with Yasmine's daughter. Because when my husband leaves this world, I am going with him!'"

Sergei pulled a handkerchief from his pocket and twisted it in his hands.

"It was then that Sergius recognized the man standing over him. Micah Samaan. A glassmaker. A friend."

He stopped again. Swallowed. Took a sip of his tea.

"By now, Sergius could feel his life ebbing away. Through a haze of flickering candlelight, burning incense, and fading eyesight, he saw his wife withdraw the dagger sheathed in his boot and press the tip to that tender place on her neck that he loved to kiss. Sergius had fallen in love with her the first time he'd seen her. His tiny volcano. He'd always been accused of being a bit too serious, but she was his very own Scheherazade. She could act out a story and have him laughing so hard he had to gasp for air. She could look up at him with those dark eyes, soft as velvet, and have him weeping in gratitude for her adoration. And she made love to him with a ferocity that astounded, gratifying him like no woman ever had before. She was everything. More than everything.

"Micah tried to grab the knife. 'This is madness!' he cried. 'I don't even know if the alchemy works, and I will not cut him without his permission.'

"I struggled to speak and the change in my breathing must have caught their attention because Cyrine bent over me, tears falling on my fevered skin. I had no use for alchemy or magic or blind faith of any kind excepting the strength of a man's arm and the warmth of a woman's body. I was a man of the world and to my mind, magical gods and saints and prayers whispered on a dying man's breath were made of nothing but wishes and fear. But it broke my heart to think of Cyrine plunging that knife into her tender throat. So, I forced the air from my lungs and managed to say, 'Do it. For my wife. Do whatever must be done. Before it is too late.'

"And so I watched as my friend Micah Samaan, the Alchemist of Aleppo, took my dagger from Cyrine's trembling hands and sliced off the tip of one of those lovely fingers that had for years touched my body with such tenderness and passion. I watched as he twisted the point of my blade into her wrist and collected her blood. And as his knife bit into my skin and cut through my bone, I cursed every god and priest and pretender, every charlatan who promised life everlasting and profited off the gullible and hopeful. I cursed Micah Samaan most of all. No longer my friend, he was my tormentor, promising my beloved things I knew for a certainty no sane man could believe.

"I closed my eyes, prepared to die. There was no need to bleed me as I was already covered in blood, the gaping wound of my eviscerated body already putrefying. But still I felt him dip his fingers into my wound and the world went dark. I heard him chanting:

> *Bind Cyrine and Sergei one to the other now and forever. Feed the Earth from that which is subtle, with the greatest power. It ascends from the Earth to the*

*heaven and becomes ruler over that which is above and that which is below. Feed the Earth with blood and bone for time is ephemeral and only love is everlasting.*

And then I remembered nothing more.

"Until sometime later when I awoke in a boy's body. A beggar boy sleeping in a sheep's pen. A boy with no history, no family, no money, no friends. Somehow I managed to survive. And then one day I saw a familiar man walk by and I knew. It all came back in one sickening jolt. I knew who I had been and how I had died. I had a man's lifetime of experience in a young boy's body, and I set out to make something of himself with two goals: find my wife and make Micah Samaan pay. I never found my wife, but I did find Micah. Michael. By that time, I realized revenge was useless, and eventually, Michael became important to me. A friend. A brother." He looked up at Kat. "A lover."

Kat didn't move or make a sound of acknowledgement. Maybe it was still all too much for her to truly understand. Maybe she hated him. Maybe she was jealous. Sergei had no idea.

He picked up the journal and ran a thumb over the leather cover. "I didn't write much during the war. It would've been dangerous as an agent of the Crown, working with Allied Forces in North Africa. But I wanted you to know that I'd found your lodestone. The vessel Micah made for Yasmine, on display in a museum " He smiled and his gaze held Michael's. "You were an old man when I gave this to you, but I knew the next time we met it would be in London."

"It was your way of telling me where I needed to be," Michael said, "and somehow, by the fates or the gods or whatever alchemy rules over all of us, my father emigrated, met my mother, and here I am."

"So, here we are." Sergei repeated. "Including Katherine Musgrave—or Yasmine as she was first known and then later as your beloved Emmaline. And perhaps other names that are not known to me…or that neither of you can remember."

"And yet, there is one missing still," Michael said.

Sergei closed his eyes as if in pain. "Cyrine. I've never found her." His voice caught. "Not once. It's the curse. When you used my blade to cut me, I cursed us all and my refusal to believe has followed me ever since." He went to one of the windows and looked out at the lengthening shadows. "But somehow, I always find you." He huffed out a sad laugh and turned back to Michael.

"Except once," Michael said.

"Except once," Sergei repeated. "In 1640, I had been in Constantinople for a time and when I returned to Aleppo, I went to the Samaan house and to the glassworks to find you. You were gone. At least that's what they told me. In my arrogance, I sought to intimidate your household and went back, this time wearing the full regalia of my position as a Timarli Sipahi. I must have acted like a madman because your brother threw me out, and no one would tell me where you were. I searched among the glassmakers and alchemists, witches and viziers, occultists and necromancers and charlatans, anyone who might have heard of you. And then one day, an old woman, blind and barely able to walk, found me in an alley and beckoned to me. She told me you'd gone to England to find your destiny."

"Elias's grandmother," Michael said. "She claimed to speak to the spirit of the Alchemist."

"I asked when you would return, and she told me to be patient. *Time is ephemeral,* she said. *The past is always with you and the future is always with you. Keep your eyes open and you will see.* And it was later that very same day, that I saw her. A woman's reflection in the glass of a shop window. *My Cyrine!* My heart nearly stopped. It was her. I knew it was her. But when I turned, she was gone. Maybe she'd never been there. Maybe I had indeed gone mad. You were lost to me, I was desperate, heartbroken, and alone. My position offered me no comfort. My wealth failed to console me. That night, in a run-down hotel near the souk in the Old City—across from the towering Citadel of Aleppo, I put my pistol in my mouth and pulled the trigger."

"Jesus," Kat said as she choked back a sob.

In a soft voice, Michael said, "And later, when I returned from England, bereft and alone, I followed you into that darkness. But now," Michael said, leaning forward. "You have hope. I can feel it."

"There is a woman…" Sergei shrugged and chuckled at his foolishness. "It may be so much smoke and mirrors, but I have a feeling." He shook his head and sank back into his chair. "I've not even met her! I know her name. I know her history and have read her CV so many times, I have it memorized, but still… God, I sound ridiculous. After all these lifetimes, a schoolboy with a first crush."

"Not ridiculous," Michael caught Kat's hand in his and threaded their fingers together. "Never ridiculous."

"But I can't find her without your help. Without—"

"I know." Michael drew Kat's hand to his mouth, pressed his lips to her skin and then pulled his fingers free. "Wait here." He stood, stepped out of the room for a moment, and then returned. He set the wooden box he'd found in his father's office on the coffee table before Sergei.

Sergei sucked in a breath and shot to his feet, eyes wide, unable to speak.

Michael sat beside Kat, and said, "Michael Samaan, the last Michael Samaan, my father's uncle, gave this box to my father before he even came to the UK. It's been here since my parents bought this house."

Sergei stared down at the box, engraved with the same motifs he'd drawn in his journal all those years ago. For a long moment, the room was utterly quiet except for the *tick tock* of an old clock on the mantle. "How did you not feel them?"

"I think I did. I told you I've never been quite right, and I suppose having these in the same house I grew up in went a long way to making me feel I was going insane. My worst nightmares just tucked away in my father's desk. No wonder that room always gave me the heebee-jeebies."

"And they're all there?"

Michael nodded. "Along with the Alchemist's manual." Michael opened the box and turned to Kat. "Will you do the honors?"

Kat reached out and removed the tufted cushion with the book in it, Sergei and Michael riveted to her every move. She set the book aside and pulled off the velvet cover to reveal the spheres, the colors shifting beneath their surfaces like storm clouds in a high wind.

Kat sat beside Michael and they watched as Sergei Badawi—powerful billionaire, influential investor, and counselor to royalty and heads of state—fell to his knees. He reached out a trembling hand and tenderly removed the first sphere on the top right from its velvet cradle and held it in his outstretched palm. The streamers of color sped faster and faster as if a tsunami of power had been unleashed beneath the clear surface.

He looked up at Michael, eyes glistening. "I feel it. *Mother of God, I feel her.*"

And then, his fingers closed around it, he clutched it to his chest, lowered his head, and wept.

# FORTY-NINE

Holding a single candle for illumination, Elias followed the map Emmaline had used as a bookmark in the volume of poetry she'd handed him in the sitting room after dinner. He and Roland had been at Hartley Castle nearly a week and opportunities to spend time alone with Emmaline had been few and far between. Now, he hurried toward the flickering torch at the end of the passageway, inhaling the smell of cool dry stone and damp earth. He imagined cooks and kitchen staff bustling about to and fro, preparing daily meals or special banquets for the family, functionaries, and guests living upstairs.

How could life go on when everything had changed? The alchemy. The magic. The thought of it all nearly brought him to his knees in wonder. And in fear for what he had wrought. What others might be going through—or not. How the others may be floating on the ebb and flow of time, tossed about like so much flotsam and jetsam. Alone and angry. Afraid of an eternity of the same.

His thoughts turned to Syria, to Sergius, the man he'd left behind without a word or even a note. Of course, he'd been off on campaign somewhere, fighting someone else's battles with his sword arm and his keen intelligence, struggling to live with the curse he'd brought down on his own head. He would wonder where Elias had gone. He would feel abandoned.

Elias pushed those thoughts aside. Tonight, he would have Yasmine in his arms again. Finally. He had thought it would never happen, and now? To have found her here in the middle of this island nation so far from home…it was a miracle, one he had wrought with his own hands.

Days earlier, on their ride, the truth of their shared desire had been evident in the drawing Gerard had made and given Emmaline. It was beautiful and revealing and Elias wished he had a copy of his own to gaze at in the privacy of his bedchamber.

"Elias." Her whispered voice came from the shadows.

He stepped toward her and then her arms were around him and his mouth was on hers, claiming her for all time. "My love," he breathed the words against her lips.

"Wait." She pulled away from him. "Follow me." She lifted her torch from the bracket and led him farther down the passageway until she reached a wooden door. He stepped forward to lift the latch and followed her in, pushing the door closed behind him.

"We'll be safe here. No one will visit the wine cellar in the middle of the night. Come, see what I did." She took him by the hand and led him toward the back of the long room, hurrying beneath the arched stonework of the ancient roof. She turned right and wove through racks of barrels and bottles until she reached her destination, a small alcove better suited for storing peat or cast-off barrel staves than a midnight tryst. She tucked the torch into the nearest bracket, slipped her feet out of her boots, and stepped toward him, barefoot, on the cool stone floor.

Elias stared. Almost as if he were afraid that moving too quickly would break the spell she had woven around his heart, he bent slowly to set his candle holder safely on the ground and rose again to look down at her. He cupped her face, his dark eyes full of love and longing, then knelt and pulled her down to kneel with him amidst the pillows and nest of blankets she had made for them in their alcove hidden from the world.

His voice cracked as he whispered, "Do you truly know me?" He didn't realize he was crying until she wiped the tears from his cheeks.

"I know you. I don't remember everything. But I remember how I felt when you looked at me. How you smiled the first day we met in the market and how it transformed a world that had so long been full of fear and violence into a place where joy and delight was a possibility." She pressed his hand to her heart. "I felt you here. Like a glowing coal warming every part of me. You made me feel radiant. Beautiful. Wanted. And I remember how you welcomed my daughter, even though she was the abandoned child of a brutal man."

Guilt gutted him at the memory of how he had abandoned her daughter to his brother's wife as he delved deeper and deeper into the dark magic that had made their reunion possible. Later, he had tried to make up for it. Had tried to do right by her child as well as...the other children. *He'd had other children!* How had he forgotten? He would have to confess these things. Tell her about the other woman he took as wife. But not now.

"And I remember how you held me at the end," Emmaline whispered. "How you sprinkled rose petals on my pillow and showed me the glass vessel, our lodestone, and promised it would lead me back to you."

"It worked. The lodestone is here, with me." He slipped his hands under her robe and slid it off her shoulders and down her arms until it pooled behind her. "You are mine. And I am yours. Now and forever." He tugged at the drawstring of her chemise and held her gaze as it loosened and he drew it up over her breasts, caught briefly on the peaked tips before he pulled it off completely.

"Now and forever," she whispered and leaned her head back as he bent to trace his tongue along the slant of her collar bone and then down the valley between her breasts. "I remember our garden." Her hands molded to the back of his head, pulling him closer. "Where we would hold each other under the pine trees." She moaned as his tongue wandered up over her breast to pull her nipple into the wet heat of his mouth sending swift drumming pulses of need ricocheting through her body. "I have waited lifetimes for you to find me. Do not make me wait one minute more."

Elias bit back a groan and thought his heart would burst from the wonder of it all. As if she were as breakable as blown glass, he lay her back on the blankets, made quick work of his clothes and finally, *finally!* stretched out beside her. Yasmine and Michael. Emmaline and Elias. As one. Skin to skin. Nothing between them. Not time. Not distance. Not death.

# FIFTY

Sergei Badawi and his retinue were long gone, headed back to the city in a *whoosh* of rotor blades and blinking lights. Leila and George had headed home as well, but Michael and Kat slept together that night in Michael's childhood bedroom, under plastic stars pasted to the ceiling, glowing like little beacons of light. Or rather, they didn't sleep. At least not until nearly morning. They didn't make love, either. They simply lay together, legs tangled, arms around each other, holding on tight as the magnitude of what they'd experienced settled over them.

It was early, not yet 7:00, when Michael's phone buzzed. He reached over to see who was calling. DS Rao. The absolute last person he was interested in talking to. Still, he accepted the call.

"Mr. Samaan?"

"Yes."

"I wanted to let you know we were able to track the shooter's car. CCTV caught the number plate after the woman cut from the path behind the woods and then turned on to the road just past the old abbey ruins south of here. We tracked her to her hotel, and  should have more information very soon."

"Do you have a name?"

"The vehicle's a hire car. The name on the contract is Marie Viviano. Does that sound familiar?"

"Viviano? No. I've never heard it before in my life."

Viviano. Michael rolled the name around in his mouth. Marie Viviano. Had that been her maiden name back then or was it something she'd adopted this time around?

Michael had just stepped out of the shower when he got another call from DS Rao, this time to report that they'd tracked Marie Viviano to The George Hotel in Wallingford, and that when he and two constables had knocked on her door and asked about the shooting, she'd gotten belligerent, spit in Rao's face, kicked one of the constables, and refused to talk to anyone but Michael Samaan. So, he'd dressed and headed to the police station, leaving Kat asleep in bed with a hastily written note on the bedside table.

Now, Michael was about to confront Marie, for the first time in…he didn't know how long. He couldn't remember how many times their lifelines had intersected, how many times she'd demanded that he end it all for her. He did know that this was the first time he had it in his power to do what she asked. He could end it. Forever. But this time, he would make sure he knew what she wanted. No more playing god.

He'd managed to convince Rao and his superior to let him talk to Marie alone. Of course, they would be observed through the one-way mirror of the interrogation room, but he didn't want anyone in the room with them and he didn't want any equipment recording their conversation. Now, Michael sat on the opposite side of a bare metal table in a cinderblock interrogation room and waited for a handcuffed Marie Viviano to say something.

After a long period spent simply staring at each other, Marie's expression went from cold condescension to unadulterated hatred. "God, every time I see you...." She shook her head and coughed out a contemptuous laugh.

"What were you looking for at my mothers' place?"

"What do you think?"

"How did you know about the books?"

"I don't care about any bloody books." She practically spat the words. "I care about my life sphere. That magical little talisman *you* made that keeps *me* coming back over and over again until I am fucking sick and tired of it."

"Do you remember any of it?" Michael suddenly needed to know. "What happened in Latakia?"

She snorted out a laugh. "I was nearly dead! Besides, why do you care?"

"I care."

"Oh, so you're a regular do-gooder, are you? Caring for the poor and downtrodden."

"You didn't look poor and downtrodden then and you don't look poor and downtrodden now. Your husband was obviously wealthy, and I hear you're now driving a Range Rover and staying at The George Hotel."

"So then, what? You want to assuage your guilt?"

Michael held his body still, tried to not let nerves and emotion get the best of him. "There's no chance of assuaging my guilt. I just want to know if you remember."

She let out a disgusted sigh. "Let's see, do I remember my power-hungry father and money-grubbing mother forcing me to marry a man I loathed, a man Marthe, my beloved twin who had never been quite right in the head, had been fucking for months?"

Twins. That's why Lionel Millhaven's mention of twin granddaughters had initially caught his attention.

Marie went on."A man whose child she was already carrying. Do I remember Marthe insisting that she accompany me on my first voyage with my new husband since I had a tendency to sea sickness and she could care for me? The answer is yes. I remember all of it. And I remember poor, strange little Miriam insisting she not be left behind."

Marie leaned forward, pinning Michael with her cold gaze. "I remember finding my twin and my husband in bed together the first night we left Venice. Not that I cared. They could fuck themselves silly as far as I was concerned. She shook her head in disgust.

"Once we arrived in Latakia, she asked me to take a walk with her. Said she knew I was unhappy. Said she had a solution that would make us both happy. So, we walked along the edge of the quay and she entertained me with some cock and bull story about sisterly togetherness and then I turned my head at the sound of footsteps just as my husband—her lover—bashed in my head. I fell to my knees, and he kicked me in the stomach. Rolled me into the water like the carcass of a dead animal. And Marthe just stood there and watched."

"Holy hell." Michael slumped back in his chair and stared at her.

She shrugged. "It was bound to happen. I was not what my father wanted. I fancied myself in love with the eldest daughter of my father's most hated rival. My powerful father couldn't have that, could he? So, he hurriedly married me to the son of one of his loyal retainers, the man my sister wanted. Nicolo Scarpa. So she plotted to get rid of me. And poor stupid Nicolo didn't want to be saddled with two bothersome sisters, especially since one of them was already carrying his heir, so he went along with her plan. It was, as they say today, a win-win all around. If it weren't for Miriam, they would never have been discovered." She huffed out a laugh. "My father was convinced Miriam was a demon spawn. Too intelligent to be his child, that's for sure."

Michael was appalled. Had she ever told him this story before? He knew it had been common for fathers to sell daughters to wealthy men and sons to the church or the army. But that didn't make it right. How was it that her whole family could be so malicious? He remembered the look on her husband's face. Dismissive. He remembered the impatience. The arrogance. The way he'd looked at Marie's sister—Marthe, nearly a carbon copy of Marie—with the knowledge that the two were bound together in a horrible crime. At least that's how Michael remembered it now. Even later, after it was done, it was difficult to articulate to himself what had truly happened. What he'd been forced to be a part of. That's what you get, Michael told himself now, for living in an opium-induced fog.

"I looked them up the first time I came back," Marie went on. "Died in a resurgence of the Black Death in 1362.

The whole lot of them. Even poor Miriam. And they're still dead. Except for my loving husband, who I keep having to track down and kill over and over again. It's getting boring, Michael. Too repetitive for words."

"You don't know how sorry I am."

"Doesn't matter how sorry you are now. What matters is what you did then. I could hear everything, you know. It happens sometimes. People are dying or appear to be in a coma, but they can hear. You could barely talk. Every word slurred into the next like your tongue had slipped on ice and tumbled down a hill. I wonder you could even hold the blade in your trembling fingers as you brought the knife down on my finger."

He choked back the bile as the memory washed over him. Stars filled his field of vision, his face went hot, sweat beaded on his skin. He wiped his sleeve over his face and sank back to lean against the cold wall of the interrogation room. He looked up through bleary eyes to see Marie Viviano staring at him, a smug look on her face.

Michael put his hands on the table and leaned over Marie. "I have your life sphere. I know where it is now."

"I didn't even know about the spheres until I'd already cycled through two lives. I kept ending up in fucking Aleppo, looking for something with no idea what it was. Just like your pal, Sergius. Sergei Badawi. He was the one who told me."

"I'll destroy it for you if that's what you truly want."

"Listen to yourself, you bloody bastard. '*I will destroy it for you if that's what you truly want*,'" she mimicked. "As if you still think you are God Almighty. Jesus, you make me ill. How many times have I asked this of you?" She watched his face and then barked out a laugh. "You don't even remember, do you?"

He picked up the chair and sat back down across from her. "No. I don't remember. I didn't always know where the spheres were."

Her face went red. Eyes bulged. "You couldn't keep track of them because they didn't fucking matter to you!" Her spittle flew across the table. "You and your lover weren't tied to them. All you had to do was keep your precious lodestone intact and you knew you'd find her again someday. But not us." She shook her head in disgust. "Think of all the times Sergei begged for your help. At one time or another, we've all demanded or threatened or begged for our life spheres, but you couldn't even be bothered to remember where you stashed them. You didn't want to remember because *oh woe is me I did a bad thing and it gives me bad dreams and so I'm just not going to fucking think about it!* Well guess what? We never had a choice. We. Never. Had. A. Choice."

"That's not—"

"Shut up! It's my turn now and you're going to sit there and listen to me."

He put his hands up in surrender.

"I've spent this lifetime trying to get your attention, to prove that I can reach you. I can hurt you just like you hurt me. Standing on the dock while you set sail for Orkney. Didn't make it far, did you? Learning to ski just so I could track you on the slopes. I particularly enjoyed watching Ski Patrol drag your ass down to the lodge. Slipping belladonna in your beer. Again, off to hospital you went. Even nudging your car off the road. Too bad it wasn't you in the driver's seat."

"You're fucking insane."

"Oh, you have no idea. You may think you've found a happily ever after, you and your American, but I can end it just like that." She held her hand up and snapped her fingers. "How'd you like to find her fingertip delivered to your doorstep?"

Michael leaned forward, face twisted in rage. "You touch her and you're dead."

"I've been dead, Michael. Your threat doesn't impress me."

Jumping to his feet, he jerked his chair around and gripped the back, as if poised to throw the damn thing against the wall. "I know what I did was horrific. Do you not think I've been haunted by those memories all these years? These lifetimes? But at least I did it for love."

She threw her head back and barked out a laugh. "For love? Is that what you tell yourself?"

"Your husband begged me. Your sister! I thought—" Even as Michael said the words, he knew it was a lie. He knew it had been a murder. He had been party to a murder, and he'd done exactly what the murderers asked. With no thought whatsoever for the victim.

"Give me a fucking break. If you ever loved anything, it was your own intoxicating power over the alchemy of resurrection."

"No." He heard himself protest, heard himself say the word. It wasn't true. It couldn't be. Or at least it wasn't true at the beginning. *It was about love.* It was about Yasmine. Then it was Cyrine and Sergei and then, only then did the spiral into the dark enslave him, only then did the magic take hold of his mind.

"So, here are my terms," she said. "You get me out of here. You do not press charges. We destroy my fucking life sphere—I want to see it done—and you do not go near me after it's done, or you and your precious family will—"

A surge of something ugly hit his bloodstream. Yes, he'd done an unspeakable thing then, but his father was dead now because of this woman and he wasn't coming back. Talk about playing god. Marie had killed his brilliant, curious, cricket-loving father in an act of revenge. She'd left his mother a widow, almost killed his friends by sabotaging their boat and leaving them bobbing about in the North Sea. Maybe he'd been a monster in the past, but she was the monster now.

"You dare threaten me? We're sitting in a police station. I could tell D.S. Rao about the hit and run that killed my father, have you arrested for murder."

"What good would that do you?" Marie scoffed. "There's no proof and they'd never be able to hold me. Besides, you were the one I was after, so it's really your fault."

"You may have been after me, but he's the one who's dead! No second chances for him." He leaned forward, the power of pure, undiluted fury coursing through him like a living flame. Fury and regret. For who he had been. For what he had done. For what he felt capable of doing in that moment. "So, you better bloody well leave my family alone. You better go far, far away and if you hurt anyone I care about, you will die a death a thousand times worse this time than you did the first time. And you won't be able to come back to haunt me."

"Oh, I'm so frightened. Will you have Badawi the Billionaire sic one of his security boys on me? You know I blasted 50,000 volts into the chest of the last one who got too close. If you bother me, I'll do worse next time, so when this is over, you better *all* stay the hell away from me."

"Believe me, no one wants to be near you. You say your sister was a demon spawn? I'd say she had some stiff competition. Sounds like it ran in the family."

She looked him in the eye. "You have no idea."

# FIFTY-ONE

It was another perfect day. A full week since they'd had the opportunity to be alone, Elias and Emmaline were up at dawn and before the air even had a chance to think about warming, they were nestled together before a crackling fire in the tiny, old woodsman's cottage Roland had told Elias about. A cottage, Elias suspected, Roland and Gerard had visited very recently, based on the wood left in the grate and the bundle of rumpled blankets left in a pile on the thin mattress pushed up against the wall.

Close to the river, the melodic sound of water flowing over rocks hummed in the distance. Sunlight filtered through a broken shutter as they lay together, just the two of them. Touching. Talking. Dreaming. Wondering what would come next for them when they told Emmaline's stepmother they wanted to marry. Wondering if her father would give her permission to marry a man from so far away, he might as well have been born on the moon. And wondering what they would do if permission was not granted. Hoping for acceptance, but making plans for what might come next if the worst was to happen.

They'd packed a breakfast of cheese and bread, but they hadn't opened the hamper yet. Food could come later. After.

Elias played with the laces on her gown, loosening them, his fingers yearning to touch her again. Emmaline trailed kisses down his neck, blowing little puffs of warm air against his skin. And then the sound of their horses, tethered outside, moving. Agitated. Trying to break free.

Elias was immediately on his feet, pulling a blade from his boot just as the door banged open and five men crowded into the small room.

"I believe you're outnumbered," one of the men said, stepping closer and looking around the room. "Nothing good will come of attempting to use that bit of steel, so I'd just slip it right back in your boot. Or hand it over to one of my companions.'

Elias stood his ground. "We're not carrying any money."

"Money would be a bonus, but that's not what I'm after. I've looked long and hard for you, Elias Samaan," the man said, nodding to one of his associates to move toward Emmaline. "Tracked you. Hunted you. You may not remember me, but I certainly remember you. I thought you were mad. I thought the rumors of your skills as an alchemist were overwrought and, quite frankly, ridiculous. They said you could heal people. Bring them back from the dead. Give them life eternal. Little Miriam spoke of the Alchemist of Aleppo as if he were Christ Jesus himself, wielding power over life and death. If I'd had one thought that any of what she said was true, I never would've allowed her to convince me to call for you. All I wanted was to put on a show so she would report back that I did everything I could to save my wife. If not for that life, but for the next. But I did not actually want my wife saved. Or, god forbid, tied me to her forever. After all, I was the one who wanted her dead in the first place."

"Who *are* you?" Elias demanded, trying to back up to protect Emmaline. On a nod, one man took Elias's knife while two others grabbed his arms and held tight. Elias jerked backward toward Emmaline only to see her yanked to her feet and clasped to the chest of one of the other two men.

"The woman was unnatural,' the obvious leader said, ignoring the question. He spoke in English with a heavy Italian accent, but Elias understood him perfectly. "My wife was *in love* with a woman. She spit in my face when I tried to kiss her the first time. Not that I wanted to kiss her. Her curst father had made a deal with my bastard of a father, and it was declared that we should marry lest I be disinherited. But I'd already been fucking her twin for months and had gotten her with child. Marthe. She was more than willing. But, damn their father. Marie was the one they offered up for marriage while Marthe was promised to the convent. Probably because Marthe was most likely insane like little Miriam. The world would've been better off if they were both kept in a locked room. For reasons I never understood, the old man would not budge even though I said I would take her. Marthe, not Marie. But Marie was for marriage even though marriage was the last thing she wanted, and Marthe was for the church, even though she was lusty as a whore in heat. Does any of this sound familiar?"

"Latakia." Elias whispered. He was white as a ghost. "Nicolo Scarpa."

"Ah, you *do* remember," Scarpa said, nodding to his companions. Two lengths of rope were produced and as his arms were yanked backward, almost pulling his shoulders out of their sockets, Elias noted that the men all stunk of onions and ale and sweat. "I thought it was all the delusional ravings of a mad man," Scarpa continued, as the men tied his elbows together behind his back, "but you really did it. You bound me in some diabolical way to that bitch I was forced to marry. She's dead, you know. I've killed her again," Nicolo sneered. "But this time around, she told me about the life spheres. Now, I've come for what belongs to me. You give me my life sphere or your lover dies."

"'I don't have it! They're not in England. I don't even know where they are." Elias winced as one of Scarpa's companions bound his hands, pushed him down into the one chair in the room, and then bent to tie his feet to the chair's legs.

Elias struggled to kick himself free even as the highwayman pulled the rope taut. He felt his arms being tethered to the back of the chair.

Nicolo stepped right in front of Emmaline, pressed the tip of his blade into the soft spot at the base of her throat. "I don't believe you," he snarled at Elias. "Such precious pieces, these magical spheres. The very souls of your victims. You'd have to be mad to not carry them with you always."

"I swear, I don't have them! I don't even know where they are."

"One more chance," Scarpa pressed the blade into Emmaline's throat.

"'I swear on all that is holy," Elias pleaded, his body struggling to break free of his bonds.

"Holy? There is nothing holy in this entire world," Scarpa spat the words. "If you don't have them with you, I'd wager you've got them hidden away at your workshop. I'm sure that brother of yours knows where they are. Or maybe his wife knows."

"I would tell you if I knew, but I swear I don't." Elias tried to keep his voice calm, placating. "I hid them away long ago so that they wouldn't haunt me anymore. And I don't know…I swear I don't remember. But when I go back, I'll look for them. I'll find them. I'll give you yours. I swear."

"You swear." Scarpa laughed. "For some reason, I have difficulty believing you. No, I don't think I'll wait for you. I'll take my pleasure here and then go back to Aleppo and have a talk with your brother."

And then, as Elias struggled and screamed and begged, and Emmaline cried out, biting and kicking and cursing, Scarpa sliced open the front of her gown and pulled it wide, revealing her breasts. He fumbled with the front of his breeches, yanked up her skirts, and then plowed into her, pushing the man holding her back up against the wall of the cottage. And then the others took turns as Elias wept and thrashed unable to look away and unable to do anything to save the woman he loved.

And when they were done, Scarpa slammed a meaty fist against the side of her head and laughed when she fell unconscious. Then, keeping an eye on Elias, he pressed the very tip of his blade into the soft skin below Emmaline's breastbone and pulled it slowly down her to her waist.

Then further. And watched with sick glee as blood seeped from the wound."

"She may live. She may not." Scarpa shrugged, getting to his feet. "It matters not. Either way, she's marked. Ruined. For you and for every other man. Her family will never let you near her again."

He sheathed his knife and wiped his hands on his shirt. "They may even hang you for the villain who did these despicable things to her. Such a lovely young thing. What a shame. If you want my advice and want to escape the hangman, I suggest you don't tarry here in the north." He strode to the door and then turned back one more time and looked Elias in the eye. "See you in Aleppo, my friend." And then he strode out the door, leaving it wide open to any creature that might be drawn by the scent of blood.

∞

Elias couldn't focus. His mind circled around and around and around until Roland finally sat down beside him and took his hands in his. Roland was talking, his voice low. Urgent. But Elias had no idea what his friend was saying or how long he'd been in that chair—*in that hell*—before Roland and Giles had found them. Useless. He'd been useless. Unable to protect her. Unable to look away.

"She's breathing!" Giles cried out. "It looks like she's lost a lot of blood, but I believe she may yet live." He gathered her up and wrapped her in blankets to take her back to Hartley.

Elias knew he was weeping. And in some distant part of his mind, he heard the words Roland was whispering to him, that things would not bode well for him if he was still around when Emmaline's father and brothers arrived. If Emmaline survived, Roland told him, he may still be hanged as a rapist and despoiler of the Musgrave name.

"I know you love her, my friend," Roland said, "and I can see that she loves you. But you can't remain here. I know you've been with her, and you have to think of her now. What if she's with child? Her father won't care if it's your child—a child conceived in love—or the child of her rapists. He will send her away as soon as possible. I'll do what I can to watch over her and will get word to you as to how she fares. But, my friend, as much as it pains me to say this, she is lost to you. You must go. And you must go now. Take my horse and leave before it's too late.

And so he'd run. With the sole purpose of his life now to escort Nicolo Scarpa into hell. Later, how many days later, he didn't know, he realized he'd left the lodestone behind. But what did it matter? Yasmine was dead. Emmaline was dead. Or soon would be. Even if she lived, she was lost to him forever. He would be dead soon too. But not before he found Scarpa.

Finally, weeks later, Elias did find him. In Aleppo. At the glassworks. The man was holding a knife to his brother's throat, demanding the Alchemist's spheres. Elias crept up behind him, pulled him off his brother, dragged him out to the street and, in front of shocked neighbors, shopkeepers, and merchants, he gutted the man for a thief and left his body for the dogs.

Before he could even clean the blood from his blade, Boutros told Elias about Sergius, the Sipahi cavalryman who had come blustering about looking for him. Had he been a friend? Boutros wanted to know. Elias couldn't answer. A friend, yes. And something more.

Sergius been found dead, Boutros was sorry to have to tell him, with the back of his head sprayed against the wall of a tiny room with a window overlooking the Citadel.

"Then all is lost," Elias whispered. He handed his filthy blade to his brother and walked away.

After asking in the souk, Elias found the same room Sergius had occupied. He sat for hours in the same chair Sergius had sat in. He stared out the same window, watching people come and go up and down the ramp to the Citadel's gate. There was nothing left for him but to hasten the coming of his next lifeline. Another chance at another chance. So, as dusk fell, Elias wept as he picked up his own Wheellock pistol, a gift from Roland, placed it in his mouth, and followed Sergius into the dark.

# FIFTY-TWO

The next day, Michael, Kat, Sergei, and Marie Viviano stood before the open door of the 400-pound Hub furnace, mesmerized by the glow and the heat and the promise of annihilation. It had taken Sergei one call to the owner of Skylark Glass Studio to arrange to rent the studio for the afternoon. Located just off London's Bermondsey Street, a fashionable area full of shops, galleries and restaurants, they'd all agreed to meet at Skylark at noon. But now, faced with the magnitude of what Marie wanted to do, none of them seemed able to take the next step.

The plan was for Michael to reverse engineer the creation of Marie's sphere using the instructions the Alchemist had written in his little book all those lifetimes ago. Instead, they all just stood there, as if held captive in a trance, each lost in their own thoughts of what it would be like if none of this had ever happened. Each wondering what it would mean to undo everything and to know that the next time death came calling, it would be for good.

It was what Marie wanted. But what about the others, the other lovers the Alchemist had bound together? Now and forever. What were their stories? How many of them would want forever to end?

Michael had been reluctant to have Kat come along—he didn't want her anywhere near Marie—but she'd insisted, claiming it was all her fault to begin with. They'd argued after he'd returned from the police station. Their first real fight. Michael had found Kat sitting in his bedroom holding the drawing of Emmaline and Elias, staring at it with an unreadable expression on her face. He'd pulled her into his arms and held her close, and then he'd described his meeting with Marie. Kat listened, but she could tell he was holding back. She hated that she had to push and push until he finally admitted that Marie had threatened her. Had threatened his whole family.

"You cannot protect me by hiding things from me!" she'd said, frustrated at his refusal to come clean on the ugliness of the confrontation. Still frustrated that he hadn't yet explained what had really gone on between him and Sergei over all those years, lifetimes. She'd bet big money on the fact that it was more than just a long-time friendship. There was something more there. He was keeping her at arm's length, and it was pissing her off.

Michael clasped his hands behind his neck and stared at her. "Last night, I told you everything I remembered about when Marie died, when I performed the ritual and made her life sphere. I was party to a murder, Kat," he said in frustration. "You have no idea how sitting across from her made me feel. How sickened I am by the whole thing. By the idea of peeling flesh off bone. Of grinding bone to powder. Of mixing and chanting, of losing myself in the ritual and calling on the darkest forces to—"

"And you have no idea how sickened I am that it was Yasmine who pushed the Alchemist to do all this in the first place!"

"Jesus, Kat. No! We've been over this. I was already playing with spells and magic and alchemy. I was the one with the arrogance to think I could control the forces of life and death!"

"And I was the one who was too selfish to face the prospect of losing you once I'd finally had a taste of happiness! I was the one who didn't want to let go. I was the one afraid to die. The one who wanted forever."

"I was the one who promised too much, who went too far."

They'd gone round and round, each attempting to shoulder the blame for the beautiful and terrifying and unspeakable things they'd set in motion lifetimes ago until Carys interrupted them with a loud rap on Michael's bedroom door.

"You're spoiling teatime," Carys said through the door.

Michael had yanked the door open and glared down at his mother.

"Talk about arguing over spilt milk," Carys said, addressing both her son and Kat. "Solicited or not, here are my motherly words of wisdom: you both are to blame. Arrogance, desperation, love, whatever you want to call it. What the two of you unleashed six hundred years ago has had untold consequences on countless lives. Now, you need to stop all the self-flagellation, wearing of hairshirts, and acting like martyrs and start dealing with it in the here and now. You need to stop arguing about who is to blame for what happened in the past and decide what you are going to do with the time you have together now. In this lifetime."

And Kat suddenly realized that Carys was right. That her whole life she'd been grappling with this haunting sense that somehow, in the dark recesses of the past, she'd set things in motion she couldn't control. That things had spiraled away from her and that she hadn't been there to do anything about it.

She now knew that as Yasmine, she'd left Micah to carry out a selfish deathbed request and had ruined his life—and the lives of so many others. Repeatedly. *For six hundred years.* All her life she'd been afraid that time and tide could roll in at any moment and sweep her off her feet again, leaving others to deal with the consequences of her actions. So, she'd held herself close, kept far away from the edge, refused to give more of herself—or ask more of anyone else—than she thought she deserved. It had been a sort of punishment, and she was through with it. And she knew, with a cellular certainty, that turning away from Michael now, worrying about his relationship with Sergei, wondering who the other pairs of lovers were and what secrets Michael still held in his heart or kept locked away in his mind was not the answer. Embracing this, this miracle of science or magic or whatever, was the answer. They could keep discovering each other, keep exploring the nature and resonance of their connection, maybe someday make that trip up to Carlisle and visit the ruins of Hartley Castle. But she couldn't turn away. They were in this together.

And so, together, they had dealt with it. Michael asked Sergei to make the arrangements, and Kat asked to look over the Alchemist's notations with him. After all, she was a scientist. She understood about lab notes. Together, they would figure out how to go forward.

Now the four of them—Michael, Kat, Sergei, and Marie Scarpa or Viviano or whatever name she claimed—stood staring at the open furnace like lost children fascinated but afraid of the dark. The enormity of what they were about to do, weighing on each of them.

"What now?" Marie said finally.

Michael cleared his throat. "So, it turns out, there's really not much to it. The hard part is making the damn things. Unmaking them is," he raked both hands down his face, "as easy as Frodo throwing the ring into the fires of Mount Doom."

"Frodo didn't do it in the end," Sergei said. "Gollum did."

Marie snorted in disgust. "You two." She cast a dark glance at Kat. "They'll be your problem from now on. I can't wait to be rid of them."

Michael raised an eyebrow at her. "Then why don't you go ahead and do the honors."

"Me?" She turned to him. "You want me to throw it in?"

"I told you. I'm done playing god."

"More like you fancy yourself Frodo while I'm cast as Gollum." She turned and looked Badawi up and down. "I guess that makes you Samwise Gamgee, loyal sidekick." She turned to Kat. "I'm afraid you don't feature in this story."

Kat didn't rise to the bait, but Michael said, "Okay, Gollum, are you going to do it or not?"

Marie stared at him a long moment, and then shrugged.

"Remember," Michael said. "You end it for yourself, you're ending it for Scarpa too."

She rolled her eyes. "Jesus Fucking Christ. That's precisely the point."

Michael walked over to the work bench on which he'd set a ZERO Halliburton Special Edition briefcase. He entered the combination and opened it to reveal the smaller metal box holding the even smaller engraved wooden box. Boxes within boxes. Lives within lives. Nesting dolls, he thought absently. Maybe their current selves were merely the largest nesting doll, hiding the secrets of all their past incarnations. He wondered what Kat would say to his genius nesting doll theory of genetics.

He opened the wooden box, set aside the book, to which he'd now grown accustomed after having poured over it with Kat late into the night, and revealed the two rows of small spheres. One indentation was empty. That life sphere belonged to Sergei now and Michael knew he had it locked away in a safe at his home on the other side of London.

"Look at all of them," Marie said, awe and disgust lacing her voice. "Look at what you did."

"We don't need to revisit what a despicable human being I was. Then or now," Michael said with a wave of his hand. "It's old news. If you want to do this, do it, and let us get on with our lives."

"Fine." Marie reached out and grabbed the last sphere Micah, the Alchemist of Aleppo, ever made and held it in her hand. The roiling storm of colors clouded the surface and then the swirls turned even darker and darker, shadows moving across the sphere until the whole orb was black as night and emitting a low hum in her hand.

"Fascinating," Sergei said. "Mine didn't do that."

"Yours was made from love, compassion, and desire," Michael said, his voice rough with emotion. "Hers was made from malice and murder."

Ignoring them both, Marie held the dark orb in her palm for a long moment, then turned, strode to the furnace and threw it in so hard it *clanged* against the back of the crucible. "There. Done."

Kat stared at Marie. "Do you feel any different?"

Marie pinned her with a dark look. "I feel free." Then she turned, wound her way around worktables and display shelves, yanked open the door, and disappeared down the street.

∞

"What are you waiting for?" Sergei glanced from Michael's face to where his fingertips rested lightly on the Alchemist's book of instructions.

Michael looked up as if startled awake. "I don't know if I can. I know I should, but—"

Sergei studied Michael's face. "It's dangerous having an instruction manual for resurrection and reincarnation floating around in the twenty-first century. There are too many unscrupulous people who could do worlds of damage if they knew such a thing existed."

Michael shook his head. "More dangerous than in the fourteenth century? You were the soldier. You've been a diplomat. A spy. You know better than anyone that the world has always been full to the brim of unscrupulous people. Besides, it'll hardly floating around. It'll be locked up in our safe."

Sergei glanced back toward the door. Marie was gone and Sergei, for one, hoped he never saw hide nor hair of her again, but there was the issue of her vile, totally repellent husband. Eventually Marie would die, and she would take Nicolo Scarpa with her, whether by her own hand, by another's, or by the natural process of aging. And that would be that. And Sergei and Michael and Kat and everyone else whose hopes and dreams were encapsulated in the remaining life spheres would go on living and dying and loving and losing and suffering loneliness and heartbreak for as long as the magic held. And no one knew how long that would be.

Sergei stifled a shudder. But until that time, Nicolo Scarpa was a wild card. He watched the emotions on Michael's face, his hand still touching the Alchemist's book. If Michael destroyed it, if he tossed it into the open mouth of the furnace like Marie had tossed in her sphere, no one else would be able to wreak such havoc on so many lives with such powerful alchemy. And that would be a good thing.

*But still…how could one destroy such knowledge?* What if, someday, some scientist discovered how to control the process? What if a geneticist like Kat Musgrave learned how to help people live longer, healthier lives, or somehow use it to cure disease? *What if, what if, what if?*

No. Sergei could not see Michael destroying the book. Even when Michael told him he was taking it to Skylark to do just that, he didn't believe him. Watching Michael now, he knew he'd been right.

"Michael." Kat touched a hand to his forearm. "You said destroying it was the right thing to do. Have you changed your mind?"

"Not necessarily."

"Then what?"

Michael let out a long sigh. "It probably *is* the right thing to do, but I can't bring myself to do it. Not today."

"Will you ever be able to do it?" Kat's face was etched with concern.

"I have no idea." Michael looked at his two lovers—one who had captured his imagination and his heart and one who had become his closest friend and confidant—and gave them both a faint smile. "Maybe, eventually, one of you will have to do it for me."

Sergei and Kat exchanged a glance. "Well, if we're done here," Sergei said, gently closing the lid on the wooden box. "Let's go home. We've got plans to make."

# FIFTY-THREE

"Quit fidgeting." Kat cut Sergei a glance. "For god's sake, you're worse that my nieces and nephews on Christmas morning."

It'd been over two weeks since Kat watched Sergei's helicopter land in Carys's backyard and the complicated nature of his relationship with Michael had been revealed. She was still coming to terms with their past and was, she had to admit, at least a bit jealous of their time together over the centuries even though it had been fraught with heartache. She wondered if she would ever know the full extent of their relationship and what had happened after Yasmine had died. After Emmaline had been attacked.

The past had not been kind to any of them, yet here they were. Together for the first time in hundreds of years, and she knew this gift of time was precious. She was determined to make it count, and if that meant accepting the past for what it was and embracing the present for all it could offer, she was determined to give it her all.

And that's why she was at the V&A with Sergei, hovering about the gallery where the Luck of Edenhall was so beautifully displayed. For the past two days, all of Sergei's restless energy and attention had been focused on what to do when Dr. Celeste Simpson of Toronto, Canada, by way of the Corning Museum of Glass, returned to her fellowship at the V&A.

Through his contacts at the museum, Sergei had discovered that Celeste had spent nearly a month back in Canada dealing with the aftermath of her father's death, moving her mother into a nursing home, and putting the house she'd grown up in on the market. He'd also learned that Celeste's first day back at the museum would be today. Sergei had been a wreck ever since. The man was forty years old, had made and lost several fortunes over several lifetimes, had been a soldier, a diplomat, and a spy, and was as worked up as a teenager gathering the nerve to ask for a first date.

Kat found it delightfully hilarious. She relished reminding him of how intimidated—and angry—she'd been the night he'd crashed the dinner party at Hempstead House and proceeded to badger Michael in an effort to get him to remember their past. Now she was helping to orchestrate a meeting to see if Celeste Simpson was the woman Sergei thought she was. Sergius's wife. Cyrene. And to discover whether or not the woman remembered the past.

Kat had been appalled when Sergei told her he'd had Celeste's flight tracked from Toronto to London. Had Lindhurst follow her cab from Heathrow to her rented flat. Had someone watching her place 24/7. Just to make sure she was safe. "Stop being a creepy stalker!" Kat had protested only to have Sergei gape at her.

"But what if something happens to her and no one's there to help? What if there's an accident? What if she's hurt? What if—"

"She's a grown woman who has obviously done fine without you so far," Kat shot back. Abject fear had painted his features then, and Kat suddenly realized what he was truly afraid of.

"But what if something hapens and I have to wait another six hundred years?"

Kat didn't have an answer to that.

∞

Sergei still wasn't sure if Celeste Simpson was his Cyrine. No, he was sure. Or, at least, he was pretty sure.

That was what he told himself at two in the morning. At three. At four. And while he was swimming laps and running on the treadmill and eating breakfast and doing every single other thing a man did to stay alive. Memories of Cyrene and speculation about Celeste occupied all his thoughts, and in some self-deluded corner of his mind, he fancied that he occupied hers too. But, he scolded himself, how could he imagine such a ludicrous thing when he'd never even seen her in real life? Never talked to her. Never heard her voice or watched the way she moved across a room. *Bloody hell, he was driving himself crazy.*

So, while Michael was giving a presentation on the books to Liz Bridewell's staff in some conference room upstairs, Kat and George and Leila, who came to finally see the Luck for themselves, were staking out the gallery with him. If Celeste was who Sergei thought she was, she was sure to make her way down to the gallery on her first day back. She would be drawn to the Luck just as he had been. Just as Michael and Kat had been.

Only instead of dressing in one of his bespoke Saville Row suits, Sergei was wearing jeans, one of Michael's old Cambridge sweatshirts, the running shoes he never wore outside his personal gym, a ratty old baseball hat Carson had loaned him, and a pair of oversized but very weak reading glasses Carson had picked up at the chemist. And he hadn't shaved in three days.

"Remind me why I'm dressed like this," he groused. "And why I need an audience for what very well may be my complete humiliation."

"You were the one who said you wanted to get a look at her without her knowing," George said with a laugh. "How else did you propose to do that without her recognizing you? Lie in wait outside the museum's offices to see if she'd come out for lunch and then dive for cover?"

"Of course not, but still...." He blew out a breath. "I feel ridiculous. Besides, she's Canadian, so she might not even know who I am."

Leila eyed him up and down. "That's like saying she might not know what Jeff Bezos or Elon Musk looks like. Besides, despite the silly glasses, I think you look rather handsome. Casual. Approachable. Not at all like some snooty billionaire."

Sergei arched a brow. "Have I ever been 'snooty' to you?"

George gave her a gentle elbow poke in the ribs. "Careful darling, or he might not support your next art project. Rich benefactors are few and far between."

"You're the only rich benefactor I need." She touched a fingertip to the end of George's nose.

"Oh?" Sergei said on a laugh. "I'll have my accountant tear up that check."

Leila rolled her eyes. "I don't even have a new project in the works, so there."

Sergei gave here a teasing look. "What about orchestrating a grand wedding to your future earl."

"Turns out that between our two mothers, I'm not orchestrating much at all."

"Hush!" Kat hissed. "Someone's coming."

While Leila and George separated, each putting on a good show of browsing the gallery alone, Kat hurriedly took her place at Sergei's side and dragged him into position so he could see the Luck without appearing to be staring at it. She looped her arm through his and pointed at some random object as though they might be any ordinary couple enjoying a leisurely afternoon at the museum.

Behind Kat, Sergei could see a woman descending the stairs. Could *feel* her approach. She wore low-slung heels, trim slate-grey slacks, and…he waited, not breathing while she made her way down the steps… a white flowing button-down blouse topped by a knee-length grey sweater. Understated. Comfortable. Professional. Then she began to weave her way toward the Luck. Her face was shaped like a heart, high cheekbones tapering to a delicate jawline and featuring a perfect rose petal of a mouth. Her hair, Sergei realized, was the color of maple syrup. *Did he think that because she was Canadian or because he wanted to know if it would pour through his fingers with slow, sugary sweetness?* It was cut short in a bob that was longer in the front and swung like sheets of silk as she walked. *So that's how she moves through a room.* Now he knew.

Sergei's heart hammered against his ribs like a battering ram. "Don't stare!" Kat whispered and nudged him toward the next set of objects in the case they were supposedly admiring. Sergei's feet moved but his eyes were fixed on Celeste Simpson.

Celeste stopped and looked up. Her gaze snagged on the intensity in Sergei's dark eyes. Kat squeezed his arm and brought his attention back to her. "Don't freak her out. Remember, I ran out of here like a dazed lunatic when I first saw Michael."

"Shh," Sergei hissed and glared at her. Then, out of the corner of his eye, he saw the quirk of a smile on Celeste's face as she moved forward, stopping at the Luck's case. She stood for a moment, staring down at the beautiful glass piece that so obviously captured her attention, and then she looked up again and found Sergei's eyes on her. And that's when she really smiled, her whole face lighting up as if some stage director had flipped the switch on a beam of light designed to illuminate her and only her.

He was done for. He extracted Kat's arm from his and strolled as casually as possible directly toward Celeste. "It's a beautiful piece, isn't it?"

Her voice was like the smoothest whisky, like peat and moss and air and sky and rain and life and he nearly swooned and then laughed inwardly at himself even as he wondered if he'd survive the moment with all his faculties intact. All the pent-up emotions of the past six hundred years seemed to want to crowd into the same space in his heart and he was suddenly frighteningly angry at the fragility of life, thinking that if he'd died right then and there, he'd have to start all over again and he might never find her again and it would kill him and the cycle of heartbreak and loss and loneliness would just go on and on and on.

"For some reason," she continued, "I'm drawn to it."

Sergei nodded, trying to look casually interested in the Luck. Over the centuries that he'd lived and died, he'd met some of the most powerful figures in history. But now, he felt completely out of his depth. He thought of his Cyrine and how she'd taken ownership of his heart, control of his household, and had been every bit as decisive and determined as the most renowned generals and kings and politicians he'd ever known.

"I'm doing a six-month fellowship here," she went on, since he was apparently unable to form words. "I've always loved glass, old glass, especially. But really, I came for this." She shrugged. "It's so beautiful and its history is so delightful and mysterious that ever since I learned of its existence, I've wanted to know the real story of how it was made and how it arrived here, in England. The story *behind* the story. You know what I mean?" She pinned him with a look that penetrated down to his marrow and made every fine hair on his body stand at attention. "What about you? And your friend? Are you fans of the Luck of Edenhall?"

He wondered if he'd ever be able to make his vocal chords work again. He swallowed, started to say something. Nothing came out. He wet his lips and tried again. "My friend," he managed at last, turning toward Kat only to realize that she, along with George and Leila, were making their way to the steps and that now he and

Celeste Simpson were alone. He swallowed again and when he spoke his voice was rough.

"As a matter of fact, my friend's partner is upstairs giving a presentation that has to do with the Luck. He's discovered who made it, you see. Part of a family legacy. Ancient records discovered from a glassmaker in Aleppo, Syria. A man who claimed to be an alchemist."

She held his gaze as her head tipped back ever so slightly and then down again in a slow-motion nod that spoke volumes. "An alchemist from Aleppo. Well, that *is* an exciting discovery. I trust he'll be presenting the information to all of us soon. I'd die a thousand deaths to know the details of that story."

Her tongue darted out to wet her bottom lip and then her teeth followed suit, scraping over the rosebud swell and Sergei felt the blood in his head rush straight to his groin. And God Almighty, when was the last time that had happened? Yes, he'd just turned forty, but lately he'd felt like he was twice that. Now, he felt like he was fourteen and getting his first glimpse of a woman's breasts. And he was certain, finally—*finally!*—that he'd found her, his fiery little volcano of a wife. And that, in a twist of fate, she'd found him.

He'd briefly considered bringing the life sphere with him today, but at the last moment he'd decided it was too risky. He kept it locked in a secret safe in his home office, and now was immensely thankful he'd not brought it, that the pull of its power hadn't affected him—or her. Instead, they simply looked at each other and knew.

"Since your friends appear to have abandoned you," Celeste said, that deliciously sultry voice wrapping around him, "I wondered if you'd care to have a cup of tea with me. In the café?"

"I'd love nothing more, but…" He knew if he went into the café or even past the information desk, that someone would recognize him, would say his name and greet him with deference. Sporting a scruffy beard and wearing glasses and a baseball hat wouldn't fool the people upstairs who knew him as a wealthy benefactor, always impeccably dressed. "I'm afraid I have something rather embarrassing to confess." He pulled the baseball cap off and raked his fingers through his hair. Then he took off the inane reading glasses and stuck them in a pocket. "You see, I'm a bit underdressed and out of sorts, and I would hate for you to be surprised by—"

She stepped forward, eyes blazing with intent. "I don't care about how you're dressed, if you're clean-shaven or wearing a full beard, if you're sporting a turban, a tricorn, or a top hat. I know who you are."

A stab of painful self-doubt sliced through him. Did she know about his money? His gifts to the V&A? Was that what all this was about? Had he been mistaken after all? "You do?"

"I do. I also know that once upon a time you had a diminutive wife who barely came up to your shoulder but who was full of spit and fire and who refused to give up on the lifetime of love she'd been promised. Don't ask me how I know this because that's the one thing I don't know. But," she reached up to smooth the thick hair he had just mussed, "I do know that she has waited a lifetime—life*times*—for that promise to be fulfilled."

"She has?"

"And she's tired of waiting."

"She is? Do you…? Are you sure…? That you…?" Holy hell, he'd forgotten how to speak in complete sentences.

"Yes, yes, yes and yes."

"But I thought, I don't know…"

He let out a strangled moan and wiped a hand down his face, unable to control the feelings slamming into him from every direction, overwhelming him, threatening to choke him. He had a sudden vision of Michael smirking and rolling his eyes at his inability to form coherent thoughts and then how he would reach out and pull him close and hold him tight, reveling in the unbridled joy of this moment right along with him.

"I thought I'd have to prove it to you. That you wouldn't remember the way I've remembered. That I'd never find you."

"Ah, well. It seems I've been cursed—or blessed as the case may be—with a very good memory. Remarkable, really. So, let's just say, the Luck of Edenhall brought us together and that this time, finally, we found each other."

"What happened, Cyrine? Celeste. After I was gone. I need to know. Were you safe? What about our son?" It was the question that had plagued him for lifetimes, what had her life been like after he was gone.

"Did Micah never tell you?"

"Micah or Michael?" His brows drew together, puzzled.

"Either, both."

Now Sergei looked confused. "No."

She bit her lip, looked away for a moment, and then turned back to him, and taking his hands in hers, she led him to the bench behind the display case where they sat together, side by side.

"We survived your dreadful brother. For a time. After you were gone, he came to lay claim to everything you owned. Including me. Like Penelope waiting for Odysseus's return, I delayed and delayed and delayed all the while our son grew into a bright, adorable little boy. Chubby as a pasha. Black eyed and mischievous. But one day, your brother decided I'd mourned long enough and he…he tried…"

"God, did he…?"

She shook her head. "I knew the day was coming and prepared for it. I took Lukas and we fled. We went to Micah. He was not well, but he was…better. It was after Marie and Nicolo Scarpa and—"

"Wait. You know about them?"

"Yes." Her voice was low. Reassuring. "Micah was just coming back to himself. He took the life spheres deep into the tunnels beneath the citadel and hid them. With his little book. Somewhere no one would find them, he said, so no one could ever be tempted to do what he did. I asked him why he didn't destroy the whole lot, but he said he'd promised Yasmine, and he couldn't betray her. And that he didn't want to betray you or have your last wishes made in vain."

She held his hands tight in hers. "Sergius, there is something you must know about that time. I went to Micah and he took us in. It was Micah who raised your son along with Yasmine's daughter. We married and he cared for us, protected us with his name and his honor."

A blinding surge of almost incapacitating jealousy and betrayal sliced through him followed by a breathtaking wave of relief and gratitude. Sergei raked both hands through his hair and gripped his skull as if his fingers were staples holding it together by sheer force. He looked up into her eyes. "He should have told me."

"Don't be angry at him. I made him swear not to say anything because it was *my* place to tell you if we ever met again. And, besides, he may not even remember. He was never really quite right after all he'd done. Remember also that he was obsessed with Yasmine. It was always Yasmine for him. Just as it was always Sergius for me."

"But all these lifetimes of worry about what happened to you and Lukas. I needed to know. Holy hell, it was the not knowing that's driven me mad."

He took a ragged breath and shook his head as if trying to shake the facts into place. Did knowing he and Michael had been lovers make Kat as crazy as the revelation that Micah and Cyrine had been lovers made him? The thought of Micah making love to his wife—*Dammit, he was being childish and stupid.* He and Michael had turned to each other for solace and comfort and Micah and Cyrine had done the same. Emotional closeness and physical release were human needs. He had to let the jealousy go.

"But knowing he protected you and gave you and Lukas a home," he said. "I don't think I can never thank him enough for that."

"I owed him too," Celeste said. "I was the one who pushed him down the path toward madness. On her death bed, Yasmine made him promise to use his gift, but he never intended to do it. He said it was a blasphemy to use the gift he made for her for anyone else. But when you lay dying, I pushed and pushed and after you were gone and he was broken, I knew it was my fault. I owed him. We helped each other survive. Nothing more."

Sergei scoffed at that. "Nothing more. You were a beautiful woman with an indomitable spirit. It's impossible to believe he felt nothing for you."

She smiled at that. "And you? Have you been celibate all these lifetimes? Have you never cared for anyone else?"

Sergei thought of all the women he'd known, of all the times he'd taken comfort in other arms, in Michael's arms. He shook his head and held her gaze. "No. I'm not a saint and I was not celibate, but I never loved anyone like I loved you."

"Then you know. Micah and I came to care for one another because we needed each other and because we had hope for the future. That he would find Yasmine and I would find you. We cared for Yasmine's daughter. We raised our Lukas. *Your* Lukas. Our son became a Samaan and we told him everything." For the first time, her voice faltered. "Lukas loved both his fathers. The one who brought him into the world and the one who protected him in it."

Sergei swallowed hard. "All these years. All these lifetimes. All the things Michael and I shared…I never dreamed we shared you and our son." He dragged a sleeve across his face. "And now, I have our life sphere in my keeping. Michael gave it to me."

"I'm glad," she said, wiping away a tear with her thumb and touching a fingertip to his lips. "But I didn't need it to know you. To *feel* you in here." She pressed a fist to her heart. "I came to the V&A for the Luck and for you. I've been waiting to know you. And, yes, I want to know everything about who you are today, and I want to know about your past as I'm sure you want to know about mine, but for now, we've both done enough weeping. We have time to share our stories. We have time to live and love. Fully. Finally. After all, what was it the Alchemist of Aleppo said?"

Once more, Sergei swiped a sleeve across his face and then he cupped her chin and gazed into his past, his present, and his hope for the future. "Time is ephemeral. Only love is everlasting."

# FIFTY-FOUR

A press release announcing that a young art history lecturer from a local university had discovered among his family's papers the name of the fourteenth century artisan who had crafted the much-loved Luck of Edenhall was issued by the museum a month after Michael's negotiations with the V&A were finalized. The fact that philanthropist Sergei Badawi was underwriting the curation and conservation of the Samaan Glassworks Collection and that it would be available for study ignited new interest in glassmaking, old books, and the history of Middle Eastern practices of accountancy and commerce. A gala event unveiling the collection would be scheduled for the fall and was sure to be the premier event on London's social calendar. Especially since the sister of said art history lecturer was soon to be wed to Viscount Hempstead, himself a lecturer and somewhat of an expert in old books.

Michael, Kat, Sergei and Celeste debated whether or not to issue a second release, one from the Badawi

Foundation itself. It wasn't that they argued about it, per se, but that they couldn't decide how to describe what they were up to. How do you announce the formation of a new institute to study an ancient alchemical text that held the key to resurrection and reincarnation? Michael didn't even know what his old scribblings meant anymore. Like any good alchemist worth his saltpetre, he'd written in code and drawn cryptic illustrations that could mean any number of things.

"I may have been an alchemist in that lifetime," he said, "but I'm a simple art historian in this one. I'm not even sure I want to remember everything even if I could."

"Then why not destroy it?" Celeste had asked, already knowing it was a question Michael, Kat, and Sergei had discussed repeatedly.

"Because I can't," Michael answered, repeatedly.

Sergei had nodded in agreement, and Kat remembered that before disappearing, Marie had warned her that Michael and Sergei were 'her problem now.'"

"Then why not try to remember what it all means?" Celeste had asked. Repeatedly.

"Because I'm afraid to," Michael answered, repeatedly.

Sergei had nodded in agreement at that too, and Kat and Celeste—Yasmine and Cyrine—agreed they had their hands full with these two men whose shared history made them a formidable pair.

But the more the four of them talked, the more they were determined to at least try to leverage their experiences for good, and, besides, the idea of destroying knowledge was anathema to all of them. Perhaps they could leave a legacy of new knowledge and discoveries for the future. Something they could all build together. Believe in together. That's why Sergei decided to throw his money and support behind a new scientific institute dedicated to the study of any of the myriad outlandish ideas that might come from thinking too long and too hard about what they'd all been through.

And Kat had agreed to help. While Michael could go back to writing his book on the history of Samaan Glassworks and Middle Eastern glassmaking and Celeste could work with him on studying the evolution of the craft and how that applied to her own interests in religion and ritual, Sergei and Kat would run the institute.

And they would all wait to see who, if anyone, came forward looking for the Luck and seeking a long-lost love. After all, there were four more spheres sitting in their tufted, velvet beds waiting to be claimed.

In the meantime, as George and Leila and Carys— often, interestingly enough, accompanied by Dr. James Tully—got caught up in wedding plans, Kat took Michael home to Tucson to meet her family.

After an evening of Bea and Isabella cornering Michael on the couch and foisting family photo albums on him, gleefully pointing out the most embarrassing pictures of Kat they could find, they enjoyed a dinner of guacamole-topped enchiladas, refried beans, and Spanish rice along with prickly pear margaritas and locally brewed beer.

Finally, as Bea took herself off to bed and Kat went with Isabella to tuck in and read stories to the kids, Craig and Michael settled around a firepit in the backyard of the tidy Musgrave ranch. And beneath a dark sky studded with brilliant stars and with the chirping of crickets and the occasional hoot from nearby owls as background music, Craig apologized for his wife and mother pouncing on him like hungry hyenas.

"It's quite all right," Michael said with a low laugh. "Kat warned me."

Craig offered Michael another beer from the cooler nearby. "I hear you ride."

"Competed for a while. Jumping. I was sort of a crazy man for a time. Rugby. Rowing. Skiing. Sailing."

"An adventurous risk taker or a man with a death wish?" Craig asked.

"Kat warned me about you too," Michael said with a laugh. He pitched his voice a bit higher. "My brother doesn't say much, but he sees everything."

Craig laughed and held his bottle up to clink Michael's in a toast. "Just sayin' this is all very unusual behavior for Kat. Goes to London for a conference and comes home a month later with a man who looks at her like she's the key to…well, everything. Gives a big brother reason to wonder what exactly happened in London."

"A lot happened in London," was all Michael would say. "And she *is* the key, your sister. She's the key to my happiness, at least."

Craig smiled at that. "So forthcoming."

"I have a sister too, you know," Michael said.

"So I hear. Marrying a viscount or somesuch."

"Marrying a good man who loves her."

Craig nodded at that. "We've got trails on the ranch, cut up into the hills. Kat and I can take you out first thing tomorrow. Give you a little taste of what the Sonoran Desert looks like from the back of a horse."

Michael smiled, imaging riding behind Kat, watching her body sway in the saddle. "That'd be great."

"We've got to get on the trail early, so we can get back before it gets too hot."

"Up with the dawn. I'm fine with that. Kat promised me some proper sightseeing too. And I want to see her lab at the university."

"Her boss is gonna be sorry to see her go," Craig said, his voice even. "Seems like a risky move, Kat taking a job at a brand new institute run by some fancy billionaire investor. Totally unlike her."

Michael leaned his head back to look at the stars. He heard the *swoosh* of the sliding glass door opening. Footsteps and muffled laughter. Kat and Isabella's voices coming closer.

"Look," Michael said, "you obviously love your sister. And you know what she's been through. The dreams and the therapists and the worries about her—well, let's not be coy here—about her sanity." He took a swig of his beer and turned to look at Kat's brother.

"Let me tell you this one thing: Katherine Musgrave is fine. Better than fine. For the first time in her life, she knows exactly who she is and what she's about. Someday she may tell you what happened in London, but in the meantime, just know that going back to the UK, starting up the Badawi Institute, and being with me—*marrying me*, someday soon, hopefully—is her choice. It might not be something she'd have done in the past, but it's most definitely the right choice for her now."

A hand came down on Michael's shoulder and squeezed as Kat walked around to slip into the chair beside him.

"Craig and Isabella, "Kat said, "I know this has been a shock to the system and that you all have been worried about me. Believe me, *I've* been worried about me." She laughed softly and reached out to take Michael's hand in hers.

"Over the past month, I've worried more about losing control and getting swept away than I ever have before, even in my darkest days. But you know what? I *am* in control now. I *do* know, finally, who I am. And those things about myself that I'm still not sure of"—she felt the echoing thrum of the silvery birthmark on her abdomen—"I can work through. But right now, you need to know that the choices I'm making are the right ones." She smiled at Michael. "They feel like destiny."

He held her gaze and quirked a smile. "Almost like they were foreordained."

∞ THE END ∞

Remember...

*Time is ephemeral. Only love is everlasting.*

# AUTHOR'S NOTES

Many years ago, my grandmother showed me some family documents that a cousin, who's surname was Musgrave, had sent her. Buried among the many births and deaths and other family tree information was a note about the Musgrave family of Eden Hall from the north of England. Intrigued, I did some Googling, and that's when I first discovered the glass goblet known as the Luck of Edenhall, now on display at the magnificent Victoria & Albert Museum in London.

The Luck's information on the V&A website noted that it was made around 1350 in either Syria or Egypt, but how it came to be in the north of England in the 17th century remained a complete mystery. This tidbit was particularly fascinating to me because I just so happened to have married a man whose father was born and raised in Aleppo, Syria. I decided the Luck *had* to be from Syria and I, a distant relative of the Musgrave family, *had* to write a story about it. *(Almost like it was destiny!)* Thus, was born *The Alchemist of Aleppo*, my origin story for the Luck of Edenhall. And, in 2022, I was finally able to visit the museum and see the beautiful—and mysterious—piece for myself.

# ACKNOWLEDGEMENTS

Every writer knows that a book is much more than a product of one person's imagination. From people, places, and events that inspire us to the beta readers and editors and designers who help shape the final product in all it's many stages of development.

Before publication, *The Alchemist of Aleppo* had been swirling around in my brain for at least a decade and had gone through countless iterations and re-imaginings. Because I'd already spent time in England, I had a good sense of what the country felt like, and thanks to my father-in-law, I was able to visit Syria before the Civil War.

I studied Arabic in college and had read extensively on Middle Eastern history, and so, from the moment I set foot in Aleppo, I was entranced. The history of the city and the beauty of the surrounding countryside completely drew me in. And the amazing welcome my husband's extended family showed us as they hosted us and acted as tour guides was truly heartwarming. And inspirational. So thank you to the Makansis of Aleppo.

Through the whole long process, my husband Jason, and our two daughters, Amira and Elena, put up with me going on and on about the story and asking them to read (and re-read!) myriad new versions. So thank you to them for their patience.

Thank you also to my sister Karen (an even more voracious reader than I am!), and to my niece Jennifer and my friend and colleague Colleen, all of whom were willing to take a look at the story in it's development stage.

And thank you to editors Heather, Ariell, and Stacey, each of whom helped make the manuscript better.

Finally, a grateful shout out to the Victoria & Albert Museum where lucky visitors like me can enjoy and be inspired by pieces like the beautiful and enigmatic Luck of Edenhall.

Find out more, including what's coming next, at:
www.kristinamakansi.com

 kbmakansi

 kbmakansi

 kbmakansi.bsky.social

# ABOUT THE AUTHOR

Marie K. Savage (a.k.a., Kristina Makansi) studied government, international relations, and education, but her career has been in writing, communications, and marketing. Since 2011, she's been the principal editor as well as the interior and cover designer for Blank Slate Press and Amphorae Publishing Group, a small independent publisher.

She's also a freelance editor and designer, and between her various projects, has worked on 160+ books. Titles she has worked on have garnered starred reviews from *Publishers Weekly* and numerous accolades, including Benjamin Franklin awards, IPPYs, and a Gold Medal for Outstanding Book of the Year from Independent Publishers.

Her first solo book, *Oracles of Delphi*, was written under the pen name Marie Savage, and she is co-author, along with her two talented daughters, of *The Seeds Trilogy* (*The Sowing, The Reaping,* and *The Harvest*). Her most recent novel, *The Trouble with Roommates*, is a contemporary romance set in the time of "#metoo" and Covid-19.

She currently works in communications at a major research university and lives in Arizona with her husband (also a writer), and two extraordinarily derpie doxie mutts.